MAGNOLIA

Magnolia

A NOVEL

by

Agnita Tennant

RENAISSANCE BOOKS

Magnolia: A Novel

By Agnita Tennant

First published 2015 by
RENAISSANCE BOOKS
PO Box 219
Folkestone
Kent CT20 2WP

www.renaissancebooks.co.uk

Renaissance Books is an imprint of Global Books Ltd

ISBN 978-1-898823-18-6

British Library Cataloguing in Publication Data
A catalogue record for this book is available from the British Library

Typeset in Bembo 12 on 14 by Dataworks.
Printed and bound in England by CPI Antony Rowe

Contents

MAGNOLIA

by

Ronald Duncan (1978)

From where these birds
Which perch upon the bough
Leafless, but for their white wings
Of ivory or alabaster

Now furled, so spruce, so still?
What dark wind swept them?
Across which seas?
Drawn by what instincts?

Migrating from where to where?
Or are these not birds, nor flowers,
But hands in prayer
Clenched in brief hope
Wrung with long despair?

Reprinted courtesy Ronald Duncan Literary Foundation

PART I

Chapter 1

Letters

I often stayed on late in the office. My colleagues and the caretaker thought I was studying. I liked the quiet hours after a busy day. Sometimes I read but mostly I turned over things in my mind and wrote up my diary even though there were things I could not frankly put down.

It was going to be my last night. I wrote several letters to various people and went over the names of those whom I would have liked to invite to my wedding had I been fated to have one. There were too many. Instead of writing individually I left a few words to each in a notebook. Finally I wrote to the Director.

The Office
8.00 p.m.
24. 11. 1959

Dear Professor Kang,

I have a confession to make.

For the past two years I have led a secretive life that amounts to a disgrace to myself and a betrayal to all those people most dear to me, my family and friends, yourself and my colleagues who cared for me and expected great things of me, and to an extent, to my beloved country. Things came to a point, where I have no choice but to take my life.

I had started it with good conscience, and even now my conscience stands clear. God is my witness. When I entered it in my innocence, I didn't think it would turn out to be like this.

Ah, how lucky I thought I was when you offered me this job a few days before my graduation three years ago. How single-heartedly I loved my job, my colleagues, and the noble ideals that you had set out to achieve through this institution, until this strange fate befell me as if out of the blue.

Even though I have long since bid this world farewell, now I feel as if I am speaking to you in person and it makes me weep all over again. Memories of the happy times I have had here, the eyes and smiles of my dear colleagues rouse afresh in me the deepest love. Even the inanimate objects in this room like desks, cabinets and pictures seem to come alive and cling onto me. But there is no other option, I must go my chosen way.

I am so sorry, dear professor, please forgive me. Farewell, and a happy, long life.

Yours truly,
Sukey Yun

P.S.: For the last thing I do in this life, I am going to visit a certain clergyman to make a confession. When the winter is over and spring comes round, the mirage shimmers along the ridge lines of the hills, and your heart, too, beats warm with the pulse of spring, would you like to call on this man and ask about my mysterious death?

His name is Father James Osbourne at the Anglican Clergy House, Anp'yŏng.

I folded the letter, sealed it, and stood up. Coming round the partition, I glanced around the office, empty now except for the furniture. There were five or six desks. In my mind's eye, I could see the owners of each. Miss Pak – as she had been my senior, by a year, at Y University I called her 'Miss Park ŏnni', ŏnni meaning 'elder sister'; the one in the left corner was now taken up by Miss Pae, but I could not help thinking of its previous owner, Miss Chŏng, a graduate of E University, very pretty and affectionate towards me. As she was a year younger she called me 'Miss Yun ŏnni'. She had gone to America three months ago; the funniest of them all, Mr Hong had the nickname of 'Bull' because of his extraordinary physical strength; slow-moving Mr Chin who preferred to be called by his nickname of 'Mr Bear'; with a child-like grin, Mr Yu was a thin, agile and very clever man. His general knowledge was amazing and we called him 'Dr Know-all'.

Altogether, we made a congenial bunch. I pulled at the knob of the door that led to the Director's room. It was firmly locked now, but during the day it was left ajar, and Dr Kang pressed a bell on his desk when he wanted me. How many scores of times did I cross that doorstep everyday? Next to it on the right was the Conference Room, and behind the Conference Room and Director's Room were the Korean Classics and Music Collections. Upstairs on the first floor were the Reading Room with mostly English books on open shelves, a Periodical Room with two hundred journals from the USA and other Western countries, and a small microfilm room. I knew the inventory of each room off by heart for there was hardly an item bought or brought in without my knowledge. I had been the first member of the staff of the Korean Academy, which had been founded almost at the same time as my graduation. I had been very lucky to get a job in such a prestigious place.

One day a couple of months before my graduation I had bumped into Dr Kang in a bookshop in Chongro. As we walked out he asked me whether I would care to have a cup of coffee with him at the tea-room across the road. I thought he had asked me more as a formality than for any particular reason. Even though I had agreed I felt awkward as I sat opposite him across the table. Apart from attending his lectures for two terms I hardly knew him personally. He had returned from America the previous year with a doctorate and taken up a post as a lecturer at my university, so I had been one of his first students. He was a handsome man nearing forty but not married. After living in the States for over ten years he spoke Korean rather clumsily during his first years back. He seemed to have forgotten some Korean vocabulary while keeping almost intact, the native accents and dialect of North Korea where he had originally come from. His awkward expressions during his lectures often made students burst into uproar.

Though knowledgeable on his own subject, he had few words when it came to small talk, and it took him some laborious moments before breaking the silence.

'Why did you choose political studies?' His question came as if he was accusing me for not having chosen a more feminine subject.

'I don't know.'

'What will you do when you leave college?'

'I would like to find a job, and save up to go to the States to continue my studies.' Then I added, 'I have no wish to become the first woman President, so don't worry about that if that's what is worrying you.'

'I am going to need some sort of secretary cum librarian in my new job. I wondered if you might be interested?'

Suddenly the dull atmosphere became animated. He went on to explain about The Korean Academy. It was to help scholars, who having lost their books and study facilities in the war, found it hard to pursue their research that the new institution had been set up, and he had been appointed as the Director. Membership would be limited to post-graduate students and scholars of high standing. He stressed that it was non-political, a pure research institution. Its main function for the present would be to run a reference library with a comfortable reading room; exchange programme of scholars with other countries; and provide grants for the publication of learned papers, and so on. I would be required to supervise the Reading Room as a Reference Librarian and to assist the Director as his secretary. I instantly accepted this unexpected good fortune and started work two days after the graduation ceremony. That had been three years ago. The Korean Academy, backed by generous financial assistance from the American X Foundation and the support of scholars throughout the country, had grown into an organization of great importance in the post-war period of Korea. To me it was paradise. My colleagues were all promising young people, graduated from the best universities and picked from the top of candidates list. We were a congenial bunch, full of mirth, hope and enthusiasm, and proud of our happy atmosphere at work.

I locked the office door and went down the few steps that led to the caretaker's room. Mr Shin was in the middle of reading the evening paper, but at my approach came rushing out, as if on full alert, to take the keys from me.

'You've been studying late again, Miss Yun,' he said. 'Take my advice and slow down a bit, or you're going to break down one of these days.' He added with mock severity, 'tut tut'. His good-natured smile was especially heart-warming tonight. I handed him the white envelope and directed him to give it to the director as soon as he came in on Monday afternoon.

'He will be out teaching during the morning,' I said.

'Yes, yes,' he said unsuspectingly.

'Goodbye then,' and feeling like bursting into tears, I added cheerily, 'Have a nice weekend.' The street was dark in spite of the occasional street lamps. The sky hung low with no moon and no stars. It might start to snow any moment. I walked and walked around the streets like a lost soul. While the poison was in my handbag, death was within reach. No need to rush with it – the chance was to be had only once. Two more days to endure! By the time Dr Kang reads my letter I would no longer belong to this world. How would he react to it? But what would it matter to me once I had gone? Nevertheless, I could not help conjuring up the scene: I could see his troubled eyes through his black-rimmed spectacles. Thrusting back a lock of black hair that perpetually fell over his forehead, he would frown. Then leaning his right elbow on desk, he would rest his forehead between his fingers, the thumb on the right temple and the third finger on the left. He would let out a heavy sigh, then press the bell rather harshly, perhaps twice, even three times. Miss Pak would feel that she should go in instead of me, but before she had time, he would stalk out himself. The staff would immediately sense something was terribly wrong.

'Does anyone know what has happened to Miss Yun?'

They would be perplexed. Mr Hong would give a sigh of relief thinking 'Is that all? She's just absent without leave. She should know better what he's like. "Always remember the difference between official matters and private ones. If you are called away from the office make sure we always know where you are, etc., etc."'

'Well, I could easily have made something up. Told him that she had phoned in and said she was not well.' At the thought of this sanguine friend I smiled to myself. Meanwhile Mr Chin, feeling that he ought to say something would cautiously speak.

'She is not in today, sir, but she hasn't been in touch, most unlike her.' Getting no clue from them he would call Miss Pak to his office as she is my closest friend. She might tell him that since I came back from a holiday at the spa town of Onyang a couple of years ago, I seemed to be harbouring some secret but it was only a vague impression, and she was not at all sure. He would show her my letter. She would turn white.

'We can't just sit here and talk like this, sir. We must do something. I will ring her sister.'

By that time my sister would have read my letter to her, but at the thought of her reaction to Miss Pak's call, I burst into tears. Please God, don't let them make too much of a fuss about me when it's all over. I walked into a coffee-shop and sat in a quiet corner. The experience of the past two years came floating before my mind's eye so vividly, like a film.

Chapter 2

Fate's Favourite Child

The snow was getting heavier by the minute, flakes as large as a child's fist. It fell on the top of the ever-deepening layer already on the ground. Houses, trees and all the other objects you could see stood still under its thick cover. It was the most enchanting scene that I had ever seen.

Miae and I were looking down on the courtyard from the window of our hotel room on the first floor. From the radio floated the mournful, sweet melody of Negro spirituals sung by Maria Anderson, making us feel sad and sweet too. In three hours' time we would be catching the train back to Seoul.

Onyang was a famous spa town. Newly-married couples came here for their honeymoon. But for us it had been a few days of farewell treat. We had been the closest of friends since high school days in the provincial town, Chŏngju. We were the famous duo who sang duets at school concerts, she alto and I soprano; we were the dynamic chieftains leading our classmates in all aspects of school life. We frequented each other's houses, treated like members of each others' families. Our friends and teachers used to tease us calling us 'The pair.' Our ideals were of the loftiest, and to achieve them we worked hard with some proud results. On leaving high school we entered the universities of our choice through competition rates of twenty to one or more, the only two girls from this provincial town to get into the first-rate universities of Seoul. Miae went to the Law College of the Seoul National University and I to the College of Politics and Law of Y University. Surrounded by congratulations and encouragement from friends, teachers and families, we subconsciously had believed that our future paths would be as sunny and smooth as they had always been. There seemed no reason to believe it to be otherwise as long as we kept our heads clear.

Even though we now went to different colleges at opposite ends of the city, we scarcely passed a day without seeing each other. We were no longer a couple of chattering young girls, we were thoughtful intellectuals, brooding over serious matters like politics, life, God and love. Analysing, criticizing and then sometimes uncertain we often talked all through the night. Four years of college life, when it came to an end, seemed like a fleeting dream. It was during the last two that certain events had altered Miae's life and these same events were to turn the course of my life also.

She had a brief but passionate love affair, which ended tragically. Though my closest friend, I learned that in matters of love there was nothing I could do to help except to comfort and support her choice of action whatever it might be. She had, after much anguish and inner struggle, chosen to enter a Catholic convent. Her parents were atheists. They declared that they would rather see her dead than a nun. Unknown to them who were conveniently out of the way living in the country, the arrangements went ahead so that in September the following year she was to enter a house of the Carmelite order in Taegu. Now that her path became clear she no longer wept or looked miserable. Knowing her as I did, I was certain that her decision was final. Whatever her motives may have been, I thought, it was an admirable choice to become a nun. At the end of December that year I got my monthly pay plus an equal amount of bonus from The Korean Academy and I thought it would be an excellent idea to spend the bonus on Miae to mark the grand finale to our friendship. I remembered that she had expressed a wish to get away to somewhere even for a few days. I took a week's leave and decided on Onyang as our destination. It was our first ever holiday and I could afford a few days of luxury. I had chosen the most expensive suite in the hotel, and we enjoyed ourselves doing nothing in particular, and eating the most delicious things.

The radio music ended, and an unbearable sense of finality followed. We exchanged a sad smile, and then started singing a song of farewell in two parts.

Beyond the lake, the moon is setting,
while on the hill behind the dawn breaks,
Your eyes full of love, your face a vision of an angel
You smile as you say goodbye.
Jenny, my Jenny, must you go?
Jenny, my Jenny, how shall we part.

Our song came to an abrupt stop as down in the courtyard below our window we saw a smart gentleman emerging from the hotel entrance. We recognized him at once as Mr Kwŏn who we had met briefly the night before. Wrapped up in a sage-green overcoat with a hat and well-polished black shoes, he went across the courtyard and out of the main gate. He had around him, I thought, an air of poetic melancholy, probably reflecting my own mood.

'I bet he knows we are watching him. He's just too proud to look up and say hello to us,' I grumbled.

'You fancy him,' said Miae, and imitating the voice of an old spinster, the domestic science teacher at high school whom we used to hate, added, 'You'd better watch out. All men are hungry wolves.' Merrily we laughed and went back to packing.

'Still, I think he is a gentleman. What I can't understand is how he dared to walk in here in his pyjamas. I was outraged. I nearly told him to get out.'

My mind was in a strange state so that I wanted to talk about him, whether it be praise or derision.

'Knowing we were two women from Seoul, he thought we were the frivolous kind. That's all.' She said curtly.

I had known her when she had been a very sensitive yet positive and forceful girl, and then had watched the process of change taking place in her. When she had been hit by the bitter experience of love, she seemed to droop like frost-bitten grass, gradually losing interest in her surroundings. Recently she seemed to have recovered her reason, but remained cool towards the outside world.

'I expect he's just a simpleton and came over as he happened to be dressed at the moment.'

In my mind I went over what had happened the previous day.

It was very quiet in the hotel in the afternoon. We seemed to be the only guests in the whole establishment. Lying on our beds, we were singing our favourite songs one after another, between the usual chatter. Suddenly there was the sound of running footsteps and the hushed voices and laughter of people along the corridor outside. We took it as the male and female staff having a bit of fun among themselves, taking advantage of the quiet afternoon. Then there was a loud crash on the door of our room as if someone had been thrown against it. Then a dead silence as they made a stealthy retreat only to end up with a loud cry at the far end of the corridor. We did not take any notice and just carried on singing.

In the evening the maid who brought in our meal said, 'I am very sorry we disturbed you this afternoon,' and added 'This is an apology from Mr Kwŏn, who is one of the guests from Seoul,' and handed me a business card which said on one side: 'Tong-hi Kwŏn, Lecturer, S Women's University.' On the back, scribbled in a flowing style was: 'To the guests of Room 16. Our play got rather out of hand this afternoon. Though I hope you'll understand as I hear you are from Seoul, I do apologize for the disturbance.' Then the girl went on to say, 'He wants to know whether you'd mind if he came to say hello in person.'

We exchanged a playful glance. 'It won't do any harm,' we quietly agreed. On further inquiry we learned that he was on holiday doing some writing. 'Writing?' We were hooked by curiosity. Besides, we thought, a university lecturer can't be a person to be on guard against. But the real reason for accepting Kwŏn's self-invitation lay deeper. Miae and I were momentarily reminded of Mr Hyŏn, our mutual friend and hero.

Having just come out of the hot spring, our hair was still wet. Miae had hers permed short but mine was long and straight, loosely brushed over my shoulders. We were wearing the traditional Korean costume, *ch'ima* and *jogori*, hers of black satin and mine deep sea-blue silk. Mr Kwŏn followed the maid in his pyjamas with blue and white stripes. He looked around and said, 'This room is freezing.'

After examining the fire-pot in the middle of the room he said to the maid, 'Look, it's going out. Take it away and fetch another, full of bright red coals.' He used a familiar tone, as if to his own housemaid.

After we had exchanged our names he said, 'I know you are from Seoul. Which college are you at?'

'Miae did Law at Seoul National, and I did politics at Y.'

'Gosh, women bachelors of law and politics!' He said. I told him briefly about my job and then the conversation came to a halt, which was quite unexpected. In our experience with Mr Hyŏn such a thing had never happened. This man is a fool, I thought, in his silly pyjamas.

'What were you doing this afternoon?' I said, 'For a moment we thought the Red Army was on the loose bashing things on its way. Do you like running about with kids?' I said this in a contemptuous manner, just to provoke him so that he might try to defend himself, but all I got from him was a grunt of 'Oh, yes, very much.'

Another awkward silence followed.

'What subject do you teach?' asked Miae.

'English literature.' Then we were faced with another dead end. I longingly thought of Mr Hyŏn. He would never have let us down like this. He used to make us feel so natural and at ease. The strength of our relationship had been its sexlessness. The way he treated us was such that the delicate feelings which might exist between unmarried men and women were kept out of the way. We had talked freely about all sorts of things.

While the awkward silence went on, my mind drifted from the present scene as I continued to think about Hyŏn.

We came to know Mr Hyŏn through our sixth-form teacher, Mr Chang. When we were going to Pusan, then the wartime capital, to sit our university entrance exams, Mr Chang gave us a letter of introduction. Mr Hyŏn would help us find lodgings and getting around in a strange city.

'He maybe an even greater help to you, Sukey,' he had said, because he did the same course as you are going to take at Y.' Mr Chang told us in great detail what a remarkable man Hyŏn was. He came originally from North Korea, from a wealthy gentry family. Only he and his elder brother had managed to come over. As poor refugees they had been through great hardships in their early days in the South. His elder brother, determined to give his younger brother a good education, had sent him to school while he worked as a labourer and then as a market trader. Hyŏn proved to be a brilliant scholar and got through his school years always at top and every year winning a scholarship of one kind or another. Now he was a lecturer at a college in Pusan.

With all this knowledge, we met him as if we had known him all our life.

The exams took place at individual college sites. Probably because he was a graduate of Y, he was always hanging around the campus during the three-day exam period. He came to see me at breaks, and at lunch time he bought me something to eat, asking me what questions there had been and how I had answered them.

Once we started university life we did not see him very often. It was only when one or both of us needed his advice or help that we went together to his room at his college or to the modest house where he lived with his brother's family. We were always warmly welcomed. On such occasions we greatly enjoyed his company. We went on talking for hours on end. When our bottoms ached or our legs felt cramped from sitting for too long on the hard *ondol* floor, we got up and went out to a nearby tea-room to continue. He was not only good at serious debate but also at making us laugh – we often laughed until our sides ached.

Our friendship continued in Seoul after the capital was recaptured.

In the depth of her affair Miae would discuss with him openly the relationships between men and women. On such occasions I felt left out and immature at not being able to contribute, but study-wise, I benefited greatly. In my third year I won first prize in a competitive debate organized by the Political Students Association. In my final year, I contrinuted a lengthy article entitled 'The Neutral Diplomacy of India' to the Association's journal, which drew many complimentary remarks. On both occasions, needless to say, I owed much to discussions with Hyŏn.

In the previous year he had accepted an exchange scholarship from M State University in the United States. Occasionally when I was feeling lonely, I thought of him or rather, the thought of him made me feel lonely.

All through the time we had known him it had been rare for either of us to see him alone as if there had been an unspoken rule between us. Then a week before his departure to the States, I happened to bump into him in Myŏngdong. I was alone. It was a dusky evening in early autumn. The leaves on the trees were beginning to fall and drift about. He asked me to join him for dinner at a restaurant that we were just passing. He had finally got the visa that very afternoon. The whole procedure had been so complicated and tediously prolonged that now it was all complete, he felt as if he was going to be ill.

I don't remember how it happened, but after dinner I found myself walking beside him up the slope that led to the Namsan Mountain. I had noticed earlier that evening that his face was thinner and wan. Now he looked completely forlorn. I had never known him to be like this.

'You look very odd today.'

'Why?'

'I don't know what it is, but you look sort of sad and lonely'

He looked down at me with one of his gentle smiles.

'The season's to blame, I suppose. It's a sad and lonely time, isn't it.'

We walked on along the parapet until we came to a point from which we could see a large part of Seoul sprawled out below. Through the blanket of mist, lights and rooftops of all sizes and shapes stood out like hundreds of flowers in a flower-erbed. Around us the darkness grew stronger every minute and it looked as if an intoxicating scent was rising from it. We stood in silence. I thought I ought to say something to restore the cheerful atmosphere to which we were accustomed. There seemed to be a lot to talk about yet nothing important enough to break the silence.

To my relief he started humming the tune of a film that had been very popular, 'Love is a many splendoured thing.' I knew the lyrics in Korean translation but not in English. Soon I learned them from him and we walked down the hill quietly singing it in English. When we were at the foot of the hill that verged on the main road, I foolishly put a blunt question to him, 'I wonder why you don't get married.'

He wasn't particularly impressed with it but I took one step further and asked what sort of woman would be regarded as ideal. In fact, these were questions that now and again had occurred to Miae and me. To my surprise he answered it with sincerity.

'Firstly,' he said, 'a girl with a normal family background, not necessarily rich, but brought up under both parents among sisters and brothers. I think such a girl would have a natural and balanced character. I am scared of neurotic women riddled with complexes.' 'Secondly,' he went on, 'a girl of above average looks, and thirdly – I am being exceedingly greedy – an educated woman who can take an interest in my studies and read English texts with me.'

The effect of these plainly spoken statements was such that I felt faint, as if a dagger of ice had pierced my heart. I was so embarrassed at this unexpected reaction on my side that the next moment I blushed deeply, thanking the darkness that hid it from him. What hurt me most was 'normal family background...with both parents.'

My mother died when I was five. I was brought up by my father and grandmother until my father remarried when I was eleven. My family was full of complexity and going through a particularly difficult phase at that time. It was obvious that I belonged to a different class from such girls as he desired. As for my looks, assuming myself a born scholar, I paid little attention to them and never once thought of myself as beautiful. Unreasonably, I was upset with him for not having given the answer that I wanted to hear. Why couldn't he have said, 'I would like someone with a good brain, nice personality, well educated and with average good looks?'

He offered to see me off at the bus stop, but I politely declined and walked away. Not only did I not tell Miae about it but I carefully avoided even talking about him. On the day of his departure, I excused myself from going to see him off at the airport. When Miae, after going to the airport alone, told me that he had asked after me, I quickly turned my head blinking away my tears. That had been three months ago.

I was comparing the blissful silence I had shared with Mr Hyŏn at Namsan that evening to the awkward one of this moment with Mr Kwŏn.

Shortly he took his leave, saying, as if he had suddenly remembered, that his father was sending his car to take him to Seoul in the morning. If we'd like a lift we were welcome, he said. I slammed the door behind him as I stuck out my tongue as a gesture of contempt.

'What an idiot!'

'He's like a zombie,' said Miae. We rolled with laughter.

'He must be a prince in disguise. Chauffer-driven car indeed!' Private cars were indeed a rarity in these times, in the restoration period of our war-torn country. We wondered whether we should accept the offer of a lift. In a way it was tempting. Just to think that we could sing all the way to Seoul while being driven through the beautiful, snow-covered scenery. But in the end, before we went to bed, we decided against it to show him that we were not such flighty girls to accept an offer like this from a man who we had only met briefly.

No sooner had we called the maid and ordered two first class train tickets in the morning than was there a knock on the door. It was Mr Kwŏn in a smart suit of dark grey. He looked even more subdued than the night before.

'Good morning Mr Kwŏn. You've been out early – we saw you,' we greeted him cheerfully.

'The snow is so beautiful. I went for a little walk.' Then he added, 'I'm afraid I have an apology to make.'

'What about?'

'My father phoned me early this morning. He needs his car for the next two days, so it would be Wednesday before he could send it.' He looked troubled.

'Oh, please don't worry on account of us. We have already got our tickets anyway.' We were pleased with ourselves. We set off in good time for the station, and had a cup of coffee in a tea-room. A few minutes before the train was due, we saw him walking into the station with a suitcase, but we had completely lost interest in him.

'I just remembered I have a meeting tonight. So here we are, together again.' But we did not look on him as our companion. Besides, his seat was far away from ours, so that we never spoke to him all the way. Outside the train, the world lay in total submission to the reign of snow, deep under its cover. The sky was grey and heavy, and snow continued to fall.

Quite unexpectedly, Mr Han was waiting for us at the station in Seoul. Miae looked very pleased. As she handed her bag over to him she gently brushed the snow off his shoulder, and said, 'I wonder how you knew we were coming back today. Are you well?'

I walked a few steps behind them. He was a law student, a year behind Miae at her college. I knew him as an admirer of her, but more as a younger brother than a boy-friend. He had been strongly opposing her plan to enter the convent.

After a week's leave, I went back to work. It was now early February. The last of the severe weather still hung on, day after day. Miae's calls at my office became scarce. At one time she had popped in almost daily, but now she made her appearance once every three or four days, sometimes only once a week. Even on these visits, she did not stay as long as she used to, lingering on into coffee or tea breaks. Our meetings after work also became rare, but I did not worry too much as I thought she was preparing herself for the great event in September. I was busy myself brushing up my English and the national history as I intended to sit for the government exams that qualified students to go abroad.

Nearly a month had passed since our return from Onyang. One day, a few minutes before the closing time Miae turned up, out of breath.

'I thought I had missed you. Come with me, I'll buy you supper.' She looked happy and excited. Outside Mr Han was waiting. The three of us went to a Music Room. One table away from Han, she sat opposite me and started in a whisper. 'I hope I am not turning into the type of women that you and I despise.' She said that recently she had been seeing Han everyday. He had proposed to her and was awaiting her reply. If she accepted him he wanted to become engaged in March. She knew it was wrong but could not resist his love. I thought I ought to look pleased but felt a sort of betrayal. I wasn't at all sure about my feelings, when I said, 'It's entirely up to you, dearest. All that matters is your own happiness. As long as you don't abandon our principles, you can't go wrong, can you?' By 'Principles' I must have meant the rationality that we had so highly upheld. Then the three of us had supper and I came away.

Next day I had a phone call at the office from Mr Kwŏn, the man we had met at Onyang. He said that as The Korean Academy was much being talked about among his colleagues, he was intending to come and see it himself, bringing a friend with him.

'What would be a convenient time?'

'Anytime between 9 a.m. and 5 p.m.'

'Is it true that Dr Kang is the Director?'

'Yes. Do you know him?'

'I haven't met him personally, but he will know me when I explain who I am.'

'Very well. Hope to see you soon, goodbye.'

He never came and I had nearly forgotten him when he rang again in the middle of March. He said he had been in Pusan on family business.

'It is such a lovely weather. I wondered if you and your friend would like to come out for a little walk tomorrow. The Academy is closed on Sunday, I expect?'

Though reluctantly, I accepted his invitation. Indeed it was beautiful spring weather. When I went to Miae's next morning wearing my favourite dress she was in bed thick with flu. I brought up the subject of Kwŏn, but she did not show the slightest interest. Going out in her condition was out of the question. Besides, Han was due to call on her shortly. Wishing I hadn't promised to go, I went alone to the appointed tea-room.

'Hello, Miss Yun, how good of you to come.' He was obviously delighted to see me coming alone. He started to explain why he had to be away for so long. For family reasons he had to change his job and arrange a transfer to Pusan University. Fortunately, he said, the Chancellor was a close family friend and was only too pleased to have him as a member of his staff.

'We won't be able to see each other so often now,' he said in a solemn tone.

'You make it sound as though we have done before,' I said jokingly. He was instantly cheered up by my light mood.

'Sukey, you are not as simple and straightforward as you look, are you?' I noticed him dropping off the respectful 'Miss Yun' and calling me by my first name.

'By the way, did you ring me at the college?' he asked.

22

'Why should I?'

'There was a message on my desk saying a lady had phoned. I thought it might be you.'

Then he fell into silence and sat there thoughtfully like an object up for inspection. And inspect him I did. With strong eyebrows, large, expressive eyes behind gold-rimmed glasses, a high straight nose and a firm mouth, it was an attractive face. His light coat, shirt, tie and tie-pin showed a refined taste. As we stepped out of the tea-room, a breeze ruffled his tie and brought a whiff of a scent of the lily of the valley. The idea of a man using scent would have repelled me before but it seemed to suit him. I liked it. We walked up the slope and stopped at the spot where I had stood with Hyŏn on that particular evening of the previous autumn. I compared the two men bobbing up and down on my horizon, the one with a mature, rich personality, heroically encountering the whole world, and the other with the look of a fairy-tale prince, trimmed and polished, nervous and rigid, and probably pampered by rich, adoring parents. I longingly thought of Hyŏn, but at the same time felt resentment. He hadn't sent me or Miae so much as a single postcard since he had left.

To change my mood, I said, 'Miae is going to be engaged soon,' and told him briefly how she had been set on becoming a nun, but had been miraculously won over by Mr Han.

'It shows that the power of love is stronger than the persuasion of parents or friends.' This rather trite statement moved me deeply. Only when I look back do I realize that Miae, my long-time comrade and support, having fallen in love and deserted me, had left me emotionally vulnerable. Subconsciously, I must have felt a need to fill the gap she had left. Things were out of my control. I was ready to be impressed by anything he said.

'So that's why you look so forlorn today,' he said. I ignored this and walked on.

'You are from Yonsei University? I expect you've got plenty of boys after you.'

'Well, if I had gone to a co-ed school because I was boy-hunting, no doubt I would, but I didn't. Why? Do I look like that kind of girl?'

'No, I didn't mean that. But surely you have at least a steady boyfriend?'

'No, I haven't actually.' I strongly denied his supposition, and as I did so, I suddenly felt very shy. By denying this so emphatically had I not invited him to court me?

He bought an expensive lunch, and as a token of thanks I offered to buy the coffee. Sitting opposite him across the table in the coffee shop, I suddenly knew I was falling in love with him. That evening I told my sister Sŏnhi about him.

It was the time when everybody was trying to pick up the pieces from the ashes in the wake of the Civil War. Poverty stricken, most people went hungry. For parents who had daughters of marriageable age, the highest they could hope for was a man who had no debts, a house of his own, however small it might be, and who was able to keep his wife decently fed and clothed. A chauffer-driven family car, elegant clothes, good looks and a job as a college lecturer, these were conditions good enough to win my sister's consent for a further relationship with him.

'You really are a lucky girl. You've always been Fate's favourite child, haven't you?' She was very happy for me. 'Just think how lucky you were to get your job just like that when there is a years' backlog of unemployed graduates all over the country...'

She started talking about those several occasions in the past that had shown how lucky I was, as if to reassure herself that nothing could ever go wrong with me in future.

While I was at college, my father had gone bankrupt. The beginning of each term had been a time of great anxiety for the family because of my registration fees. They were an enormous sum of money for a man in debt. Many times, in despair, I was prepared to leave college and get a job instead. Then the day before, or a day after the closing date a handsome sum of money, for quite unexpected reasons, came into my troubled father's possession. Similar miracles happened several times. As he handed the money to me with no grudge, father said, 'You were born under a lucky star, child. Fated to carry on with your study, eh? Remember to do it well.'

My sister and I lay in bed side by side till the late hours, reminiscing before we blissfully fell asleep.

Chapter 3

Sitters

In the shadow of a large apple tree, sitting on a straw mat, my sister, Sŏnhi and I were playing at being grown-ups. She was six, two years older than me. She was always the mother and I had no choice but to be the father. While she prepared the dinner, mixing up clay, bits of flowers and leaves, and chopping up raw apples that had fallen off the tree, and arranging them on the dinner set, I sat behaving myself, stroking a dust pan and pretending it was a briefcase. I even remembered to cough lightly as if clearing my throat.

'Dinner is ready.' She brought in a wooden board loaded with plates and bowls stuffed with pretty 'food' not a scrap of which was edible.

'You must say "it looks good".' She kept instructing me. As I said it I pressed my lips tight so as not to show a smile. The new tea set that father had brought with him from Seoul yesterday was very pretty and came in very handy, but I was dying to have done with this tiresome dignity and run wild.

'You must say, "It was delicious". Don't you know how to be dad? Shall we swap it now, and you be the mum, and I'll show you how to do it properly.'

'Oh, no thank you,' I said to myself, 'I've had enough of being grown-up.'

When the long, long summer day was over and the sky in the west was blushing deep it was time for the real dinner. Round the corner of the house, mother appeared carrying the baby strapped on her back.

'Come on, dears, dinner time. Go and wash your hands first.' Her voice was so gentle. I don't remember her face ever showing anger. While Sŏnhi packed the play set, I shook dust off my skirt and ran off to the cowshed where my father was giving out some instructions to the workers.

'Father, dinner is ready.'

'Righto!' said he. I made a mental note of the expression for tomorrow's dinner with Sŏnhi.

Holding my hand, father almost dragged me to the bubbling spring, where squatting down he washed my face and hands vigorously. I wished he would not let the soap suds get in my eyes. It hurt.

The large round table was out in the middle of the living room because all the family was together tonight. My father had taken a job with a newspaper company in Seoul and was away most of the time these days, leaving the running of the huge orchard virtually to mother. Then, insisting that children should be educated in the capital, he had transferred my elder brother, Hyŏngsŏk, to a reputable school there. When he left home we had all cried, and the house felt empty for a long time. Yesterday he came home with father for the summer vacation. He received a hero's welcome, and he lavished presents from Seoul on the family.

'Hyŏngsŏk's no ordinary chap,' my father said. 'You should see the way he sticks at his studies. This term he's missed being top by one point, but it is not the sort of thing one expects of a boy straight from the country.' Father looked proud.

'School work is important,' said mother, 'but what about his health? He looks so much thinner.'

'I know, he's gone thin. It was his first time away from home. His uncle and aunt are really so kind to him, but he's been homesick, especially at the beginning.'

'Hyŏngsŏk, did you miss me?' Mother stroked his head, and turned away her tearful eyes. 'Still you have got two more years to work hard, and then the year after that you ought to get into Kyŏng-gi High school, oughtn't you? That is your father's wish.'

Father had been a Kyŏng-gi boy himself, but he got involved in the nationwide protest march of 1919 against the Japanese annexation. He was suspended from school and put in prison. After his release he went to Japan and continued his study at Waseda University, and he cherished the one wish of seeing his own son at Kyŏng-gi.

'Next year, I think, we ought to move Sŏnhi to Seoul as well,' said father. 'I have been thinking about it a lot. For the children's sake we must eventually settle in Seoul ourselves. To do that, this orchard will have to go. It is hard work for you as it is now.'

'Is Myŏngsŏk asleep?' He changed the subject.

'Yes.' Mother's voice was low.

Myŏngsŏk, just over two was asleep at one end of the room. When the supper table was taken away, the kitchen maid brought in a large wicker basket laden with sweet melons. They were bright yellow, the skin smooth and thin. Putting aside the sweetest looking one for father, mother said, 'Children, take your pick.' My brother picked out a big one, and so did my sister. Not being a big eater I picked up the smallest and yellowest.

'Let's see who's got the sweetest,' said father. 'They say that one who is good at choosing a sweet melon is also good at choosing a spouse.'

'Taste mine,' 'taste mine, too,' we all held out our melons to father. Sampling a bit off brother's he said, 'It's very sweet, 'and then to Sŏnhi, 'This is very sweet too.' Lastly taking a bite of mine, he said, 'Look, this is the sweetest. She has the right way of choosing – you taste, mother.'

'Um, it's delicious. She was the last to choose, and picked the sweetest!'

'Let me try,' 'give us a bite,' my brother and sister begged me. Proudly I handed my melon to my sister, 'You have two bites,' I said, and then to my brother, 'No, you can't have any,' pouting.

'Why?' They all looked at me.

'Are you sulking about something, darling?' asked mother with a smile.

'You wouldn't let me stay with you.' I gave my brother a sidelong glance pretending I was still angry. They all burst into laughter.

'Silly idiot. It was all because you were making such a fuss about nothing.' He explained what had happened.

'This afternoon we went into the orchard to see how black-berries were doing. We saw this gorgeous dragonfly darting about. She kept pestering me to catch it for her. If I'd had a net I would have, but without one how could I? She started being silly and crying. I told her to go home. I'd forgotten all about it.' Once more they all laughed.

'She was sitting on the ground, crying, so I coaxed her and brought her home, mummy.' Sŏnhi explained her part in the drama.

'She's like that,' said mother to father. 'Sometimes she brings up some little thing that had upset her ages and ages ago, and goes on and on about It. I don't know why she does it.'

'Because she's a clever and sensitive girl, that's why. Mark my words, she will be somebody when she grows up. Look at the way she has chosen that melon.' He laughed and I was instantly happy.

'It's thanks to Sŏnhi that I've kept my sanity. She's so good and never causes any trouble. She's so reliable and practically looks after Sukey. I am sure I don't know what Sukey will do if Sŏnhi goes.'

'Let's have a song contest. Come on, who would like to start?' Father thus changed the atmosphere.

'Hyŏngsŏk, you go first,' said mother as she patted my brother on his shoulder, but he seemed suddenly to have gone shy, or feel that he was too old to do such things.

'No, not me. But mum, you do it, with dad. Your favourite, "I wandered today to the hills, Maggie..."'

The melody of 'The Song of Maggie' had been deeply rooted in our minds since our infancy along with the gentle voices of mother and father. Even now I feel like crying when I imagine them, young and in love, singing it together as they dreamed of their future, happily married, bringing up a brood of happy children.

Sŏnhi and I stood against the wall and sang 'Clementine.' Father clapped loudly and praised us. 'They've got good voices just like their mother. I have a mind to send then to a music school!'

Then all the family sang together a song from the gramophone record:

The sun has gone down from the top of the hills,
'Caw, caw', cawing the crows are homewards too.
We'll meet again tomorrow, till then adieu,
Let us to our mama's welcoming arms.
Join hands together and stand in a ring, then
Let them go at one, two, three.
Bow your heads for a goodbye now,
Let us to papa's welcoming lap.

As the last song was coming to a close, Myŏngsŏk woke from his sleep and joined in the fun, keeping the rhythm with his hips while rubbing the sleep out of his eyes. His rosy cheeks were dimpled and, fully awake, his eyes were like two bright stars. We adored him. Now joined by the youngest member, the family fun gained a new momentum. Myŏngsŏk liked music. When in a good mood he would go on singing to himself making it up as he went along, picking up bits from here and there from the family songs, the gramophone, or the labourer's singing, keeping time with his head. This particular evening, he sang his latest song in which some mysterious words recurred. Mother interpreted them:

Daddy's train's gone away, chuff, chuff, chuff,
The toffee man went away and never, never, never comes
again...

'What a clever boy!' Father gathered him in his arms and said, 'That is a very good song. His rhythm is right and a good tune too.'

Suddenly there was a commotion outside the door. Opening it, we saw in the courtyard, Samsu, a casual worker from the village, blubbering.

'Please come and save her, sir. My wife, she is dying. She's been whimpering with tummy ache since lunch. Thinking it's the old worms playing up again, I let it be, and now she's...'

My father cut him short.

'Is it upper or lower stomach? Has she been sick? Is she hot?' He told mother to fetch the first-aid kit while he put on his shoes.

'Let's go and see.' They disappeared round the bend into the darkness.

On both sides of the house were paddies and beyond them the vast orchards. At the far end of the front yard and behind the house grew all kinds of fruit – peaches, pears, persimmons, plums, grapes, dates, chestnuts and walnuts.

The village was called Sapsuri. The village and its surrounding countryside in Kangwŏn Province, now a part of North Korea, was to my father, his kingdom and Utopia. He had built up this community with his blood and sweat, and youthful idealism to practise his passionate patriotism.

When he came back from Japan with his hard-won graduation certificate, he found his country, now a Japanese colony, a difficult place to find a job that suited him. Besides, young intellectuals like himself were under constant police surveillance. After a long, frustrating search for a job, he had decided to serve his country by living amongst the uneducated farming folk and enlightening them. With all his inherited money he bought a hundred acres of land here and developed it into a flourishing orchard and farm.

He started night classes and taught ignorant people to read and write. Over the years he had become a sort of sage. He was a friend, teacher, scribe and solicitor, and a mediator when there was a row. He even treated minor ailments.

When he made up his mind to forsake his Utopia, it must have been a heart-breaking decision for him. He could do it only because, to his mind, the education of his children was a matter of highest importance.

The day came when my sister, Sŏnhi was to be taken away to Seoul. When we set out in the morning to see her off there were six of us, the whole family, but after we had said goodbye to my father and his party at the eastern gate of the village, there were only three of us on our way back home, mother, Myŏngsŏk and me. Many nights I went to sleep sobbing, and then pitiably cried out in my sleep calling, 'sister', or 'I want my Sŏnhi,' making my mother weep.

One day I wandered off by myself to a place where I used to go with Sŏnhi to play. It was where the look-out shelter was in the middle of melon plantation. A four-feet-square platform with straw roof was propped up on four wooden stilts. You climbed on it by a ladder left there slanting against the side of the platform. As I climbed the steps of the ladder, I longed for

Sǒnhi so much that I thought my heart would break. Even now I vividly recall the sensation – a first taste of sorrow in my life. The next thing I knew was that I was lying in bed back at home, conscious of the presence of some women around me.

'If it wasn't for the thought of Sǒnhi how could she dare to go off that far on her own?'

'They really are a peculiar pair, aren't they? I've never known any girls quite like these two.'

'Since Sǒnhi went away, I just can't relax for a minute for the worry of this child...' It was mother's voice. I opened my eyes and saw her two large sad eyes looking down into mine.

I must have had slipped off the ladder. Apparently a village woman found me lying on the ground unconscious and brought me home, carrying me on her back.

Chapter 4

A Chronicle of April

1 April. When I met Mr Kwŏn at the tea-room 'Rose' we felt quite natural as if we had known each other for a long time. He made me sit beside him and ordered the coffee without asking me whether I wanted it or not. He had by him a red-covered book which turned out to be Grace Metalious' *Peyton Place*. When he saw me eying it he said, 'It was sent to me by a close friend from the time I was in America. Would you like to borrow it?' I was delighted. Besides, I now knew that he had been to America. I was dying to ask him which state, and for how long, but I refrained. I might have appeared vulgar to show too much curiosity in someone else's private life. But I am sure his experience will be helpful when my time comes. Probably his polished manners and the refinement in his clothing are thanks to his American experience. He praised me twice today. I know it is a weakness but when he praises me I get excited and silly.

'You look very nice in that dress. It reminds me of a fashion model I knew once in the States.'

'Goodness!' I thought as I blushed. I was wearing my marine blue dress with a black satin belt tied in a bow at the back. I had a matching pair of high heeled shoes. As we came down the stairs I caught my reflection in the long mirror on the landing. With a black handbag slung over my shoulder and red-covered book tucked under my arm, I did look nice. From a few steps behind, he said again, 'You do look smart, Sukey.'

I turned to face him, and looking up said with mock severity, 'You shouldn't make complimentary remarks to a lady's face.'

'Oh, I am sorry. I do apologize.' He bowed from the waist. His quick and witty reaction made me laugh and he delightedly chuckled in his turn. We went to a Western restaurant. He asked me whether I liked dancing.

'Like it?' I said, 'I can't take the first step,' as if I was proud of myself.

I thought he might say 'That is not like you, Sukey, modern woman as you are.' In which case I would have said, 'It is not as if I object to dancing itself. I would love it. It's just that I am waiting until I have a boyfriend with whom I can learn it properly.' But there was no need. He rather praised me as he nodded his head and said, 'I am pleased to hear that. It is just like you, Sukey.'

'I expect you are good at it?'

'No, no. I am like you. I have had many chances to learn but somehow missed them all. I was thinking you might be able to teach me.'

Is this not evidence of his innocence and shy personality? I felt as if I could relax my guard a bit. After dinner we went to a cinema to see a Korean film entitled 'Money'. It was ten past eleven when we came out. He called a taxi, put me in the back seat, sat himself beside the driver and told him to go to Tonamdong, and then turning to me he said, 'That's where you live, isn't it?'

I closed my eyes as I leaned my head back on the seat. The love scenes from the film came floating back. I wondered why he did not sit in the back next to me. Some men would have done. In a way I was glad it turned out that way. Only by keeping a respectable distance until the right time comes can we have the right kind of relationship. I would hate myself if I were to fall into a blind passion. When the taxi had passed the Samsŏn Bridge, I had to rouse myself from my reverie, to give the driver directions to our house. Kwŏn said that the new term starts in the middle of April, and he ought to be at his new post in Pusan by the tenth, at the latest. The thought of seeing him off at the railway station for it is a certainty now that I shall be there, made me emotional. I want to make the most of the remaining days and enjoy his company.

'You must be tired,' he said as he helped me out of the car and lightly patted my cheeks with his fingers.

'Good night and thank you for a lovely evening.'

'It's my pleasure. Good night,' he said and waved as he got into the car.

2 April. The first thing I meant to do when I got to work was to ring him. But when I entered the office the telephone was already ringing. It was him. I could not hide the delight from my voice.

'Oh, is that you? Did you sleep well? How is it that you always answer the phone? Is it near you?'

'Yes, it's just on my desk.'

'So I can ring you often, can I?'

'Even if it wasn't, you can ring me as often as you like.'

'Didn't you get a scolding from your sister for being late last night?'

'Scolding? Why, I'm not a child, am I?'

He chuckled. I could see his face. I love him when he does that.

'I've only just woken up. I am ringing from my bed. I have the phone just above my pillow. Are you busy?'

'No, I am not. 'I wanted to hold onto the phone. 'What are you going to do today?'

'I have to go into college, of course.'

'Even on holidays?'

'Yes. I've got a lot to tidy up in my office.' Then he said, 'It's my mother just peeping round the door to see why I am lying in. I will ring you later. Bye for now.'

Before my eyes floated his room; a large *ondol* floored room, maybe a combined bedroom and study. Apart from the sliding doors that face the inner quarters across the wooden floored hall, the three walls will be lined with books from floor to ceiling. A desk with an adjustable lamp stand and a small bed-side table with a telephone and a night light on it. A loving mother frequently popping in and out to make sure he's all right...

After work I met him again at the tea-room 'Rose'. I've learned some more about him and his family. There has been a shortage of sons in his family and the family line had been maintained by only sons for the past six generations, and now he's the heir of the seventh. He has both parents and a younger sister doing English literature at Ewha Women's University. He told me about her at length. Apparently she's a tomboy and spoilt rotten.

'She tells me, 'he said, 'she and her friends have started some kind of a club and appointed me as their adviser, can you believe it? It's their monthly meeting tonight, and I am expected to be there at seven-thirty. She kept popping in and out of my room even before I was fully awake to make me promise to be there.' He went on with a smack of his tongue. 'I shouted back and told her I didn't want to have anything to do with such a cheeky bunch of girls. Why they didn't even ask my opinion beforehand, and besides, I have a date tonight.' Then he produced a crumpled piece of paper. 'This is what she left on my pillow before she went out.' In careless scrawl it read, 'It's all up to you, dear brother, whether you come or not, but really I don't believe that you'll let me down. The meeting place is "Liberty Salon", in case you've forgotten, at 7.30 p.m. Your darling sis. Mirim.'

I smiled to myself. It reminded me of my ways with my own sister. These spoilt younger sisters! Then I thought if I were to develop a relationship with him, his sister would be an important person. Either I get on well with her and she will be my ally or she will set herself against me and play the devil's advocate. Don't I know the importance of a sister-in-law to one's married life in this country!

'Of course, you must go,' I said. 'I am unconditionally on her side.'

So he conceded to the two women and went to the meeting. Before we parted he invited me into a florist's we were passing by and asked me to choose some flowers for myself. The small shop was filled with things like lilies, camellia, carnations, azalea and forsythia, but I did not fancy fully blown ones. It was sad to think that they would wither in a few days. I rather fancied the idea of watching over some buds growing into lovely leaves and flowers. I picked up a lump of roots with small, pointed tips – lilies of the valley. When I came home I put them in the flowerpot just outside the window. I shall water them everyday and have the pleasure of seeing them grow day by day.

3 April. He phoned during the morning. He has to go to a party tonight to welcome a friend who has just returned from America.

'Would you care to come with me?' he said. I briefly thought about it. It did not seem to be right to appear in public with a man I hardly know.

'It's just like you. I thought you might say that. I won't insist against your wish.' Then he said, 'What about the fifth or the sixth? The fifth is a public holiday, isn't it? Have you any plans?'

I looked up at the calendar on the wall. The fifth is Arbor Day, followed by Sunday.

'If I can have the car on the fifth, I thought, it would be nice to drive out to the suburbs. Besides, my sister wants to meet you, she really does. Do you mind if she comes along?' I thought to myself: what a lovely idea. I think I'll get on famously well with her as she's supposed to be a tomboy like myself. I already feel friendly towards her. I said, 'I shall be delighted if she can come.'

'Even if I don't speak to you tomorrow, I'll expect to see you at the usual place then, at 10 a.m. Is that OK? Make sure you have some idea of where you'd like to go.' I smiled to myself at his tone of voice, which sounded like an intimate command.

'I'd rather leave the programme of the day in your hands,' I said and heard him chuckle.

5 April. I packed lunch for three with great care and went to 'Rose'. He was alone.

'Where's your sister?' I had put on clothes and shoes with her in mind. I had hoped to secure some sign of approval from her.

'I am ashamed to say that she's made herself unavailable. Apparently mother scolded her severely about something yesterday. She just walked out and did not come home last night. She's terrible, she's spoilt and so wilful causing us serious headaches sometimes.' He clicked his tongue disconsolately and said, 'I couldn't call off our plan simply because of her, could I?' He was right, I suppose, for there are only a couple more days before he goes to Pusan, but I could not hide my disappointment.

'How sad. I really wanted to meet her more than you. Don't you have to do something to bring her home?'

'No, it's nothing to worry about. We're quite used to her ways, refusing to eat or leaving the house until she gets what she wants. Sounds awful, doesn't she? But when she is nice, she's the sweetest thing in the world. Would you like to see her picture?' He produced a snapshot from his wallet. A young lady in tight-legged trousers of three quarter length with a check-patterned blouse, and a wide-brimmed straw hat was leaning on a walking stick as she brightly smiled by the wheel of a water-mill. An attractive face with large eyes and straight, high nose resembled that of her brother. I handed it back. 'She's lovely. She takes after you, doesn't she?' He just smiled.

'Now, where would you like to go?' He said briskly as he looked at his wrist-watch. It was past half past ten.

'They brought in some plants at home yesterday. I picked up a couple for you and me to plant somewhere.' What a romantic idea!

'What are they?'

'Magnolia.'

'Magnolia! Wonderful!' Filled with childlike delight I clapped my hands. 'To plant magnolia, it would have to be some hills, do you think?' Then I remembered Samgak Mountain. I knew it only through Kim Naesŏng's novel *The Lovers*. The last scene is set on this mountain and it has left a deep impression on me. Its protagonist Kang Chiun and the heroine, Yi Yŏngsim, walk up the steep paths of this mountain, deep in untrodden snow. Their bodies and souls sealed in one accord, unconscious of the time or place or what lies ahead them, and rolling over in the snow, picking themselves up and propping up each other, they plod on towards the summit, leaving a trail of endless foot marks. I fancied seeing this mountain. As I walk up the valley towards the highest peak today, I thought, my own soul may be sealed in one aspiration – love.

'Samgak Mountain – I've never been there but I've always wanted to go.' Thus our destination was settled.

We got into a covered jeep with a driver waiting inside. There were two saplings in the back about a metre high, like two switches of equal length and thickness.

'How did you find a pair so alike?' I was impressed.

Once out of the city and past the Capitol Building and Hyo-jadong, the surface of the unpaved road was rough and it was full of sharp bends. Sitting on the back seat with the lunch box on my lap, I was thrown up and down each time the car bounced. I also had to mind my handbag that kept falling off the seat, and the saplings bouncing over from one side to the other. The driver noticing my plight in his mirror said, 'May I suggest, sir, you go to the back and give the lady a hand. She's got too much to cope with.'

'I am sorry, it never occurred to me.' He stopped the car, came over to the back seat, and took the lunch box and the plants off my hands. The driver turned round and smiled as if he was pleased with what he had done. Sitting so close to him I felt nervous. I tried hard to hold myself upright but as the road was getting rougher we were constantly thrown against each other. When it was a smooth going I could hear him breathing. I could not face his eyes so I kept mine fixed on the landscape outside, hoping he did not hear my heart beating fast. What will I do once we are in the woods with not a soul around? He seemed to be calm. Why can't I be like that? He would laugh at me if he knew what I am like. I took a deep breath to compose myself.

In no time we were at the foot of the mountain where the car could go no further. He gave the driver some money as he said, 'Thank you and goodbye.' It seemed to be an excessive tip for a private driver but I could not dwell on such matters.

'Have a good time, sir, and the lady too.' He gave us a meaningful wink and turned away. Just the two of us, and not a soul around. We entered a pine wood following a narrow path. It was a beautiful day. Birds darted about chirruping as if welcoming some distinguished visitors. Yes, we are rather special people, I thought. We shall behave as fit for such people.

As the path grew wild and dangerous I fully recovered my calmness. I was happy now that I could behave naturally with him.

'Are you sure you can make it to the top?'

'Of course, I can.'

'The one who gives up first will be the loser.'

'And the loser will obey the winner.' We heartily laughed.

We walked on up a steep rocky path, passing in and out several pine woods until we came to a little stream. We had a rest here, eating some chocolates and sweets I had brought in my bag, and started climbing again. The higher we went the more breathtaking the view became. Range after range of hills all round you, dells and woods below and crystal streams weaving through the ravines, and a torrent nearby, all in one view. I slightly shivered with awe.

By now, we were both panting and drenched in sweat. The trouble was that we were not properly dressed for climbing. Each time we had to clamber over a rock, he turned and put out his hand to help me but each time I declined. I wanted to show him my independence.

When we reached a spot from which we could see the summit just above our heads, we found a Buddhist temple and a small homestead.

'Should we plant the trees here first,' he said, 'have some lunch and then go up the top?'

'I was just going to suggest that. To make sure they come to no harm, it would be nice to plant them near the temple compound, and ask the people here to keep an eye on them.'

He went up to the main Hall and asked for the abbot. A man of about fifty came out, joined his palms as he bowed from the waist and said, 'Welcome to our temple. What can we do for you?' We stood side by side and bowed in greeting.

'As it is Arbor Day today, we've brought a couple of saplings hoping to plant them somewhere here. We came to ask you if you would be able to keep an eye on them.' He said it so smartly, so politely yet with such dignity I was proud of him.

'Ah, is that so. That is a good idea,' said the abbot. 'Have you chosen the site?'

'No, not yet. We'd appreciate it if you could help us. It would be nice if it was in front of the Main Hall.'

'What are they?'

'Magnolias.'

'Ah, in that case, it's an excellent idea to put them there,' he pointed the rectangular flower-bed in front of the Main Hall. How splendid! I was congratulating myself on our luck. Just imagine, two splendid magnolias growing in front of the Main Hall of a temple. We will often come together to see how they are doing. Two monks came out from the inner quarters and started digging at either end of the flower-bed. When the holes were ready we took one each and planted them helped by the young men. After covering the roots and filling in the hole I smoothed the soil, treading on it to make it firm. I gave the plant a final jerk and watered it generously. I think it will grow into a splendid tree and produce magnificent flowers.

'It is in commemoration of a special occasion. I would be obliged if you would take great care of them,' he said. The term 'commemoration of a special occasion' roused a strange excitement in me.

'Of course, I will,' said the abbot. He looked pleased too. We were now being treated as honoured guests. We were shown into a room attached to the kitchen where we could eat the food we had brought. From outside it seemed a low-lying shack but it was spacious inside, cool and clean. There were two sets of sliding doors, one leading to the kitchen from which we had entered the room, and another looking out onto a small courtyard. We opened the latter, and across the courtyard, a splended scene came in view. Ridge lines of lower hills dense with trees stretched out as far as to the distant housing estate of Chŏngnŭng, the houses like a group of playing cards shimmering in a mirage. The doors to the kitchen slid open and a woman politely pushed in a small table with some side dishes of vegetables, two spoons and two sets of chopsticks, and two bowls of cold water. As a token of thanks, I handed her the spare lunch box. When she withdrew, I sat opposite him across the table. We smiled at each other. I was happy that all had gone well so far.

'This is not very good but I prepared it with care, so I hope you enjoy it, ' I said as I handed him his lunch – rice tightly rolled in dry sheets of laver, with savoury centres of beef, eggs, dressed spinach and pickled turnip, then sliced into mouth-size pieces.

'It's delicious. I didn't know you could cook so well.' He finished his quickly and had some more of mine. Now that my stomach was full, I was overcome by drowsiness. My legs ached and every joint in my body seemed to be melting like candle wax. I longed for a nap.

'I shall be very ill tomorrow. It's my first climbing you see.'

'I must say I was impressed. The dogged way you followed me was wonderful.'

'I didn't follow you. You just walked a couple of paces in front of me, that's all.'

He gave his charming chuckle again. 'You and your pride. I know your type. You can't bear to be second or defeated, can you?' I smiled and shrugged my shoulders. He guessed right. I am like that. Being second rate or defeated has rarely been part of my experience so far.

By now I could not keep my eyes open. As I leaned back against the wall they just drooped shut. When I forced my eyes open I saw, a couple of feet away, his burning eyes looking into mine. His face was tense as if he was going to have a fit.

'When you are alone with a man in a room, make sure the door is left open. You can't go too wrong if you think he is a hungry wolf. A tired face of a woman arouses a particular temptation in a man, so ideally you should meet him in the day time rather than in the evening.' These were the words of the domestic science teacher at high school as she gave the last, special lessons to the school leavers. How Miae and I hated her guts. But at this moment her voice rang in my ears sweetly. I sat up straight and smoothed my hair and clothes. He must have sensed my alarm.

'You must be very tired. Look, I'll go out for a stroll and leave you to yourself so that you can relax and have a good nap.'

I don't know how long he went out for but I must have instantly dozed off. When I woke up I felt refreshed. I went out into the courtyard to look round for him. Some distance away I saw him sitting on a flat rock, his back against a large tree. I felt guilty. He really is a gentleman. He would have waited there for as long as it took for me to sleep and feel rested.

'Mr Kwŏn —' I called loudly as I ran up to him. From there the conquest of the summit was easily done. The view from there was breathtaking but the summit itself was bare, just a few large rocks and a strong breeze. There was no need to stay long.

'We might as well go down,' I said. 'The pleasure of the moment of a conquest does not last long, does it? Yet for this brief moment of happiness we've come all that dangerous way taking hours.' It was meant to be a casual remark but he seemed to be impressed by it. He uttered a moan-like 'Mmn,' followed by a deep sigh.

Following the advice of the people at the temple we took a short-cut down. I found coming down was much easier than going up. I was pleased that it had been such a good day. We walked on in silence for some time. I broke it.

'What a good climbing course this is. I shall come here often now,' then went on chirpily, 'Whose tree, do you think, will do better?'

His response was quite unexpected. 'No doubt yours will, Miss Yun.' He sounded solemn and formal.

'Why's that?'

'For one thing, you will come here more often, I suppose.'
I thought he was thinking about his going away to Pusan.

'Miss Yun,' he said. 'While I'm away, will you look after my
tree as well as your own?' His face and voice were so solemn
and tragic. What did this sudden change mean? Cautiously I put
in 'Will you be in Pusan all the time from now on?'

'Well, all being well, I hope to come back within a year or
two at the most but...' he trailed off in a weak voice.

'It looks as though this is going to be the first and the last
time that you and I will come together.' I added imitating his
tone of voice, 'Mr Kwŏn, would you look after my tree as well
as yours in my absence?'

He looked at me with inquiring eyes.

'By the time you are back I shall be in the United States. I
hope to be there by next spring at the latest.'

I hoped he would challenge my phrase 'the first and the last
time,' by saying something like 'We can still come together when
you are back from America,' but all he gave was a deep sigh.

'Whichever one of us it is, each time we come, shall we
agree to leave a white stone beneath each other's tree?' My
mind was full of imaginary incidents like fairy-tales that might
evolve from the magnolia tree.

In the middle of a gentle slope not far from the housing estate
of Chŏngnŭng, we passed a huge beech tree. Beneath it was a
bamboo grove. Out of season the bamboo was not lush but its
dry leaves had fallen and were scattered thick all around like
straw matting. It looked a comfortable place. No one suggested
it, but we simultaneously sat down, leaning our backs against
the tree. The sun seemed to be in a great hurry. One could
almost hear its striding footsteps as it sets. Trails of smoke from
cooking supper drifted over the houses. Feeble light lingered
on where we sat. Not a bird twittered nor a leaf rustled in the
bamboo grove. Blissful calm.

Then I saw rising on the horizon a mushroom of black cloud.
'Oh, dear, we are in for a shower,' I said.
'Why, are you afraid of gettingg wet?'
'No, I'm not afraid, it's just a nuisance to have to walk about
in wet clothes. Let's hurry up and get under some shelter.'
'No,' he said sulkily. 'I want to stay the night here.' I thought
he was being unreasonable.
'I don't want to go home. If I fall asleep, just leave me and
you go home.' With this he flung himself down on his back
and closed his eyes. He could have been an unpredictable and
moody child when he was young, I thought, and smiled to
myself. As if coaxing a child I put my hand on his shoulder and
gently tapped it. 'Please stop being silly. Just tell me what you
want me to do.'
After a long silence he called me formally, 'Miss Yun.'
'Yes, Mr Kwŏn.'
'Can you recite a poem for me?'
'A poem?'
'Yes, please.'
'What poem?'
'Anything that might comfort a lonely soul.'
The first thing that came to my mind was a translation of
Yeats' 'Innisfree.' I recited it once and having no response from
him repeated it once more:

I will arise and go now, and go to Innisfree,
And a small cabin build there, of clay and wattles made:
Nine bean rows will I have there, a hive for the honey bee,
And live alone in the bee-loud glade.

And I shall have some peace there, for peace comes dropping slow,
Dropping from the veils of the morning to where
The cricket sings;

There midnight's all a glimmer, and noon a purple glow,
And evening full of the linnet's wings.
I will arise and go now, for always night and day
I hear lake water lapping with low sounds by the shore;
While I stand on the roadway, or on the pavements grey,
I hear it in the deep heart's core.

'Thank you, Miss Yun. That was lovely,' he said as if he was awaking from a dream. 'I have been foolishly wishing that my body was purer so that I could join in a perfect happiness. It has been bliss to be with you for the last few days.' After a long silence he raised himself and sat upright and said, 'Would you care to hear my life story?' I was tense with curiosity.

'Your youthful vivacity with no trace of shadow gives me the illusion that my dead wife has come back to me.'

'Dead wife?' It made me start. Ignoring my surprise he went on, 'Shortly before I went to America, I used to go to S Girls' High School as a part-time lecturer. I fell in love with one of my pupils there. I was confident that I could make her the happiest woman in the world. She was not particularly beautiful but had an attractive personality. She made me think of a crock filled with clear water. I loved her for that. But my mother, who is wilful and perverse, did not like her. She could not accept a poor widow's daughter who was not a great beauty as the wife of her only son. While I was away in the States my mother played all sorts of mischief to make her give me up. The letters I wrote were never once answered. When I came back she was not among the people who welcomed me at the airport. That evening my mother threw a big party to which she had invited many smart young ladies but it all meant nothing to me. Then the telephone rang on the table by which I was standing. She had taken poison and been taken to the Severance Hospital but there was little hope for her. I rushed there at one breath and broke down by her bed, crying uncontrollably. Apparently after seeing me at the airport from a distance she had gone home and committed the deed straightaway.'

I felt my eye-lids smarting as tears rose to my eyes.

'I didn't leave her bedside for two days. Miraculously on the third day she came round. After she came out I married her at once. But she was not at all like what she had been before. She had lost all her former vivacity. With lustreless eyes and limp body she carried on for another two months before she died.'

As he came to the end he closed his eyes. I thought he might burst into tears but it was I who broke into sobs. It was not only the dead woman I felt sorry for but my heart ached for him. Beneath his gentle manners, to carry such a sorrow! He opened his eyes and smiled at me. 'Silly Sukey, you are crying. I'm sorry if I have upset you. Shall we go now?' He pulled me up by my hand. When we came to the house where I lived with my sister in a rented room, he put out his hand for mine, which I readily gave him. He held it tenderly in his hands and said, 'Good night. You must be very tired,' and added, 'Can I see you again tomorrow or would you rather stay at home and have a rest?'

I didn't know what to say. Two more days and he will be gone. I wanted to make the most of the time left. On the other hand, I was really tired. I thought I needed a day's rest to be at work on Monday. Just then I heard some one moving behind the gates. I quickly pulled my hand out of his grip, said in whisper, 'I'll see you at the usual place at eleven', and ran into the house.

6 April. 3 a.m. I have been lying awake all this time. My limbs and whole body ache and I am dog-tired but sleep would not come. Like a pond disturbed by throwing a stone in it, I cannot calm myself. At the temple, he went out of the room so that I could relax and rest while he waited outside. He could love, with such faithfulness, a plain-looking woman with poor background. He is a man of few words. Most of the time he lets me dominate the conversations with trivial matters while he just looks on me with admiring eyes. He has some respect for women. He is a personification of goodness and truthfulness. If he wants me I think, I shall give him the whole of myself at any time. In this way am I sealing my fate? Yes, I am ready to accept my fate if it is that.

I finally dropped off after more or less making up my mind. Once gone off I slept soundly. When I woke up it was half past ten. I got myself ready in a great hurry, omitting the breakfast, and got a taxi to 'Rose'. Even so I was half an hour late. Leaning back on a chair he sat with closed eyes. As I sat opposite him with a guilty look he opened his dreamy eyes and said, 'So you decided to come?' There was no need to explain why I was late. I just smiled.

'I knew you were tired, but I thought you may not want to see me anymore, a worthless man like me...' He did not look as sad as he had yesterday so I stopped him briskly. 'No more moping, please. It's too nice a day to be stuck in a dark corner of a tea-room. Let's get out of here.' This seemed to cheer him up.

'I thought a day at the seaside would be nice, after a day in the mountains, unless you are too tired?'

'A day in the mountains followed by a day at sea! How wonderful.' I gave him an admiring look as I clapped. 'Where will that be?'

'Inchŏn would be just right for the time we have. It's already twelve.' He stood up and went to the counter to pay. He had a camera slung over his shoulder, and looked very smart from the back. I was proud of him. On the way to the bus terminal, I was slightly taken aback when out of the blue he asked, 'By the way, what sort of salary do they pay you?'

I teasingly said, 'A gentleman asking a lady about her salary!'

'It's just that I am thinking of taking on an assistant and wondering how much I should pay her.'

'Seventy thousand Hwan.'

'That's not bad, is it?'

'Besides, we get a quarterly bonus of the full amount.' He thoughtfully nodded his head.

The seat for two on the bus was not quite big enough to be comfortable. We sat side by side, our shoulders touching. I felt as if I could feel his warmth coming through my layers of clothes, but soon I realized that I was the only one who was so self-conscious. With his eyes fixed on the view through the window and his hands on his lap, one on top of the other, he sat correct and upright. Outside was mile upon mile of barley, the blades of leaves sparkling in the bright sun. When the breeze rose and ruffled them, they fell flat on one side and then the other, ripples of green waves through which our bus sped like a speedboat.

In no time we were at the beach. He arranged me in various poses and clicked his camera. The tide was low. In silence we walked over the sand toward the water's edge. It made me think of travellers setting off towards the far horizon, long, lonely shadows dragging behind them. He was very attentive to my moods. When I was just thinking of a rest, he stopped and made me sit against a large rock facing the sea, pressed the shutter once again and then came and sat beside me.

Far out the tide had turned. Myriad of seagulls hovered over it. In a rhythm of 'pull, rest, smash!', 'pull, rest, smash!' the waves surged and shattered like explosives. We sat in silence, each in their own thoughts. Mine dwelled on the love and wondered whether it did not resemble the waves, in its force and its single passion. Once started rolling it won't stop half way. It will go on and on until it reaches the shore and smashes itself.

In no time the water was almost below our feet. He stood, took a step closer to it and mumbled as if to himself, 'The water that ebbed is flowing back but...'

'You mean 'the one who departed is not?''

'Sukey, you are too clever for me!' I rose and stood beside him and we both took a deep breath. It was a full tide.

'Sukey.'

'Yes?'

'I've decided on something.'

'What thing?'

'Not to think about her anymore.'

'It is not the sort of thing that you can do or not do at will, is it?'

'What I mean is that the face I have remembered everyday for the past three years has recently become blurry. Even if I try hard to evoke it, I cannot bring it back.'

A silence fell. I thought of the poor woman. Then he said, 'It is thanks to you that I am beginning to live my life.'

'Oh, no,' I thought, 'He is going to propose.' His face was tense as it was yesterday, at the temple. I knew I was in love but I was not ready to make a decision right there and then.

'We are going to miss the bus if we don't hurry.' I gathered up my handbag and the litter from our snack. Without any fuss or protest, he followed me.

'It has been a lovely day. Thank you, Mr Kwŏn.' I knew we had got over another dangerous moment. We were now happily chattering about trivial things.

He said, 'You must be fond of the colour of the sea. I like your dress. I often think of you in that sea-blue *ch'ima* and *jogori* at the hotel. It reminded me of a kingfisher skimming over cool and clear water.' He went on, 'There was a lake not far from my college in the States. My professor often took me there for a drive or on a picnic. There was this beautiful water bird. It used to dart about over the surface of the water making merry, chirping sounds. It had feathers of that colour.' Again about the States. I was dying to ask him what he studied, and where, and how long but refrained in case he thought I was too inquisitive. I smiled to myself as I remembered what a goose he had been at the hotel in his white and blue striped pyjamas.

We stopped briefly to turn round and cast a last glance to the sea.

'Sukey.'

'Yes?'

'How old are you?'

'Twenty-four. What about you?'

'Thirty-one.' Then we looked at each other and burst into laughter. Thirty-one. Suddenly the thought of my brother, Hyŏngsŏk came to mind. He would be just that.

7 April. We are now confessed lovers. This is how I had wished it to be. He leaves for Pusan tomorrow. Before he went, I had hoped, we should make some kind of binding pledge tonight. I am too excited to write down what happened today.

When he phoned me during the morning I expressed my strong wish to see him off at the station after work tomorrow and he said he would change his plan so as to leave at seven-thirty in the evening. But when we met after work, he apologized that after all he had to go in the morning as he would be with his mother and she had already bought two plane tickets. I am afraid I can't think kindly towards her. She sounds a bossy, mischief-maker, and keeps him under her thumb. Of course I told him I did not mind not seeing him off. Unfortunately the Board meeting that had started at four-thirty dragged on until seven-thirty and it was not until nearly eight that I was with him. After dinner, a farewell dinner, we went out to the Han River by taxi and walked along the sandy beach. After a group of late fishermen had collected their tackle and gone, we were the only ones left on that vast shore. Like two dreamers we walked hand in hand, vaguely, towards the lights from the houses in a distant village on the other side of the river. The damp air rising from it felt quite chilly as I was wearing only a thin spring dress.

'Sukey, aren't you cold?' He lightly touched my cheek.

'No, I am alright, thank you,' said I but somehow I stepped closer to him and into his arm. From then on we walked with our arms round each other's waists. He again spoke of how he wished his body was purer, and asked me what I thought about love and whether I thought one should be allowed to love for the second time? I knew what he meant. He wanted my approval for his second chance to love. I had never thought about it much but words just tumbled out. 'Of course one can love for the second time, the third or even the fourth. Why ever not? I'm sure love is not a matter of the past or future. It is whether or not you love someone now; whether you can wholeheartedly keep faith with the one you love, a matter of conscience perhaps...' He did not wait for me to finish but gathered me in his arms and kissed me. In accepting this I felt as if a large column that had propped me up until now collapsing and, leaving a huge hole. As if to fill up that emptiness I attached myself tightly to him for a long time.

'I feel worthless and shameless to ask this but will you marry me?' he said and without a moment's hesitation I nodded my consent. I had well prepared myself for this. By doing so I have sealed my life!

We must have walked for miles. The lights that once looked so far away were now just opposite us on the other side of the water. We could have gone in a state of daze. I was dimly beginning to think it must be very late. Suddenly a sharp breeze from the river came and slapped me on the cheek. I pulled away from him. 'Let's go home, I'm scared.'

'What are you scared of? We have plenty of time,' he protested and sounded irritated. 'And it is the last night before we see each other again!' But I shook myself free. 'I am going to catch my death of cold!' I started off towards the embankment.

Come to think of it, he was very annoyed even though he was too much of a gentleman to show it. He said, when we bade our final goodbye, with less certainty than earlier, something about sorting out some business in Pusan and coming back to marry me very soon. I don't know what to do. I am all in a flutter. Even though I am thrilled I am sure I am not ready for an early marriage. Still we can think it over, can't we? It is my daily blessing to water and see the pointed buds of the lilies of the valley push their way through, a little bit bigger each day, like the promise of bright and happy days.

9 April. I am a fallen woman. Let the world laugh and mock at me!

Yesterday, when I got to the office, Suyŏn handed me the phone and said, 'It is the fourth call for you, always the same voice.' She seemed to sense it was something special and left the room.

'I knew you weren't be there yet, but I wanted to hear your voice so much that I have been ringing you since I woke up. Silly, aren't I?' He chuckled. 'I am just about to leave for the airport.'

We had gone over everything that we had to last night. I didn't know what to say except 'Take care of yourself, and please keep in touch. Goodbye.'

Ten minutes later the phone rang. It was him again. 'Mother is not quite ready. I just wanted to say that I love you so much. I can't bear to leave you. Shall I not go?'

I was touched but thought him unmanly. 'Don't be silly. You sound like a little boy.' But when he actually put the phone down saying that his mother was just coming out, I was sad and held onto the receiver as if expecting to hear his gentle voice still vibrating.

When two hours later he phoned yet again I was taken aback. He was being ridiculous, I thought. We have made a pledge to each other and we know that we'll meet again soon – what is there for him to be so restless about. He said he had something important to talk over with me. So, at the airport he parted from his mother and came back. I felt a momentary disillusionment. One can be infatuated when in love but this was going too far. I also felt ashamed about what had happened the night before by the River Han. When I see him tonight, I thought, I would suggest that we ought to calm down a bit and carry on our love in a more dignified and rational manner as befits intellectuals.

On the other hand I was uneasy about the 'important matter' he was referring to. What could be so important that he should go as far as to cancelling his flight? I was again detained at work. So it was nearly eight o'clock when I met him at the appointed restaurant. When we had ordered our meal, he started by saying, 'I was nearly trapped into my mother's plot.' Behind his back apparently, she had been arranging his marriage to the daughter of a business tycoon in Pusan. It had been his mother's intention to introduce her to him in the evening. As his mother sensed something was going on between us, he had guessed, she might plan some mischief against me. He had to warn me of this in person. He would go to Pusan tomorrow to sort out a few things, staying away from his mother, and come back on the 12th to discuss our marriage arrangements.

I felt as if I had been hit on the head with a hammer.

'Our love and trust in each other will win in the end, blah, blah, blah' he went on talking something like this but I couldn't hear a word. When I recovered my senses I felt bitter. So, his mother is against me, is that what he's saying? Am I not good enough to be his wife, a second wife? Who does she think she is? How dare she? Outrage made me feel like screaming but I kept a calm face. Why, in the first place, had he not introduced me to her before he made any advances? I had so much to say but words failed to come out.

'Mother produced this out of her handbag on the way to the airport.' He handed me a photograph, the size of a visiting card, of a beautiful woman. It was rubbing salt into my injury. My hand shook with jealousy on top of the outrage. I was dying to hurt him to the quick by words or deeds or both as revenge for my pain. I handed it back to him and said very calmly and clearly, 'That's the best thing that can happen to you. I haven't the slightest inclination to enter into competition with this woman or fight your stupid mother. Goodbye.'

I walked out of the restaurant and briskly and blindly set off down the road ahead me. When it turned out to be the way to the River, I sharply changed my direction to shake off the memories of last night and took another course. I don't know how many turnings I had taken before I found myself going in the direction of Tonamdong. When I was close to home, I turned back again. I had been weeping and could not go home with a tear-stained face. I had been aware of his footsteps behind me for some time now. When I veered into a cul-de-sac they quickened and as he snatched me into his arms I broke down and cried.

'I didn't know you were as weak as this,' he said. 'As long as we are sure of our love, what is there to be afraid of?'

I was calm when we resumed our walk. He talked about various possibilities about our future, living away from his mother. For instance we could go and live in Cheju Island. A close friend of his is running a large dairy farm there and would welcome him any day as a business partner.

'But you must be starving, silly girl,' he said. Indeed I was. I was cold too, my teeth were chattering. We went into a shabby soup place, which was about to close for the night. We ate a bowl of meat soup each. When we came out the preliminary siren for the curfew was sounding. He caught a taxi just rushing by. I leaned on his shoulder and closed my eyes. It dropped us in front of a hotel. I could not believe my eyes. The prolonged shriek of the siren for the curfew shook the black night. With a keen grasp of the situation, like a well-trained dog, the waiter said there was just one room unoccupied. Once in the room and the door was locked from the inside the inevitable took place. I could not blame him entirely but I was certain that we disgraced ourselves. It was not a proper way to go about love. My lofty pride was thrown down onto the ground and trodden on. I was quietly weeping but at least I was sure of one thing – nothing could now separate me from him.

This morning I was too ashamed to face the world let alone my colleagues. I sent in a message that I was unwell and came home. I had to invent a lie for my sister. I told her that his mother and sister were so keen to meet me that I went to his house, enjoyed myself very much and did not realize how the time went until the curfew siren went.

A face floated before my eyes all day. It has superseded the entire world. What would I not give to have it by me now. In the afternoon I went to see Miae. We hadn't seen each other since her engagement party on 30th March. She was wild with delight when she saw me.

'What a super surprise! You're still alive then? What wind brings you here?'

'Silly cow! Who's talking? Why couldn't you drop in while you were in town? Anyway, that was a splendid party, wasn't it?'

'Did you enjoy it? Thanks a million for all the things you did for me that day.' We heartily enjoyed our reunion.

'How is Mr Han? Has he got a job yet?'

'Yes, at X Bank. He's just started – last Monday.'

'That's good.' I took off my shoes and entered the room, which seemed to have been converted to a sewing room. A middle-aged seamstress from the country was deftly turning the wheel of the sewing machine.

'What's all this? You haven't even fixed the wedding day yet, have you?'

'Well, I'd like it to be in the autumn but apparently his mother wants to have it done before May. In any case, my mother thinks it would be best to have everything ready in good time.'

We walked upstairs and stood on the verandah overlooking the garden with its thriving shrubs and trees. Her father's transport business must be thriving to have bought a house like that in an expensive, residential area. As I rested my gaze on one end of the evening sky I was comparing the rising fortunes of her family and the declining luck of my poor father. I envy her. I live on a tight budget. Buying ordinary clothes to wear at work is hard enough let alone getting a trousseau ready! What am I to do?

Miae was very happy. She told me that she had started learning to play the *kayakŭm*. I asked why out of all instruments she had chosen that.

'It's Han's favourite apparently,' she said. 'He says he can't take to noisy Western stuff, and would like to see me plucking the strings of a zither in a traditional full skirt of pastel-coloured gauze. Funny, isn't he?'

'It sounds a very refined taste,' I said as I turned to face her. 'Miae, don't laugh, but I may even beat you to it.' I needed courage to bring this up.

'What? With Mr Kwŏn?' She was surprised.

'Umn.' My mood of melancholy of a few moments ago had completely cleared. I told her about everything except what had happened in the hotel – a day in the mountains, a day by the sea and the night stroll by the River Han. As I did so my heart ached with love for him.

'You sneaky minx! So you've gone through it all.' She clapped her hands and rolled in laughter. We chattered on like this for sometime.

'So what is going to happen now to our beloved study?' Miae said. It's true, our studies have been our lovers. Books and dreams have set us apart from our friends and contemporaries. There had been little room for men in our hearts.

'Of course, we are not going to abandon it altogether, are we? Let's carry on,' I said. 'We have to be different from the others. Probably, I shall go to post-graduate school next year. I fancy a transfer to English literature. Then in a couple of years' time, I would like to go to America preferably with him...' I said this with confidence then but now I feel less certain. The thought of his mother bothers me.

10 April. I have been counting the ticking of the clock virtually all day. Counting down for our reunion had started forty hours too early. Forty hours, thirty-nine... After work I went to Chongro 4th Street and roamed around the district for nearly two hours hoping to find his house. I looked into every alley, but could not find one that fitted what, from his casual remarks, I had imagined it to be like. It's foolish of me, of course, to set out in search of a house without knowing the number or the name of the head of the family. But then I didn't mean it seriously. Even if I had found it I would have had no courage to knock on the gate or anything like that. I just missed him so much. I would have been happy just to be around the house that he goes in and out everyday. Finally I knocked on the door of the District Office, which keeps open late.

'I am looking for the house of a man with the name of Kwŏn. He lives around here, I am certain about that. He's a lecturer at S University, his father is a businessman, his mother owns a number of buses, and by the way, he has a sister who is a student of E University...Would you happen to know such a family?' The clerk gave me a pitying look. 'You might ask for Mr Kim of Seoul City. You won't find a house in that way.'

I don't blame him. I turned round with giggles. What an idiot I am! I shall tell him when I see him. It will make him laugh.

11 April. Overnight the world has changed. It's wrapped in layers of suspicion. My head is filled with cotton–wool–like substance and I can't think clearly. 'Social evil' is a familiar term I hear almost every day of my life, but I have little experience of it myself. Probably my world so far has been too secluded. I have no immunization to it. Still, how can you doubt such a good and sincere man and place him in the context of social evil.

Miae's advice was from the bottom of her heart, I know, but sadly I see that a chasm has opened up between us. She had called me in a cheerful voice just to say hello but when I told her what I did last night her tone changed.

'When you decided to go and look for his house you must have had some idea of its whereabouts, near some landmark like a big building or a shop or a large chimney. As you know I had lodgings around there once, and as far as I can remember I can't imagine a big private house tucked away anywhere among all those shops and shop-keepers' houses in that area.' Once again I appreciated her rational mind in contrast to my woolly and emotional temperament.

I hesitated for a few seconds but had to tell her about the phone calls too.

With longing and peculiar curiosity I had dialled the number he had given me. If anyone answered I would just hang up. If someone sounded nice and said hello before I put it down, I could simply say that I was a student of his and could I speak to him. It rang. I was all nerves. No one answered it. It was a relief. I tried again and again through most of the morning. I was beginning to be irritated. In the end, I phoned the enquiries and was told that the number was not registered. My heart missed a beat.

The bell in the Director's Room rang. I was unable to stand up. So Suyŏn went in on my behalf. I gritted my teeth, got the number for S University and dialled it. The operator's kind voice said, 'I am afraid most teachers are away because it is still the vacation.' Like a drowning man holding onto a straw I interpreted it as a positive admission that he belonged there. I asked to be put through to the Registration Office and confirmed that he was not on the teachers' register. I wanted to die. I crawled into the conference room and collapsed onto the sofa. Suyŏn came in bringing in a cup of coffee.

'Good heavens, ŏnni! What is the matter? Should I call the doctor?' She was in a flutter. It was then that the office-boy put his face round the door and told me that Miae was on the phone.

'I think you should stop seeing him before your affection for him grows any deeper,' her voice was now decisive yet solicitous. 'What is the use of loving a man who lies to you whatever reasons he may have.'

She does not know the thing that I need to hide from the world. How disillusioned she will be when she knows it. Something like a lump of lead in my throat was choking me. I could not speak.

'Han has some friends working with the newspapers and in the Police as well, the Criminal Investigation Section in fact.

I have a good mind to let them investigate the case and teach him a lesson.' Her voice was now cool. But such words as newspapers and criminal investigation made me cringe. I could see before my eyes such headlines as 'Professional Fraud – Fake College Lecturer Seduces Female Graduate.'

'Please don't tell Han, Miae. I will make another investigation and sort it out myself.' My voice sounded cowardly, as if appealing for her mercy.

'Alright then, I won't. I will trust in your good sense,' she spoke curtly and rang off. I still can't believe he's a fraud. He must have had his reasons. Until I know them I can't just dismiss him like that.

It is late but I can't sleep. Unable to bear it alone I told my sister the whole truth. I thought she might slap me in the face but she took it with unexpected calm. 'I am going to be ill,' she said before she went to bed, pulled the cover over her head and sobbed. She's now asleep. I have a feeling that he will never appear before me again. My love – has he gone forever leaving sorrow in my heart? Leaving the saplings of magnolia and the buds of the lily of the valley as the only proof that he was there? The rapture of yesterday turned into sorrow today. Why did he do that? Why did he have to deceive me? He didn't have to lie. I would have given him my all without all these lies. I am thinking of taking my life.

12 April. Sŏnhi is ill. Every time she has a shock she seems to go down with sickness. She needs several days' quiet. Whether he will come back or not I have a duty to my work. I thought I ought to clear up all my drawers and files to make it easy for my successor after I have gone.

In the afternoon, the Director went out to go to the X Foundation leaving his office for an hour or so. 'When the cat's away the mice will play.' My colleagues behind the partition broke into lively conversations. Mr Hong banged on the partition and shouted, 'Miss Yun, how long?' meaning how long will he be away.

'About an hour,' I said. Long enough to pool a small sum of money, and one of us go out and get some snacks. In normal circumstances I would have joined them chattering as loudly as anyone else, but today I went on with tidying up my drawers. Miss Pak came round to me.

'Are you all right? You don't look well.' I like her sisterly ways towards me. She pulled up a chair by my side and was about to say something but on second thoughts closed her mouth.

'So, Miss Chŏng's going soon, then,' I had to break the silence as I was the hostess and she the guest.

'Yes, isn't she clever? She has arranged it all so quietly with no fuss, no showing off.'

'Having her sister and brother in America must have been a great help, I suppose. I shall miss her.'

'So will I.' Then she said, 'What about you? With the man you met in Onyang. I thought you were getting on well with him for a few days?'

I didn't know how to reply. Two days ago I would have said, 'We are going to be married soon,' and told her all about it.

'Um, we are in love with each other. He's away in Pusan at the moment.'

'Good. What's he like? '

I could not hide my tears rising to my eyes. 'We love each other but he has a wife and a child.' At this rate, I shall soon be a master liar myself. There was now no need to restrain my tears.

'Oh, I am sorry.' She heaved a sigh.

'Ŏnni, don't tell anyone, will you.'

'Of course not, but I am terribly sorry. Try to forget. You couldn't have developed too deep an affection yet.' She clicked her tongue as she left me and went back to her desk. At that moment the telephone rang.

'Hello.' My voice sounded weak. A woman's voice said, 'Is that Miss Yun I am speaking to?'

'Yes, I am Sukey Yun.'

'That's handy,' she said. What an arrogant voice. 'It is about Tong-hi Kwŏn.' I tensed up. At first I thought it was his mother.

'You had better give him up. He will not be seeing you today. I've been with him in Pusan.'

'May I ask who you are?'

'You don't need to know who I am, but I am telling you this for your own good. All I can say is that I loved him before you and I trust your good character.'

I could not make sense of all this and I was thoroughly confounded. Then a few minutes later the phone rang again. This time it was him.

'Oh, Sukey. I've just got off the train and run up the stairs in one breath.' He was obviously panting.

'How are you? You are quiet? Sukey? Sukey?' I didn't know how to respond to this. On hearing his voice all my suspicion and anger melted away, I could not wait to see him. If I was honest to myself I should have said frankly, 'You have been lying to me. Liar!' But I had developed some cunning in the last few days. I have learnt to handle certain circumstances with caution and strategy. If he knew that I suspected him and was angry he might decide not to see me again. I could not risk letting him slip away. I pretended innocence and cheerfulness.

'So, you are back. Did you have a good time? How's your mother?'

'I have so much to tell you. I'll see you at "Rose" at seven.'

When I saw him the expression on my face probably betrayed a mixture of hatred and love. He looked a bit thinner. I thought

I would sort it out there and then, the questions of love or deception, and life or death.

'You have been lying to me. Why?'

Like a deer struck by an arrow his countenance instantly crumpled. 'I knew you would be like this.'

'But why, why did you have to deceive me?'

'Please say no more. There are reasons, which I hope to explain to you in due course. All I can say is that only our love can solve all the mysteries,' he said imploringly. I noted with curiosity his words 'There are reasons.'

'I left home today,' he said. We looked at each others' blank eyes.

'I haven't eaten anything all day. Shall we go and eat first and then I will tell you all about it.'

We sat in a Western-style restaurant and ate our meal in silence. I could see his hands holding the knife and fork were visibly shaking.

I was taken aback when what he called his new lodgings turned out to be a room in a small hotel. Since that night I had come to harbour bad feelings about such places. In the room there were one suitcase, a small writing desk and a small transistor radio on top of it. The *ondol* floor was pleasantly warm, over which his bedding had been neatly laid out. An elderly inn-keeper and his wife came out and offered him a courteous greetings and went away. Music floated from the radio.

'I want you to understand this, Sukey. I have thrown away all the comforts of life for your sake,' he said as he gripped my hands. 'You trust me, don't you? I will tell you everything tonight.' His face was full of love, enough to melt away the last trace of suspicion and anger. As my tension loosened my body became sloppy. Languor came over it and I could barely sit upright. I felt like throwing myself into his arms and abandoning it to his caresses.

A beep came from the radio. It was the time signal announcing nine o'clock. It was like an alarm bell to shake up my numbed reason. 'You must not allow yourself to spend the night here.' It was a stern voice of my conscience. I sprang to my feet. 'I must go now. See you tomorrow.'

'What do you mean?' He was confounded. 'No, you can't do this to me. I won't be left alone.' He whispered like a feeble child at first. But when he saw me putting on my coat and picking up my handbag he stood in the doorway blocking it. 'If you go, I shall leave Seoul tonight and never see you again.'

'My sister is very ill.' I pushed him aside and stepped down to the courtyard. 'Good night, Mr Kwŏn. I will see you at "Rose" at ten o'clock tomorrow.' I did not wait for his reply and ran out of the gate.

When I was finally through the long alleyway and stood at the edge of the main road I saw him coming after me calling 'Sukey, Sukey.' Like a lunatic I ran across the road stumbling forward and stepped onto the pavement on the other side of the road. Now we stood opposite separated by a dark main road like a deep river. As I stood there I repeated to myself, 'Please forgive me, please forgive me.' I had to get on whatever came first, taxi or bus, but it was a quiet road and nothing came. From the pitch black sky, drops of rain began to fall. His body standing on the other side of the road like a statue started moving towards me. He was coming to implore me once more to stay with him.

'Father, save me from this moment.' Unawares, a prayer leapt out of my lips. I repeated it again and again. He was half way across the road when an empty taxi came sliding round the corner and stopped before me as if in a response to my prayers. Its door briefly opened and shut and it slid away. A scurry of rain beat on the rear window. He stood rooted on the spot. I desperately waved at the rain-splashed back window but whether he saw me or not, he did not return it. The car turned a corner. 'Poor man. He will be wet through standing there fixed on the spot.' I felt heartless. 'He will never appear before my eyes again.' At this thought I burst into tears.

13 April. When I woke up I knew this was the day on which I had to make a final decision. As if I were faced with a difficult maths question my mind was clear and my mood just rightly tense. By the time breakfast was over my mind was made up. 'He is not a common fraud of no conscience. He must have some reasons. There is no doubt about his love for me. As long as I can trust that he is not a villain I will forgive him and help him out of his trouble.' I wondered whether he would turn up now that he knows I suspect him.

'You'd be wise to take my advice. You shouldn't go. There is no need even to reconsider it. He's a liar and that's that.' My sister had been coaxing me all morning but when I said to her 'I won't be long,' and set off she exploded in anger.

'If you are not back by midday, mark my words, I will kill you and myself.'

He was waiting for me. I was thankful but not in the mood for a cheerful greeting.

'How's your sister?' he asked with a rueful face.

'She's not too bad. It has been too big a shock for her delicate nature. From our childhood, I have always been a cause of worry to her.'

'She must hate me. Can I go and see her today?'

'Well, she's virtually my guardian, so you should but...' I could not say that she hated him. Besides I wanted to get on with the business to hear his explanations, consider them carefully, draw my conclusions and go home to look after my sister.

'Do you know any quiet place where we can go to and talk things over?'

I felt like ridiculing him by saying, 'What fantastic secret do you harbour to need such a place?' But I refrained.

'You are quiet today. Where would you like to go?'

'We'd better go to the Secret Garden, then,' I said. It was only partially open to the public but I had a special pass.

Once the residence of the kings, the Royal Palace Gardens were now as quiet as a tomb shrouded in a mystic atmosphere. Ancient trees, their trunks as thick as several arms' span, stood with solemn dignity like sentries. I thought of them as witnesses to the lives of the generations of kings and queens and their attendants who had strolled here weaving multifaceted human dramas. As we passed beneath them I fell into a fantasy that for every word I uttered and every footstep I took now was like planting seeds that I would reap some day in future. The azaleas and the forsythia now at their peak were in delighted coquetry with the fresh, glossy leaves of the shrubs.

There was no human sound around. Only the chatter of birds as they darted in and out of the trees and bushes. We walked in silence through the woods looking for an even more secluded spot. Being in the middle of a wood with not a soul around inevitably made us feel closer. At last we stopped beneath a huge beech tree. I had noticed that he always carried under his arm a large brown envelope filled thick with papers. You could see from the open top that for the most part it was manuscript paper. After rustling through them he produced a folded white paper and handed it to me. It was a long poem. I sat down as he directed on a seat he made for me with layers of newspaper and his handkerchief on top. I read.

Star-counting Night

The sky through which the seasons pass
is full of spring.

MAGNOLIA

With no fears or worries, I think
I can count all the stars, the stars of spring.

One by one, they are impressed
in my heart. And,
If I fail to count them all
It is because the morning is drawing nigh;
it is because there will be another night tomorrow;
and because my youth is not yet finished.

To one star, memories
To another star, love
To another, forlornness
To yet another, yearning
To another, poetry
And to another, mother, mother,

Mother, I give a sweet word
to each star. Names of the girls
Who shared the desk with me at junior school,
Names of foreign girls like Pai, Kyong, Ok;
Names of the girls who have already become mums;
Names of the poor neighbours; a dove, a puppy, a song, a deer,
and names of poets like Francis James, or
Rainer Maria Rilke.
They are far away
Like the remote stars,
And you, mother, are in North Chianto.

With a yearning heart for a certain thing
I inscribed my name on the ground
of a slope on which descended

The starlight from the many stars.
And then, buried it over with the earth.

Do you know why
The insects chirp all through the night?
They are sorrowing for the shame of that name.

But when the winter is over and
spring comes to my star,
Like the grass on a grave revives green,
On the slope where my name is buried
Grass will thrive with pride.

1958. 4. 12. K.

When I finished reading it he calmly gathered me in his
arms. The sad and beautiful spirit of the poem had moved me
deeply. A man who can write a poem like this can't be a bad
man, I thought. I was overcome by a great sense of relief. I
held onto him tight. I was ecstatic, but it was after hearing
his confessions that I became even closer to him and resolved
that no amount of suffering or even death could separate us
now.

'Sukey,' he called as he held my face in his palms and looked
into my eyes. 'By telling you this I am putting my life in your
hands.' He went on looking into my eyes.

'Do I not look forlorn?'

Yes, he did look forlorn and pitiable. He made me think
of a deer having a momentary rest behind a rock, after losing
its mate on a hunt and still being chased by the hunter. His
eyes were filled with fear and loneliness. I nodded. The lingering emotion from the poem I had read a minute ago made
my heart ache. It echoed like the sobbing of a soul that had
been separated from its loved ones, roaming in a dark valley

of desolation, and cherishing a remote dream. Then it crossed my mind. Could he be? I shot at him a questioning look.

'That's right,' he said. 'I am a lonely man with no family. My home is in Hamhŭng in the North, My real name is Changho Yu.'

My heart missed a beat but I did not show him my surprise or embarrassment. I am known to be cheerful and tomboyish, but when faced with a crisis or a shock I am extremely calm and self-possessed. That is my peculiar characteristic. I calmly heard him through to the end.

He is the only son of a high-ranking government minister in North Korea. His family had lived in Seoul before the country was liberated from Japan in 1945. In that year he graduated from Kyŏng-gi High school. After that his family went North. There he studied law at the Kim Ilsung University and went to Moscow University where he gained a Master's degree. He was noted as a capable man by the Central Communist Party and eventually appointed a leading figure in an underground operation in the South. He was not keen but knew he had no choice. If he had refused to go he would be killed anyway. So why behave in a cowardly way? When it was finally decided, his intellectual mother, a graduate of the Japanese Women's University, went for a month without food or sleep.

His father, a strict disciplinarian from the army told him at the last moment, 'Changho, your country demands this of you. If you save your life in a cowardly manner, you are not my son, remember that.' In the previous year, he had entered the South through Inchŏn, leading a group of three men, all of his age. He had successfully completed his mission. It had been fairly easy. His only remaining task had been a safe return. Then he saw me, fell in love at the first sight and decided to give up the idea of going back.

'I went to Pusan and bade a final farewell of my colleagues. If only I had got into that jeep, I would be home by now. They were very fond of me, like a big brother. To the last minute they pleaded with me to change my mind but I said "no".' His large, expressive eyes closed as he said, 'When the jeep started moving, strong-willed as I am, I could not help tears rising to my eyes.'

By now I had come to fully realize the situation. I was having an affair with a spy. Fear gripped me. I was shaking despite my effort to be calm. He went on to explain his position. As for his own security he was absolutely confident. He belonged to an extreme elite group completely different from those that had infiltrated spies in the past.

'They are blind idiots. It beats me how they can be so stupid. To send down spies in chains in a time like this. If one is caught, the rest are bound to be hauled up like a net of fish,' he said contemptuously. 'I won't tell you the details because if I did, it would only upset your sensitive nature and cause you unnecessary distress. Just trust me. I would not have started this if there was the slightest risk.' He went on, 'The most important thing is that we have left no clues behind whatsoever, not so much as the tip of a hair.'

I had no wish to know anything about it. On the verge of a nervous breakdown as I was, I felt I needed protection from knowing one more fact. I weakly smiled to myself as the phrase formed in my mind, 'Blessed are the ignorant for they shall be spared of worries.'

He was also sure that his financial position was fairly good. The remaining fund from their operation amounted to some five million Hwan, which was in the hands of some practitioners of Chinese medicine in the form of the medicinal material. He could draw on it gradually as time went by. Then one day the country will be reunited, he believed, within three or four years at the most. It has got to come in one way or the other, or the country in a state of strangulation as it is, will just fade away.

'There, I have told you all. I feel such a great relief. I have long wanted to be delivered from such a dreadful life. All I wanted was to lead an ordinary family life with a good wife like you. However, I won't blame you if you report on me.' Whether he noticed my nervousness or not he went on, 'You are all to me. I don't mind dying so much. Just that I have had you for a few days makes me the happiest of men.'

Then something crossed my mind. According to his account I must be the only woman who knew him in the whole realm. Who was that woman who rang me yesterday? I told him about it expecting he'd be surprised but he gave his charming chuckle.

'Ah, that. I arranged it. She's the maid at the inn where I am lodging at the moment. I hope to stay on there, you see. It was a way of proving my identity.' I must say, I was impressed by his meticulous planning.

A long silence fell. As though even the birds were tired of calling to each other, the entire wood was as quiet as death. The only sound was the rhythmic booming of my heart. It was the sound of the engine of a ship that was about to sail and change the course of my fate regardless of my own will and wishes.

I closed my eyes. I was to listen to the voice of my conscience and to decide on the course of my action from now on.

As an individual, I have lived a very happy life. I certainly belonged to the privileged class in my country. At school I was a studious, exemplary pupil; at work an exemplary employee working hard and conscientiously; and in society a law-abiding, responsible citizen. Along with all these favourable conditions, I passionately love my country. The patriotism that has been bred into me ever since my childhood flows through my arteries never ceasing. Would I ever dare to commit a deed that betrays my motherland? A spy, an enemy against my country – could I love such a man?

I opened my eyes disturbed by a rustle. A squirrel had come up from somewhere and was staring at us from just a yard away, probably puzzling out whether we were some still objects or living things. We had been that still. I looked up at him. Expressionless, his eyes and face showed he was very tired.

'Poor man!' I was overcome by a sudden upsurge of emotion of pity.

'Even spies must have basic human goodness and conscience.' I began with this hypothesis. He has his beloved mother and father back in his home. How much he must have missed them, especially his mother who went without food or sleep for a month for the worry of her beloved son. On autumn nights when the moon was bright and the crickets cried all through the night did he not cry himself to sleep for the love of his mother? Knowing perfectly well what kind of punishment awaits him in this country, he chose to remain here for his new-found love's sake. What a fairy-tale-like story!

What will become of him if I now abandon him? There is no doubt that I love him. We are not, by origin, aliens to be afraid of each other. Due to an unnatural division of the nation we now belong to opposite camps but surely this is not going to last long. One day soon we will be one nation and we could be lawfully married husband and wife. He says he is completely freed from his past commitment. Our love for one another can be in no way against human conscience. Apart from the political past, we can establish a happy relationship.

'You can't undo what has been done, but are you sure that you won't be swept into it again?' This is the only guarantee I wanted of him at the present.

'I swear in the name of God,' he said.

Chapter 5

At The Threshold of a New Era – Memories of a Childhood

Following my father's conviction that children should be educated in the capital, our family left the orchard village of Sapsuri and moved to Seoul when I was five. My impression of the village on the day of our departure was that of a big funeral. The whole village buzzed. Everyone in sight along the ten *li* road to the railway station, as we rode on a horse-cart, was weeping. Mother, holding Myŏngsŏk in her arms, was crying all the way, her face buried in her handkerchief. Father who had me on his lap sat upright with a rigid face as if he were cross, his lips tightly pressed.

Our new house in the capital was in Sajikdong, on high ground, which was reached by what seemed like more than a hundred stone steps. It was small compared to what we were used to but great fun. It was there that for the first time I saw electric light and was amazed. From the verandah, I could see below the parapet, a black dome, like a huge umbrella sitting on the top of a building. When I was told it was the roof top of the Capital Building I was amused. Everything was wonderful.

After moving to Seoul mother lost her health. I often heard her saying the water from the tap disagreed with her. She missed the country and most of all, she said, the water from the spring at the entrance to the orchard.

For me life in Seoul was full of fun. In the morning, after father had gone to work and my sister and brother to school, mother, carrying Myŏngsŏk tied on her back, often went out with me exploring the city. We went to the market, department stores and sometimes went to visit my aunt on a tram. On Sundays all the family went to the Anglican Cathedral behind the Tŏksu Palace. On summer evenings, we went out to the evening market along the pavement of the main road.

My elder brother, Hyŏngsŏk soon became the gang-leader of the kids in the alley. I was proud of him. Some evenings all the children gathered at our house for concerts. The hall was the stage, draped with bed-sheets as curtains. Under direction of Hyŏngsŏk we put on plays, sang and danced.

Mother, eight months pregnant had a still-born baby and became seriously ill. She was bedridden for a long time. My grandmother or my aunt came to give a hand. With the onset of winter came the pickling season and piles of cabbages and mooli were brought in but left for several days unattended in the garden, covered with straw mats to keep the frost out. One day Myŏngsŏk, then three, fell ill, running a high temperature. Grandmother tried to take him to the doctor's, but he would not be separated from his mother, crying. Mother got out of bed, quickly dressed, called for a rickshaw and set off, holding him on her lap.

Our family practitioner was in Angukdong, not far off from the Capital Building. Either the rickshaw-man misheard the name of the street or he was mad. Or I suppose it was one of the trickeries of fate. My mother inside the carriage, wondering why it took so long, looked out of the peep-hole and saw that they were going in the opposite direction and had gone miles out of the way. She had been exposed too long to the severe cold. That night she became very ill unable even to turn over. The doctor called every day. The atmosphere at home was as heavy as lead.

After giving birth to me and mothering me for five years my mother departed this world. I was too young to remember much about her but the last few minutes that I was with her have meant a great deal to me throughout my life. It represents my memories of her, her love of me, and serves me as the pointer of my conscience that prompts me to be good through all my life.

As on other days, father had gone to work and my brother and sister to school. Since mother's illness had taken a serious turn Myŏngsŏk had been taken away to be looked after by my aunt. I was alone with mother. I sat close to her. She had been very still until she stirred and called me. Her voice was weak.

'Darling, are you there? Can you get me the chamber pot?'

I fetched it for her. As I did so, unaware of myself, tears came to my eyes and rolled down my cheeks. As she propped herself up in bed she said, 'Are you crying, my pet?' and gathered me into her arms. I did not mean to cry but could not help sobs rising and my whole body shaking. She embraced me tighter.

'Don't cry, darling. There's a good girl. Mum'll soon be better.' Her voice was very gentle. 'When I am better,' she went on, 'We'll go shopping at the Hwashin Department Stores and buy some lovely shoes for you, and some nice biscuits too...'

I let myself go and cried freely and then, feeling such comfort in the warmth of her embrace, I felt drowsy.

At that moment someone came in. It must be either my grandmother or aunt. I was ashamed of myself for holding onto my sick mother as I came out of the room but once out I was sulky at being pushed out of such a bliss. Squatting in a sunny patch on the verandah and with my back against the wall I must have nodded off into the sleep that I had failed to get in mother's arms. When I awoke, there were my father, brother and sister all weeping. I have no memories at all of the few days that followed. On the day of her burial, I am told, I was crying like one possessed. As the hearse was leaving the house I was pounding on the floor crying 'I want my mummy' and 'I want to go with my mummy' until I passed out. I often heard father telling this story to various people.

'I can never smack her, even when she's really naughty. When I raise my hand that scene comes back.' Probably it was because of this that father was specially gentle and patient with me out of all his children.

In the year after her death, there came several happy events in the family. My brother entered Kyŏng-gi High school as his parents had wished, my father was promoted at his work and I started primary school. We went to visit mother's grave. Hyŏngsŏk was wearing his school uniform with the badge. Father bought expensive sweets and biscuits besides the food for lunch. He had planned a family picnic by the grave, but no sooner had we got there than my brother broke down at the foot of the grave calling, 'Mum, you could have waited another year and...' The outing started and ended in tears. Being a Christian family we did not offer sacrificial food like other families did but we often visited the grave, and on the anniversaries of her death we all sat round at midnight to say prayers and sing the hymns that mother used to like.

After mother died grandmother moved in to look after us. Under her management the household became very tidy and well organized but it lacked homely comfort. A strong disciplinarian she fussed about such things as table manners and the way we addressed our father, and how girls should behave, and boys. Sometimes her iron rules were intolerable but father unconditionally obeyed her, setting an example for us to follow. She had been widowed young, and had brought up two sons, my father and his elder brother, single-handed and successfully. She was very proud and righteous.

When I was nine she arranged a second marriage for father to a woman who had been briefly married before. She was a simple-minded, good-natured woman from the country. It was obvious from the beginning that she tried hard to make a good wife and a good mother. Grandmother retreated to her elder son's house and the stepmother loosened the household rules. Everybody seemed to be accepting the new situation and trying to adapt to it except for me. I never relaxed and felt comfortable with my stepmother. Sometimes I purposely chose to do things that would displease her. I openly showed my contempt, dislike and dissatisfaction. It is not that I really disliked her but it was rather a kind of psychological twist. She was endlessly patient with me and put up with all my wiles. If she had severely scolded me or smacked or beaten me, I think retrospectively, my childish wilfulness might have given way to docility. Or if she had been given more time, my whims would have run their course and her efforts might have been rewarded, but it was my fault that her marriage to my father came to an abrupt ending.

One evening I cried and sulked for some reason, refused to eat supper and went into the spare back room and sat squatting there for a long time. When it was getting dark my father came in and without saying anything just raised up my face. I buried it in his lap and cried uncontrollably.

'Why are you being like this, my child? Why do you hurt your father so much? What is it all about?' He repeated this several times.

After a long time I stopped crying and said, 'I don't like our new mother.'

His arms stiffened and held me tighter but he did not speak. It was just then that real wickedness got the upper hand. I thought I could take it a step further. Something amazing, which sounded quite dramatic but was not from the bottom of my heart, leapt out of my lips. 'Don't you miss our dead mother? Probably you've forgotten her,' and I cried again, a semi-dramatic weeping.

It was later in the night that the performance produced its effect. The commotion continued all through the night in the inner quarters where father and mother slept. Now and again sounds of father shouting, something being smashed, and mother crying with some words in between, were heard. '...a woman that dies leaving behind her brats should be punished thoroughly wherever she's got to...Unless she's possessed by that woman's soul, can it be words out of her own mouth? A brat of barely ten?'

The row between father and mother went on for a few more days until finally she left.

As the days went by I silently suffered the consequence of the breakdown. My little heart was remorse-stricken with the thought that my wickedness had been the cause of my father's unhappiness.

That year my father became the branch manager of the X Newspaper in the Ch'ung'chŏng North Province. Leaving Hyŏngsŏk in Seoul in a lodging house near his school, my family moved to Ch'ŏngju, the provincial town and into a house much bigger than the one we used to live in Seoul. There were the inner quarters where our family with grandmother, once again the mistress of the house, lived. They were joined at one side, through a corridor, to the offices, and at the other end of the office block, joined in right angle were the servants quarters where the delivery boys and two housemaids lived. Across the yard from the inner quarters were the visitors' rooms. Father set up his study here and spent most of his spare time buried in books and papers. He was master and mentor to the paper-delivery boys.

'Knowledge is power. Your future depends on how well you cultivate your minds now,' he encouraged them to read and think deep. 'A poor harvest through failing to sow the seeds in the right time can cause sorrow of one year, but if you miss your chance to learn at the right time, sorrow will follow you for the rest of your life' he told them as he gave them personal instructions according to their individual aptitude and ability.

What with several young men and a couple of female helpers on top of our own family it must have been a large household with many mouths to feed. With food shortages and the constraints of the last years of the Second World War, these were indeed hard times for the grown-ups, but looking back they were the happiest times for me. These memories are as vivid as if they had happened but a year ago. I was doing well at school and at home the atmosphere was always warm and pleasant. Harmony reigned throughout the big household.

With the help of the menfolk in the house, father made a big, circular flower-bed in the centre of the courtyard. Exquisite flowers bloomed throughout the year and the shrubs flourished. Scattered here and there in the garden were trees that bore apricots, persimmons, dates, pomegranates and chestnuts. On the land behind the kitchen there was a vegetable plot and its produce was a great help in overcoming the shortage of food.

My younger brother, Myŏngsŏk who had been with my aunt and uncle in Seoul since mother's death was now back with us. A darling boy amongst three elder cousins, all girls, he was used to calling their parents 'mummy' and 'daddy', and now at his own home he kept calling his own father 'uncle' bringing a wry smile to father's face. With eyes sparkling like stars, and cheeks rosy and dimpled, he was a beautiful boy. He now started at the primary school for boys, and Sŏnhi and I were transferred to girls' school. Among the country children wearing shapeless clothes and dragging rubber shoes Sŏnhi and I made an odd pair with our navy blue sailor suits with snow-white silk ties and leather shoes. Every morning father did up my tie for me.

Father often took the three of us for a walk along the embankment of the River Mushim that skirted the western side of the town. The water was clear and its banks adorned with magnificent cherry trees and weeping willows. On the grass below the embankment black and white cows grazed leisurely. He held Myŏngsŏk's hand always, and mine as well sometimes. He made us sing songs and told us stories or sometimes walked in silence.

He took us on picnics, for which granny made us special, packed lunches. Ostensively we were going to pick wild herbs. We went beyond the town to the hills, and deep into the woods. Now and again we picked tender fern shoots or other edible leaves and wild garlic but we most enjoyed our lunch by a bubbling little stream, and splashing about in the water. Father with a boyish grin carefully turned over a flat stone, and gave a cry of delight as he lifted with his thumb and forefinger that held a crayfish. He quickly handed it to me and started chasing another one that was scurrying away. 'Cor! It's fast!' We were all excited with the chase. A little way up it escaped among some dead leaves and small stones by the edge of the water. 'That must be its den – let's see.' He stealthily removed the stones one by one, and there it was. When he finally caught it and held it up in the air we all let out loud cries of triumph. All that we brought home, wrapped in a handkerchief, was a handful of wild herbs and three little crayfish which all went into the soup pot of soya bean paste for supper. The crayfish added a fishy flavour above all other ingredients. We all agreed it was delicious.

When the school holidays came we could not wait for Hyŏngsŏk to come from Seoul. Meeting him at the railway station was the most exciting moment. Having probably inherited father's weak sight he was already wearing dark-rimmed glasses. Each time he seemed to have grown a head taller.

He was handsome in his school uniform. We were proud of him as we all walked home followed by a coolie carrying his bags on a *jige*.

My father who was gentle and delicate with his daughters had quite a different way with his son. It was quite Spartan. He sent him to classes for Karate, fencing and swimming, and punished him for the slightest wrongdoing. When Hyŏngsŏk spoke back to grandmother and upset her, father ordered him to roll up his own trousers and to stand straight, and caned him until red weals stood out all over his calves. At such times I was shaking all over as I whimpered but Hyŏngsŏk stood up to it with his lips pressed tight, never uttering so much as a groan. He looked heroic and I worshipped him.

'An honest, honourable and manly boy' was father's motto in bringing him up. Probably, in this way, from his childhood any element of feebleness or cowardliness was eradicated from the formative process of his character.

At this time he was at the threshold of adolescence and yet very much a child at heart. On the way home from the station he was excited at the prospect of seeing us, his younger sisters, opening the presents he was bringing home. He could not wait until we got home.

'Yours is a set of pretty beads,' he whispered. 'It's in there.' He pointed to one of the bags that were being carried by the porter.

'Sŏnhi's is a pair of stockings, long silk ones. Shh, don't tell her until she opens them herself.'

But when he challenged the authority of grandmother he looked so grown up. 'Your way of bringing up the children is called despotism. You should try to understand their psychology a bit, granny.'

She would be outraged at this. 'What insolence! Is this how that useless school of yours teaches you to behave to your elders? I've always thought it was a waste of money that your father earns with his blood and sweat.'

'Please leave my school out of it, granny. To disgrace its honour through my deeds is unbearable.'

Being away from home meant that he had some money to spend as he chose. Now and again he took us to a baker's shop and gave us treats with cakes and ice-creams. At such times, he was generous and happy. He seemed to be enjoying the privilege of being the eldest of the brood. He told Myŏngsŏk, 'Don't tell granny that we ate cakes outside, will you?' Myŏngsŏk eagerly nodded in agreement. As soon as we got home, he ran straight up to her and said, 'Granny, we didn't eat any cakes outside,' with an uncertain shake of his head. Father could not help smiling, and even granny smiled as she pretended she was cross and said to Hyŏngsŏk, 'You think I am not feeding your brother and sisters properly, don't you, silly boy?'

Approaching fifty, father now had white hairs among the black. With his head laid on a wooden pillow in a sunny patch on the floor of the verandah, he often called and asked me to pull them out. Parting his hair this way and that I searched for them and plucked them out. I liked doing it. I thought it was like looking up at the night sky with a lot of stars and giving them names one by one. He fell into a sweet sleep while I was messing up his hair.

It was about this time that the possibility of his remarriage was being whispered among the grown-ups. The prospective bride was an elderly spinster, Miss Lee who was the head teacher at the municipal kindergarten. During one of these hair-plucking sessions, I gave my father my heartfelt advice as I fingered through his hair. 'Father, please don't turn her out this time, will you?'

'Silly child.' He gave one of his sad smiles. I might not have put it over-elegantly but it came from the bottom of my heart and with solemn resolve that for the sake of my father's happiness I would do anything for the new stepmother.

In 1945 he remarried and two months later Korea was liberated from Japan. I was eleven, in my fifth year at the primary school. My elder brother, Hyŏngsŏk was graduated from Kyŏng-gi. Setting his heart on taking the earliest possible opportunity to go to America and studying medicine there, he came home, confined himself to his room and studied day and night.

My stepmother was a graduate, which was rare for women in those days. Born and bred in Seoul, she had an unusual background. She had lost her own parents when she was young, and her nearest relation was an aunt, an elder sister of her father. This aunt, Lady Lee, had been one of the royal concubines of the late King Kojong. Compared to the life she once had led as the King's favourite, her present situation must have been infinitely desolate but to the ordinary people it was glamourous. She now lived in a large private residence near the old palace with a lady-in-waiting and half a dozen servants. Our new mother had been her favourite niece and she was delighted with her marriage to my father. Mother came into our house with a magnificent trousseau. The royal lady, who since her retirement to a private life had scarcely had any chance to meet intelligent men, instantly made my father her pet and made a great fuss over him.

After the liberation, father threw himself into the world of politics. The offices once used for the newspaper business now became the meeting place for people who were concerned about the country. There was a constant bustle of people talking, shouting or whispering. Sometimes father sat with them around a drinks table in his study and talked through the night in a dense clouds of cigarette smoke.

This question has puzzled me on and off all through my life: why a woman like my mother who had such favourable conditions had chosen, out of all marriageable men, my father who was fifteen years her senior and a father of four children from his first marriage? Either it is another example of fate's wiles or it bespoke of the enormous charm of my father's personality, which would outweigh his disadvantages.

Mother brought a series of changes into the house. Grandmother went back to her elder son's house in Seoul. The housemaids grandmother had trained and who had served the family well were replaced by a woman of mother's choice. Now that the newspaper boys had all gone away, the servants' quarters were refurbished as children's rooms, and we went down there along with wardrobes, furniture and the old sewing machine that had belonged to our natural mother.

Apart from meal times we had little chance to go into the inner quarters where mother had set up a cosy nest as befits a smart bride. It became a strange place to us. When we went there for our meals we did not feel comfortable lest our dirty feet might soil the clean floor or we might spill something on the silk cushions.

She was never unkind to us but she did not make any effort to be warm towards us so that she lacked the kind of motherliness a child would expect of a mother. In this way our relationship started with a tension like that of a taut rope at a tug-of-war. Regardless of her position as a mother, as a newly-married woman she had every right to make her new home according to her own ideas and tastes. I had accepted her as my mother with a resolve to put her comfort before my own for the sake of my father's happiness. We had not openly talked about this but it was obvious that Hyŏngsŏk and Sŏnhi also felt the same – never to cause displeasure to our special stepmother. We were good to her and tried to show somewhat exaggeratedly how happy we were to have a mother.

However, it was too much to expect this of Myŏngsŏk. Soon he became a nuisance to her, a discordant note in the harmony of the family life. He had always been the most endeared and adored member of the family. Cossetted by granny with her stock phrase of 'poor lambkin who lost his dear mother at the tender age of two,' Sŏnhi and I had never once smacked him even when he was naughty. If we were seen doing this by granny we would have been in trouble.

Wetting his bed now and again had not even been considered as a problem, but mother could not take it. When it happened she made a big fuss, and ordered the maid to hang up the mattress with wet patch on the washing line. 'I've never heard of such a thing. An eight-year-old child wetting his bed. Unless he has no control...' At such times Myŏngsŏk looked deeply miserable.

He had a habit of being awkward about his meals. Under granny's regime, if he suddenly asked for fish in the middle of eating chicken, she sent the maid to the market to get it and cook it for him at once. It looked as though there was nothing he wanted and could not have from his granny. But overnight the situation had changed, and he could not adapt to it. Now if he made a fuss at the meal table mother frowned and Hyŏngsŏk threatened him. If he persisted in sulking, Hyŏngsŏk lifted him up, took him out of the room and put him on the top of the garden wall. Frightened and humiliated Myŏngsŏk cried pitiably as he tightly held onto the top of the wall. Sŏnhi and I laughed as if we enjoyed the sight.

Deeply involved in politics by now, father was frequently away and we rarely sat with him. Myŏngsŏk's school reports got noticeably worse but no one tried to understand why or help him.

Whether it had been through goodwill or as a concession of the weak we had taken unguarded first steps, and in the tug-of-war competition the one who made a weak start was bound to remain weak and be dragged to defeat. Within a year of mother's installation, Sŏnhi and I, when we were at home, became like her maids, running to and from fetching things and putting them back – for which we were rarely thanked. Medically diagnosed as barren, she had a somewhat sensitive constitution and things got worse. After she had recovered from typhoid fever, we were told that she was not to lift heavy things, not to be upset, and she was to take plenty of rest. She ordered us to do things and if what we did was not exactly to her liking she became irritable. When we sulked she got angry and its effect lasted till the evening when father came home. We could not win. We learned to become submissive to the extent of being servile, 'for the sake of father's happiness'.

Two years after setting up his goal of going to America, Hyŏngsŏk accomplished all the requirements that qualified him to go abroad as a student, and he went off to the United Stated. I left the primary school and entered the Girls' High School where Sŏnhi was already.

In the first general election that the Korean people had ever known my father was elected a Member of Parliament. The whole family was delighted. The most exciting thing for Sŏnhi and me out of this exultation was that we were to have a short spell of freedom from our parents while they sold their property in Chŏngju and were buying a new family house in Seoul. For the convening of the National Assembly on 31 May father and mother went to Seoul taking Myŏngsŏk with them. They were to stay in temporary accommodation, which was hardly big enough for the whole family. Besides, father thought it unwise to disturb our study by taking us away in the middle of the term. If we could be trusted to be left on our own, he would rent the outer wing of the house of his friends, Mr and Mrs Kim for us to stay there, cooking our own meals. Father said it would only be a couple months before the summer vacation. When our parents finally decided on this plan, Sŏnhi and I were overjoyed though we concealed our happiness. To be free from mother and to be on our own!

During this separation father came down several times to see how we were getting on. He saw that we had made a cosy home in which we were happy. We were doing well at school, and obviously not missing mother. What had originally been meant to be a couple of months was extended to two years for one reason or another before we finally joined the family in Seoul.

While father as a Member of Parliament and an in-law of a former queen, and mother as the wife of a Member of Parliament enjoyed their prestigious life in Seoul, Sŏnhi and I, leading a simple life in the country were the happiest of girls. We thoroughly enjoyed the taste of freedom. When we did not feel like cooking or bother with lighting a fire in the kitchen stove, we ate a cold lump of rice from the previous day with a bits of *kimchi* and chilli sauce, and slept curled up like shrimps, getting warmth from each other. Free from the worries of being asked, 'Why are you so late getting home?' we stayed on at school and played tennis till we were exhausted. We enjoyed the choir practices after school. Sŏnhi sang alto, I soprano. The fun of singing often continued until we were home and well into the night as we sang what we practised at school, in one spirit in two parts. We had a rather distinguished music teacher as our choirmaster and learned an ambitious repertoire and often gave concerts at the civic hall or sang on the local radio.

Sŏnhi was by nature domesticated and I was more boisterous. As in the days when we had played being grown-ups at Sapsuri orchard with our toy tea-set, she was always the one who cooked our meals, washing and tidying up the house while I did nothing but study or fool around. I bore with pride such nicknames as tomboy, rascal and hoyden − in other words, a boisterous, fun-loving girl.

Chapter 6

In the Valley on the Dark Side of the Sun - 1

Our parting from Hyŏngsŏk had not been memorable. There had not been as much as a farewell dinner. He had just gone off as casually as if he were going to Seoul. It occurred to me when I was a little older that had our mother been alive she would not have let his going abroad pass like this. That had now been ten years ago. In the early years he regularly wrote to father but his letters suddenly stopped. We made enquiries to his former college but they could not help us as to his present whereabouts. We had now been out of touch for some seven years. During this time the country had been through the Civil War and as a family we were having difficult times. Even if we had been in touch it would have been difficult for us to understand each other's situation but after seven years of no communication, he was felt in our heart like a legendary character, so vivid and at the same time so remote.

Sometimes, particularly when we were in difficulty, Sŏnhi and I missed him with aching hearts. When a tall young man of about thirty wearing dark-rimmed glasses passed by I felt like running after him calling out, 'brother, Hyŏngsŏk!' and holding onto his arm. Sŏnhi felt the same, she often told me so. Then one day, his image came close and helped me to get over the hurdles in the way of stepping over the threshold into a new era – was it yet another of fate's wiles?

After his confession Mr Kwŏn and I walked out of the Secret Gardens as if nothing at all had happened. Outside, dazzling sunlight poured down from a clear blue sky but it was dark to me. I felt as if the passers-by saw through our secretive selves and were regarding us with watchful eyes. I wanted to go straight home, but he took me into a nearby goldsmiths and bought me a gold ring as the token of our betrothal. When my friends got engaged they were given diamond rings or at least platinum. Gold rings were only for country bumpkins. Such thoughts crossed my mind but I was too embarrassed by the knowing looks of the shopkeeper to dwell on such thoughts. I told him to go back to his lodgings but he insisted on seeing my sister and hailed a taxi. I was self-conscious about my ringed finger. It seemed to symbolize the end of the free life I had led until now, but at the same time it gave me a sense of security, of belonging to someone greater than myself. As we were closer to home, I worried about bringing him and my sister face to face. What on earth was he going to say to her? If she knew his secret, I was sure she would pass out on the spot. I must hide it from her by all means. Within the last few hours a thick wall had been erected between us, the closest two persons that one could ever imagine.

The taxi stopped in front of our house.

'Please don't tell my sister about it.'

'Leave it entirely to me. I will wait in the tea-room across the road. Will you go and bring her over?'

As she opened the gate for me, the landlady said, 'Your sister must be very ill. She was sick again only a minute ago.' I felt as if she was accusing me. Still conscious of the ring on my finger I went in nervously.

'I am sorry to be so late, sister.' I went close and felt her forehead. It was uncannily cold. Her hands were cold too, and her lips were blue.

'Shall I call the doctor?' I said but I knew that what she needed most was calm and peace of mind.

'No, don't. I'll be alright by tomorrow if I have a good sleep tonight.' Her voice was weak. 'Have you seen him?'

'Umn,' I said, but I did not dare to add that he was waiting outside. Conscious of my ring I kept my left hand behind my back. Five minutes passed, ten minutes and fifteen...it was passing fast. I stood up and pulled back the curtains. Bright light streamed in. She turned over and looked up to the sky as she narrowed her eyes as if they were hurting. Beneath the windowsill outside, I saw the soil in the pot of the lilies of the valley was parched. I had forgotten to water them for several days.

'Why don't you change and eat something. You must be hungry,' she said.

'The thing is that he is waiting outside. He insists on meeting you.'

Her face instantly crumpled with irritation. I was painfully aware that I was striking another blow while knowing perfectly well that she needed a quiet.

'What? Him? You must be mad. Why on earth do you want to bring a man like that here?'

Perhaps because she was too weak, her voice was gentle.

'He knows you are virtually my guardian, and insists on seeing you to apologize...'

I was well aware that such words as 'my guardian' touched her tenderest emotions. Often when I wanted more than a fair favour of her, I used this to remind her of our somewhat fatal attachment and would get great concessions from her.

'My beloved sister, you are my pride, worthier to me more than my own life. Probably I was born to be of service to you' She often used such phrases in her letters. 'Until I see you a successful, happy woman, I swear, I shall never choose to go my own way', meaning her own marriage.

'Even so, how can I see him in this state? I look awful,' she said as she began to dress and pat her face with a pad. 'So, he is alright, is he? Did you find out?'

'Umn, you will understand when you see him.' Unable to say much about him I mumbled in a vague sort of way and gave her a hand with dressing. Her eyes caught my ring. 'Good heavens!' She exclaimed. Her forehead once again creased in a frown. By the time she was ready, nearly half an hour had gone by. I was getting anxious as I thought it was not safe for him to be sitting alone in a public place. I had put aside such questions as our future and how to find security for him. I would have time to think about them in the night.

I put my arm round her to keep her from falling.

'I am sorry to keep you waiting for so long. You see, my sister is not really well enough to come out,' I spoke cheerfully, and introduced them.

'I am very pleased to meet you. Please forgive me for not having called on you earlier. It was greatly remiss of me,' he said. I could sense that she was impressed by his self-possessed and dignified manner, and by his good looks.

'She looks bad now but when she's well she's a very good-looking girl.' Again I spoke in a cheerful voice as if I had not a scrap of worry in the whole world.

'Shush, Sukey! Don't be silly.' She gave me a sharp, disapproving look.

'I have heard so much about you from Sukey. I'm hoping to see a lot of you, and benefit from your advice,' he said.

'That's nonsense. I am no better than her. There's only two years between us and we grew up more like twins. We had to support each other as our own mother died when we were young. I have rather spoilt her, I am afraid. I hope she will get better guidance from you.' She was choosing her words carefully to the effect that she had little inclination to make friends with him.

'I have found her to be an extremely intelligent woman.'

'Yes. It may be silly to sing the praises of your own sister, but I must say she's the brightest thing I know. She's been so

good and led such a faultless life, not a step out of place, until...'
I could see that she was attempting to get to the core of the
matter and accuse him, but could not quite finish the sentence.
Instead she ended it in a slightly different tone. 'As much as she
is clever, she's stubborn, that's the trouble with her. There's no
match to her in willfulness.'

'Yes, I am already deeply impressed by her strong will-
power. Once she sets her mind on something she'll never rest
until it's accomplished. Don't you agree that it's admirable? I
hope to learn that from her.' He looked at me with a benign
smile. I was happy at the way things were going.

'So, your home is in Seoul?' She was making another attempt
to get at the truth. Her face was deadly pale but her eyes were
burning with her determination to find out. They had been
fixed on his face for a few minutes and then dropped to my
ringed finger as demanding an explanation. Feigning calm, with
a false smile of happiness, my mind was anticipating the outcome of the interview with a tremor like that of a defendant
awaiting the judge's sentence.

'That's right. I was born and bred here. I went to Hyojai
Primary and left Kyŏng-gi in the year of liberation.'

'My goodness! You must know my brother!' An instinctive
move to avert the crisis made me throw this in. This immediately relieved the tension.

'You told me that your brother was in America but I didn't
know he was at Kyŏng-gi. What was his Japanese name?'

'Masyama Kenjo.'

'Masyama, Masyama?' As he turned over Hyŏngsŏk's Japanese name as if to jog his memory, her tautness visibly loosened.
Her expression took on a pleading look and her eyes were on
his lips.

'Of course, I knew him! Sure enough, that chap was
Masyama!'

Her eyes lit up as her pale face flushed. I observed every second of this process.

'I seemed to remember he had a tiny wart like a black sesame seed just beneath his left ear?'

I did not remember noticing such a thing but it did not matter.

'It's very likely,' I said. 'What was your Japanese name? Do you think my brother would have known you as well?'

'Toyota Junichiro. He's unlikely to recognize me, because, you see, I was in the Japanese class.'

'I've never heard that there were any Japanese in Kyŏng-gi,' Sŏnhi said as if doubtful, but in a more friendly tone of voice.

'Towards the end of the war they set up a special class for Japanese boys as a way of emphasizing 'Japan and Korea are one body'. You may accuse me as pro-Japanese, but my father was working in the Governor-general's office, you see.' He went on, 'So his Korean name's Yun Hyŏngsŏk, eh? Whereabouts in America is he now?'

'We don't even know that. We've been out of touch for seven years now,' she said. 'We have tried everything we could think of to trace him but without any luck. We've almost given him up.'

'Oh, don't give up. I will do what I can. I have some friends in America and several of our Kyŏng-gi old boys are doing quite well there. To begin with I will make enquiries through them. There will soon be some news in one way or other.'

'You are a graduate of S. University?' Sŏnhi turned the subject. She was not going to give up her interrogation.

'Yes, the College of Education. The Dean of the College, Dr Kim is like a father to me. In fact I was at his house last night.'

'Ah, another lie!' I thought. The Kyŏng-gi story might be true but S University and Dr Kim and his house is an utter lie. Unaware of myself I heaved a deep sigh. Sŏnhi now looked relaxed and I thought she almost trusted him.

'For the last couple of months, I have been in a terrible plight,' he said. 'I can't tell you how much I suffered. If it had been due to my own fault, even in the slightest degree, I wouldn't grumble, but it was all because of a dear friend of mine. Another two months, and it will all be over. I shall be so relieved.' Then he said. 'You look very weak. I don't want to disturb you with the complicated stories of my circumstances, now, but I will tell you all about it some day. For the time being I want you just to trust me.' He was about to stand up but she was not going to let him get away so easily.

'All my life it has been my hope to see my sister the happiest woman in the world. Because of our unfortunate family situation we live away from our parents and being the elder of the two I feel I am responsible for her. If we lived at home they would not just sit and watch her go astray... and our own mother would not have liked it.' But she was no match to him, she could not detain him against his wish. He stood up and said, 'I have got to meet a friend so I must go but hope to see you again soon. Please get well quickly,' and added in a confident manner, 'You can leave Sukey's happiness in my hands now.' Then turning to me, he took some notes out of his wallet, 'Look after your sister well, and get her something nice to eat from me.'

He breezily left the room. Again I heaved a sigh. I felt as if I had been given two months' reprieve.

We ate our supper in a lead-like silence. When we went to bed she did not tuck in the quilt on my side as she had done until now and at once turned over with her back to me. Suddenly I felt like crying. I was overwhelmed with loneliness as if I had been dropped on a desert island from which I was never again to return to my sister.

Indeed I had entered a new era. To be comforted in your loneliness by crying, or by opening up your heart to a friend to pour out your sorrow belonged to the previous era, the era before you stepped into the valley of darkness. I was fast learning that a sad story that you can talk about with somebody was, in comparison to one that can't even be breathed, neither sad nor really serious.

How was I going to manage from now on harbouring this enormous secret? I was at a total loss. I held my breath as I pretended I was asleep. One thing after another, all sorts of thoughts came flooding into my mind, and kept me awake. Sŏnhi had been so still and quiet I thought she was asleep. Towards dawn I heard her say, 'Ah, how nice it would be if he was a trustworthy man like a brother to us.' That was all she said and she again fell into silence. It was as though she had been awake all night toiling with her thoughts, turning them over, shaping and chiselling them into this one sentence.

The windows were turning whitish. Had he been all right overnight? I wanted to go at once and see him but it would be a long time before the curfew would be lifted. How can a man who has been a spy dare to sleep in the room of a hotel with an eye-catching signboard? Should I marry him straight away? Even if we had to live in a hovel it would be safer for him as a married man. But what about his identity? I may be able to bluff my family by sheer willfulness and bullying but what can I tell my friends about him? As far as money goes we may just be able to manage on my salary alone but the world will want to know why a good-looking and presumably well-educated man like him can't get a regular job.

It would be easier if he were lame. Cut off one leg and walk on crutches? Then people would want to know why a woman like me suddenly decided to marry a cripple. Shall we leave Seoul so that I can get a job as a married woman? That would be easier in a place where I am not known. But it would be all the same. Wherever we go and whatever I do I can't completely get away from the question of what my husband does. Everyone has a social class, to which they belong. A shoe-shine boy, a coollie, even a beggar going from door to door with his bowl belongs to a class of a kind. Is it not a time when people need, more than ever before, a clear proof of identity? What am I to do? What am I supposed to do with a classless man?

When it turned seven Sŏnhi got up, saying she ought to go to work. I told her that I had some typing to do for Dr Kang before he came in, and went out before her. I went to the nearest telephone box. The man who answered at the hotel, had somewhat a haughty tone.

'Kyŏng-woo Hotel.'

'Can I speak to Mr Kwŏn of S University?' The haughty voice said, 'Who are you?'

I put the receiver down. 'What is to come sooner or later has come,' I thought. I could see it. Three or four detectives stood around in the courtyard while another one searched his room. The man with the haughty voice would be constantly reporting the development to the headquarters. He would also check all the incoming calls and try to catch anyone wanting Mr Kwŏn to take them to the police station for questioning. Even though I put the phone down probably they already know me as the first and most important associate of him. What a daring thing to do for a former spy to stay in a hotel in the city centre.

'This is the end.' As I reached this conclusion my throat was parched and hot air gushed out of my nose and I felt giddy.

Has he been handcuffed? Probably he's already behind bars. By this evening my name would be in the papers as an accomplice of a spy. Astounded my friends would pass the news to each other and whisper.

'Sukey is a spy. I can't believe it, can you?'

'As they say "You can see what's at the bottom of ten-foot deep water but not one-foot deep into the mind of a person".'

Some minutes passed. I was now resigned to my fate. Things would take their course. My fate was not my own. It was God's providence. I was now calm. I picked up the phone and dialled the number again. The owner's kind voice said, 'Kyŏng-woo Hotel.' I asked for Mr Kwŏn.

'Mr Kwŏn? Just a moment. I don't think he's up yet.' I let out a deep sigh of relief. I realized how early it was. I told him I'd ring back later.

When I went there, on foot, he had just had the breakfast table brought in.

'Ah, you were all right then?'

'Why? Why shouldn't I be? I told you never to worry about me.' He sounded extremely confident but when I told him what I had been through within the last hour or so and expressed my anxiety about his staying in too public a place he easily consented to move to a quieter place. He said, however, he had not much money on him because, as he had told me before, his money in the hands of some herbalists was not going to be available immediately. As if to assure him that money was no problem, I withdrew a large sum, without a moment's hesitation, from what I had saved for going to America.

I had often been tempted to use it for my father or Myŏngsŏk, who were now hard up but I had resisted the temptation. Rationally, I told myself, I cannot save them from their poverty by offering occasional charity. Unless I was prepared to sacrifice my whole future for them, I must not touch my savings.

That evening I dressed myself like a married woman and we went as a respectably married couple to a Buddhist temple in a quiet spot a few miles north of the city. We convinced the hostess that he was a lecturer with delicate health. He needed a quiet and restful place to complete a book he was writing. It was a lovely old establishment surrounded by serene pines and people were very kind. I wistfully thought how nice it would be if we were lawfully married and on our honeymoon.

When we were kids, father taught us not to lie. It was the most base and detestable habit, he said. Sometimes you may lie with some good intentions, but it would be better if you did not. Probably because of this, lying had not entered into my life until now. During the last few days I had turned into a master liar. But though my lips had spoken lies, in my heart of hearts, I had been most solemn and sincere. I was pouring out the noblest essence of my life to maintain my integrity, and guard what seemed to me the most precious thing in the world, love, a love that had chosen to land on dangerous ground.

At the first light of the dawn the birds' chorus started. I sat up and opened the sliding door. The courtyard was wet. It must have rained overnight. As there was no bus, I had to set off now to walk a mile to the nearest bus stop. I had to be at work on time. He was fast asleep and there was no need to wake him. I left a note to say that I hoped he would like the place and that I would come and see him in a few days' time. The scene of a fresh early morning in early spring that would have delighted me in the past only saddened me now. I wished I could have stayed in the temple as his wife.

To me, now nervously peering out from the valley of darkness, those on the sunny side looked happy. My colleagues were amicable, every one of them. My assistant, Suyŏn, who had been sorting out the post approached me with a smile as bright as a peony. She held a letter hidden behind her and said, '*Ŏnni*, what will you give me for this? Shall we book for a dinner at the Bando Hotel?'

It was the long-awaited letter from Boston University in the United States, a letter confirming my admission with detailed instructions as to what I should do next. She had known about it from the day I had typed my first letter of enquiry. She expected to see me jump with joy. Instead she saw my serious look and quietly withdrew. How I would have rejoiced a month ago! My life that had been running fairly smoothly so far was set to change its pattern and play all sorts of tricks on me from now on. The thought made me shudder. From now on, I thought, I must watch out for my expression, and guard against giving sad or serious looks that might attract attention or provide some clue to what was happening to my life.

At lunch time Miae called in. It was only ten days since we had seen each other but what had happened in that time had already set us a world apart. With a forced cheerfulness I bought her lunch.

'It's turned out that he's a married man with his wife alive and kicking. It was a good job that it came out before we went into a deeper relationship, wasn't it?' I was becoming an ingenious liar. Miae was fairly quiet. Two days later I had a letter from her.

Dearest Sukey,

....I was not sure what to make of such a sudden change in your attitude since our last meeting only a few days ago. I felt a kind of sadness. Even though it was for a short period, you were so much in love. Am I to believe that you could give him up so cheerfully? I suppose it applies to anything. When a course of action changes its direction too suddenly, whether for the good or bad, it makes the by-standers uneasy. I am not the one to give you advice except to repeat the old motto that we together have upheld so firmly. 'Always use your reason and conscience as the key.' Honestly, I know very little about this affair of yours: how deep you went, how much you are hurt or what you are really thinking about it. All I can say is that you were not your normal self, and hope it will not be long before you fully regain your peace of mind. Love, Miae.'

On the third day I went back to the temple to see how he was doing. I had remembered him saying that a gentleman could not always hang about in his Western suit at home. So I had obtained the traditional Korean clothes for a man, *paji* and *chogori* in silk with a waistcoat.

Contrary to my hopes of seeing him well settled, he was thinking of moving back into the city. Staying in an isolated place like this would draw more attention than in the city. Already a police officer from the nearby substation had twice been to check his identity. He told me to send up a taxi the next morning with a message that his father was seriously ill and he ought to come home without a minute's delay.

'It has got to be a jeep with opaque windows,' he said. 'It's the only way I can get past the sentry box without attracting any attention.' I knew the type of vehicle he meant because we had used one when we went to the mountains to plant the magnolias.

The next day he was reinstalled at the Kyŏng-woo Hotel as a long-staying guest. Fortunately he seemed to have obtained respect from the elderly proprietor and his wife. Not only did they treat him as a special guest but all the other staff looked up to him as a V.I.P. But I could not relax for there was the nightly inspection of the hotel guests by the police officer from the district police station. Every morning I left home early, hardly eating any breakfast, and called in to make sure he had been alright during the night. On the way home I called in again briefly. Unable to shake off the fear that his arrest and my ruin could come at any time I could not have any hope or plan for the future. To get through another day without any incident was all I could wish for.

'A fairy prince who has thrown away all his comfort and luxury for the love of me, only a plain woman. He passes his days in a mean hotel room waiting for the brief reunion with me.' Such thoughts turned me completely into a slave of our love. I would do anything for him, come what may.

One of the strictest rules at the Academy was that under no circumstances should we lend the books to anyone to be taken out of the premises. Not even members of staff could take them out of the Reading Room. Now and again a professor with a membership card came and pleaded with me to allow him to take a book out just for one night as it was vital for him to consult something in it but I would say curtly, 'I am sorry, but it is against the regulations.'

Now I broke this sacred rule. I smuggled out four thick cloth-bound books. 'After all, they are under my supervision,' I said to myself. 'As long as I conscientiously bring them back no harm can be done.'

They gave his room a look more like that of a scholarly man. They could tell any onlookers that he was a lecturer. Sometimes he was so engrossed in them, he did not turn round until I went right up to him and tapped him on the shoulder. He told me that besides being fluent in Japanese, Russian and English, he could also read and write with fair competence, French and German. I thought I would look out for some chance for him to make use of his foreign language skills even though it could never be an open asset.

In this way a month passed. During this time Kwŏn had established himself as an intimate friend of the proprietor and his wife, and to the staff a respected customer. His status had been raised from a mere guest to a resident and he had been given a room close to the family's living quarters. His fees were reduced to that of a long-term guest. To my great relief he was now eliminated from the nightly inspection. When in the night, the inspecting officer on his rounds, stopped before his room, Hwaja, the maid who was showing him round, told him that the gentleman was a relative of the proprietor and a lecturer at S University, and they just went past. Indeed Hwaja's contribution in securing his safety and earning him the trust and respect from all around was enormous. She was the woman who under his instructions had phoned me sometime ago urging me to give up Mr Kwŏn.

Originally from Suwon, Hwaja was of the same age as me. She had married young and been happy for two years until a few years ago she became a widow with a baby daughter. She hated to be tied down in the house with a baby, so she left the child under the care of her mother and threw herself into the world of hotel service. As she was good looking and intelligent she was very popular with the male guests. Mr Knŏwn once whispered to me that she was naughty, in fact like a whore. 'She behaves herself only with me.' he said.

Sometimes he treated her like his own servant. He was harsh with her when his room was untidy or his meal table was brought in slightly disarrayed.

'Even though I am stuck in a hotel room due to my circumstances, do I deserve to be slighted in this way?' At such times she apologized unreservedly.

At other times the two of them played wildly like two boys. He knocked her over, rolled and kicked her at which she clawed him and hit him back. It was not very nice but I did not mind. It reminded me of that particular afternoon in the hotel in Onyang, when he had been engaged in playing with the employees which became the starting point of our relationship.

For sometime now I had noticed Hwaja using the term 'For the sake of literature.' She said this at the end of a rough play or some lewd jokes. They giggled as if it were some sort of secret joke between them. I intended to ask him what she meant by it, but somehow missed the chance. My mind was always too preoccupied with the worries of each passing day and our future together. If we got through one day safely that was enough for me to be thankful, and I prayed that tomorrow might again be passed safely.

In the hotel, he was known as a lecturer teaching literature and at present engaged in writing a novel.

'Mr Kwŏn sat up until three o'clock last night writing.' Hwaja, by spreading such words earned him more and more trust and respect. I was truly grateful to her.

Minho Lee, the owner of Kyŏng-woo Hotel and his wife came from servant families attached for generations to a landlord in Kangwŏn Province. From the time they had taken their oaths of marriage in a small mud hut many years ago, both of them now approaching seventy and owning a reputable hotel in the centre of Seoul, they had cherished the hope of bringing up their only son Huni well and successfully, and in turn, being provided for by him in their old age. They had done everything they could to ensure that he lacked nothing and envied no one in the world. But as he grew up he betrayed their dreams. They wanted to see him enter a university but he left school at sixteen, and after his time in the army, a compulsory military service then required of all young men, he led a dissolute life, squandering his parents' money. He was not wicked, cunning or violent but seemed to be good-natured and easy-going. He spent his time mostly in billiard saloons, cinemas or tea-rooms, and carrying on with women.

Huni had married a woman his parents had chosen and they had two sweet little boys of three and five to whom he appeared to be completely indifferent. His wife, pretty and lady-like, never blamed him, waited on her parents-in-law with devotion and took good care of the boys, who were always clean and smart. Old Mrs Lee was so thankful to her and repeatedly told Mr Kwŏn that her only wish was to see her son and his wife as loving as a pair of nesting doves.

Taking account of the weakness in this family situation Mr Kwŏn invented an ingenious love story about the two of us. His parents, he told them, were millionaires but wicked people. His father, the managing director of the largest textile company in Pusan had several concubines. His mother was fully aware that her marriage had virtually ceased long since but she maintained her position because of his wealth. Far from being a chaste woman herself, she owned several business enterprises and she had several lovers who living off her money helped her with running the businesses. Mr Kwŏn regarded them both with sadness and contempt. He did not want to have anything to do with either of them, so he had left home five years ago, and kept moving around from one lodging house to another. Because he worked at a women's university he was under constant temptation but he had chosen me, even though I was not a great beauty or a rich man's daughter. He simply loved me for my purity and my personal qualities. Two years ago, he had sought his parents' consent for our marriage but they turned it down. I was too poor for them. They had so many offers from all round, much more favourable than mine. Of course he would not marry without their consent, but he would not beg for it either.

This story had its intended effect on the simple-minded old Mrs Lee, whom he had started calling 'mother'. She saw in our story exactly what she would have wished to see in her own son. Deeply moved sometimes she wiped tears from her eyes. In her sight I was a poor thing rejected by his parents, but a good woman. I did not care what I looked to other people as long as he was secure. Often when she brought his supper table while I was still there, she kindly added an extra bowl of rice for me.

He used even more ingenuity to make his position in that place more secure. One evening when Mrs Lee came into his room to remove his meal table he blurted out, 'Mother, I must be getting old, mustn't I, for I so much wish that I had a son.'

'Poor man. You do need a wife. It's unnatural to live like this.'

'Had I married Sukey when I first knew her, I would have a son of my own by now, just about Yuni's age.' Yuni was the younger of her son's two boys. He went on, 'I may not show it, but I love little children. When I see Yuni, I fall into a fancy that he is my own son, I'm silly, aren't I.' He gave his charming chuckle.

'I know what,' said the old woman half jokingly. 'Why don't you adopt him? His own father is as good as not being there.'

This conversation, originally a joke, took effect from the next day. Within a couple of days he had completely won Yuni over. Mr Kwŏn bought him toys and drew him pictures while making his brother Kyŏngi so jealous that the two of them fought like devils and Yuni always ended up crying after being beaten by his elder brother. Knowing that if he went to his own family Kyŏngi would hit him more Yuni stayed on in Mr Kwon's room, eating and sleeping with him and kept by his side. Yuni even began to call him 'daddy'. He took him around and made an ostentatious show of his love for him. The family and the staff thought it was wonderful. Even Yuni's own father, Huni thought that it was just because Kwŏn was a good man and his character appealed even to a little boy. Nobody knew the psychological manipulation going on in the background.

'Daddy, Kyŏngi calls you a customer,' Yuni said as he came back from the inner quarters.

'It's because he's a silly idiot. He's jealous because he hasn't got a daddy like you. If he says that again give him a big clout, then come running back to me.'

Yuni sprang to his feet, and sprinted away to give his brother a clout. Soon there was a row and the sound of Yuni crying. Kwŏn opened his door, looked out and called Yuni in a gentle voice. 'Yuni, you mustn't fight with your brother. Come to daddy, there's a good boy.'

The boy came running along and stopped crying. He picked him up as he lovingly said, conscious of the eyes of the family and staff, 'Silly child,' kissed him on the cheek, took him in and slid shut the door. Everyone including the old lady and Yuni's mother was impressed as they went back to their work.

When he was tired of sitting around, Yuni would say he wanted to go to his family. At first Kwŏn said, 'Stay here,' but if the boy insisted on going, he would threaten him, 'All right then. You go. I will be Kyŏngi's daddy. I'll take him out and buy him toys and sweets. You go and live with your granny.' At this Yuni visibly flinched, resigned and sat beside him like a well-trained dog as he watched every expression and movement of his master.

Huni, senseless in many ways but basically a guiless and good-natured man, not only never held Mr Kwŏn as his rival but freely showed his admiration for him as a man of higher social standing. When he was home which was rare he came over to Kwŏn's room for a chat and talked about his problems, ready to take any advice.

In this way, his lodgings were secured but it was a life based on lies. There was no knowing when and where it would end. Also it was painful for me to act the role of a good, faithful woman according to his script.

No longer could I turn to my sister for comfort and sympathy. Dropping in briefly morning and evening and seeing him safe was my only comfort, and the conviction that we were both making an enormous sacrifice for the sake of a rare and worthy love, was my only source of strength.

I learnt that people living on lies, in perpetual anticipation of being found out and with a disastrous ending, see omens even in the most innocuous incidents of daily life. I was boiling a kettle of water over a stove to make coffee. Suddenly the stove went dead. Another power cut. But I could not let it pass casually.

'Ah, this is a hint of fate. At this moment he's been stopped for questioning by a detective at some police station.' A sigh of resignation followed. 'It's the end.'

As a lecturer, he could not stay at the hotel all the time. He had to leave the house after breakfast and had to spend considerable time somewhere. He mainly haunted tea-rooms in the city centre. Occasionally he called in at the Academy. I took him into the Reading Room as my special guest. He could have stayed there as long as he wanted and he would be safer there than anywhere else. But he never stayed for long. I could understand, of course, that after what he had been through and with his unsettled life he could not easily concentrate on books.

Even when the power came back on again only a few minutes later, my heart, once stirred, would not easily calm down. After work I went to his hotel. He was not in. My anxiety was confirmed. His interrogation was being prolonged because they found him suspicious, I concluded. Then he appeared. He had been on a bus and it had been held up in the traffic. The ecstasy at seeing him safe turned the whole day's agony into a glowing pool of happiness.

There was a vague hope that his money dormant in some Chinese hands would be a big sum when he got it, but at present he had nothing at all, not even his bus fare or the price of a few cigarettes. From the day of his move to the temple and back to the present lodgings, I had paid all his expenses. His daily spending money and even the tips he gave the staff had to come out of my pocket. Besides he had to keep up appearances as a richman's only son and a lecturer. He had to avoid looking shabby by all means. At his suggestion, I bought him two smart suits, a raincoat, and a table and a leather chair for his room.

In less than two months I had spent all my savings which I had put by for the days when I went to America, and for the first time, I had to ask Mr Chin, the accounts manager, for a pay in advance. It could not go on like this much longer.

I often speculated on how we ought to use his lump sum when it materialized. We ought to seek ways of living without telling lies, and I should help out my father who was floundering in poverty at the moment. Now that I had given up the idea of going abroad, there was no reason why I should not support my father with my income. I would tell him everything and seek out ways of making Kwŏn an accepted family member. It seemed possible as long as we had some money and he proved to be truthful.

One morning my father came to see me at the office. It had been a long time since I last saw him. He sensed at once that there was a change in me.

'You don't look well,' he said. But his own appearance was terrible. He had suddenly aged, and his hatless, snow-white hair shocked me. Even though it was early summer it was quite cool but sweat poured down his face. I took him round to a tea-room and sat him down but I could not think anything to say. He again asked why I looked so pale.

'Probably because I sit up too late with my study, I suppose, but I am all right, really,' I said.

'Study you must, but not to the extent of damaging your health. I hope the procedure is all going smoothly?'

'Yes.' I answered firmly.

'So, what sort of a man is he?' My sister must have told him about Kwŏn, not the details but just that I had a boyfriend.

'He's a graduate of S University, with no parents or brothers or sisters. But he seems to have some money and we are likely to go to America together.'

'Liar, liar.' My inner voice screeched at me.

'Depending on how things turn out, we could marry in America or after we came back...We'll have to wait and see.'

Powerless now to exert his paternal authority as he would have done in the olden days, he seemed to have decided to leave it entirely to me.

'Even so, try to make an opportunity to introduce him to me.' He rose to his feet. 'By the way could you spare me some money to buy a couple of pounds of beef? It is Lady Lee's birthday tomorrow and I feel bad to be there without taking anything for her. I have troubled your sister too often...'

I would have given him anything, but all I had in my purse was just enough for two cups of coffee. My frustration, which had been accumulating for some time with no outlet, suddenly exploded.

'Father, how can you ask me for money? Don't you know I am desperately trying to save up to get to America, not even eating properly or buying any decent clothes? My friends, lucky as they are, go to America and to Europe with such ease. Money causes no problem for them because their parents provide them with everything...'

'I know,' he said, instead of clouting me and saying 'You ungrateful hussy!' 'I understand, but you don't need to be so angry, do you? I will go then. Look after yourself.' He turned and went.

'Ah, if only I could have given him the bus fare.' I could not contain the tears streaming down my cheeks.

All day, the image of father in the days when he had been at the height of his political success kept coming back, and then his decline, painfully reminding me of the vicissitudes of human life.

Early in 1950 father had managed to sell his house in Chŏngju and bought one in Myŏng-ryun Dong, one of the smart residential areas in Seoul where Sŏnhi and I were reunited with the family. During the past two years Myŏngsŏk had grown beyond recognition. He was so excited to be with us again he never left our side. He had so much to tell us about what had happened during our separation, and so much to show us in Seoul, which he seemed to know so well. He was almost making himself ill trying to think of the most effective ways of imparting all he knew. We had known him as the best looking of us all but now Sŏnhi and I were rediscovering how handsome he was. When we were going round sightseeing he made a striking contrast to us. We spoke in the drawling dialect of our province while he spoke smartly with the best Seoulite accents. Countrified, our faces were tawny and quite plain next to his like a marble sculpture with ivory skin, rosy cheeks and straight nose. His fingers were long and slender, and when he smiled his cheeks dimpled.

To an outsider ours was a picture of a perfect, happy family but in reality rarely a day passed without some trouble or other. Myŏngsŏk and our stepmother were like two discordant notes and they clashed. Mother's irritation, set off by his disagreeable behaviour resulted in quarrels between her and father which usually ended up with Myŏngsŏk being beaten by father. The beating seemed to be forgotten in one day but the ripples of the quarrel between our parents lingered on for several days. Father's belief in a strict upbringing for boys might have been successful with Hyŏngsŏk but not in the case of Myŏngsŏk who was by nature extremely delicate and sensitive. Also he did not have the protection of an adoring mother in the background like Hyŏngsŏk had when he was little. Myŏngsŏk's development was beginning to diverge from the normal course. Reprimands or beatings did not seem to have any effect. To father's dismay he lied and bunked off school. Being unhappy at home he tended to roam around the streets. Instead of coming straight home after school, he got on any bus or tram to get away and the money for the fares was usually the change from school, which he should have returned to father. When he came home late his hands and clothes were filthy and mother complained that he was producing too much washing.

In March that year mother, who had been diagnosed as barren, gave a miraculous birth to a healthy baby girl. She was named Chinhi and became the darling of the family, everybody making a great fuss of her. It made Myŏngsŏk even more unhappy as he felt left out and jealous.

When the Parliament was dissolved in 1950 my father did not run for the second general election. Instead he took up a job as a managing director of a Fire and Marine Insurance Company. He was also engaged in the founding of President Rhee's Liberal Party and became responsible for recruitment in the Ch'ungchŏng North Province with which he had close connections. S County of that province had become the object of his political ambition, a laboratory for testing his political ideals and his ability. Susim in S County was our ancestral village where the graves of our ancestors lay. Farmers throughout generations, most of the villagers bore the name of Yun and were related to each other. Father was born and spent his boyhood there. As 'a relative who had been a success in Seoul,' he had earned much respect and affection from the villagers and his relations. He commanded a strong influence on them. Making this village the starting point, he thought, he might be able to materialize his ambition of developing an ideal farming community there. He had started writing a book entitled 'The Prospect of Promoting Korean Agriculture', into which all his spare time and energy went.

In June that year the Civil War broke out. Seoul was occupied by the Communists for three months until September when the UN Forces recaptured it and pushed the enemy north, only to retreat again abandoning the capital in January the following year. The war continued until 1953.

There was scarcely a family whose life was not affected by it. My father was hit by the tragic loss of his elder brother and his mother.

Because the outbreak of the war came so suddenly, most of the citizens of Seoul had had no chance to escape. My father survived for three months hidden in the cellar of Lady Lee's house but his brother, Chun-kuk Yun, a professor of literature in S University was captured and taken away by two men with guns who burst into their house, and he has never been heard of since. He left behind his wife and three daughters. Our grandmother who had lived with them was brought over to our house when father came out of the cellar in September but she had become deranged with grief. Whenever she caught sight of father she would say, 'Go out and see if your brother's coming.' When she was given something nice to eat she could not swallow it. It choked her. She accused father for not trying hard enough to find him.

'He must be somewhere in Seoul for where else could he go?' At such times she seemed to have forgotten that there was a bloody war going on. At other times she gritted her teeth and swore, 'Communist bastards, you make my eyes shed tears but the time will come when tears of blood will run out of yours.' Over-excited by her own anger, she would pant for breath and collapse in exhaustion. It was too pitiable to watch. A woman who had been so upright and dignified all her life, her sons' pride and prop, had been reduced to a mad woman.

Father's love for her did not falter. He accepted all her unfair accusations in silent submission. When she told him to go out and look for his brother he would go out even in the middle of the night as if he really meant to do what she asked of him.

Apart from his grieving mother, he himself was harrowed by the love of and sorrow for his brother. When they had lived in their ancestral village, Susim – two little boys and a young widowed mother – the trio had been upheld by their relatives as an example of a good family. Many touching stories were told of how the two brothers had supported and helped each other as poor students in Japan. Their mother had lived on looking forward to the day when her two sons would be grown up, each with his own family. She died in the autumn, a sorrowful death calling 'Chun-kuk, Chun-kuk', to the last moment.

By the end of the year the war situation was deteriorating. Father arranged for mother, Myŏngsŏk and baby Chinhi to go south to one of our closest relations in Susim, and moved his head office to join with the branch in Pusan, the wartime capital in South, but he decided to remain in Seoul with Sŏnhi and me to the last.

On the fourth of January 1951, the evacuation order was declared in Seoul. To catch the last southbound train we walked across the centre of the capital as all forms of public transport had broken down. The city in anticipation of disaster was a desolate sight. We had packed as lightly as possible but were carrying stuff on our backs and in both hands. We were becoming refugees, not knowing what lay an hour ahead, but I had never felt happier for I was with the two people dearest to me. I hadn't the slightest concern for the things we were leaving behind but felt like singing a picnic song. Father talked to us all the way of the several miles to the station. Times have changed and I have grown old since that day but his voice as he spoke then always rings in my ears vividly as if it had been only yesterday.

All around us were waves of people and cleaving through them now and again went trucks loaded with household goods.

'...If I had loved material things I could easily have done that myself. Instead of walking with my young daughters in this bitter cold, I could have gone comfortably in a car. But I have chosen this way because I want to fall and rise with the fate of my country. Poor, ugly and mean it maybe, but it is better to have your own country than suffer the sorrow of a people without it. In this turmoil, what would happen if everyone wanted to ride in car?'

A man who had left all things of value behind, his briefcase was filled with nothing but the manuscript of the book he was writing.

At last the station square came into sight. It was seething. What I heard him last say before we reached the crowd was something about an unconditional, parental love.

'...honestly I don't expect from you anything except that you both marry into good families and be happy with your husbands. It hurts me to think that you've had a sad childhood with your stepmother...How many more years will you be living with me...' His words were lost as we were sucked into the waves of people.

We had to climb up the window ledges onto the top of the train, squeeze in and sit down amongst a swarm of people trying to find something to hold onto when the train jerked. Only then did we release a sigh of relief. 'Phew, we are lucky to be here at least. A lot of people are going to be left behind.'

The train started moving at midnight but it trotted like a sick horse. It jerked and halted, jerked and halted all through the night and in the morning we found ourselves stationed at Yŏngdŭngp'o, only two miles away from Seoul. We had spent the night holding onto each other under a blanket. All around us was covered in thick frost and the food we had brought with us had become solid lumps of ice.

After he dropped off Sŏnhi and me at Susim to be with mother, father had to push on further south to join his company in Pusan.

We had been cut off from him for several months before he sent us some money through a messenger and instructions as to our schooling. He had heard some schools were opening in Ch'ŏngju, our old home town. Mother was to take us there, rent temporary accommodation and see to our transfer to the right schools. By the time he himself turned up we were well settled down there. He had managed to secure a two-roomed accommodation which was hardly suitable for the whole family. Even though he had come to take us all with him, seeing Sŏnhi and I were happy at school he changed his mind. There was little point in disturbing us, he thought, particularly Sŏnhi who was in her final year. He believed that it would not be long before we all returned to Seoul. He went back to Pusan taking mother, Chinhi and Myŏngsŏk .

Sŏnhi and I were free again. In the following year Sŏnhi left school and got a job at a bank. Father continued to send us money by various means, but we would have been comfortably off now even if he hadn't. The recapture of the capital, which had once seemed near took another couple of years so that when I went to University it was not to Seoul but to Pusan.

Prior to the next general election in 1954 father received delegates representing various sectors of the S County of Ch'ungch'ŏng North Province, pleading with him to run for election. The petition from Susim and its surrounding districts especially had a convincing solidarity of support. As his book was nearing its completion he had a clear vision of developing a progressive farming community there. He needed some political power behind him to realize this plan. He gave his consent.

Counting on his contribution to the founding of the Liberal Party he had expected that there would be no difficulty in obtaining the party's official nomination for his candidacy. However, there had been changes in the personnel of the party and things were different from its early days. To his surprise he was turned down. Nevertheless his supporters were adamant. They wanted him to run independently. They were certain that he would get a landslide victory.

During the second half of the campaign, however, the tide turned. The official candidate of the Liberal Party had changed his tactics. He was pouring out money and it was reported that some of father's supporters were seen eating and drinking with the other man's supporters.

Father was not a rich man with a stored wealth, nor had he rich friends to turn to for help. But once started you had to carry on, you don't give up a battle half-way. He started borrowing money in every possible form without considering the consequences. However hard he tried he could not turn back the tide. In the end he was miserably defeated.

Our family fortune had gone downhill and into a bottomless abyss. He was in serious trouble over the money he had borrowed. The debt grew bigger and bigger as cumulative interest was added to it and the hope of ever paying it off diminished day by day. Mother had also borrowed money, as much as she could from her friends. Good friends of a few months ago now became aggressive and insulting. Creditors came and rattled the gates at first light to catch father before he went out. Neither father nor mother had any experience of being in debt. They kept on borrowing money regardless of the rate of interest just for momentary relief from the threat that surrounded them, getting deeper and deeper into the mire. They had reached a stage when father's whole month's income as a managing director was hardly enough to pay off the interest. Not satisfied by coming to the house, the creditors now went to his office making a dreadful row. The Board of Trustees advised him to resign and he became a jobless man.

In these circumstances, I carried on at college. I took it for granted that it was up to father to see me through the course.

Each morning he gave me the bus fare and added a coin or two saying, 'You must have a bite of something for lunch even if it is only a small bun. If you go without, you'll become ill.'

(To my father who gave me education in this hard situation, I ultimately failed to give a small sum of money for a couple of pounds of beef!)

My family tragedy did not end there. Myŏngsŏk was causing father great distress. Now fifteen and no longer a timid child, he defied father and was in open conflict with mother. He was not entirely to be blamed either.

Even in smooth circumstances adolescence is a difficult time, a phase of discontent and uncertainty. Myŏngsŏk was now constantly falling behind with the school fees. His school friends from the new industrial middle-class families were spending money like water, buying cameras, watches, bicycles or smart clothes, and going on outings, but already five feet tall, he was a pathetic sight as he set off to school in his black school uniform that he had worn for the last two years, faded and short at the sleeves and ankles, and tight round the chest. He played truant, and often came home smelling of alcohol.

Sŏnhi who had stayed on in Ch'ongju after I went to college was in dire straits too. She also had borrowed rather a large sum of money to help father's election campaign. The interest was threatening her livelihood and she kept sending distress signals to father but got little help. Eventually the house went, but by that time things had got so out of hand that Sŏnhi did not get a penny from it.

We would have become homeless but for Lady Lee. She offered us one wing of the guests' quarters as our temporary home. Mother, mortified, objected to the idea saying she'd rather die than face the servants there. On the day of the move she went out early in the morning taking baby Chinhi with her and I helped father with the shameful move.

The old Lady, who had always been gracious and good to us, patted my shoulder as she said, 'My child, don't feel bad about it. Until better times come, live here and think of it as your own home.'

When mother turned up late that night, she was called in and was severely reprimanded by her aunt. She came down with tears in her eyes to vent her humiliation and anger on me. 'Where do you think this is? How dare you bring your family in here? I would rather sleep on the street if I were you.' That was enough. There and then I made up my mind to become independent. It was to be the last night that I slept under the same roof as my parents. Next day I sorted out my things, bade an amicable goodbye to my parents, Myŏngsŏk and Lady Lee and left. The only place I knew I could go to was Miae's. Before her parents bought a house in Seoul, she had lived alone in a rented room. I was always welcome there and had often stayed with her in the past. But things were different now for I was coming as a homeless person. It hurt my pride. I would look for a job and if necessary take a year off college. But Sŏnhi intervened. She would not let that happen. She would see to that I continued with my studies, she was adamant. Despite her debt for father, she provided me with money for the college fees, lodgings and other expenses. In my last term at college, she was transferred to the main office of her bank in Seoul. We rented a room and lived together. Now we rarely saw father.

It was the day of my degree ceremony at the University. The congregation was in the amphitheatre. Among the proud and happy parents and friends that already half filled it, I caught the glint of father's glasses. I felt an impulse to run to him, bury my face in his arms and cry. At the same time the wicked streak in me that had turned out my stepmother those many years ago surged up writhing. I pretended not to see him. Even from a distance I could see he was wearing a traditional Korean outfit, a loose, full-length coat of cotton material, obviously old but well-pressed.

'How silly,' I said to myself. 'Why can't he put on a Western suit like other parents?' Shortly before the ceremony started he came over to me. Whether it was because of tears or the sun on his glasses his eyes flashed. I put on a cold, hard face and said, 'What did you come here for? I didn't think my graduation had anything to do with you or mother.' There was no change in his proud and loving look as if he hadn't heard me. He went back to his seat as the ceremony was about to begin. I swallowed a sob as a streak of tears ran down my cheeks.

I was being carried away by memories of the day four years before when the results of my matriculation had been announced. I had passed it against heavy competition. How he had stood with tearful eyes before the notice-board. Quite out of his characteristic austerity and frugality, he had put me into a taxi, took me into town and bought me an expensive lunch. After that we went to his office where he proudly presented me to his boss and colleagues. That evening he had said to me, 'If you had been a boy, I would have nothing to envy in the world, even if Hyŏngsŏk was never to come back and despite my anxieties about Myŏngsŏk.'

When the ceremony was over I dismissed him in the same cool manner. My true self had so much wanted to cry in his arms and at least have my picture taken with him. Along with memory of rejecting my first stepmother, it remains one of the saddest of my memories.

Since leaving his last post, father had remained a man without a fixed job, a hanger-on at Lady Lee's. During the first couple of years while he still had some hopes of better fortune, he had been able to hold onto his self-respect, but now hope was rapidly diminishing and he was getting old.

Myŏngsŏk continued to cause him pain and embarrassment. In a household ruled by court conventions, a boisterous young man could not fit in comfortably. When the baby Chinhi cried the lady-in-waiting came down and said, 'Shee!', with her forefinger on her lips. When Myŏngsŏk raised his voice and quarrelled with his parents the servants raised their eyebrows and frowned. Soon he fell out of Lady Lee's favour and once that happened he was no longer welcome there. Father put him into a cheap lodging house, but unable to keep up with the fees he had to move him to even cheaper ones. Sŏnhi and I advised him to try and find a job and earn his keep or to be humble and put up with the ways at Lady Lee's, but he could do neither. We tried to have him with us for some time but it did not work. His six-feet-tall body took up half the room when he lay down and he was quite unruly. He often became violent when he could not have his own way. In the end we concluded that he had to remain under father's charge. When we moved into a new rented room, we did so without giving him our address.

Chapter 7

In the Valley on the Dark Side of the Sun – 2

When Myŏngsŏk and I were together we often fought like devils, but he was my own brother, sharing the flesh and blood of the same mother and father. No sooner was the moment of wild fury over than I felt silent remorse and pity. The thought of my own mother chastised me. Were she alive, would she allow all these sad things happen to her darling son, let him fall into becoming an unloved, and humiliated hanger-on?

He was being difficult mainly because he was denied all his basic needs, and partly because he was too immature to come to terms with reality. But I thought, the time would come, sooner rather than later, when he came to his senses and pulled himself together. Then he would want to be independent. About six months before, I had started a little saving scheme to be able to hand over to him a small lump sum when he showed a desire for independence, whenever that might be. I pasted up a large tin with paper, made a slot on top and wrote on the side 'For Myŏngsŏk.' I kept it behind the sliding door leading up to the attic room. On returning home each day I emptied my purse and put in all the loose change. Sŏnhi was touched. As a sign of her support she put in not only loose coins but now and again notes as well so that it was getting quite heavy by now. When it was full, I would empty it at the bank and start again.

The twentieth of June was Sŏnhi's birthday. For the last two months, since Sŏnhi's meeting with Mr Kwŏn I had felt like being on probation. An awkwardness had settled in between the two of us. We were cautious with each other and rarely had intimate talks. The promised day when his secret would be revealed had already passed a week ago but she had not yet pointed this out. I wished so much that we could spend her birthday carefree and comfortable in the way we used to be. The day before, I thought, I would miss my visit to Mr Kwŏn and go home straight after work to get some food ready for her birthday.

On that day, I dropped in, meaning just to say hello and go. But when I got there, the landlady told me that he was ill. 'He's feverish,' she said. After making sure nobody was around he briefly told me that he had been questioned by the police. They took his camera and radio away for investigation. He was waiting for them to come and arrest him at any moment. He said I had better go home at once.

'It looks as though the dreaded thing has come at last. As for me, I deserve it, but for you, I don't know what to say. Sukey, don't you regret it all?'

I held his hands tightly and buried my face in them. 'Ah, what a terrible fate,' I thought. I had been ready to die long since. The question was how. I can't bear any thought of pain or cruelty. Just stories of someone being tortured or the sight of blood makes my stomach turn and I feel faint. If I were to be exposed to such things, it would be a blessing for me to be able to take my own life painlessly.

'Lord, grant only this to me – to give my sister a happy birthday tomorrow,' I offered a silent prayer. I should have time to write to her tonight, I thought.

From under his pillow he took out a piece of paper folded into the size of a postage stamp. 'This is the only thing I can leave to you,' he said. Inside was a short strand of hair, an inch-and-a-half long.

'My mother came to see me off at the airport, but we could not find a word to say to each other to the end. At the last moment before getting aboard the plane I threw myself into her arms and blindly plucked her wherever my hands touched her. This is the proof of that last scene, a hair from her armpit.' His voice was solemn and tragic. 'Once arrested, I have no doubt that I shall be hanged. But you, dear Sukey, will probably get three years or so of imprisonment as an accomplice. Don't try to hide anything, tell them everything as it happened. Keep this until the good times come and then go and find my mother.'

I gave him once again my pledge of love that death could not put asunder. I had prepared some money for Sŏnhi's birthday but I gave him every penny I had and left him.

On the way home, the sense of an imminent danger was dimmed by the more urgent task of 'giving Sŏnhi a happy birthday,' which would be the last from me. When I got home I laid my hand on the tin for Myŏngsŏk. I craftily cut it from the bottom and got the money out. At first I took only notes so that Sŏnhi would not notice its lightness, but it did not seem enough, so I took out a couple of handfuls' of coins as well. Of course I would mention this in the letter. On top of the original idea of a chicken and some beef I went to a silversmith and bought a brooch.

Sŏnhi's birthday was Sunday. I thought I would stay with her all day. For the past two months I had rarely had breakfast because I had to call at his lodgings before going to work. Even on Sunday or holidays I spent the whole day with Yuni. We had little money to go out with and in any case I felt it would be safer to keep away from the crowds. I usually spent time playing with him in his room and when the landlady called in, chatted with her on soulless subjects. Sometimes he would say, 'Mother, tell Hwaja to go and get some ice cream, one each for every one,' or 'Why don't we all have a snack of steamed dumplings?' and handed over some money. Everyone, including the girl helping in the kitchen, had a share and thanks to such a meagre generosity his popularity grew.

As Sŏnhi sat before the breakfast table prepared by me, for the first time in months, in fact the first time ever, she was obviously moved. She was making a big effort to be nice to me, as she used to be in the past that was lost. As if stroking the taut strings of a violin, or playing the piano without touching a broken key, the morning passed without incident.

Earlier on, I had phoned Mr Kwŏn and had found out that after all he was safe and that he had recovered his radio and camera. He sounded quite cheerful. As if I had no worries in the world, I started cleaning the chicken.

'Sukey,' Sŏnhi called as she looked out of the door. 'The tin seems to be lighter than it was.' My heart skipped a beat.

'It can't be,' I said not looking her in the face.

The house in which we rented a room was a traditional Korean one with tiled roof, so stylish and large that it stood out in its poor neighbourhood. As you entered the gates there was a gate-room to the right. When you crossed the threshold you were in the main courtyard. On the right were the living quarters consisting of, in order, a study, a large wooden floored hall and at the far end the inner room where the lady of the house lived. These quarters were fronted with sliding glass doors along the whole length. At right angles to the inner room was the kitchen. Attached to the kitchen on the other side was a visitor's room with a verandah and sliding glass doors and this was the quarters where Sŏnhi and I lived. Opposite our quarters, across the courtyard was a separate wing with three small rooms, originally, I guess, for servants.

The house had been built by a Mr Lee, once a promising poet with a roaming habit. A victim of Korea's traditional marriage customs, Mr Lee was married as a boy to a woman much older than himself. They had one daughter between them and his nomadic life started as soon as his parents died. With his inherited money he travelled all over the country and went to Japan and Manchuria or wherever his fancy took him. Each time he turned up after a few years' absence he had brought with him a baby wrapped up in swaddling cloth. In this way his wife had three girls to bring up besides her own daughter. She did not complain nor did she ask about their mothers. As far as she was concerned they were just her husband's children.

Ten years ago he had come home bringing with him a baby boy and built this house. They called him Chiun. His father never went away again but, by now approaching sixty, he was seriously ill. He had been bed-ridden for five years before he died. All his money had gone on the doctors and all that was left for his wife was the house.

She kept going by letting the rooms and taking in boarders. Her own daughter, over forty now had long since married and the two elder step-daughters had been married while their father was still alive, and now only the youngest daughter, a college student, and Chiun, who was ten, remained.

Chiun was a good looking boy but gave his mother endless trouble. He was provided with loving care and plenty of pocket money but he lied, stole little objects out of the house to sell at the market, and emptied his mother's purse. A good, kind-hearted woman, she could never raise her hand to beat him. She was only sorry for herself, she said, as she often came into our room and told her life story. When she was upset, she wrung her hands or beat her breast as she suppressed her sobs and wiped away the tears with the end of her sleeve. We became very fond of each other and we called her auntie while she addressed us 'nieces'.

'It's Chiun, I'm sure,' Sŏnhi said as she shook the tin. 'There is no one else in the house who would do such a thing. I'm going to speak to auntie about this.'

'Still, you can't do that with no proof.' While I mumbled this, she had already seen the bottom of it that had been craftily cut open.

'Look at this, just look! I could murder him.'

She was about to dash to the inner room. I grabbed her hands as I collapsed before her. 'Sister, it was me!'

For the first time in my life I had committed theft. I could not add that it was for her birthday.

The volcano had now erupted. Without a word she slapped my cheeks several times. Lest the commotion was heard in other rooms I bit my lips and repressed my cries. Tears flowed freely. Sŏnhi whose face had turned white started shouting.

'A woman earning seventy thousand Hwan a month puts her hands on a piggybank? Is it possible? Because I believed you were saving up to go to America, I never asked you for penny. I even told you, if you save as much as you can and still it isn't enough, then I would make it up even if I got deeper into debt. You've been cheating me! Do you think I haven't noticed you're going short of money?' She poured it all out in one breath and went on.

'How much have you got in the bank? The money for which we all sweated blood – didn't you learn anything from all the torments that father and I went through? Pouring it all out on some fraud you picked up in some corner.' Her voice was growing louder.

'Besides, why do you keep telling lies? You told Miae he had a wife, and father that he was going to the States with you. Which is the truth? The promised two months are over. You must come out with the truth. What kind of bastard is he? Where the hell did he come from? I'm going to go and drag it out of him. Do you think I don't know the hotel you go in and out of? You despicable, dirty bitch!' She was becoming hysterical.

'I am so ashamed of you. Go and kill yourself before I do it for you.' She took my hair by the roots and dashed my head against the wall again and again. I no longer needed to be afraid of the noise. I snatched my head out of her grip and threw myself onto the floor, hitting some hard object with my head in doing so. I felt blind and I thought I was dying. Then we went on crying loudly till we were exhausted, stopped for a few moments and cried again. The landlady came over in a fright.

'My God, what is the matter? You, the older one, you should control yourself, you can't behave like this. All this time I've known you, I've never heard so much as a cross word pass between you, and now this... What on earth is the matter?'

'If you don't know what she has meant to me,' she said, 'you'd never understand it, aunt. 'After a while she sent the landlady away saying that we would be all right now. She stared at me, stretched out on the floor for a long time and then started combing her hair.

'As they say, "A pagoda built with devotion and care collapses in this way." How cruel God is. Get up now and let's go and sort this out. If I can't do it myself I will call father.' Her voice reached me as if it was from another world. I was falling into oblivion. I had no desire to go on living. Death was an eternal nothingness and at the entrance to it I felt no sorrow, no pain and no love. How long was I in this state? Suddenly the door to eternity was shut before my face. I was turned back to reality as I regained my consciousness. The first thing that appeared on my horizon was him. 'What will become of him if I die? A man who chose the land of death for the love of me?' Unless we die together, I had to protect him from danger and to do that I had to live.

If I made a clean breast of it to my sister my suffering would be alleviated for a burden shared is a burden halved as they say, but I could not do that. It was for her own good that I was guarding the secret. Once she knew it, either she would report it, or if she could not because of her love of me, then she was taking it onto herself, and becoming a criminal, an accomplice. I must protect her from it whatever the cost.

I could not let her go to him now. I held onto her hands and pleaded. 'Please, sister. Trust my conscience. He's not a bad man. You'll understand it one day but I just can't tell you now. I will swear in our mother's name that I won't do anything disgraceful or that goes against human conscience.'

It was dark outside. Either won over by my pleading or too exhausted herself, she did not insist on going to see him. For the first time in a long while she tucked in my side of the quilt. All through the night I was ill. I woke up several times screaming from nightmares and each time I saw her sad eyes looking down on me.

The three years of my high school days in Chŏngju where Sŏnhi and I lived as refugees seems the happiest time in my memory. I can't imagine any girl with two doting parents could have been happier or more contented than I was, living with my sister on her earnings as a bank clerk. Her devotion to me was probably not only sisterly love but combined with a form of maternal love. She did everything a mother would do for her daughter while I returned her love with pride, honour and hopes for a bright future. I won prizes at school for good work, sang solos and duets at concerts, won prizes at speech competitions. At such times she seemed to be more pleased than I was. I did not wash so much as my own socks or handkerchief. All I did was school work and reading as many books as I wanted. When I applied for Y University at the end of my high school, she did not believe that I could win a place there. The day when

I came home with the news of my pass was the climax of the glory with which I could reward her love.

When I had to leave her behind in Ch'ŏngju to go to university, we cried our eyes out. In the holidays I was back with her. Even at the time when she was hard up because of father's debts, she lavished her money on me. She bought me, on credit, clothes, shoes and anything that she found I was in need of, and helped me with the registration fees.

On the winter vacation of the year that I had left Lady Lee's residence, I was faced with homelessness. I had decided to stay in Seoul and look for a job instead of going down to Sŏnhi as I thought I should not put any further financial burden on her. I had nowhere to stay.

An economics student at the university, Okja invited me to join her in her humble accommodation. At first I was reluctant to accept as I knew she was even harder up than I was. She was virtually living on what her boyfriend could spare from the money his parents sent him from the country. In holidays he went home and she lived in a poor rented room in Yŏnhi-dong, a village behind the university. To take advantage of her seemed 'taking out a flea's liver to eat', as they say, but I accepted it in the end.

Yŏnhi-dong is now a prosperous suburb but in the 1950s it was a hamlet with about a dozen thatched cottages among paddies and vegetable plots.

Okja's was the outer room of a tumble down hut at the farthest end of the hamlet. We lived literally on boiled rice with soy sauce and dry laver. But we were happy. We were young and we had the future, and we got on so well with each other. Our only luxury was fuel. We could stuff the kitchen fireplace with as much firewood, dry twigs and leaves, as we wanted. The hot *ondol* floor was so comforting in the bitter winter nights. Lying on our stomachs, we read poems all through the night until the oil burnt out in the lamp. In the desolation of these winter nights I was carried away by the beauty of the soulful poems and it lingered on long after I had closed the book. One such night, amidst the rustling of fallen leaves, I heard my name being called, 'Sukey,' as if from a dream.

'It's my sister!' I sprang to my feet and rushed out. Okja thought I had gone mad and was frightened. In the pitch-black outside stood Sŏnhi with Miae. Miae had known I was in Yŏnhi-dong but never having been there herself, she wasn't sure whether she could find me, but as Sŏnhi had to go back to Chŏngju the next morning, they had set off anyway. Once they were in the village, they had stood at every doorstep and called out 'Sukey', until they got to this last house. Out of Sŏnhi's baggage came out *ddok*, fruit and other delicious food. She gave me a lot of money as well. We had a delightful midnight party.

After our hysterical night I felt weak on Monday morning. Sŏnhi said I should stay in bed and rest. But I had to see him. Outside Kyŏng-woo Hotel I met Hwaja who had come out to get him some cigarettes, from the shop in front of the hotel. I asked her how he was but before I had finished the sentence she blurted out, 'He slept out last night in Nagwŏn-dong and came in this morning.' She gave me a wink as she smiled twisting her lips in a peculiar way.

'I see.' I replied in a casual tone suggesting that the place he had been to was known to me. When I went in he was still in bed. He seemed to be in a good mood. When he saw me he said, 'What's this sulky look about? Did Hwaja tell you something?' Without a word I demanded an explanation with my eyes.

'I had a traumatic weekend,' he said. Then I noticed a telephone set on his desk, which had not been there before. He saw me looking.

'Ah, that. I saw an old hand-set lying around in the house, so I put the pieces together.' He added proudly, 'Doesn't it look good there.' 'I have been going out to the hall to get the phone, sharing with other people. Besides, it gives an air to the room, and it will be very convenient for our private conversations, won't it?'

Still I was not happy. Something in his cheerful manner and in the general air was disagreeable to me. I needed a good explanation. I turned up my eyes to the radio and camera, which had been out of sight last Saturday.

'On Saturday, I went to the police station. I thought it would not make any difference whether they came here to take me or I walked in there myself. I just caught the chap who had questioned me earlier and confiscated them. Obviously he was coming back after seeing a woman, I could see a bit of rouge on his chin. He was in a jaunty mood. I walked up to him and said, "If you have finished with my camera and radio, I'd like them back, please", and added, "By the way, what is your name? You know mine already." He was taken aback by my audacity. He was very polite.

'Mr Kwŏn, please forgive me for causing you such inconvenience. I have checked everything, and there was nothing wrong with you. It's just that we have a rather complicated case in hand at the moment, which is driving us all mad. I hope you will understand and forgive me. Here are your belongings, please take them.' That was it. It was obvious to me that in the height of an affair with a girl, he had forgotten all about it. Investigation indeed!' He laughed scornfully and went on.

'Then the other thing blew up out of the blue, the Nagwŏn-dong affair, I mean. Would you believe it, they were back, the chaps who worked with me. This time they came with my father's personal order to find me and kill me.' A shudder ran down my spine.

'Will they do such a thing though? I was like their own brother and father to them. They frankly told me. One of them had a mistress in Nagwŏn-dong, so I went there with them, and stayed the night there, that's all.'

A man who had sworn never to have anything more to do with them had been in touch again. It was a serious breach of security and it meant that our danger had been intensified. I had kept a cool face till then but could no longer carry on like that.

'You must surrender yourself,' I said. 'Please go to the police station and do it now. They say that if you are caught as a spy your punishment is heavy but surrender and make a promise never to do it again and you can get a pardon.' Then as I calmed my voice, I held his hands pleading, 'Then all will be well. We can declare our love to the world and live an open, honourable life. I don't care if we have to live on one meal a day, as long as we are free from any danger.'

He shook off my hands and burst into anger. He turned up the volume of the radio and under the cover of the loud sound bitterly accused me.

'What are you talking about? There is no need to beat about the bush, just tell me to go and kill myself. If you have had enough of me and don't want to see me again, just say so and I'll take myself out of your sight.' At this outburst I was instantly crest-fallen. He said in a gentler tone.

'To offer pardon to a surrendering spy is only propaganda. For a crime committed there can only be a punishment, what else? And I know I deserve a death penalty. Of course I understand your anxiety but I am trying to do everything in the safest possible way. You must be patient with me.'

'But they are back again, aren't they? Is that what you mean by "the safest way?"'

'Don't worry about it. They gave me their word never to appear again before my eyes, and they went back last night for good.'

Six months had gone since we had exchanged our oath of love. We were lovers who saw each other twice a day, morning and evening but had rarely been out together for a meal or to see a film. There was an understanding between us that we had little money and it was safer to avoid places where people gathered.

I had a shock one day when I saw Hwaja passing a note to him from the nearby Chinese restaurant urging him to pay up the accumulated bills. At the same time I found out that he owed a lot to the small confectionery shop across the road. It was beyond me how he could have got himself into such a state.

Apart from bus fares every penny of my pay went towards his upkeep. All through the summer, I had been so hard up I had not bought a single blouse for myself, nor had taken home so much as a melon in season, which was Sŏnhi's favourite fruit.

Nevertheless, to keep up his appearances I could not delay clearing up his debt for much longer. I took out my pay in advance up to the limit and sold the gold ring off my finger.

One evening, we mustered our courage and strolled out into the streets near the hotel. Soon we found ourselves standing in front of an antique shop peering into the window. Inside the dimly lit shop an old man with a long white beard sat on a cushion turning over the pages of an old book. Impressed by the sight we drifted inside. A tray of precious stones caught my attention. Among them I saw an item I liked very much – a tiny ruby like a drop of blood set on a thin, 19 carat gold ring. It was not expensive but delicate and elegant. It fitted on my ring finger but I could not afford to buy it. He saw me putting it back into the tray.

'Do you like it? If you do, have it,' he said. 'How much is it, sir?'

The old man, as he took the money, gave us a peculiarly serious look as, over his glasses, his large eyes blinked slowly.

He could be a detective and you'd never know. We should never wander about in the street, by day or night, I thought. Day by day I came to love the ring, much more than the ugly one that I had sold.

As the autumn deepened a nationwide anti-spy campaign was launched. Posters and placards were put up all over the place. Street-check-ups were intensified and loudspeakers repeated the message, appealing for public cooperation, with the promise that self-surrendering spies would be pardoned. In hotels and lodging houses the nightly inspections were carried out with extra thoroughness, sometimes even twice in one night. Mr Kwŏn was now excused from them as 'a relative of the family', but if Hwaja was not there and they were shown round by another member of the staff, there was no way in which he could avoid it. The thought of him being in intensified danger every night made me so nervous that I lost all interest in life. 'If only he would surrender himself and we lived together in the light of day even only for a month, I would ask no more.' This pitiful wish pierced my heart with such acuteness that I often felt faint.

Then one day he fell ill with jaundice. One more tribulation on top of the heap already high enough to reach the sky – Where was it going to end? I couldn't carry on like this much longer, I often thought. Hwaja's probably exaggerated story made me scared. Her own father had started off with jaundice, but because he did not get the right treatment at once, he had turned black and died. While I sat in the office with false cheerfulness, my lips dried black and throat felt parched until I could almost hear the sizzling sound.

People at the hotel advised us with one accord that the herbal medicine was much more effective than the Western. So I took him to an herbal doctor, but the price was horrendous. I brushed away my worries and bravely said, 'Don't worry, you'll be all right in no time. Didn't he say that twenty packets will put you right if we start it tomorrow? It is a good job that we came before it got worse.' But where would I get the money from by tomorrow? I lay awake wracking my brain. 'If only I could live with him as his wife just one day, nurse him, feed him with food I cooked, boil his herbal medicine with my own hands and be beside him in the night and relax my tired mind and body,' I wistfully thought.

The late autumn was advancing into early winter. It got dark early and the nights became frosty. I thought of Miae who had now been married two months. I set off with no particular plan but more from habit. How often I used to go running to her when I had good news or I was in trouble. But at her gate, I stopped as I was reminded that it was my first visit to her new home. I should have brought some little present or at least a bunch of flowers.

She led me into her house with a somewhat exaggerated welcome. After a few minutes of initial chattering we fell silent. There seemed to be so much to talk about but on the other hand I realized with pain that we now belonged to different worlds. Unless I told her my secret, I could not ask her to lend me any money, and I could not betray my love for her by dragging her into my secret.

It was obvious that she was steering our conversation away from the sensitive area. Despite her insistence that I should stay for supper, as her husband would soon be home, I made an excuse and left. I was crying as I walked down the gentle slope leading to the main road. Between sobs I mumbled, 'Dear Miae, forgive me for leaving you like this. How is it that I walk away from you in this way? You will understand me one day when I am gone. It is to safeguard your security that I keep this secret to myself. Once you knew this, you would be trapped in the shadow of death. The bliss of your marriage would be shattered...to protect you from catastrophe I must go alone...'

Near the tram stop, I saw a man coming towards me. There was something familiar about him. It was Sangjin Hyŏn. I was so embarrassed, I wanted to turn back but it was too late. In no time he stood before me. I had known that on his return from the States he had been appointed as a lecturer at Y University. We went into a tea-room on the roadside and sat opposite across a small table. As if trying to read my mind, which was in a flutter, wanting to get away quickly so that I could sell my wrist-watch before dark, his eyes were fixed on my face.

'How are you, Mr Hyŏn? I am sorry I didn't go to see you earlier. I knew you were back...I am ashamed.'

Only then did he smile his old smile. 'Well, don't I know what girls are like, not worth making friends? But why do you look so terrible? You are not ill, are you? You're not married yet?'

I could not find a word. I just smiled back.

'I see, you've been to Miae's? I knew she lived somewhere around here but I daren't go and see her in case someone tries to beat me up for going after a married woman. I expect she's well. Give her my regards.'

A silence fell. He could have been thinking of the past as I was, when we had been good, innocent friends with all sorts of possibilities. It was possible that he had loved me and I him. How I wished I could confide in him about my life. Would he despise me and turn away from me?

He must have noticed that my expression off guard, was extremely grim. He tried to brighten it. 'I like your ring. Is it for your engagement? Can I come to the wedding and give an address?'

'Pretty, isn't it? This ring knows the story of my fate.'

'Fate? Happy or sad?'

'Both.'

'Are you engaged?'

'Would you give such a cheap thing as this for an engage-ment ring?' I spoke in mock severity and laughed brightly. I could not remember when I last laughed like this. 'Such words as engagement or wedding do not seem to apply to my case.'

'What do you mean?'

'Just fate.' I felt like bursting into tears.

'Why are you being like this?' His voice was sincere. 'If you are in any trouble, come and see me. My room is two doors away from the Dean's office.' He added, 'You must trust me. If there's any way in which I can help, I will.'

I gave him a smile and left. What could he do for me with all the good will in the whole world? He belonged to a different world.

Mr Kwŏn started on his herbal medicine. The landlady took it upon herself to look after him. She simmered the herbal medicine, and then squeezed out its juice for him to drink. To my amazement his room turned into a most luxu-rious sick-room. A square aquarium, the size of a television was brought in with tropic fish and a terrapin smoothly glided among the water plants, a spectacular scene of marine life. It was a get-well present from Madame Kim of the tea-room 'Black Rose'.

On his table was a large vase arranged with bright exotic flowers, and a wicker basket filled with expensive fruit, both sent by the proprietress of the tea-room 'Carnation', Julie.

I had known that he had established himself as a respected, regular customer in these places for he could not stay all day in the hotel room nor could he kill his time just roaming around the street. The thought crossed my mind that they were some-what excessive gifts for a mere customer, but I was comforted to think that he, the loneliest of all men, had gained such trust and friendship from people he met, even though only mistresses of tea-rooms.

He had often phoned me from the counters of these places obviously within the earshot of the staff. It was to impress them by showing what an important person he was. They were utterly meaningless conversations but knowing his intention I tried to make suitable replies as I imagined the scene. It went on and on.

Miss Chang's wedding, blah blah...about father's visit to Japan, blah blah...and what about taking so and so to the airport to see off his boss...

Having been brought up starved of a mother's affection, I loved it best when he talked about his mother even though not very often.

'I am sick of the lodging house's food,' he would say. 'At home, I often stayed up late reading. Mother used to bring in late night snacks, you know such things as home-made buckwheat noodles in ice-cold *kimchi* juice, or acorn jelly dressed in oil and laver done in the way only she knew. I have never tasted anything like that since I left home.' Such talk about his mother gave me a strange thrill. Shall I live long enough to see my country reunited? Will I see the day when I go with him to meet his parents and be loved by them, especially by his mother? She sounded a sensitive and caring sort of mother. I missed my future mother-in-law, a woman whom I had not seen even in a picture, so much so that my heart ached for her. I had developed the habit of singing to myself the 'Song of Unification': '*We want our unification...even in our dreams, the unification...the way to revive this nation...Give myself for the unification...Come unification, unification, come.*' Every word was wrung out of my heart until unable to bear it any more I broke down in sobs.

Christmas came. It was our custom at the Academy to have a staff party on Christmas Eve. While I was busy arranging it,

I did not forget to prepare a small present for him. It has been a painful year and the prospect for the new year was not good but I hoped to have at least a few pleasant days over the holiday.

Everybody was playful as they wrapped the presents that were to be exchanged after the dinner. I had phoned the Chinese restaurant to order the food and tell them when to bring it over. There was still plenty of time left.

The caretaker buzzed the intercom and told me that there was a lady wanting to see me. I went down the stairs wondering who it could be. It was Hwaja from the hotel. Smelling of alcohol, she said she had come to say goodbye and would like a word with me at the tea-room across the road. I had seen her only that morning and she hadn't mentioned it then. Apart from the smell, I did not like her general demeanour which was unlike her usual self. She spoke gibberish and her expression was unpleasant.

'It is not just to say goodbye – I have a business matter to deal with, Miss Yun. I am not like you, a lofty, prim and chaste lady. I might be compared more to a sand fish wriggling in and out of a muddy river-bed. But let me tell you this. I do know one or two things about the world that you don't.'

'I don't know how you will take this but I have been Mr Kwŏn's mistress for more than six months.' I felt as if I had been hit on the head with a mallet. She noticed the effect and now knew that she had the upper hand. With cruel smile of a victor, she went on.

'It all started in a rather silly way. He said he was writing a novel and he needed experience with a woman to describe his heroine. Not for his enjoyment but "for the sake of literature".' I now realized with disgust what their jokes had meant.

'I know he's not a lecturer. But when a good woman like you for whom I have great respect, has chosen him, there must be some good reason. I don't care to know what it is.

'Of course, I could report on him to the police or claim compensation from him – that's up to me, but I won't do that, I'm not that mean. It's only that I am three months pregnant. To put it bluntly I want you to give me the money for an abortion. I don't want to give birth to an unwanted child.'

I was shaking all over but could not say a single word. To her I must have been a pitiable sight. She took on a patronizing tone.

'Look, Miss Yun. With this, I want to put everything behind me and start a new life. I am sorry to upset you, but it will never happen again. I will leave your sight for good, and his too.

'You may be wondering why I don't get it out of him? It's because I hate that person, I can't stand the sight of him. He's dirty beyond words.' I wanted to block my ears.

'You should hear his conversations with those bitches at the "Black Rose" or the "Carnation" and the likes of them. He doesn't know, but I hear every word of it on the phone in the hall. It makes even me blush. When he wanted a phone I thought he had some important business matters to deal with. He paid three thousand Hwan for it.'

'Wasn't it an old set that had been lying around?'

'What old set? We went to the market and I got it cheap from a dealer I knew.

'I won't go into details, but can you let me have twenty thousand Hwan? I've got a long way to go. It's got to be now if you don't mind. Obviously you will get it back from him, the only son of a millionaire.' Her lips twitched in a sarcastic smile. 'Tell him this is the exact amount for the abortion, not a penny more. Well, I'll wait here.'

Unable to utter a word of protest, I walked out of the tea-room as if I was a prisoner with a gun pointed at my back. There was no room for rational thought. I was quite unnerved by her mentioning the police. Even if I was going to go and stab him to death myself, I had to get her out of the way first.

It was only just past four but the winter streets were already getting dark. I mechanically walked across the road towards the office but I knew it was no use going there.

'Hello, auntie!' Sudol, with his shoe-shine box over his shoulder was approaching. The sight of him warmed my frozen heart a little.

'Sudol, I suddenly need some money. Can you think of anyone I could borrow it from? I will pay it back in a couple of days.'

'How much do you need?'

'Twenty thousand Hwan.' I did not hold out any hope but to my astonishment he said, 'I can lend you that. My savings will be just about that much, I think. I've put it by to go to high school next spring. Will you wait here a few minutes?' He left his box beside me, disappeared into the darkness and returned with a bundle of paper notes. I held his cold hands tightly in mine but could hardly bring out the words, 'Thank you, Sudol.'

When she saw the money before her Hwaja's hard expression thawed.

'I've always had a lot of respect for you, Miss Yun. Now, a word of advice, as a sign of my goodwill, from one woman to another – those animals called "men" basically don't like lofty ladies. They prefer dirty women. If you mean to marry him keep an eye on his relationships with other women.'

I could not bear another moment. I said, 'Please, just go away.'

There was a row of five or six shoe-shine boys on the road just outside the Academy building. Sudol stood out by being the smallest. We called him by the pet name of 'Tot'.

It was two years since I had first met him. It had been the year I graduated from the university and started at the Academy, full of ambition and confidence for my future. On my first payday, I had treated my sister and Miae to a good lunch, and after work I was walking towards the bus stop with Miss Pak. A young man handed us a handbill about a famous physiognomist's visit to the area. It said he was at the hotel we were just passing by. It also gave information about his wide experience in this field and his proficiency in foretelling one's future. A blown-up portrait of him was posted on the gate. I had never been interested in such things but that day my curiosity was aroused for some reason. Probably it could be that in my high anticipation of a bright future I wanted to hear a word of confirmation even if it was a fake one.

'*Onni*, shall we go in and see what he's like?'

'Why not.'

So we went in. Miss Pak went into his room first and when she came out, I went. Contrary to my preconception of people involved in such a trade, a shabby crook, I was greeted by an elderly gentleman with a dignified air. He spoke of my past with amazing accuracy. He knew just by looking at my face that I had lost my mother before I was six, and I was one of four children and had a step-sister. Then he went on about my personality. I was extremely intelligent and had strong willpower and self-discipline. 'But what a pity,' he said. 'If only you were a man, you would be a President some day, but what's the use of having such a face when you are only a girl?' He was supposed to have mastered the cultures and philosophy of the West as well as the East, according to the poster but he must have rather dated ideas of these things, I thought.

'There is no law that forbids a woman becoming a President, is there?' I said jokingly. He gave a roar of laughter and said that when he saw people with a good physiognomy, he was happy and spoke more for the same money. I quite like him. He went on to say that I was fated to live away from my parents and within a year or so I would be going off on a long journey. I assumed that he meant the fulfilment of my dream of going to America. Once I decided that it was the case I was no longer interested in what he was saying about my marriage and how many children and so on. As I came out I was over the moon, as if I had been told by God himself that my dream would soon come true.

I walked on in bliss. I could not believe that there could be ugliness or sorrow in such a blissful world. At that moment I saw a small hand put out before me that belonged to a little boy, a beggar.

A few minutes later, I found myself sitting side by side with him on the stone steps leading up to Ahyŏn Church. This was Sudol. He was hungry, he said. I bought him a pitta bread filled with sugar syrup that they cooked and sold by the road-side. While he was eating it I asked him about himself. Another commonplace tragedy of a family hit by the war. He had lost his father and his elder brother during the war and now lived with his mother and five-year-old sister in a shelter under a bridge. His mother had been earning their living by selling things from the basket which she carried on her head, going from house to house, until recently when suddenly she became ill and couldn't get up, so he started begging. Then he said that if he had a little capital he could set up as a shoe-shine boy and would be able to support his mother and sister.

While he was talking I scrutinized his face. It was a sweet face with intelligent eyes. I could also see that he had not yet picked up the habit of lying or exaggerating.

'How much do you need to do that?'

'About three thousand Hwan will be enough to begin with, I think.'

'I can give you that.'

'Pardon?' He was startled and looked at me incredulously.

'It so happens that I have some money to spare. Something tells me that you are a good boy, and you will go far.'

I opened my bag and counted out three thousand Hwan from my pay packet and added another couple of notes telling him to buy some food for his mother and sister. As if in a daze, he had walked away in the opposite direction. A few minutes later he came running after me.

'I forgot to say thank you very much, aunt. Can you tell me your name and where you live?'

I smiled into his eyes. 'You don't need to worry about such things. I won't ask you to pay me back. If we live in Seoul maybe we'll meet again. Goodbye and good luck.'

I had completely forgotten about it until late one autumn evening he had walked up to me as he called, 'Auntie,' just as he had done tonight. He had a shoe-shine box over his shoulder.

'It's Sudol!' I was so pleased to see him. He hadn't grown a bit since I last saw him. His head now shaven showed up his unusually round face and eyes. He reminded me of an acorn fully ripened by the autumn sun and nightly frost. I took him into the Hanil restaurant and ordered *mandoo* soup. I wanted to hear how he was getting on. At first he was ill at ease as he carefully picked up his spoon.

'Auntie, aren't you ashamed to be seen eating with a boy like me?' He looked up at me with uncertain eyes.

'Sudol,' I said. 'You must never say such things. I want you to know that you and I are equal human beings. I am so pleased to see you again. Tell me how you are getting on.'

'You are a strange lady,' he said and shyly smiled.

'How is your mother? Can you polish shoes nicely now?'

Relaxed at last, he was eating his soup with relish. He told me he enjoyed his work. When he had first joined the central controlling body of the shoe-shine boys he had been allocated to the South Gates district but now he had been transferred to the West Gates area which was his home ground. His mother had recovered soon after we had met in the spring, so she was back on her round, and as far as daily life went they could manage on her earnings. He saved his money to pay for the high school, an evening technical school for working boys in the spring.

Since that day he had worked with other boys on the roadside in front of the Academy. All my colleagues called him 'Tiny Tot' or just 'Tot', and were all his regular customers. Whenever he saw me he came and stood before me with an intimate call of 'Auntie.' If I had to go out for lunch unexpectedly, I called him in to the store-room and gave him my packed lunch and after an office party or a special event, I wrapped up the leftovers and gave them to him.

In no way could I stay on for the party. As I apologized to my colleagues for letting them down I told them that I was being called away for an urgent family matter. I got a taxi and soon stood before Kwŏn. What I had felt like doing was just to stab him and then myself and bring the whole thing to an end but once I was face to face with him, it was different. In a sharp and cutting manner, I told him what had happened. He leapt up as if he was going to dash out at once, swearing and cursing Hwaja. 'I am going to grab that bitch and make her eat her words. I can't take her insolence any more!'

According to him, she had been trying to seduce him all that time.

'I kept it to myself not to cause you more worry on top of other things, but she's been a pest. A few days ago she came into this room in her night dress. I slapped her on the cheeks and called her a bitch. Since then she has been plotting against me. In fact, I was the one who told the landlady to get rid of her. She has been going in and out all the men's rooms so who can tell whose child it is?'

Then he changed his tone and said with a much subdued look, 'I know I am a useless hanger-on, stuck in a lodging house, but is it right for you to associate me with a woman like that and insult me in this way?'

When I saw his dejected look, my extreme hatred and repulsion were replaced by sympathy and love. I mentioned his relationship with the mistresses of the tea-rooms in a gentler tone and expressed my wish that even though we had to lie to other people, there should be no lies between the two of us.

'Even though ours is like a love growing in a thorn bush, I wanted it to be perfect in the eyes of God. Our thoughts should be united in one and even our breath,' and I added 'There can't be honour, nor glory in this love because we are living on the dark side of the sun, but I don't want it to be against my conscience, I want it to be something worth our sacrifice.' By now I was sobbing uncontrollably.

'Thank you, Sukey,' he said. 'If I went home I could have all the comfort in the world, but I think you are worth more than the whole world could offer. You have no idea how I treasure your pure heart. Think about it rationally, Sukey. What would it matter if there were a hundred tea-room madams? As you know, to camouflage my identity and not to give the impression of being a loner, I have to make the most of the one or two people I know, making it look like twenty, and by frequent telephone calls disguise my isolation. If I was stuck in here giving the impression of being a lonely man, the old man will be immediately suspicious and phone the college, won't he? That's all. I am not hiding anything from you. However if you don't want me any more, I am always ready to leave you in peace.'

Just then, the landlord called out from the hall, 'Mr Kwŏn, a phone call for you.'

'Thank you,' he said. The call was put through to him. He gave me a wink as he whispered, 'It's the "Black Rose".'

Shamelessly I brought my ear close to the receiver.

'Is that you, Madame?' he said repeatedly but there was no reply from the other end until there came the sound of a deep sigh.

'I am with Miss Yun at the moment.'

'I bloody well know,' the voice said. 'Sorry to disturb your bliss, but I won't be long anyway.' Then again a succession of deep sighs.

'Madame.'

'Don't look down on me, Mr Kwŏn. I am going to...' He did not let her finish. Instead he said, 'I must go now, goodbye,' and put the phone down.

I had so much wanted to go to the Christmas Midnight mass with him but conceded that it would be wise not to be seen together where there were too many eyes.

Avoiding the street scenes of merry-making, I chose to walk in dark patches, down dark alleys and beneath dark eaves, taking each step timidly like one who was afraid that the earth might sink. In future, I resolved, I would forgive him whatever he did. Had he not chosen to stay in the land of death for the love of me? If having him to myself meant leading him to his death, I would endure sharing him with others. Even if my share was only a quarter, a fifth, even if I had no share at all I would put his safety foremost.

The Cathedral was full. The congregation was a huge and solid mass. I could not distinguish individual faces. I chose an obscure corner to sit and wept all through the service until the Holy Communion. Probably God had abandoned me for good. On the other hand, he might be keeping a great blessing in store for me until the right time came. I had not entirely abandoned my trust in Him.

Chapter 8

In the Valley on the Darkside of the Sun – 3

A year had passed since we planted the magnolias in the courtyard of the hillside temple on Mt Samgak. That had been the prelude to our love. I had often wondered how much they would have grown. On Arbor Day, the fifth of April, I thought we would take a picnic lunch and go and see them, but an emergency cropped up like a whirlwind, blowing away all my plans. Instead, Kwŏn was installed as a boarder in the study of the inner quarters of the house where I and Sŏnhi lived.

A few days before Arbor Day, Mr Lee, the proprietor of Kyŏng-woo Hotel turned up at the Academy. It was quite unexpected. As soon as he saw me he said, 'I am right, am I not, in thinking that Mr Kwŏn teaches at S University?'

'What do you mean?' I replied, as if I doubted his sanity. My heart was beating fast.

'Please, don't tell him this but I was there on some business and I happened to see the register of lecturers and his name wasn't on it. I just wondered.' He put on a casual air but it was obvious that he had been suspicious and had gone there on purpose to check. And now that his suspicions were confirmed he wanted to terminate his dealings with him.

'I'm not surprised,' I said also putting on an air of casualness. 'What you saw must've been the register of the full-time staff. People like Mr Kwŏn working on hourly basis wouldn't be on that.' The old man, who had never been near a university, would not know enough to raise questions about that.

'If you say so, that must be it,' he said. He then went on to tell me an astonishing story. Apparently Mr Kwŏn owed him two hundred and fifty thousand Hwan for his lodgings, which was about the equivalent of four months' salary for me. Apparently he had not paid a penny for a long time now. I wondered how he had got himself into such a mess. We had agreed to pay his board at the end of each month. Even though at a reduced rate for a long-term guest, it still took a large part of my income but I had given it to him every month without fail.

'Knowing his temper, I could not speak to him directly, so I came to see you. I would be obliged if you could put in a quiet word for me.' These last words shook me out of my daze.

'Yes, of course, I will,' I said cheerfully. 'As you know he's not a poor man. He just doesn't think about money matters, that's all.' I added that in fact he might be thinking of moving out, as a friend of his had been persistently asking him to come and live with his family in Hongje-dong. It was an inspiration, laying out an escape route for Kwŏn.

After showing the old man out, I slumped into an armchair and closed my eyes. It was foolish of me not to have seen this coming sooner or later. I should have got him out of there a long time ago. In the first place, it was not safe for him to stay in one place for long and in any case I could in no way afford to keep him in an expensive place like that. I was wracking my brains all night to know how to get hold of the two hundred and fifty thousand Hwan and find him cheaper lodgings. I tossed and turned in agony until towards the early hours of the morning an idea came. I remembered that a student who had been lodging in the study at our place had left about a week ago and the room was still vacant.

'Sister, I have a favour to ask. Please let him become a lodger in this house, in the study.'

Sŏnhi did not immediately reply.

'I am sick of going in and out of that hotel. I give you my word that I will not behave in any way that might embarrass you. I'll keep a respectful distance and never go into his room.' She neither agreed nor objected but in a mocking tone of voice said to herself as she turned over, 'She's crazy.'

I was relieved for at least it was not an outright objection. It seemed as good as a consent.

During the past ten months, while I had been gasping for breath as I dragged myself under the weight of the cross of my love, some significant changes had been taking place in my sister's life. For a long time she had been regretting that she had not gone to university herself. It had been due to the war-time confusion, to being in debt on behalf of father and for her noble undertaking of seeing me through university. As soon as the pressure of her debt was lightened, she took the first opportunity of enrolling as a student of Korean literature for a two-year course at an evening college. She was a keen scholar and worked harder than the young ones straight from high school. At the same time she had accepted a proposal from a man who had constantly been courting her for several years. She now planned to marry next year, when she would be graduating. She went out with him after she finished night school and came home only just in time for the curfew. Fully immersed in her own busy life, my existence might have been little more than a nuisance, a withering flower thrown into a ditch with no hope of revival. Where there was no love, it seemed, there was no hatred. Now that she had given me up she hardly bothered to tell me off or reproach me. She looked onto me with cold, indifferent eyes.

In the morning I asked our landlady whether she would care to take a new lodger whom I knew well.

'If he has your recommendation, I have no hesitation,' she said. 'As long as he pays his bills, I don't really mind who it is.' Once he was there, I swore to myself, I would make sure he did not fall behind with his bills. Thus the first hurdle was overcome fairly easily but I still had the second. Where on earth would I find the money? I needed a lump sum of at least two hundred and fifty or three hundred thousand Hwan.

At the end of another sleepless night, I thought of Hae-ryŏn Chang, a friend from high school. I knew that a dozen or so of my high school friends now living in Seoul met once a month and ran *kae*, a kind of monetary club. The principle was to put in small sums of money for a length of time and get it back in a lump sum, taking it in turns among the members. It was a good way of saving and very popular among housewives at this time. Hae-ryŏn organized *kaes* of varying sizes and supervised the smooth running of them. The lump sum thus earned was usually lent out with interest.

Hae-ryŏn could not believe me when I told her that I wanted to borrow three hundred thousand Hwan.

'I will pay it back within the month,' I said with little conviction. She said that she had no money to lend me at the moment but could give me a tip. It was *kae* day tomorrow and it was Miae's turn to take the lump sum, which amounted to five hundred thousand Hwan. Unless she was going to use it immediately, it would be loaned out anyway, so she might let me borrow it. The next day I went to Hae-ryŏn's house at lunch time, where my friends met. They gave me a noisy welcome for I had not seen them for years, but soon settled down to business. Hae-ryŏn collected everyone's due, counted them twice and handed over to Miae five bundles each of a hundred-thousand Hwan. The transaction was over within fifteen minutes. A luncheon party at a Chinese restaurant was to follow for which Miae would pay. Her attitude towards me that day had been cool from the start. I mustered my courage but my voice only came out in a whisper. I asked her if I could borrow some of her money.

'I have a use for it somewhere else.' She said curtly and led the way out of the room.

It was drizzling with rain outside. As I walked away from my friends in the opposite direction I was crying, my tears blending with the rain. In the evening I went back to Hae-ryŏn and almost begged her. She forced me to join a three hundred thousand Hwan *kae* she was about to start, and lent me the sum I wanted with interest of ten percent per month. From now on I would have to put in a regular sum to the *kae* every month until my turn came, and when it came I would probably have to hand it back in payment of what I was now taking with the ten percent interest.

I got him out of the hotel at last. He told the owner and his wife that he had been persuaded by a close friend to join him and his family in Hongje-dong. We now lived in the same house but all we shared with each other was the roof. The conditions here were even more constricting than at the hotel for we had to maintain a strict respectability so as not to cause embarrassment to Sŏnhi before the eyes of the other lodgers.

Within a few days I had fallen into the net of an enormous debt, the same monster that had led my father to his destruction, and strangled the bloom of Sŏnhi's youth and sucked her blood. My monthly salary was hardly enough to cover the interest, the instalment for the *kae* and his lodging. Where was it all going to end? In the night I lay awake and trembled with fear. But there was in me a conviction that I was doing the right thing, that God was with me and that to love perfectly was to offer oneself as a perfect sacrifice. As long as I believed in my love I had strength to carry on.

At six o'clock in the morning I took the washing to the stream at the foot of Yonhi Hill, on the outskirts of the village. It was mainly his clothes. As an unmarried woman I could not openly wash a man's clothes in the view of other lodgers at the communal pump in the courtyard. Even though it was April the water coming down from the mountain spring was icy. My fingers, unaccustomed to washing, hurt at first and then went numb. That I was washing some man's clothes at a stream at dawn – it was like a bad dream. Until then I had hardly washed even my own socks or handkerchiefs. I would have to hang them out in the room while Sunhi was out and put them away out of sight before she came in so as not to provoke scorn or even hysterics.

It was a comfort though to see him settled in the house safe and beyond the police inspections. He had succeeded in gaining the complete trust and respect of the landlady, and got on well with her family, Yŏnok, her daughter, and Chiun, her trouble-making son. She often got carried away in long conversations with him as she confided her sorrows and troubles to his sympathetic ear. He, in his usual insinuating way had won the trust of the boy, Chiun. His mother was full of praise for Mr Kwŏn saying that he was a good influence on the boy. Since he came to her house, she said, Chiun had considerably improved. Often when Chiun was having a row with his mother, Mr Kwŏn would say, 'Chiun, you must not upset you good mother in that way. Come along with me. Let's go for a walk.' When they came back from a long walk, Chiun was a different person. Only Sŏnhi was icy towards him, plainly showing her hostility. It was embarrassing for me. After all he was my friend as far as everyone could see, so why she behaved like that they would wonder. But I could not blame her. How wonderful it would be, I often dreamed, if Sŏnhi and her fiancé and we two could get on well and the four of us go out happily together. But that would never be.

As spring advanced and the days lengthened, requests for the extension of the library opening hours came through the 'suggestion box'. At the staff meeting we discussed this and agreed to extend them by four hours to nine in the evening until September. The decision was followed by the question of staffing during these hours. Unless we took on extra staff, which was agreed to be impractical, we would have to take it in turns among ourselves. No one was keen on that idea and I volunteered. My colleagues were not surprised because the supervision of the Reading Room was my job anyway, and they took it for granted that I wanted to use the quiet evening hours for my own studies. It was assumed that there would not be too many readers at that time of the night. The director expressed his concern about my health and said I should call for help at any time that I felt unfit to stay on. Behind my bravado, all that I was thinking of was the extra money.

At five o'clock sharp, my colleagues who had been like a happy family brood all day gave a mechanical 'Cheerio', 'See you tomorrow' or 'Don't work too hard', and left without so much as a backward glance. Left to myself in the empty room I felt forlorn. I went up to the Reading Room and took my seat behind the counter. As predicted, there were only half a dozen readers, who knew well enough on which shelves to find the books on their subject. Occasionally one or other of them would come up to me to ask for help with finding their material, or to see back issues of certain journals kept in the store, or to use the microfilm. Now and again I stood up and walked up and down the room as if to demonstrate that I was in charge, stopping before a shelf or two to put something right. Most of the time I read my books, got carried away in reveries or sorted out my tangled thoughts and feelings and wrote in my diary.

4 July. I am wild with joy. Dare I be happy? Can I really believe that my toil is over? He has got a job! Have I passed the test God set before me and about to enter a new heaven? It does not matter if his pay is a pittance. Even if it meant that he had to pay to go out regularly to be a man with a job I would have been happy. At least we can now plan our life together instead of me steering and charting out the course of the life of two persons alone.

For several days, he had been busily going about with a tiny newspaper cutting that advertised some jobs. I did not hold out any hope – a man with no definite identity, how could he apply for any job publicly advertised in a paper? But behold, yesterday he came and showed me a letter of appointment and an identity card as a member of the staff of M Education Insurance Company. It had opened a branch in the Sŏdaemun district and was looking for a number of office workers and sales persons. He had applied as a college lecturer, with me as a referee. Apparently he had gone to see the Branch Manager in person and was accepted on the spot. 'We are looking for hidden talents like yourself,' he was told. His title is Deputy Branch Manager. He is to supervise the work of over twenty sales staff and recruit them as he sees fit.

I went to see him at lunch time. His office is in a rather ramshackle alley off the main road, about ten minutes walk from here. He was sitting at a desk with a telephone and beamed at me.

Recently Sŏnhi's hatred of him has reached a new peak. She frequently breaks into cries of 'Unless he's a spy or an ex-convict, why can't he get a decent job instead of scrounging off a poor woman?' At such times I would hold onto her hand and, begging like a slave, ask her to lower her voice. While she is in the house, he says, he dares not come out of his room. He can smell the poison in the air, which even penetrates through the closed door.

When I showed her the letter of his appointment and the identity card this morning, she said scoffingly, 'Hmn, at last you're in luck. Hope you'll be happy.' Yes, I will be happy, I will show you how happy I can be.

6 July. He came to see me at the Academy bringing the Branch Manager with him. I welcomed them politely and showed them round the Academy, explaining everything. When the guided tour was over Mr Kwŏn said, 'Is the director in?' sounding as if they were close friends. He probably knew that he wasn't.

'No, I'm afraid he's not. He's teaching at Y University this morning.'

'That's a pity. I just wanted to say hello as I haven't seen him for sometime.' Then he said, 'Can we have a cup of coffee?'

'Yes, of course.' I took them into the meeting room and asked Suyŏn to take it in for them. Unfortunately he went a step too far. He asked me to issue a membership card for his friend there and then on his recommendation. I said that I could not do that and he went away looking displeased. But he was really naughty. He knows perfectly well how strict the regulations are. Some time ago when he asked me to get him a card I fully explained to him. As for him, I said, he would be admitted at any time without a card as my special guest.

As if making a critical decision, it was hard to turn down his request. I don't know what sort of qualifications the manager has. If he has the right ones he can apply for a card in the proper way. If he hasn't, tough luck, he shan't have it. I am not going to resort to an underhand way just to show off how important Mr Kwŏn is. Of course, if the membership card was my personal property I would have given him one without a murmur of objection, but my job is sacred to me and I will not sell it cheap. I hope he appreciates my position and feels better by now.

15 July. Merry sounds of laughter ring out from his room. It looks as if Yŏnok and Kijŏng are playing cards with him. Kijŏng is a childhood friend of the youngest daughter of the landlady, Yŏnok. Her parents keep a small chicken shop at the entrance to the market. After leaving high school, Yŏnok told me, Kijŏng went to a technical college but gave it up half-way through, and is now looking for a job. Mr Kwŏn says that he may be able to take her on to his sales staff. That's why she is trying to earn his favour. She has been hanging round here rather a lot lately. If I wanted, I could go over and join them in the game but I feel rather depressed, so I sit here in my room with doors closed. Kijŏng is tall and heavily built, and wears rather showy clothes. As I came home yesterday, I saw her with him in front of the house. She was wearing a crimson sleeveless blouse, a white flared skirt and red high-heels. He introduced her to me. My arrival seemed to have interrupted them. She said she had better go. She gave him an artificial, sensuous smile, screwing up her eye, and walked away, her enormous hips juddering from side to side. What a flirt!

28 July. Long past his home time. Where is he? What is he up to? My nerves are on edge, tormented by all sorts of imaginations. My ears are pricked for the familiar sound of his footsteps, firm and precise, on the concrete slabs. I trust his love as I trust my own, but after a stressful day my patience wears thin and my hopes give way to despair and misery. I brood on the occasions and incidents, one by one, that have been hurtful. It hurts. Fussy and fastidious by nature as I am how did I put up with all these failings and shortcomings of his? Sŏnhi's flustered face with glaring eyes floats before me, her merciless abuse ringing in my ears. 'Stupid woman! Once you start sacrificing yourself, you end up as a complete victim. Pound yourself to powder and you won't get a scrap of reward.' Unable to bear it any longer, I went out for a long walk. It is eleven and he is not yet in. If only he wasn't such a liar it would be more bearable.

8 August. He comes home late every night, but he always has convincing explanations. Today I caught him red-handed, thwarted his plan and trapped him in his den. I feel miserable about it but I shall not relent until I put a stop to his lying. It is up to him now to apologize and make peace with me.

He was telling me that a member of his staff who runs a peach orchard in Sosa had invited himself and the manager out for the day. He was getting ready. I was about to put in 'Can't I come with you?', when a little boy popped his head round the gate and called, 'Mr Kwŏn, my sister says she's waiting at the bus-stop,' and disappeared. At one glance I could see that it was Kijŏng's brother. Since she has been taken on to his sales staff, I often heard from Yŏnok and Chiun that they saw the two of them getting off the bus together, or strolling by the foot of the Yonhi Hill. It did not bother me as I thought there was no harm in workmates going about together.

A few minutes after the boy had gone he came out of his room, put on his shoes and went out. Curiosity made me follow him. Just as I stepped over the threshold, I heard a nasal female voice saying, 'You are late. There's only twenty minutes before the train goes.' It was Kijŏng in tight-fitting, three-quarter-length trousers and a broad-brimmed straw hat on.

'Just a moment.' I grabbed his sleeves and pulled him back inside the gate. He looked a little embarrassed. I slapped his cheek. 'Bastard!'

'It's the end, it's the end,' he muttered to himself. He went out to send the girl away, came back and shut himself up in his room for the rest of the day. It's up to him now.

12 August. He phoned from the tea-room, 'Carnation', and asked me to come out for a minute. When I went out and found it was only to introduce me to a new member of his staff, I wasn't pleased. It is too much to be called out in office hours just to help him to show off to a girl. Hisun Chŏng, looking neat and modest, greeted me and said, 'I am so pleased to meet you. Mr Kwŏn has told me so much about you.' There was little I could say. When I had finished a cup of coffee, he said I could go and I did.

13 August. My birthday would have passed totally ignored by the whole world but for Chaehong Lee. Shortly before closing time, he quite unexpectedly turned up at the office. It was the first time that I was genuinely pleased to see an old friend since my life in the shadows began. As I have never sought out any of those on the sunny side, I rarely saw them. Friendship is a mutual thing. If I never turned up at alumni meetings or friend's weddings why should they bother to remember me. I don't blame them. I shall soon be forgotten. Luckily it was Saturday and I had no evening work. We sat in a coffee-shop. He said he had suddenly remembered it was my birthday and realized that he had not spoken to me for ages. He had seen me often in church but as soon as the service was over I always seemed to slip out like a hare. Starved for human warmth and on the verge of total collapse I nearly broke down in tears. He had remembered my birthday, which had been ignored even by my sister and my lover. Naturally we drifted into memories of high school days in Chŏngju. He had a clear memories of one particular birthday of mine there, he said. That year it fell on a Sunday and Sŏnhi invited a few members of our Youth Club for lunch. We had a feast in our tiny room. The food, entirely her work was sumptuous and plentiful. Even now I wonder how she managed to produce such a treat in those days of shortage. He said he had never enjoyed the food better before or since.

He talked about his father who had been an Anglican priest in Seoul and had been taken north during the Communists' occupation. His father sounds a wonderful man. I talked about my uncle who had met with the same fate as his father's. How I miss him, my dear uncle! Again we drifted to our days in Chŏngju. Like me, he had come there as a refugee, with his mother, it being her native town. He went to the Boys' High school while I was at the Girls'. Only a year older than me he was even then tall and well-built and rather mature for his age. He was a leader with a strong faith. He had revitalized the Anglican Youth Club, which had been a name only, making it a flourishing organization with more than thirty members. We had regular meetings and choir practices. At Christmas we put on a Nativity Play, and went carol singing after mid-night mass, walking round the whole town to sing at the doorsteps of every church member until we collapsed in exhaustion in the early hours of Christmas morning. He was also fond of debate, like myself I suppose. How we used to be engaged in heated discussions on all sorts of subjects, which we had continued into recent years back in Seoul until my clandestine life began. When the month of May came round in Chŏngju, and with it the acacia season, the hill on which the church stood commanding a view of the whole town, was covered in the white, sweet-smelling flowers. How pleasant it was to walk up the spiral paths through the acacias, some times running out of breath to get there in time for the service. As I sat opposite him, these memories came back so vividly that it was as if it had all happened only a month ago.

Chaehong also had some news about Fr. Osbourne, with whom we used to have English conversation classes, meeting twice a week when we came back to Seoul. Just fancy, I had forgotten all about him. Come to think of it, it was Chaehong who had organized this with him, a missionary who had just arrived from England. There were about eight students in the class, and we had got on well together and had some lively times. It ended after two years when Fr. Osbourne left Seoul to take up a parish in the country. I knew from the Church News that he started an orphanage in Anp'yŏng where he is now, and a small leper community in a hamlet near Ch'unchŏn. Now Chaehong tells me that he is trying to purchase some land for the lepers in the surrounding area with a view that eventually they would become a self-sufficient community, rearing animals and growing their own crops.

'As you know,' Chaehong said, 'Father Osbourne is not a man of robust constitution. You can tell just by looking at him. He is working too hard, I fear that he might damage his health.' Apparently Chaehong spent a month with him in summer in the leper colony. Now enrolled with the Anglican theological college, I have a feeling that he wants to become a priest following in his father's footsteps. He asked me several times why I looked so emaciated. I had to give some reason, so I said it was probably because I have been worrying about Myŏngsŏk, my younger brother. Once I mentioned his name, I felt a lump rising in my throat. My heart ached for him, my poor brother. What a perfectly useless sister I am! Busy putting out the immediate fireball dropped at my feet, I am ignoring my own brother who is going through a terrible time.

We went into town and Chaehong bought supper and I the coffee. The first real treat I have had in a long, long time. As we parted he emphatically said that if in any way he could help he would be happy to do so. It is now past ten-thirty. Kwŏn has not come in yet.

20 August. News of Myŏngsŏk in the Army Hospital. Is there ever going to be an end to his suffering? My mind goes back to the time of his call-up, last spring. After moving out of Lady Lee's residence and staying at cheap lodging houses one after another, he had been wandering the streets like a vagabond without a Resident Registration Card or any document concerning his conscription status when one day he was stopped and questioned at a street checkpoint. He was taken as an avoider of military service and was made to enrol there and then. When this happened our family breathed a sigh of relief. We live in a society in which some parents sell their land or family heirlooms to send their sons to university for the privileges of postponing conscription while they are enrolled as students, and a shorter period of service as graduates. At first I inwardly blamed father for not only failing to send him to college but not equipping him with proper documents. Then I came round to see it differently. After all, all young men have to go through it sooner or later, and the sons of richer and more privileged parents than ours have to go, don't they? I felt better.

Then this shameful and painful memory! One day I met him in the street near the Academy. A tall man in army uniform stalked across the road calling, 'Sister!' I grabbed hold of his hands. 'Myŏngsŏk! Myŏngsŏk!' I could not find another word. He seemed to have grown taller since I last saw him. I had to look up to catch his eyes. I took him into a nearby bakery and ordered hot doughnuts. He gobbled them up one after another. It was when he held the fifth that he smiled at me happily and said, 'Why don't you have one?'

'I'm not hungry. Are you having a hard time?'

'No, not particularly. After all everyone else is going through it.' He had incredibly matured.

'The army has made a man out of him,' I thought. Then he told me how the Y University's consolation party came to visit people from there.

'It was a spectacular sight. They all gathered together and had a picnic and sang the university anthem.' He was excited as he told me this, as if it had been for him. 'Of course I knew it word by word from you, didn't I?'

There was no trace of bitterness in him for not being a part of it, but it hurt me. As I thought to myself, 'If our mother was alive, you could have been a part of it.' A sharp pain shot through my heart.

'I've got a few day's leave, but as you know I can't stay at Lady Lee's. I wonder if I could stay at your place?'

'Of course,' I said only to regret it the next moment. It was the wrong answer. It was the time when, a few months after Kwŏn had moved into the house, the battle of nerves between Sŏnhi and myself had reached its height. In no way could I take him home.

I told him to wait there for a moment and went out of the shop. After thinking about it hard, I wrote him a note:

Forgive me, Myŏngsŏk. I had momentarily forgotten that I am in no position to take you to my place. Please do not ask me why. One day you'll know. For now just pretend I am not there. Be brave and do not despair. In three years' time when you come out of the army I will give you a hero's welcome. Until then don't seek for me. With this money, find a decent inn, buy some food that you fancy, and treat yourself to a film or two.

With Love, Sukey.

I asked Sudol to take the note and money to Myŏngsŏk, feeling mean and worthless, and detesting myself. I hoped and prayed that he would settle down with the army life but he did not. I heard that he was getting himself into trouble by repeated desertion. It was not as if he had a caring family or a girlfriend who he was dying to see. It was only to roam the heartless streets of Seoul. Nobody understood why he did it, but he did. Sometimes father took him back and other times his sergeant came out in search of him and escorted him back. I was too much of a coward to dwell on the punishment to which he would be subjected on his return. I had to grit my teeth to keep my imagination from running riot. A few days ago he did it again and was beaten up until he passed out and then taken to the Army Hospital and put into the mental unit under the assumption that a normal person, fully aware of the punishment, would have enough sense not to do it again, and that's where he is now. I must go and see him at once.

22 August. I suspect that I am being cheated again in some sinister plot. Earlier on when I asked him to go for a walk with me he said he was too tired and retired into his room. But somehow or other he has slipped out during the evening and only just came in. It is half-past eleven. What is he up to? And where has he been? Am I being foolish? Is my dream of perfect love no more than a childish illusion? Probably Sŏnhi is right. She sees and smells falsity in his every movement, gesture and word, she says. I might as well hope for a withered rose to bloom again as for a revival of his conscience. I want to kill, kill him and kill myself.

23 August. I stole two hundred Hwan from Sŏnhi's handbag. It was the first, deliberate act of theft since the incident of the tin last year. It was for the bus fare for the two of us and his cigarettes. He has been promising to give me some money when he was paid in August, but I have not received a penny. On the contrary, he is scrounging off me for his bus fare. Where is it all going to end? I am scared.

24 August. He said he wanted to go to bed early tonight. I have long since acquired the habit of sitting on this spot on the verandah from where I can see the door of his room across the courtyard. I sit here turning over my thoughts until the light goes out in his room and I guess he's gone to sleep. Tonight, for some reason, he seems unable to sleep, the light goes off and then comes back on, goes off and then back on again. What is he doing?

26 August. The chirping of the crickets has started long since. Tonight it resounds in the moonless and starless darkness, rousing in my heart feelings keener than usual. Sŏnhi who had been to the Army Hospital to see Myŏngsŏk spat out, 'He asked why you can't pay him a visit.' These words keep coming back. For a whole week I have been hoping to have some money to spare so that I could take something nice for him to eat, but I could not make it. I deserve the curses and insults of Sŏnhi, and the scorn of the whole world.

15 September. It is all over the newspaper as the main news story. The gold smugglers that have recently been arrested had direct links with a gang of spies that was rounded up a short while ago. I well remember the reports on the secret agents. I had been concerned and actually had asked him whether he had known any of the people. He had exploded in anger as he said, 'I've told you to forget about such things. I have no connections with such a past!' Then he had gone on to say more gently, 'They are all crazy bastards. In times like these, how dare they come down in droves? They deserve to be arrested and tortured to death.'

Today he came to see me shortly before five o'clock. He was out of breath and had a look of one being chased. He said briskly, 'What shall I do? I'll do what you tell me to do –

whether to risk the danger and get my money back or abandon it altogether?'

He took a deep breath and went on, 'I am on my way to get it but it is in the form of gold.' I understood it all. I told him to give it up. How often had I dreamed of the day when I would hold in my hand a lump of that money, clearing up all my debts and live with my shoulders straight again. I must be either brave or scared to death or both to give up instantly that cherished dream. In fact I feel much better now that I have thrown away cleanly the thought of that unwholesome money.

5 October. I had just come in and was about to change when Chiun announced a visitor. A man wearing dark glasses stood outside the gate. I thought it was a detective. Since the gold incident a couple of week ago I have noticed that Kwŏn has been behaving restlessly. He never told me anything but several times he was still in bed when it was time to go to work.

'You must be Miss Yun. I have come to talk to you about Mr Kwŏn.'

'What has to come has come,' I thought as I quietly waited for his next word.

'Unless he returns the insurance money collected so far, along with the account book by tomorrow, the Branch Manager says that he will start legal proceedings.' When he came in rather late, I told him, in a threatening tone of voice, about the visitor from the company.

'Legal proceedings, indeed, crazy idiots!' he said. For once, I thought, we should sit together and have a long talk about the situation we are in, and comfort and encourage each other. But he said, 'I am extremely tired. Please, can I be left alone? It is all for your sake.' Then he put the light out. He knows that I could not stay on there without the light what with the landlady across the hall and other eyes in the house. He meant to chuck me out! He did look tired. What has he been up to? It looks as though he has been given the sack.

2 November. Finished reading Victor Hugo's *Les Miserables*.

3 November. On wings of imagination I float about in some dramatic scenes. It may only be the extension of the emotional response to *Les Miserables* that I finished yesterday.

Suppose he was put in the position of Jean Valjean – if he was placed in circumstances in which his past was not questioned, and he was given a chance to exert all his energy and ability to the full, he might find his resurrection.

If he was to work for people in more unfortunate circumstances than himself, say, orphans and lepers...The thought of Fr. Osbourne came to my mind. If only Mr Kwŏn could be brought into the world of Fr. Osboure to live with him, learn from him the teachings of the Christian Church, and partake in its great humane projects, he could, I am sure, prove to be a hero. If only that was possible... In some distant future, his past may come out and he may be handcuffed, and brought to the court, but taking into account his act of repentance, his resolution to make a complete break and the good work he has done for the poor, the court will be sympathetic towards him and the judgment be lenient.

I broached this idea to him, without going into details of what I had in mind. He should be given a chance to think about it in his own way. His response was vague, neither keen nor entirely rejecting it.

'Would you like me to write to Fr. Osbourne and ask?' I said.

'Well, do you think it is possible? Of course, if he wants to have me I will consider it.' Then he said, 'Why don't you write to him and see what he says.'

4 November. I have written to Fr. Osbourne. I could not tell him all the truth about Mr Kwŏn but chose the words carefully so as not to tell lies.

Dear Father Osbourne,

It is hard to believe that it is four years since I last saw you. Even though I have been completely out of touch with you I often thought about you and the pleasant times we had with you at the English class.

Since my graduation in 1957, I have been working in this place, The Korean Academy. As far as the job goes I could not be happier. This is a rather unique research institute and we have many foreign scholars and visitors coming to see our library. I hope you too will visit us when you are in Seoul.

The reason I am writing is to introduce my boyfriend to you. He is a healthy man of thirty one with intelligence and education of, I should say, above average. At present his social position is insignificant, and he is looking for some quiet job. He has little ambition to become rich or famous and seeks a job quiet but worthy and humane.

I wondered if you need a man like him for your orphanage or some other charitable establishment you are involved with.

As for his religion, I am afraid to say, he knows nothing about Christianity but like a well prepared soil, I trust, he is ready to take and absorb the teachings of the church. For his remuneration, bed and board will be sufficient.

Looking forward to hearing from you,

Sincerely Yours,
Sukey Yun.

12 November. On the way home, I bumped into Chaehong at the Sŏdaemun roundabout and we went into a nearby tea-room for a cup of coffee and sat there for about an hour talking about this and that. After parting from him I was walking towards the bus-stop, when I saw Kwŏn among the rush hour crowd. He was walking with a woman just turning left at the crossroads. I quickened my steps and went after them but soon lost them around the bustling bus-stop. Just then I saw a bus bound for Shinch'on, our home area, leaving. As I had searched so thoroughly among the crowd, I thought he could not be anywhere else but on that bus. I don't know what I wanted him so desperately for, but I caught a taxi and hurried home. He wasn't there. I was too agitated to settle down. I caught the bus back to Sŏdaemun. Foolishly, I felt sure that he was still around there and I searched in every possible place, every tea-room, restaurant and bar. He was nowhere.

With the evening darkness came a pitch-black despair engulfing me so tightly that I felt smothered. Still I could not abandon the search. If I hung around there long enough, I thought, I would get some clue in the end. I emptied my pocket to buy a ticket in the Cinema by the bus-stop. I did not care what the film was about but surveyed as far as I could all the downstairs seats and then looked upstairs. As I slumped into an empty seat without bothering to glance at the screen, tears welled up and flowed freely as if I was watching a great tragedy.

There was no need to sit there for long. I came out and began to walk aimlessly. By the parapet of the bridge opposite the tea-room, where I had been with Chaehong earlier, I was stopped by a familiar call of 'Auntie!'

Under a flickering lamp Sudol was selling chestnuts roasting them over a charcoal brazier. It is his mother's business, he told me, which she had started a few weeks before, but late in the night, a couple of hours before the curfew, he takes it over so that she can go home and rest. I wished I had some money to buy some. If I had, I thought, I would buy the whole lot so that he could go home and rest too. What a tough life he leads – polishing shoes all day and selling chestnuts in this cold night street.

Feeling a bit silly, I squatted down beside him leaning my back against the parapet. I knew he lived underneath some bridge but didn't realize it was this one. It was getting late. Home-goers' lonely footsteps had long since stopped. Still hopeful, he now and again called out into the air. 'Buy some chestnuts, hot roast chestnuts.' The wind from beneath the bridge was bitter. My toes and fingers were freezing. Polished by the wind the sky was clear and the moon was full.

He had been quiet for sometime when suddenly he broke the silence.

'Auntie, I saw uncle today. He was coming out of the Kukjae Cinema with a lady and they went into a Chinese restaurant.' His voice was solemn.

'You can't have. It must have been someone else. He's not well today and in bed.' I wanted to protect his honour and dignity.

'Yes, it was him. I went close up, you see, because I thought the lady was you.' I could no longer hide my curiosity or try to save his face.

'What sort of lady was she?'

'About your size, wearing a chestnut Burberry coat.' It must be the woman he was with earlier on. In the darkening light and from a distance I could not be sure about the colour of the coat but it had looked dark, almost black.

'Can you remember what time it was?'

'Around half-past nine. It was shortly before I went home. I worked in the Kwanghwamun area today, you see.' It was not due to the chilly wind, but my whole body broke into violent trembling. The preliminary siren for the curfew wailed. I did not want to go home.

Regardless of the siren, Sudol called out again, 'Chestnuts, piping hot chestnuts!' Then he spoke to me again. 'Auntie, he is a bad man.' I could find no words. Probably encouraged by my heavy silence instead of protest, he went on, revealing some dreadful facts about Kwŏn.

'I have seen him many times going around with a woman holding her arm – often they were different ones.' He must have heard me gasping as he went on. 'And in front of them, he orders me about as if I am his servant, making me polish not only his shoes but hers as well, all free, and sending me on errands. He has borrowed small sums from me several times, about two thousand Hwan altogether and never paid me back.'

'Sudol, is this all true? Why didn't you tell me before? Oh, dear, it was my great mistake in the first place to introduce you to him. I am sorry, Sudol.'

'I did not want to upset you. For your sake, I thought I would put up with it.'

'Silly child!'

'He is a bad man, isn't he?' He was asking the second time for my agreement that he was bad.

'Yes, he is. Let's stop having anything to do with him from now on.' For the first time, to a humble little boy, I have opened up my heart that has been shut tight to the world, and broke the bastion of my creed, 'He is not a bad man.'

The moanful sound of the curfew resounded in the frozen, night sky.

'Auntie, you must go home.'

'It's too late for that. Sudol, would it be possible for me to sleep at your place tonight?' He looked nonplussed and then said, 'Even so, how can you sleep at a place like ours. Go to the inn.'

'No. I just want to talk with you a little longer if you don't mind.' I could not tell him that I had no money to go to an inn. As he packed up his things, he said, 'A few days ago, I saw him quarrelling with a woman in a tea-room. She was very angry with him and he looked ever so harassed.'

'How old did she look?'

'She could be about his age or a bit older, I just couldn't tell. She was wearing a full-length traditional skirt underneath an overcoat, and rather fat.'

I must say I was impressed by his sharp observation. I would never have noticed such details. Or was he doing it consciously to be of some service to me? He went on, 'I did not go inside but hung round the doorway and just eavesdropped. They seemed arguing about money. I heard her say in what sounded like a Chollado accent, "I don't bloody care about you, but I want the money at once".' The description didn't fit Julie nor Madame Kim. Who could it be? I am totally lost in a fog of doubt and disbelief which is getting denser and denser. 'I must get myself out of this. I must give him up. He belongs to a mysterious world far beyond my comprehension,' I thought.

I was walking side by side with Sudol to his home. There was no trace of anyone around the path beneath the bridge. Suddenly, out of nowhere, a female figure appeared ten yards before us. At first, I thought it was his mother coming out to meet him. Then I sensed something uncanny about her. When she came up to within a few yards of us she abruptly held up her arms into the air as her mouth broke into a grin. Her teeth flashed white as they caught the light of the moon. It was a mad woman. I shuddered with a fright.

'What do I do if she springs on me, in this narrow path?' Momentarily this thought flashed through my mind, but she brushed passed us quietly. Revealed beneath her short jacket, her midriff was white illumined by the moonlight.

I have heard a lot about slums, poor quarters and cardboard-box houses but it was the first time that I actually stepped into one. It must be a community of fair size. Seen from above it may look like a dumping ground of cardboard boxes. Looking at them closely the houses were low like crab-shells, clustered together.

Sudol stood before one of them from which light seeped out.

'Is that you, Sudol?' A gentle voice called out. As he pushed aside a straw-mat door he said, 'Mother, I've brought auntie Yun with me. She wants to sleep here tonight.'

'What?'

I stepped in front of Sudol briskly and said cheerfully, 'I'm terribly sorry to cause you this trouble but I got carried away talking with Sudol and didn't realize how the time was passing. Could you please let me stay for the night?'

'Even so, how can you sleep in a squalid place like this?' As she protested she came forward and grabbed hold of my hands. What warm hands they were though rough! A whiff of warm earth like that of the ploughed earth in the thawing spring sun greeted me. A space of barely six-foot square. But the walls were pasted with paper and the floor was warm.

Sudol's mother pushed aside a little girl sleeping at the warm end of the room and sat me there as she extended her belated thanks for my help to Sudol. She called me the benefactor of their family.

'When Sudol came home that day, bringing the medicine and some *ddok*, and showed me the money saying that a good lady had given it to him, I couldn't believe it at first. I thought he had stolen it.'

From beneath a quilt lying on the warm floor, she took out a bowl with a lid on and pushed it towards Sudol. As he lifted the lid, the rich aroma of dumplings cooked in *kimchi* soup assailed my senses. I swallowed the saliva in my mouth taking care not to make noise. He emptied the bowl in no time, and no sooner had his head touched the floor than was he fast asleep. Soon the regular breathing of his mother showed she was asleep too.

As an honoured guest I lay at the warmest end of the room, my coat being used as my cover. When I was sure that everybody was asleep I let out my repressed sorrow. It ran wild clawing at my heart. I didn't care if I died there and then.

Some time had passed when I heard someone outside singing a medley of songs rather badly. 'Moon, moon, the bright moon,' 'Moon night of Silla,' and 'Moonlight on the castle ruins.' The snatches of the songs were all about the moon. An uneven voice with uneven rhythm grew more and more high-pitched until it broke out in a cackling laughter.

'Ugh, that crazy woman, she's at it again,' Sudol's mother who I had thought was asleep muttered to herself and clicked her tongue. I gave a light cough as a signal that I was not asleep. It was thus that she began to tell me about the woman in a quiet drone so as not to awake the children.

She has been around the neighbourhood for over three years now. It is a poor community and most people find it difficult to eat three meals a day but they are kind-hearted and let her be. 'So the poor thing somehow manages to be fed and clothed,' she said. She is not completely mad and whether she has lost part of her mind or was born an imbecile, she has spells when she is quite normal and she gives a hand to the others with washing or carrying water from the communal pump.

Even though she is insane, she is a gentle soul and has never been violent or harmed anyone. Her madness comes out usually in the night, and she's particularly bad on moonlit nights.

'That's like me,' I thought. 'My emotional tide reaches its peak on a night like this.'

After a pause, Sudol's mother went on in an even lower voice,

'It is a foul world. You'd never believe this but some bastard laid his hands on her and made her pregnant. Last summer, she was going around with her tummy as high as Namsan Peak. When she laid herself down on the roadside and slept with her mouth hung open, she was a pathetic sight.' She went on. 'Then she gave birth to a baby a couple of months ago on a market stall in the night. As soon as it was born someone took it away from her. In a way it was just as well for how could a mad woman bring up a child? But when she found out it was gone, she cried until she was hoarse.'

I am going mad. I want to. If, in madness, I could shake off the cumbersome burdens of convention and dignity, and the label of an intellectual, ignore people's eyes and fling out the pile of rancour in my heart, that would be most desirable.

This night, out of all nights, when I am on the brink of madness, closer to it than ever before, it is odd that I should hear the story of a mad woman. On top of it all my thoughts of Myŏngsŏk pile up with peculiar poignancy.

Sŏnhi's words after she had been to see him at the mental ward of the Army Hospital ring loudly in my ears, every word.

The ward was large and the most wretched place she had ever seen she said. The patients wore the uniform pajamas and there were so many of them. Some sat on the bed chuckling to the ceiling; some stared out the window through the bars with angry faces; some sat on the bed with blank faces; and some, restless like caged animals, shuffled up and down the ward from one end to the other. Myŏngsŏk was among them. Probably because he was so happy to see his sister, he kept breaking into broad smiles, which made her shudder as if it was a symptom of madness. He was very docile, saying 'yes' to everything she said. His eyes that had once looked wild when he was frustrated and angry were meek and gentle and reminded her of when he had been a sweet little boy. He asked after father and me saying that he so much wished to see me.

And I failed to go and see him during a whole month while he was there. Once I had gone so far as to the doorstep of the unit but lost the courage to go in with an empty hand.

On his dishonourable discharge from the army as a 'person unfit for the military service', in September, father had persuaded one of our closest relatives in Susim village to put him up until such time as father had his own house. Would such a time ever come? Myŏngsŏk still seems to be in endless trouble in that damned village. I honestly think they are picking on him. 'He's lazy; he's not polite to the elders; he does not help with the farming, and so on.'

My poor brother who had been beaten to near death; my brother who on his leave, with no place to go to or family to give him love and welcome, had wandered round the heartless streets of Seoul like a tramp. If my mother were alive would she sit back and just watch such fate befall her darling son?

I am going mad. I want to be mad so that I can fling out all my rancour in a savage manner and bite off the heads off all the wrongdoers!

13 November. I came home late on purpose. For once he was in before me. As I walked across the courtyard and entered my room I saw him giving me a questioning glance, demanding the explanation for my absence last night. Good. I ignored him and slammed the door after me. The landlady is around and the people in the other rooms are in. He would not dare come across here.

I will be cruel to him; I will make him suffer; and I will make him see that I can be unfaithful too if I so chose. Until he realizes how he has wronged me, comes to apologize, and answer and clear up all the suspicions that are choking me and driving me mad let him stew in his own juice. Who's the woman with a Cholla accent? Who's the woman in a chestnut coat? I want to kill him. I flopped down on the floor and had a good cry.

How is it possible that such sweet, precious, devoted love can come to this? What went wrong? What can restore a love that's gone sour?

15 November. He has gone. I pray for his safety. God, bless him.

I had resolved, on the way to work, to break the dreadful silence of the past three days tonight. It has been unbearable. It felt like being lost in miles upon miles of darkness.

Shortly before noon, he phoned. From the way he was panting I could guess he was on the run. In a whisper he said, 'Sukey, I am being chased. If I don't see you again...goodbye. Don't worry about me.' I am deeply touched that he took the trouble to phone me in such an emergency. If he was caught somewhere, I would be arrested too before nightfall.

I hurriedly tidied up my drawers and files, leaving instructions, where needed, so that someone else could carry on with my work with as little inconvenience as possible.

When I finished it, I collapsed over my desk. No tears came, just a dull headache and nausea. Miss Pak came rushing to me and other staff followed suit and came and stood round me. I saw Dr Kang's tall figure bending over them all with a worried look. He instructed Miss Pak to take me to the hospital and another to call a taxi, but I said I would like to go home first. He followed me as I was escorted down by Miss Pak, saw me to the taxi and paid the driver.

Ever since I got home, I have been awaiting, with the ticking of the clock as my only company, the fatal moment that will come at any time.

It is now past midnight. Is he still on the run? O, God, please deliver him to safety.

18 November. A restless three days have passed. If he is still free, I thought, he might have dropped me a line under a pseudonym. What did he mean when he said, 'If I don't see you again...?' Has he safely gone over the border and to the arms of his mother?

He who has been in need of a shelter where he could breathe without fear has gone and now that he's gone someone has come up offering him such a place. I had a reply from Fr. Osbourne. He says that he does not need a helper at the moment for his work but if my friend is the sort of man who would like to meditate, study and lead a quiet life, he can come and stay with his disciple, Mark Cho, who is preparing himself to enter a monastery.

22 November. A bolt out of the blue.

A woman introducing herself as the sister of Hisun came to see me. I can't believe it. Apparently he has eloped with Hisun. I can't bear it any longer. I will take my life.

23 November. 'Any news from Mr Kwŏn?' asked the land-lady.

'I meant to tell you, auntie,' I stammered. 'He is not likely to come back for some time. I will clear up his room this evening.'

In the morning I walked to the bus-stop with Sŏnhi. I felt I ought to say something. Since his disappearance, for a week now, she has never questioned me about his whereabouts but has been observing me with kind eyes.

'He's gone to look for a job. He was determined that he would never appear before me until he got a decent job.' As I said this in a natural and even proud tone, I had to turn my face to hide the tears rising to my eyes.

'That's good,' she said. 'He should have done that before, you know.'

Sŏnhi phoned and asked me to meet her at the tea-room Napoli after work. Now that I have decided to die nothing seems to matter. Human joys or sorrows don't mean anything. If I have a little bit of will-power left it is to alleviate the sorrow I have caused my sister, to make the last few hours with her a pleasant memory.

At Napoli, Sŏnhi and her fiance Chinmo Yu were waiting and greeted me warmly. When I saw them together I thought wistfully how nice it would be if I could live another year, see their wedding and after that call him, '*hyŏngbu*', brother-in-law. But it is not to be. After supper at a Western-style restaurant, we saw a film of *La Traviata*, but I took in little, as I sat dutifully through it.

24 November. Hisun's sister came again. She gives the impression of being a happily married housewife. What she has revealed to me is horrific. It is like a nightmare, and I wish I could wake up from it.

For some time before their elopement, he and Hisun had been madly in love. Apparently he made out that I was the incarnation of a jealous devil, planning and plotting all sorts of wicked schemes to break up their relationship. Besides me there are several other women including Kijŏng and Yŏnok, all competing for his love. I and my sister became enemies over the love of him. I can well imagine how these fictitious stories of rivalry could have made a simple country girl like Hisŭn determined not to lose him.

Hisun's sister also told me that they were planning to get married. So they had signed a contract to buy one of the housing association houses newly built in Pulgwang-dong area. As they needed the money straight away but his salary was not due for another week or so, she borrowed it on behalf of him from a friend of hers and gave it to him.

They had fixed the fifteenth of November for their engagement party. All the family and friends had gathered and waited for them to turn up for the one o'clock ceremony when she rang to call off the party, saying that they were setting off on a journey. Since then she hasn't been seen.

Hisun's sister has made enquiries with the housing association and found out that he had never made any contract with them. She has also discovered that he is not a teacher at S University. So, she said, she came to me to get some information about his identity, about his family and his background. She was using tactics of half-threat and half-coaxing. I wanted to shout to her face, 'Hisun is not a baby, she should know what she's doing. As far as I am concerned she snatched my lover away from me and I hate her. How dare you come and harass me?' But I had to refrain because I must not say anything about his true background. It seems obvious that the woman in chestnut coat that Sudol saw was Hisun.

All is over.

In the mood of a caretaker sorting out the costumes and equipment at the back of the stage after the performance, I wrote a dozen letters, and a few words in a notebook to many more people. For the last thing, when I came home, I wrote to my sister. As soon as I started writing tears fell down uncontrollably, dropping on the writing paper. There was too much to write in a letter but I can't tell this to her face. What is the point of writing? Is it worth doing?, I wondered.

24 November 1959

My dearest sister, Sŏnhi,

As the sounds of trams and motorcars grow faint and distant, the night is getting deeper. I am sitting here staring at a point in the darkness. Did you know that the love and generosity you lavished on me during the last few days was melting down my frozen heart, starved of human love?

I have a horrendous story to tell you but I don't know how to start. Apparently he has seduced a woman and eloped with her. You will say, 'What did I tell you?' Yes, you're right and you've been right all the way along. I am sorry, forgive me.

But you know what he was to me, and I still love him. There is some secret that I have not told you. If you had known it you'd have hated him less and understood me better, and our relationship would not have been altogether so painful. But I had to keep it from you because I loved you too much to involve you in this death trap. I could not tell this to anyone, and it was hard to keep the secret to myself.

I am going to see Fr. Osbourne in Anpyŏng, make a clean breast of it, go to confession and receive the holy sacrament. Then I will go.

I am sorry, sister, that I have to go in this way, but there is nothing else I can do. I am too scared to see his mistress' sister who came yesterday and told me about her seduction and demanded information about his background. She will come again and again. I can't face it.

It will be a painless death, I promise, so don't worry. I shall go as if I am falling asleep. But when I am gone, pray hard for me, I will owe you that. I betrayed your love and disgraced myself but you are the only one in the world to pray for my soul.

I am in a dreadful state of debt, about 300,000 Hwan. Monthly interest and instalments for the kae — my financial affairs are terribly complicated but I kept you out of it from the beginning and need not tell you the details. I have left letters and notes to the people concerned.

I still believe in him and love him. I believe that he had to do what he did because he was forced into it. With a human conscience he could not have betrayed me in this way.

If he comes to you, probably in the distant future, with tears of repentance in his eyes, seeking your forgiveness, please forgive him, and tell him that I loved him to the last.

How cold I am. I am shaking all over. There's a black hole, the size of a pingpong ball in the middle of my heart. It's getting bigger and bigger, a monstrosity. It is going to suck me into it. Oh, this horror.

Sŏnhi, don't cry, I'll be all right, soon, when I am calmed down.

Be happy with Chinmo for ever.

Sukey.

PART II

ஜ

Chapter 9

Confession

'Ladies and gentleman, we are now approaching Anp'yŏng. Passengers for Anp'yŏng are requested to check their belongings and prepare to alight.'

The clear voice of the bus conductress jerked me out of the reverie that seemed to suck me into eternity. From the start I had felt no sense of the nervousness such as might accompany a first trip to an unknown place. On the contrary I had felt as the bus started moving that it was a long journey at the end of which some one was awaiting my arrival.

I stepped off the bus into the darkness of an early winter evening. It looked like a market place. All around was dark except a couple of shops still open, lit by carbide lamps. Rain sprinkled down making the clayey ground underfoot extremely slippery.

I walked into one of the shops and asked if there was an inn nearby.

'An inn, did you say?' A woman in her thirties replied in a serious, incredulous tone of voice, as her eyes examined me from top to bottom. I knew the way that country people unashamedly stare at strangers. All my relations in our ancestral village Susim were like that. A young woman with loose, shoulder length hair, wearing high heels – I was obviously an oddity. I bought a couple of apples and a small exercise book just to ease the tension.

'There is just one place I know of but I am not sure whether they could take you in,' and she kindly led the way. After turning round a couple of mud and stone walls, she stood before a dimly lit room.

'Jaya's mother, there's a guest for you,' she called, and as she brought herself closer to the door spoke in a lowered voice, 'She looks like a miss.'

I was shown into a cold room. The hostess explained that even though they were inn-keepers, they rarely had guests in the winter months, so they left the rooms unheated. I did not have to wait long before the room became warm and a meal table was brought in.

'Are you from Seoul?' Her voice implied that I should explain myself.

'Yes,' I said and told her that I had some business at the Anglican Church there. 'Do you know that there is an English clergyman there?' I asked. At this her expression brightened at once, 'Of course, I do.'

'Are you a church member?'

'No,' she said. 'Our family are not believers but everyone knows him around here. We call him "Saint", you see.' Now she was quite cheerful and friendly.

After supper, guided by the hostess, I found the clergy house. Sitting in an upstairs room with a matted floor in Japanese style, he was in the middle of consultation with his church warden, Mr Lee, a kerosene stove between them. He received me calmly but I felt that he was pleased to see me. He introduced me to his warden saying that I was the daughter of Chun-gŏl Yun, the warden at Seoul Cathedral. Mr Lee warmly welcomed me and rose to call someone to give an order to get me some supper as if it was the most natural thing for me to expect.

'It is very kind of you but I have just had my supper.'

'Where?'

'At the inn. I arranged my stay there tonight and ate shortly before I came up.'

'You shouldn't have done such a thing. Why at an inn when you are more than welcome to stay at our place?'

'I didn't want to put anyone to trouble.'

I agreed with Fr. Osbourne that I would call on him tomorrow morning at ten o'clock and left him to his friend. As I left them I felt the sharp contrast of the cool politeness of a Seoulite and the simple hospitality of country people. I had been over smart, I thought.

When I went up to his room next morning, I found him again with people, but he dismissed them saying that we had some private matters to talk about. As soon as we were left alone he asked whether I had come with my boyfriend.

'No, Father. He has gone for good.' With this I broke down in tears and could not say another word. I silently wept and sobbed for a long time. It was as if the dam of a reservoir had burst and the water was flooding over. The tears that I had repressed for two years, biting my lips not to show a sad face lest it should rouse suspicion, had at last burst forth with such force that I abandoned myself to its tide.

Fr. Osbourne sat in silence without offering words of comfort or urging me to proceed. When at last all the tears were shed and I regained my calm, I began to speak.

'First of all, I have been longing to make confession, but because my sin is of such a serious nature I could not go to just any priest. Also I have been troubled to know what to confess. One moment it seems that there is no hope of salvation for me because I live in sin and every minute of my life is adding to the pile of it, but at other times, I think that as far as my conscience is clear I can't be a sinner.'

After all that crying, I felt better. My mind was clear and serene. I told him what had happened during the past two years without faltering once, and concluded with what I felt at that moment.

'I am left with an enormous bulk of debt and with a discovery that he has committed another dreadful sin by seducing an innocent woman and disappearing without trace. It is unbearable to think of my love being trampled and betrayed in this way but what troubles me most is the tormenting question of his true identity. Was he really a spy? Is he still active? Or is he simply a fraud?'

Fr. Osbourne listened to me throughout without a word, his large, deep eyes slowly closing and opening. I caught a sight of his upper lip slightly trembling.

'If it is true that he had been a spy in the past, or even now he has a slightest link with his past, I would never feel that my life is safe in this country, and if it is the case that he is simply a liar and has been exploiting my love all this time under that fictitious cause, I just cannot go on living, life is not worth the struggle.' Here I broke down again and wept quietly for some time.

The first thing he said when I stopped crying was, 'If I lent you that sum of money, would that be of any help to you? It does not involve any interest, so you can pay it back little by little with the money you give away as interest.' But I declined the offer. I did not want financial help from him. I told him that as I don't have to continue to pay the expenses for Kwŏn, I should be able to pay off the debt myself within a year.

'At the moment, my debt, or broken love, seems a matter of secondary importance. I am dying to be freed from sin for once. I have been so desperate to make a confession for a long time.'

At last I heard what I had hoped for. He said, 'I don't think you are a sinner. You have been unselfish. You have shown admirable courage, patience, forgiveness and self-sacrifice for the love of another human being.'

I let out a deep sigh of relief. He went on to say, 'The only thing is that sleeping with a man other than a lawful husband is, according to church law, regarded as sin. So you may like to make a confession on that.'

I covered my head with a veil and entered the confessional. I was uncontrollably shaking. I felt as guilty as if I was trampling a most sacred place with muddy boots.

I knelt down and began:

'Bless me Father for I have sinned......Since my last confession I have committed fornication...'

'...I have committed fornication....That's what I did. Because of that sin I had fallen into the valley of darkness and spent those many days like a criminal condemned to a life sentence, swallowing my sorrow every minute of every day...'

My mind departed from the formality of the confession, drifted in a separate region while my body, bowed on the floor of the confessional, shook with sobs, gasping for breath. I heard Fr. Osbourne, reading the service form through, and closing it with the final blessing: 'The Lord has pardoned your sins. Go forth in peace.'

I rose to my feet and walked out of the church. Outside, in the churchyard, the priest stood waiting for me. His face illuminated momentarily, as it caught the sun just slipping out of a cloud, broke into a gentle smile. It was like that of a benign father, or that of a wise lover, or the proud smile of a boy after a heroic deed, or indeed a combination of all three. He had an expression that made people feel comfortable and intimate with him. Certainly the fact that I had opened up my heart to him for the first time and cried freely before him made me feel close to him at that moment.

There was about forty minutes left before the bus was due. I followed him into his study where he made me a cup of coffee. He lit a cigarette for himself, Azalea brand, the cheapest kind in those days.

'Are you feeling better?' He asked.

'Yes, I think so,' I replied with a sad smile and went on to ask, 'Does the church regard suicide a sin?' That was another question I had to clear up.

'Why? Are you thinking about it?'

'I have no alternative. There seems little point in carrying on. I shall be only falling into sin again and again. Besides, I have completely lost my courage to live on. The only thing that worries me is the church's view that suicide is a sin'

'Well, as you say, it is only a view, and a view is not necessarily an absolute truth that you have to abide, is it? Indeed there are many other views about the same issue. In recent years, some progressive theologians have come up with the views that suicide is not sin.'

I was amazed. I wondered whether he was encouraging me to take my life if I wanted to.

'But,' he said, 'Don't you want to live and see how it will all end?' I understood what he meant. He was not stopping me from what I wanted to do in the name of church law but simply suggesting what was the most natural way for a human being to behave. Did I not want to see the final outcome of my two years' toil? Wait and see. If things turned out to be bad, unbearably bad, then I could take my life at any time. So there was my solution.

On the bus going back to Seoul, and in the painful reality waiting there, I found myself often thinking about Fr. Osbourne. It gave me comfort to think that I had discovered him. It was like meeting with a saviour on the brink of an abyss. In him I saw the materialization of the living Jesus. An Englishman who instead of living in the comfort of his own country, had chosen a poor country and the poorest village of that country, living among ignorant people, smoking the cheapest brand of cigarettes. Happily going about amongst lepers with his benign expression and smile, he spread a message of hope.

He might not share my feelings over my broken love or sentimentalize in the bright moonlight, but I was sure that he would be my shepherd in my search for meaning and in my endeavour to lead a true and worthy life.

Chapter 10

Crime and Punishment

In spite of a bitter aftermath of an uncertain love affair and an uneasy speculation that anything might happen at any time and anywhere, I had settled into a fairly comfortable life. I who had been preoccupied with thoughts of death a month ago was now being pampered and made a fuss of by my sister.

When I came back to Seoul after the interview with Fr. Osbourne, I took back from the caretaker the letter I had written for Dr Kang and destroyed it with the other letters.

For the past two years I had hardly eaten a decent meal and had not realized how famished I had been. Now I was ravenous. I ate and ate and was still hungry. Three full meals a day were not enough, so I ate five meals and even six sometimes. I ate five or six juicy pears at once, one after another.

December was halfway through. The Christmas boom had started in the high street. One day Hisun turned up at the office, a month after her elopement. She had the appearance and air of a high society woman. She was wearing a full-length, traditional skirt under a silk overcoat. Her hair was piled up high, her face was heavily made-up and around her neck was a mink muffler. Under her arm was an alligator handbag.

I did not know how to treat her. She introduced me to a man much older than herself as a younger relative. As if he was her bodyguard he followed us at a regular distance.

I sat opposite her across a table in a tea-room. It was our first meeting apart from the brief introduction by Kwŏn during my working hours last August. As soon as we sat down, she called me *ŏnni*, and showed such a flirtatious affection for me that I was quite embarrassed.

'I deserve your anger, *ŏnni*, because I have stolen your lover but he was as much to blame. He arrested my heart at first sight and made me restless day and night until at last I had him. Now I am as good as his wife.' She cast me a coquettish glance. I realized now that she was not such an innocent girl straight from the country as I had thought at first.

'As you know, I have loved him but now he has chosen you as his wife, I have nothing more to say. I'll just bow out.' I made my position quite clear to her and truly wished that they would both clear out of my life for good.

'From what he told me about you, I thought you were a wicked woman but you're so good, *ŏnni*.' I swallowed hard to repress the anger rising up in me. The man supposed to be her younger relative sat at the other end of the room and now and again cast a watchful glance towards us.

'I see you have a ruby ring too. Was it a present from him?'

'No, I got it from an antique shop myself.' Only then did I see she was wearing a ring similar to mine, only the stone was twice as big.

'Apparently his mother had kept this for the woman who was to be the wife of her only son.' She started telling me in great detail the history of their love as if by showing how much more he loved her, she would establish her superiority.

'On the first day I started work under him, a button fell off his cuff. As I always carry a needle and cotton in my bag, I got them out and sewed it on for him. He was full of admiration saying that he had known so many women but I was the first who carried such things around.' She looked up at my face with another of her coquettish smiles and went on, 'Then I fell ill with a cold for a few days. Do you know, he stayed by my side and never left me for a minute from morning till night?' I gave an involuntary shudder at the thought of Kwŏn's manipulation of her.

'I came to Seoul from the country,' she went on, 'to get a job and now I stay at my married sister's. She has become very fond of him and treats him very well.

'You see, my parents are poor and until I came here I had never known any luxury. He treats me like a queen. He takes me everywhere in taxi.' I still could not make out what sort of woman she was. She went on and on about her love.

'We had arranged a day to be engaged. But I knew you were plotting a terrific row.'

'Me?' I raised my eyebrows but she was too carried away by her own eloquence to notice my expression.

'So at the last minute we decided to call off the party and get away from Seoul to avoid all the complications. I just slipped out of the house in the clothes I had on.

'We have been going about everywhere in taxi for nearly a month. We went to the seaside and then to the mountains.' Her last words reminded me of 'a day of the mountain and a day at the seaside,' that had inflamed my heart with love. At the same time I was surprised at the speed with which my love for Kwŏn was cooling. Now that I had been basically disillusioned by him, I could hand him over to her without the slightest regret. In fact I so wanted to wash my hands off the miserable past, to put the memories behind and make a new start.

'We went round all the famous places and stayed at first-class hotels. Then we decided to come up and see my parents and sister, before setting up a home in Pusan. We were coming on the train a few days ago when he got off at Taejŏn. He had some business there, he said, and he'd follow me by the next train, but he hasn't turned up yet.

'There is something I am not sure about him. Apparently my sister has found out that he is not a lecturer at S University.'

Then she added, 'But I don't care, nor do I envy a lecturer, as long as he's clever, good-looking and has plenty of money.'

'He has no money, not a penny to his name.' As I thought this, it crossed my mind that she was being badly cheated and that things were not going to be as simple as I had thought a minute ago.

As if at some remembered joke, Hisun broke into a titter.

'Sŏnhi Yun's your sister, isn't she?' I started. How had my sister's name come into this?

'You've become enemies over him, haven't you? Did you know she once went into his room in her night dress? – begging him to hold her just once. He slapped her in the cheek saying "Dirty bitch!" and turned her out.'

My body was violently shaking.

'Hisun! Leave my sister out of this dirty game. She has a respectable and devoted fiance. I don't care what glamorous goings-on there are between you and him but don't bring my sister into it. Since we were kids, she's been like a mother to me. She did not like him from the beginning and she has never had anything to do with him. Just tell him, as my last plea, please do not dishonour my sister's name. I had better go now.'

It was dark outside. I walked the night streets aimlessly to allay the unpleasant and complex feelings raging in me, the clicking of my high heels beating the time to my chanting of 'bastard', 'bastard', 'bastard'.

When Hisun appeared again the next day, it was with a completely different look. She was like a rustic girl just out of high school. Wearing a plain spring coat and low shoes, with no make-up on her face, she looked pale and troubled.

'Have you heard from Mr Kwŏn?'

'What do you mean? Do you think he would have the cheek to come back to me?'

'No. It's just that I have some suspicions.' Not only had her looks changed but her manner as well. Her affectionate 'ŏnni' of yesterday had become a formal 'Miss Yun', and the fond pronoun of 'He' was 'Mr Kwŏn'

As we walked along the pavement she told me that when her sister's husband found out that the eight hundred thousand Hwan she had borrowed had ended up in the hands of a fraud, he had beaten her up and he's going to turn her out. She pleaded with me to help her find him. Had I known any member of his family or friends through whom she might find his whereabouts?

'It may sound odd but I don't know a thing about his identity or his family background. I never was interested in such things. I just loved him for what he was, and when he was looking for a quiet lodging house I introduced him to my landlady, that's all.' It must have sounded false and I was deeply sorry that I could not tell her the truth there and then.

I had noticed her retching a couple times, and my suspicion was soon confirmed as she plainly told me that she was two months pregnant. I decided to be good to her and help her as much as I could. As we turned a corner there was a sudden commotion. From a dark side-alley a man leapt out and slightly brushed passed her as he ran down the road. He was followed by a several others shouting, 'Catch the thief!'

She gave out a feeble moan as she fell to the ground. I realized how frail she must be to pass out just like that. I stopped a passing taxi and took her to a nearby clinic. Her face was white as paper as she lay on the bed, rather in harmony with the whitewashed walls of the room. It made me shudder.

She recognized me as she came round and her eyes brimmed with tears. I held her hands in mine and pressed them hard. When I delivered her at her doorstep in taxi and got on the homebound bus, the preliminary siren for the curfew rang out.

'Bastard!' 'Bastard!' I had developed, unaware to myself, a habit of constantly chewing this word like gum.

When she reappeared a few days later, she reminded me of a fully ripe chillie pepper, savagely hot and biting. She had no politeness, no self-respect and of her coquetry, there was now no trace.

'I have been deceived, I have been cheated,' she hissed. 'You say you loved him so much, and yet when he was snatched away from you, you could be so calm. At first, I respected you for that but come to think of it, frankly I am suspicious of you.' She gnashed her teeth as she went on, 'I want to catch him, cut him up and chew his liver. Of course I will go to the police and get them to search for him as a criminal. He'll be caught as long as he's alive. I will tear him to pieces as soon as I catch sight of him.

'I went for the first time in my life to the so-called red-light district, to earn money because in some way or other I have to pay back the eight hundred thousand Hwan that my sister borrowed.' She broke into hysterics. I was wracking my brain to find something that could be of some comfort but to my sorrow my effort to comfort failed. I talked about God's mysterious ways and his love, and Fr. Osbourne and what sort of life he was leading. I also told her how people can become strong and wise through the adversity and trials, and how two women hurt by one man could help each other. Once or twice I thought she was paying attention to what I was saying but I knew it was only a breeze skimming over a rock.

The next day her sister came. She asked me for a photo of Kwŏn for they had decided to hunt him out through the police. I nearly walked over to my desk to get the photo out of my drawer when a voice inside me said, 'How can you hand him over to them?'

I told her that I did not have any picture of him with me but would look for one at home if she didn't mind coming back tomorrow. Without much fuss she went away. If they pressed me, I thought, I would give them a small snapshot of him. She did not come back, and soon after that I learned that Hisun had set up a cosmetic shop in the Midopa Department Store.

It was the first day of Sŏnhi's winter vacation. After work, I was to meet her and her fiance, Chinmo at the tea-room Napoli which had become their haunt.

Five minutes before the closing time the telephone rang.

'Korean Academy. Can I help you?'

'It's me,' the voice said. He had come back! How hateful, I thought. Probably to wait and see my reaction, he was silent.

'What do you want?' Still silence.

'You have no business to ring me.' I was going to put the phone down when I heard him say in a weak voice, 'I knew you would be like this,' and that voice stirred up pity in me. However hateful he was I ought to see him even if I had to kill him when I saw him.

'Where are you?'

'Honam Hotel in front of the Railway Station, Room 7.'

'I will be there shortly.'

I should have put the phone down the moment I knew it was him. Had I done that the course of my life would have taken a different turn but the moment I failed to replace the telephone Fate snatched up the chance to do yet more mischief.

The moment I saw him all my hatred melted away and I became once again a slave of love.

'Are you alright? I missed you so much. Have you seen Hisun? You must've hated me.

'I had to make use of her, that was all. I was followed by those chaps, all the time, with their gun pointed at the back of me.

'Ah, now it is really and truly all over. From now on I will live just as you want me to. Tell me what must I do.'

I told him in detail how Hisun and her sister had come to see me, and that they were going to search for him through the police but that I did not think they had yet started.

'What about if they did it today?'

I could not answer that. He seemed to have lost all his confidence and was looking up to me as his sole protector. I remembered Fr. Osbourne who might be able to consider him as an aspirant for a religious order.

I was so conscious of my sister and Chinmo waiting that I could not delay another moment. I instructed him to meet me at the Railway Station at six o'clock the next morning and left him.

When I had left home that morning my shoulders were light as feathers but now they were as if pressed down by big weights. I caught a taxi to Napoli. Even so I was nearly an hour late. I saw their coffee cups empty.

'What time do you call this?' Sŏnhi said. It was not even in an accusing tone but tears came to my eyes. I had become hysterical within the past hour or so.

'Don't be silly,' Chinmo said to Sŏnhi. 'Don't you see she's been running out of breath?' Then he turned to me and said, 'What would you like? Coffee? Or a piping hot bowl of *jenzai*?'

I quickly changed the mood and cheerfully said, '*Jenzai* please,' and added in whisper, imitating the tone of a spoilt child, 'in a specially big bowl with a extra lot of pine nuts in it.'

Sŏnhi tittered and said also in whisper, 'Freely sprinkled with freshly ground cinnamon.' All three burst into laughter.

While Kwŏn was away, I had often joined my sister and Chinmo and when the three of us were together we were very happy. When I argued with Sŏnhi over trivial things Chinmo usually took my side. I already felt close to him as if he were an elder brother.

An English teacher at a boy's high school, he had graduated from Y University, a few years before me. Come to think of it, was me who had brought them together. I had been a member of the drama group, and in my final year we presented Rupert Brooke's play *Lithuania*, translated by Professor Oh of the university. I played the role of the younger sister. Chinmo who had been a member of the group in his time, and a close disciple of Professor Oh, was one of the producers.

After the last performance, I was busy removing my make-up at back of the stage when Chinmo announced a visitor. It was Sŏnhi. It so happened that they worked in the same district of Seoul and often passed each other on their way to and from work. That's how their courtship started.

He was the only son of a rich farmer in the country. While not distinguishing himself in any particular area, he seemed to be able to do a bit of everything. Apart from his main subject, English studies, he enjoyed music, sports, and was good at general knowledge. He got on well with people from all walks of life. He was reputed to drink like a whale when in the company of his male friends, and in fights he could beat his opponents quite smartly too.

Sŏnhi, little understanding the desperation of a drowning man holding onto the straw, saw no need to give up her sweet morning sleep to go to plead with God at the early Mass. She rather admired me for getting up early to go to church. She little doubted that I had other things to do in these hours than attend mass.

This morning too, in the pretence of going to church, I was able to slip out of the house early to meet Kwŏn. Like the frozen sky and earth before dawn, our future seemed bleak. As the time passed the darkness would be dispersed by light, and the frozen winter earth would thaw, at least a little, but in our position we could not speculate any brighter future even on the basis of nature's rules. We had no choice but to plod along as far as we could go.

The sun had been up long since but the earth showed no sign of thaw, and the inside of the dingy bus was cold and desolate.

Leaving him at the inn that I had stayed before, I went straight to Fr. Osbourne.

'Father, he has come back.'

But his attitude was quite different from what I had expected.

'Tell him to go and surrender himself,' he said. I realized that my plan had been in vain. Nevertheless, I halfheartedly told him about Hisun's visit and what had happened since I last saw the priest. I appreciated that the circumstance of my visit was different from the last time. My heart had then been pure, but now I was trying to take advantage of a priest. How dare I? I was so ashamed that I could not put out the large packet of dried persimmons that I had brought for him as a present. I did not tell him that the man was waiting in the room at the inn. As I was about to say 'Goodbye', he said, 'Have you read Dostoyevski's *Crime and Punishment*?'

'Yes.' I knew what he wanted to say. The only way we could live an honest life was through his surrender, but I was equally sure that he would never do that. In that case, there seemed little point in his going back to Seoul where his arrest might be a matter of hour rather than days. At the inn we discussed, in whispers, what to do next. He said that while he had some money on him he would keep away from Seoul and look for a quiet temple where he could stay as a convalescing guest and wait until such time that Hisun's wrath had subsided. We went to the main line station where we parted, he on a southbound train while I got on a northbound train to Seoul.

As the days went by, Hisun's suspicion of me deepened. She turned up frequently at the office. Obviously I was being watched. She was trying to find some clue as to his whereabouts from me. She seemed to have given up the idea of going to the police but never the threat of doing so. She said that by pulling some strings she could have him arrested as her brother-in-law had close friends in the Criminal Investigations Team at police headquarters, but she would rather wait for him to turn up of his own free will. She even said, as if for my benefit, that if he came forward voluntarily she might forgive him. Then one day she said that he had been reported as staying in a temple as a lecturer. It was a very likely story and it made my heart beat fast. One painful day after another the time passed.

I often reflected on the term 'unconditional love'. I had first heard of it from my father as we set off as evacuees in the winter of 1951. It had sounded then a most noble and admirable thing – to love someone without any condition. But now I knew such thing could exist only as an ideal. Human love had to be reciprocal. A healthy love was one in which giving and receiving were mutual and balanced. If I loved a man I demanded to be loved back in whatever form it might take.

But what had happened to my love? I had given all my heart and soul, and all my earnings, in return of which I had been thoroughly deceived and betrayed. I felt sick at heart.

One's attitudes towards social life as a member of a community can be analysed, emphasized or criticized from many different angles. At times one can be under contrary obligations with conflicting demands. One may sometimes have to sacrifice matters of lesser importance for the sake of a greater cause. However it cannot be justified to sacrifice human values for other causes, whatever the circumstances.

The flag of victory being brandished on the ground on which the pure passion of a woman has been trampled cannot be a symbol of victory but a symbol of disgrace and cowardice that deserves scorn and condemnation.

Can acts of patriotism that disregard human decency and do not flinch from using foul means be justified?

In my country which I dearly loved, 'Anti-communism' was the national policy. When one day I had decided to love a man who had worked for its enemies, was it not because I found in that love a value that surpassed all other values and conditions? − 'A man who chose the land of death for his love.' Is there a nobler and higher human aspiration?

Had I been too simple in trusting a man who had in the first place set out to be a spy?

When he came back to me after a dreadful betrayal that had torn off a piece of my heart, I could not cast him away because of the one 'truth' which I thought we both shared − that he remained here for the love of me. As long as I had no clear proof that it had been a lie, I would never throw him away. It was most unfortunate that he had come so unexpectedly into contact again with his former colleagues, who had followed him from behind with a gun pointed at his back. He had no choice but to obey them or die the death of a dog. Wasn't it great that he had survived and come back to me?

In this way, he once again became my idol. When I first learned of his elopement with Hisun, a hole had been punched in my heart as if by a bullet. It had grown bigger and bigger until my whole heart became a desolate cavern. Had it been left to nature, it might have been gradually filled up again as time went by, with various other human concerns, but in this cavern I had now built an altar on which I placed him.

When an object of love existed remote from reality it becomes an idol. My mind seemed to be thoroughly confused about my idol and god. When I called god, it was the visage of him that floated before my eyes. As I thought of him I called the name of God. Most of the day I lived in this state.

Severe cold weather persisted without break throughout Christmas and the beginning of the New Year. Where was he now? Sitting in a drab room of a shabby inn, lamenting his sad fate? I roamed the cold streets of Seoul like woman possessed as if in search of his image. I could not pass by a beggar of about his age without looking at him closely. He could be just like that I thought.

On the tenth day of the New Year, a letter came. The message was simple. He was now settled down at J Temple in Kyŏngsang North Province and hoped that I would come to see him at once. I was tremulous at the sight of his handwriting. How could I delay a minute?

I left work early as I instructed Suyŏn to report that I was unwell should I fail to turn up tomorrow morning. I also left Sŏnhi a note saying that I was going to Anp'yŏng to see Fr. Osbourne and would be back tomorrow, and set off.

On the south-bound train, as the short winter sun set and dusk fell I began to feel nervous and helpless. The train was slow and stopped at every station. When at last I alighted at a small country station sign-posted J Temple, it was already eight o'clock. As it was a well-known monastery I had expected to see a sign pointing to the entrance to its compound. I walked up to a small inn across the yard from the station and asked the way. The host looked at me pityingly. 'You couldn't go there now, Miss. It's over ten *li*. And you say it's your first visit.' I felt despair. I was not in the position to stay overnight at an inn here. Even if it was twenty or thirty *li,* I had to get there. If I failed to catch the early morning train back to Seoul tomorrow, I dreaded to think what Hisun might do. Her vigil had been tightened of late. I asked several passers-by the way to the temple and each one gave me different instructions. I started walking along the first road I came to, bearing in mind its general direction. It was a clear night with a full moon that cast a ilvery sheen over the mountains and fields. How quiet it was all around. Eight o'clock in Seoul was still early evening but here, in the country, it was like midnight. Once I had left the main road I came to meandering small roads and I was at loss to know which one to take. I walked round a deserted skirt of hills, uphill and downhill, criss-cross paths between paddies, and suddenly found myself going through a village with scattered cottages. Dogs barked at an untimely passer-by as if ready to rush out of the gates and tear me to pieces. Afraid of dogs at any time, I flinched as I uttered under my breath, 'arrg', 'arrg!', 'help!', 'help!', and got out of there as fast as my legs would carry me.

Then suddenly I found myself alone in a vast expanse of darkness. The death-like silence all round overwhelmed me. The ridge-lines of low hills and mountains were like shadows of monsters. I fancied I was hearing the distant calls of wild animals. A wolf or a boar might leap out from somewhere. I took off my high-heeled shoes and started to run.

'Lord, have mercy. Christ take pity on me.' Thus I chanted between my breath. Small parcels that I had brought with me were now weighing tons. I was drenched in sweat.

How long had I run in this way? I felt a sudden chill as a gust of wind swept past. It cooled my feverish brain. I stopped running and looked around. I heard a bubbling sound of running water. Ahead of me I saw a large hill covered thickly in woods. It had an air of solemnity quite different from the bare hills I had passed. It must be the mountain connected with the temple. At last I was where I wanted to be. I walked further towards it, with a bubbling brook at the side of the path until I saw before me lanterns hung on the posts at the entrance to the temple.

'Thanks be to God,' I uttered to myself.

The moment I entered his room I collapsed. It was half-past nine.

He was staying in a room next to the chief abbot's, divided by a sliding paper door. It was obvious that he was being treated as a special guest. The abbot came across to welcome the late visitor. Mr Kwŏn introduced me as his younger sister, and told him that his father, who had some business dealings in the village not far from there had come in his car and I had come with him. From there, he said, I had decided that I could not go back home without seeing my brother. That's how I had turned up so late. Thrown into this unexpected situation I had to adjust my behaviour accordingly, acting the role of a girl who was a student and quite fearless.

'That's the trouble with you,' he said to me, in an admonishing tone. 'You are never afraid of anything, are you? This is not the sort of place a girl should walk about in the middle of the night.'

'That is true, Miss, your brother is right,' chimed in the elderly abbot. 'It is deadly dangerous. You may not realize it, but wild animals come down from the hills at night, of course they do.'

At the break of dawn Kwŏn was walking with me, ostensibly showing me round. Had I been a leisurely tourist, or a real sister who had come to visit her convalescing brother, it might have been beautiful, but as it was I saw nothing. It was not to see the temple that I had got up so early but to plan our future out of earshot. We had too many things to sort out before I caught the train to Seoul at eleven. All around the temple stood rows of hills shrouded in silence like guardians who had cradled and protected it since time immemorial. Their slopes were green and peaceful. But he told me that these peaks and valleys had witnessed the most ferocious battles. During the war the fiercest assaults and counter-attacks had taken place in there, and when it was over they had become a hiding place and escape route for the partisans so that even now police vigilance in this area was extremely high.

In fact, he said, he felt he could not stay there much longer. He was looking out for a chance to ask the abbot to provide him with a letter of recommendation with which he could move onto a temple in Kangwŏn Province which was linked to this one.

'I really wish to bring an end to my life in hiding,' he said. 'If you don't mind, Sukey, I may become a monk after staying there as a guest for a while.'

'That seems a good idea. I want to become a nun myself.' It seemed to be the best way of bringing an end to our troubled and sinful life.

'The thing is though,' he said. 'Hisun would not quietly give up.'

'Before you become a monk, you must clear it up with her. You must seek her forgiveness, on your knees if necessary. After all, what can she possibly do to a man who has decided to become a monk, a man whom she loved so passionately even though only for a short while?' Then I added, 'Apparently her brother-in-law is rather bossy with his wife. Because of her involvement in the borrowing of the money and all that, he's giving her a rough time.'

'If I wore a monk's habit when I see Hisun, it would be more effective, wouldn't it, 'he said. 'I will ask the abbot to arrange with someone to make one for me.' After a pause he said, 'Would you like to compose a letter from me?'

I drafted a letter written in deep regret and remorse, and he copied it out in his own handwriting.

11 January 1960

Dear Hisun,

It is the break of dawn. A monk's day starts with the recital of the scriptures before the sunrise. A thousand, ten thousand apologies in prostration will not atone the sins I have committed against you, I know, but if I spent the rest of my life offering prayers to the merciful Buddha for the expiation of my sins, I dare hope, I might be reborn a less evil being in my next reincarnation. I have been converted to the faith of Buddhism.

I have been a victim of circumstance far too complicated to explain to you. I have lived the life of an arch devil, which I now look back on with tumultuous shame. You have been the last victim of my evil reign and at the same time the angel that prompted me to break away from it.

I have no ability or qualification to take you as my wife and make you happy. After parting from you I decided to enter a Buddhist monastery, so I came to J Temple. Since then I have been under the special care and instructions of the chief abbot, and am now ready to transfer to another temple in Kangwŏn Province.

Once I am there, I do not know when I shall see the secular world again. I am shameless to write this, but before entering the temple, I so much hope to see your face just once more and beg for your forgiveness in person.

On the fifteenth of this month, I shall be on my way to K Temple via Suwŏn. Please grant me one last chance of seeing you at Suwon Bus Station at two o'clock.

A sinner, I am begging on my knees for your mercy.

Tong-hi Kwŏn.

Before I left J Temple we agreed that our future depended on the outcome of his meeting with Hisŭn. I got off the train at Pyŏng-taik, posted the letter myself and went back the rest of the way by bus.

It was not entirely unexpected but when I got home I found out that Hisun had just left after making a terrible scene. As I entered the yard all the doors opened and the faces of the lodgers looked out as if in anticipation of a great spectacle. Sŏnhi, whose face was puffy and contorted snatched my hair by the roots and dragged me across the courtyard into the room.

'You, slut! Why do you go about constantly lying? Where did you say that bastard went to? To get a job and earn money? – Not that I ever believed it. I couldn't believe a liar like that had such sincerity in him.

'A girl called Hisun has been here. In front of everyone she made a big speech about what she had been up to with that bastard – does she think it's something to brag about? If you lie on your back and spit where does the spittle fall? She was just as crazy as you are.

'What did I do? In my night dress? I will kill you, bitch!' Unable to control her anger she attacked me with her fists.

'You've been to see him, haven't you!? Come on, out with it. Where do you keep him hidden? I will report it to the police. I won't let it pass this time...'

From exhaustion and tension, my mouth felt as if it was filled with sand. I had hardly been able to eat any breakfast and had nothing since. Now my hunger made me feel faint. But there was a clear streak of light flashing within me that helped me to cope with a reality as ugly as the aftermath of an earthquake. It was the strength of my will, and the power of my faith in the truth that I alone shared with him. With this light I saw that my most urgent task was to calm down these two women. I could appreciate that what had so agitated Hisun was her suspicion that I was secretly meeting him. I must go and see her.

After a while I rose to my feet and walked out of the room. 'Where are you going?' said Sŏnhi as she came after me.

'You will soon find out.' She seemed to think I was going to Kwŏn's. We changed bus twice but did not exchange a word until we stood in front of the gate of Hisun's sister's house. As she opened the gate and stepped out Hisun was unexpectedly subdued, perhaps because her brother-in-law was in, and she was afraid that we might start a row. She was leading us into a tea-room but I declined to go in.

'Regardless of our relationships with Kwŏn, I have been trying to treat you decently from the beginning. Didn't I make it quite clear to you that my sister had nothing whatsoever to do with him? I pleaded with you to leave her alone and not dishonour her. You did not take any notice of what I said,' I spoke calmly. 'Whether or not you chase him through the police is entirely up to you. There was no need for you to go and disgrace my sister.'

Only then did she open her mouth to speak but whether because she was regretting her rash action or she was tired after the explosion, it was in a quiet voice.

'Now I trust your sister's innocence. When I first told her who I was and my relationship with Kwŏn, and she responded as if she was ignorant of what has been going on, I thought she must be lying and was a bad person.

'I phoned you at office for no particular reason and was told that you were not in. That's why I went to your house. When I found that you weren't in I did suspect you. I found your sister's attitude rather vague and evasive. If you were in my position wouldn't you have done the same as I did? I thought all the people in that house were plotting against me and cheating me. I know I am mad...' She stopped and fell into a long silence. I sensed she was fighting back her tears.

'If your sister had told me straight away that you had gone to Anp'yŏng to see the priest you were often talking about I would have understood. But she kept it to the last as if in payment for the show.'

Sŏnhi kept silent through this conversation. Under the light of the street lamp I could see the fierce anger on her face was slowly subsiding. Hisun, as if exhausted, flopped down on the pavement, buried her face in her raised knees and wept. Here was a woman who enchanted by love had given away every-thing she had. When she came round as if from a swoon, she found that it had been a stage show. The passion had gone and she was alone in an empty theatre. Enraptured by her own acting she had incurred a debt of eight hundred thousand Hwan and was with a fatherless child in her womb for it was not likely that she would ever be his lawful wife.

I gathered her convulsing shoulders in my arms, and whis-pered, 'Calm yourself, Hisun. I understand you. We are both the victims of one man. I haven't told you this but I am shat-tered too. I am just keeping quiet about it, that's all... We must be brave, and try to forget about it, that's the only way we can survive. We can be friends, and we can help and support each other, can't we? If there's anything I can do for you I will.'

'Thank you, *ŏnni*.' She said this very clearly. I thought that a sort of human bond had been established between us. By seeing her frequently and talking to her I might be able to influence her mind and lead her to forgive him in the name of mercy.

On the afternoon of the fourteenth she came to see me. 'Have you heard from him?' She said as she quickly read my expression.

'No.'

At this she was silent. I guessed she had received his letter. I had foolishly expected her to come, show me his letter and ask for my advice as to what she should do.

My fate would be sealed at two o'clock tomorrow. Uneasy and anxious, I could not stay put in the office. I went to the director to ask for sick leave. I told him I was not feeling well and might be off again tomorrow. As he gave his consent I noticed his look of concern. When I walked out the office with Miss Pak in the evening, she said, 'Dr Kang is concerned about you. He said, "Have you noticed Miss Yun's troubled looks recently?" and went on to say that as an unmarried man he did not like to interfere with your private life, but if there is anything he can do to help you in any way just let him know.' These words instantly brought tears to my eyes.

On the morrow, I thought, it was crucial that I see Hisun before she set off to Suwŏn. As if in passing, I ought at least to mention the subject of forgiving him. It ought to be before noon.

Early in the morning, I went to her house. She had already gone out. I went to the department store where she had a shop. She was not there either. Where would I find her? I went again to her house and then to the shop. I went to and fro several times between the two places until I realized it was now too late. It was one o'clock, and she ought to be well on the way to Suwŏn. Suddenly the realization came that I was faced with a fatal moment. It overwhelmed me. There was nothing else for me to do but go home. But how would I fill in the time once I was there? I walked into a third rate cinema that I happened to be passing. I had not bothered to look at the title of the film but judged from the size of the audience at this time of the day that it must be a very popular one.

It was a Korean film. There I once again experienced what can only be called a 'fatal moment'.

I stood at the back amongst the standing audience with no idea of what the film was about but at the instant the crowd parted and I cast my eyes on the screen, I saw there the fatal message materialized. Yech'un Lee, one of the leading actors of the time, wearing a hat pressed low and with a gloomy expression stood there, in a close-up, gradually filling the whole screen until handcuffs were put on his wrists with a click.

I walked out of the cinema. All was over. Ironically, it was I who had handed him over to the police. I went into my room, locked the double doors, got into bed and pulled the cover over my head. Everything would take care of itself.

It had been grim weather all day. I watched every second of the process of the light grey that had enwrapped me in the room getting darker and darker until I could not distinguish the outlines of the objects in the room. I was a being awaiting the inevitable.

What time was it? I heard a rough shaking of the latched gates, someone opening it from inside, followed by the sounds of strangers' shoes treading on the gravel and some male voices. It sounded as if there were two or three men. Then I heard one of them say, 'Which room is it?'

The landlady opened the room where he had been and one of them went in. Apart from the books from the Academy, which I had taken back, it was as he had left it.

'Is the woman called Sukey Yun home?'

The moment I heard this, I groped for the poison that I had ready by my head and swallowed it with water.

It had not been easy to get hold of the quinine. I had gone to five or six chemists to ask for it, saying I had symptoms of malaria. They had all alike looked alarmed and suspicious. One had refused, saying he did not have it in stock. Others had grudgingly handed me some powder, or tablets or capsules.

'I don't think she's home yet,' said the landlady as she had not seen me come in. Then she called across the courtyard, 'Niece, are you in?'

I sprang out of bed and ran up to the attic door. It was only an animal instinct reacting to impending danger. A wry smile rose to my face as I thought, 'Silly woman, do you think it is safer up there than here.'

At that moment I heard my sister coming home. Regardless of what met her eyes in the courtyard, her voice was clear and cheerful as she opened the door.

'Sukey, are you home?'

Pretending I was just awakened from a deep sleep I said, 'Umn —' as I stretched out my arms lazily.

'You've been sleeping. What's the matter with you?'

'I have a bit of headache.'

The men approached to our door. One of them said, 'Excuse me, are you Miss Sukey Yun?'

'Yes?' I answered innocently with one hand over my mouth pretending to repress a yawn.

'We have come in connection with the Tong-hi Kwŏn affair. Could you come with us to J police station?' They were very polite.

'Yes, all right.' I got up, gave my hair a quick brush, put on my coat and stepped out. My sister followed. 'May I come with her? She does not look very well and I am worried.'

'Yes, of course.' They all gave the impression of being kind and cheerful chaps. I felt much more at ease as we got into the jeep. I sensed that I was not being taken as a suspect. But what if they found out that I had taken poison? I had to pinch myself to look alert and smart.

'How long have you known him?' One of them asked.

'A couple of years.'

Unable to suppress her curiosity Sŏnhi put in, 'How was he arrested? Did he surrender himself?'

'He didn't exactly mean to surrender but the result was the same so to speak. He was arrested in Suwŏn.' This led them to say what they thought.

'He's the greatest of all con men.'

'He looked quite becoming in his solemn monk's habit, ha ha ha.'

'At first, I was convinced that he was a spy.'

From these remarks I could guess the situation. At least he was not being treated as a spy and I was being taken as a witness. Could such phrase as 'Fortunate in a misfortune' be an appropriate description of the case?

In the large waiting room of J police station, he was sitting on an upright chair with his eyes closed. He was wearing a hat and a monk's robe, a long, light-grey coat of cotton, and with his leather briefcase on his lap. At first glance he looked so serene and calm as if in meditation. You would not think that he was a man who had been through a severe interrogation.

'Mr Kwŏn!' I ran up to him and grabbed his hand only to realize that he was in handcuffs. It made me flinch. When he saw me two streaks of tears ran down his cheeks. I had never before seen him in tears.

'Sukey, come here at once!' Sŏnhi's stern voice made me step back. When I saw around me the interested eyes of the men who brought me, I regretted making myself a spectacle. I watched with aching heart as he raised his handcuffed hands to clumsily brush away the tears.

'Now, ladies,' said one of the detectives. 'This man's real name is Chŏlsu Kim. He's a rare example of a super sex-offender who has been all round the country luring all sorts of women – tea-room madams, college students, maidens and housewives. He had already been convicted of infamous offences, was imprisoned at X Prison in Chŏlla Province, and was released two years ago.'

He went on further to explain. 'Because his present address is in the S District, we are handing him over to the station there along with all the results of our investigations undertaken here, and the relevant papers. Soon, some one from S will come along to take him back there. It is very likely that you both will be asked to go with them and answer a few questions as witnesses.'

When they had finished explaining the situation, they disappeared behind a door into another room and there were now only the three of us in the large waiting room. Sŏnhi trying to be calm, said in a gentle voice, 'As it is Sukey's wish to forgive you, I shall forgive you too. I wish you well for the future.'

He bowed low as he said, 'Thank you –' and broke down and continued to sob, as if uncontrollably, tears streaming down his cheeks.

'What kind of tears are they?' I began to wonder. 'I've never seen him cry like this. Can they be tears of repentance? Is he sorry for the false life he has led under the mask, whether it had been due to his own choice or as a victim of his environment? Is he frightened? – He must be aching from the torture he has suffered here. Is he afraid to face another at S police station? Or is he simply acting? – To rouse my sympathy because he realizes it is now essential for his survival to secure my unreserved sympathy. But can one shed tears as freely as that unless they come from the bottom of one's heart.

Perhaps he was unaware of himself crying – an automatic, emotional reaction on seeing the only woman he can rely on in this cold and heartless world, like a boy held for a long time by a gang of bullies who suddenly sees his mother appearing round the corner? He breaks down in tears and the more she tries to comfort him the harder he cries.'

Then I realized what an inappropriate reverie I was in.

'Mr Kwŏn, have you been tortured?' I asked. He looked into my face through his bleary eyes for a moment or two and replied briefly, 'It was terrible.'

It was enough to stir up my imagination. At first he had been interrogated as a suspected spy. What sort of torture might he have been subject to? From two o'clock till now, past ten, what pain and humiliation he must have been through. I felt a sharp pain in my heart and wondered if the pain of tearing apart a flesh of your body was comparable to it.

'Have you seen Hisun?' I asked.

'She must have had detectives in hiding. She appeared alone and the moment I took a step towards her I was seized and handcuffed. We came on the same bus but did not speak. They will sue me for fraud. I'll willingly take the punishment and come out a clean man.'

As we entered the waiting room of S police station led by the two officers who had come to bring us over, the preliminary siren for the curfew rang out. We would not be able to get home tonight.

'Do you mind staying here overnight, ladies?' The officer said politely as he drew up a couple of benches close to the stove for us. After I filled in the Witness Statement Form and signed it, there was nothing we could do but wait for the curfew to lift at five o'clock next morning. Here it seemed that they were treating the whole thing as an illicit love affair or a fraud under the pretext of marriage.

Whether it was the delayed effect of the 'quinnine' or I was run down, I felt extremely drowsy. Resting my head on Sŏnhi's lap, I had fallen into a deep, deep sleep. When I awoke it took me a while to realize where I was. It was another example of 'Being fortunate in misfortune.' I was glad that I had not died after taking what I had believed to be a deadly dose. Did the chemists who had given me suspicious looks when I asked for quinine, hand me some stuff for sleep or was it that my peculiar mental power that becomes extra sharp when in extreme crisis, had overcome the effect of the drug?

It was past thee o'clock when another gentleman walked in. He was introduced to us as the head of the Criminal Investigations Department. After being briefed on the case, he came over and sat himself close to us. Accustomed to dealing with all sorts of people, he seemed to know what kind we were. He started with a courteous chat and then gradually assuming the tone of a caring father, he comforted me. Then turning to

Kwŏn he said that it would now all depend on whether or not Hisun sued him. But to his mind she was not likely to do that. A woman who had snatched away someone's lover and lived with him for some months – what good would she get out of a law suit? He concluded in gentle advice to him. 'So, if she drops the case, I should take her back and be good to her if I were you.'

If things would end as simply as that, I thought, I could wish no more.

As curfew lifted Kwŏn was led away into another room, and a detective came in followed by Hisun. No sooner was she introduced to the Head than she became flippant, joking and giggling. He knew how to treat a woman like that. He was quite a different man from what he had been to us.

'So you're the ninny who let go of your man? I'm not surprised. In future, chain him down, and live with your eyes wide open.' She burst into a cackle of laughter as if she was enjoying every minute of it. He asked her, as if he was referring to her lawful husband, 'Do you want to see him, now?'

'Yes, please.'

He called to a man. 'Mr Lee, would you like to bring him out.' Then he turned round to us and indicated with his eyes that we had better go. As Sŏnhi and I walked towards the exit, I turned round and saw a door at the opposite end of the waiting room open and he came out followed by an officer. Our eyes met. I raised my hand and crossed in the air as a sign of my blessing. What a good job he hadn't been arrested as a spy, or I would never have walked out this door a free woman.

The moment I entered our room at home I collapsed on the floor and broke down. There was no longer any need to restrain myself. I cried freely as I mumbled to myself, 'Ah, love is gone, it's all over...painful and miserable memories are all that's left behind....gone with the last drop of my passion....'

After a long, raving cry, I felt better. Tears seemed to have washed away part of the sorrow.

As I got on the bus for Anp'yŏng to see Fr. Osbourne and tell him about what had happened, I felt as if a great weight had been lifted from my shoulders and hopeful that I might be able to make a new start. Sŏnhi, who had come to the bus station to see me off, said, 'Have a good journey and come back a new, strong woman, won't you?' I smiled back at her.

Thanks to a combination of undisturbed meditation, both ways, on the bus and the encouragement I got from Fr. Osbourne, I returned in the evening in a fairly cheerful frame of mind.

A boy was waiting for me at the gate. He said he was from S police station and handed me a crumpled piece of paper. It was a message from Kwŏn. Obviously he had bribed the errand boy with a little money and sent him on an unofficial mission.

Dear Sukey,

Hisun came this morning, and after pouring out insults in a loud voice took out a law suit. I shall be detained here for a few days before moving to the Sŏdaemun Prison to await trial. While I am here I am allowed to receive private food. When I am transferred, the most important thing is for you to find out who is to be the public prosecutor and bribe him. For now, I need some warm underwear and some spending money. My mind is calm. Now there are only you and me.

Two months after his detainment Kwŏn was sentenced to a year's imprisonment, 'a lenient sentence on the account of his repentance'.

Chapter 11

In a Hospital Ward

few days before Kwŏn's trial I was admitted to hospital with acute appendicitis, operated on, and kept in there for ten days. It proved to be a significant time, not only for curing my physical illness but also restoring my sanity by going through my thoughts tangled like a mop of hair with a fine-toothed comb.

During the two months while Kwŏn was held in custody awaiting trial, I had become extremely emaciated. Even though I was now being looked after with great care by my sister and my parents, I was thinner than I had been while I was suffering alone in secret. I had frequent stomach cramps and found it hard to sleep. In the night, thoughts that had been repressed during the day would spread their wings, and doggedly fly and hover about. Also I had got into the habit of self-persecution. Even though I was not confined behind bars, I felt like a prisoner bound by ropes of sorrow. I did not deserve a warm bowl of rice. How dare I sleep on a warm *ondol* floor? I should be on a concrete floor, and on bitter evenings let the chill freeze my flesh and penetrate my bones. That's what I deserved. As soon as Sŏnhi had tucked in my side of the quilt and fallen asleep, I kicked it off and rolled over to the cold end of the room.

At such times, the stories of my father and mother came back. In 1919, the year of the patriotic uprising of the Korean people, claiming their independence from Japan, my father had been a young man of nineteen. Because of his involvement in distributing handbills he was arrested and sent to prison for a year. While he was serving his sentence, we often heard, mother had put herself under self-inflicted torture. She never touched meat dishes, and allowed herself a lump of boiled millet a day, just enough to keep her alive. In the midwinter nights she slept uncovered at the coldest end of the *ondol* floor, curled up like a shrimp. My grandmother, who had been renowned for her meanness and harshness to her daughter-in-law, was deeply touched, and put a cover over her very gently so as not to wake her, and as she did so, she shed many quiet tears. It must have been a kind of childhood moral lesson to us and unconsciously I was copying my mother.

It so happened that on the night I had the appendicitis I was meeting Fr. Osbourne. He was in Seoul for a couple of days. I knew he was a busy man and thought it very generous of him to spare one evening out of two for me. The first thing he said when he saw me was, 'It is about time you paid some attention on your own health. You don't look well.'

It took me a long time to tell him what had happened since I last saw him, but I was calm and spoke as if I was reporting on someone else's story:

Now that Hisun had sued him, I thought I was free to look after him. Keeping it secret from my family I had been sending him provisions, and under the pretext of going to early mass, I left home at dawn to visit him at the prison. In the dark cold streets not even the first buses or trams were in sight. Ahead of me, I had a three miles walk to the prison. As I trotted along my footsteps echoed in the empty streets. Whatever lofty ideals and rosy dreams might swell in my heart, in this state I could not be a cheerful sight to an observer. Besides, my eyes tired from lack of sleep drooped as if pulled down by stones. It was essential for me to get the first or second place in the queue of visitors to be able to be at work on time after seeing him.

It was easy to send him money, but taking him a parcel of clothes was difficult because I was sharing one room with Sŏnhi. It needed a nerve-wracking manipulation almost beyond one's imagination. I packed a few things to take to him in the morning, and put them out of sight, behind a suitcase. I waited until Sŏnhi was fast asleep to put the parcel just outside the first door. I had to be wary in case she stirred in her sleep and asked what I was opening the door for. Then I had to make up some excuses for opening the heavier, outer door. I lay awake until three or four o'clock when I pretended to go to the toilet, and take the parcel to the outer door. At five, under the pretext of going to the early mass, I left home carrying the bundle like a thief. Some nights I had dropped into a deeper sleep than I had intended, woken by the light, and started as I thought, 'Oh, I am late!' I sprang up and saw the time. It was only four. It was a full moon pouring down its light onto our verandah on its way to set to the west. Once spoilt in this way, sleep would not return and I waited fully awake for the arrival of the dawn.

One day during this time, I was confronted with another vicious encounter. Hisun turned up at the office bringing with her a female friend and her sister. As soon as she saw me, she said, 'What are you going about scheming his release for?'

'Scheming?' I could not understand what she meant at first.

'Don't play at being innocent, you, crafty woman. I should like to see you locked up behind bars as well.'

'Do you think we don't know that you had a hand in the eight hundred thousand Hwan fraud?' Each of them started shouting something in a loud, jeering voice on the pavement in front of the Academy. In no time at all I found myself the object of scorn and spectacle ringed by curious passers-by. The louder the women's voices grew the larger the ring grew. Having abandoned Kwŏn in a lawsuit, I had never thought Hisun would turn up intentionally to assault me in this way.

Probably she had found out that I was visiting Kwǒn, and it had galled her already embittered heart.

I was utterly at a loss to know what to do. The more you beat the drum the louder it would sound. I decided not to say anything.

'What a dreadful calamity they've suffered. I can't blame them. I can understand their anger. He's the one to blame. How much longer are they going to carry on? Until the devil in them is satisfied, I suppose. Still I am in a better position than they are. They must have lost their reason,' thus I thought as I stood, with a blank face, in the middle of a ring of spectators.

Then I saw the front door of the Academy being flung open and several of my colleagues coming out with Mr Hong in the lead.

'Look ladies!' He brushed part the spectators, stepped into the centre of the ring and went on as he straightened his broad shoulders. 'Dressed like ladies, you appear to be decent women. Do you have to behave in such a vulgar way?'

I knew he had been learning Karate, and was worried lest he might demonstrate his art on them. The women were visibly overwhelmed by his air and his physique. Even so, one of them said, 'This woman is an accomplice in a fraud.'

'If she is, you can report it to the police or sue her legally. There is no need for this kind of a bullying in office hours, is there?' He glared and bared his teeth. 'Don't you realize that you can be put to behind bars for disturbing public order and preventing the execution of public duties?'

He looked around him and gave a loud laugh. The women were utterly silenced by now.

'You can rally round here all day, or a hundred days if you haven't anything better to do, but it won't affect even the tip of our Miss Yun's reputation.' He then turned to me and said, 'Miss Yun, let's go in. You shouldn't put up with such insolence. I swear I will see that this never happens to you again, damn it!' He bared his teeth once again, waved his fist in the air and escorted me back into the office.

Once inside I locked myself in the conference room and wept for an hour. I was moved by the discreet concern of my colleagues. As if by agreement they went back to their places as though nothing had happened and resumed their work. Nobody breathed a word about the incident all through the day. For all their goodness and readiness to help me, I could not open my heart even to one of them. The realization of my loneliness hit me afresh.

I thought the director was also being extremely tactful to save me from embarrassment for he had long since guessed I was in some kind of difficulty that I would rather keep to myself. He did not ring the bell to call me for the rest of the day.

I was worried lest Sŏnhi should hear about it. If she did, she would flare up in anger and upset her delicate health, and spoil her final exams that she was going through now. I was trying hard to help her by cooking the meals and looking cheerful. I had come to the conclusion that I should stop visiting Kwŏn for the present and wait until Hisun's anger had subsided.

Fr. Osbourne listened throughout without interruption.

'The public prosecutor has demanded two years' imprisonment, and he will be sentenced in a few days' time. He has sworn to me that he will become a Christian. When I last went to see him I gave him the confessions of Tolstoy and St Augustine.'

I realized that I had taken up too much of his time telling my stories. He must be bored, I thought.

'Through my trial I have led a wanton soul into God's kingdom. That will help me a bit in my heavenward journey when the time comes, won't it?' I said and laughed to ease the somewhat heavy atmosphere. He also smiled and stood up.

'As payment for the typing you did for me last month, I would like to buy you a supper,' he said. I had typed a couple of his articles for a magazine but of course I had never expected any payment.

I had felt, since I left work, a slight discomfort in my stomach. It was coming and going. I took it for a light symptom of the stomach cramp that I lately seemed to have often. By the time we entered a Western-style restaurant and sat at a table, the pain was so acute that I could not help a frown rising on my face until with a moan I fell onto the floor. He delivered me to the hospital in a taxi. There, without delay I was rushed into the operating theatre. Unable to contact my sister during the curfew, Fr. Osbourne stayed on as a sort of guardian.

As I came round I heard my own voice like someone else's. I heard repeated mumblings of 'Our Father who art in Heaven...' 'Hail Mary...' and the voice broke into a whimper as it said something like, 'Father, I am a sinner, what must I do...' I was consciously trying not to say anything but my own will seemed to have little control over my voice pouring forth. At last I gained full consciousness. The moment I opened my eyes wide I saw, as if suspended in the air above me, the two large eyes of Fr. Osbourne. Instantly I fell into a deep sleep. When I awoke it was morning. He had gone and my sister was beside me. Soon my father and mother came rushing into the room. Mother stayed on with me for a long time after father went.

Since Kwŏn's arrest, I had become very fond of and close to my stepmother. While Kwŏn was held at S Police Station, a couple of days after his arrest, I had gone to see him during lunch hour. The head of the Criminal Investigations Department met me in person.

'I've found out that he is a bad man. Don't see him,' he said. It was as kindly voice as it had been when I first met him but it had a firmness in it.

'I know he is bad. I appreciate your concern but I still wish to see him.' I would insist on my legal right if necessary, I thought.

'Your father has been in this morning. He made me promise not to allow you to visit him.'

As Sǒnhi had realized she could not separate me from Kwǒn, she must have asked father to intervene.

'If you insist on seeing him, you'd better bring your father's consent,'he said.

My lunchtime was running out. As I came away I thought I would come back after work. If necessary, I would tell them that I had my father's approval. But when I walked out the office in the evening I saw my father standing by the roadside waiting for me. Without a word he put me on the homeward bus, himself getting on it behind me. When we got home, mother waiting for me came running to me and grabbed my hands.

'Ah, they all know about it.' I felt faint and my legs gave way. Mother spread out the bedding in the room, I went in, pulled the cover over my head and lay still in exhaustion. If they started bothering me with questions about this and that, my nerves would snap and I would die, I thought. What a good job I fainted.

After a long silence, father opened his mouth. 'An infamous criminal – it means the lowest and the basest kind of human being, not worth a penny.' That was all he said. After that there was another long silence during which I dozed off, and then he went away.

After he had left mother remained by me and regardless of whether I heard or not talked on quietly. I sensed that she was searching hard through the resources of her wisdom to find some suitable words that would comfort me.

'It is not your fault. All women are bound to go through a bitter experience of this kind at least once in their life.

'I have never done much for you and I can't do anything now either.... Whether it was due to unfortunate family circumstances or because of my lack of love, as a mother I failed to keep you, a daughter at a vulnerable age, in the same house with your parents, and left you to defend yourself like an orphan in a world bustling with wolves, and you fell a victim. I feel it was all due to my fault. Because you have been such an exceptionally clever child, I had full trust in you – I never thought you'd come to any harm. It looks as though you have been put to an exceptionally vile temptation and test.

'Still, it is a good job that it has all come out now before it went any deeper. "Being fortunate in a misfortune", as they say, or you'd have been ruined for the rest of your life.'

At first I paid little attention thinking her words could not mean anything to me but gradually I was won over by her sincerity. It was deeply moving.

From her first days in our family up till now, it was no exaggeration to say that I had never felt much affection for her. My attitude had been that though she was my father's wife, as I did not love her I did not expect it from her either. I had felt awkward in her presence and had always sought ways of keeping away from her. Now it was all changing.

I had noticed that over the past few years, with the decline of our family fortunes she had been through many bitter experiences, she had rapidly aged. Her sharp and rigid personality had become smoother and mellow.

Now I looked up at her face. There were lines on her forehead and her hair had turned grey at the temples.

'Look at this,' she said as she held up an emerald the size of a chestnut. 'Even after all these years of trouble in which we have lost everything, this little gemstone has somehow remained.' She went on to say, 'Do please swear on this stone that you won't meet that bad man again.' I looked her in the face and nodded my consent. Whether it was feasible or not I submitted myself to a deep emotion that seemed to melt down all the strength of my willfulness.

'By whatever means, I will get a gold chain and make a necklace for you. It will go well with the black sweater you are so fond of.'

'You should keep it for Chinhi,' I wanted to say but the words did not come out. Instead tears ran down my face. Mother got out her handkerchief and wiped them away.

Again now my mother stayed on by my bedside in the hospital for most of the morning. Sŏnhi came round every morning and evening and as if that was not enough, she popped in during her lunch time as well. On one of these visits, she said as if casually, 'Hasn't Hisun caused any more trouble?'

'Trouble? What trouble?'

'What do you mean "What trouble", you idiot? Do you still think I don't know about it? When I heard about it I could not bear it, I was shaking all over. I had to tell Chinmo. Don't worry, I didn't tell him anything about Kwŏn but just that Hisun had come to the Academy and attacked you.

'He said he would never let her get away with it unavenged. "Just leave it to me", he said. '

I was intrigued. Who was the informer? Miss Pak? Surely not Dr Kang himself? Sŏnhi went on.

'The next day was Sunday. I was to meet him in front of the Midopa Department Store. He turned up with two smartly dressed, handsome young men. Apparently they were his former pupils. He sent them into the store first and we watched them from a distance. As they walked up to her shop, Hisun and her friend coquettishly welcomed them. "How can we help you, sirs?"

One of the men straight went to the point. "Are you the woman called Hisun? We are younger brothers of Sukey Yun, in a manner of speaking." The two women were crest-fallen at once.

"We are rough sort of chaps. It's not our way to turn the other cheek. We go for literal revenge – a blow for a blow, an eye for an eye." He spoke rather loudly.

The second man, in a lower voice said, "Do you get it? We've come to pay you back in exactly the same way as you assaulted our sister." It was getting busy in the store and one or two customers were looking into the display cases. The harassed look on Hisun's face – what a shame, I thought, I could not show it to you.

Then Hisun said politely, "We are prepared for revenge but if you would choose another time and place, we'd be obliged to you."

The first of them ignored it and threateningly said, "I will smash it all up at one swipe," as he waved his arm in the air. The second one pulled down his friend's arm and said, "Come, if you have anything to say? Do you want to apologize to Miss Yun?" Hisun took the chance and, would you believe it, did apologize most humbly.

"I would like to send my sincerest apology to her. Please tell her that I am deeply sorry and ashamed. I was then so blind with fury that I did not know what I was doing...'"

If Sŏnhi had expected a rapturous response, she only saw a gloomy expression on my face.

'So, who told you? Was it Miss Pak?' I asked.

'No, it wasn't. I can't even remember who it was.' She was reluctant to tell me and I thought it did not matter anyway.

After she went away, I thought about it again. Even though I could understand her anger, I rather wished she had not done this. I had forgiven them all on the spot so what was the point in avenging it in the same way? On the other hand, it occurred to me that it had prevented Hisun from coming to attack me again. She had learned that after all I was one of their kind, who could resort to unpleasant means when provoked.

There was a knock on the door. I said, 'Come in.'

The head of a baby boy first came in sight from behind the door and then his whole body followed by Miae, with a large bouquet. Her first baby just over one, she was large with her second child. How we had changed in the past two years and each in such different ways! But as we chatted lively about people from our common past, the friendship that had nearly died by two years' separation revived. We were conscious of that and pleased.

No sooner had she left than in came Dr Kang and Miss Pak. She thrust upon me a large basket of fruit and sweets from the staff. I felt unworthy of such kindness.

I was so very fond of the people around me; yet because of the deadly secret that I had to keep hidden in my heart I could not freely mix with them. There was also my secret resolution to take my life when the right moment came, for I could see no way that I could ever get out of the dreadful pit that I had dug for myself. I superficially laughed and responded to their talk but all the time I was aware that it hardly concerned me. Like the sound of music from the next door, or remembering a beautiful film I had once seen, I could never become a part of it. When the visitors had gone and I was left to myself, I picked up my diary and scribbled my solitary musings.

I had asked Suyŏn to attend the trial of Kwŏn. After she had been there, she came to see me at the hospital. As she entered the room, she looked round to make sure I was alone. Even then she lowered her voice as she said, 'Ŏnni, was he the one who used to come round to the library?'

'Yes. I must tell you all about it one day. I have been meaning to.' She turned her eyes that became tearful and asked no more questions.

Suyǒn and I.

If our life here is a reincarnation of our previous life, I often fancied, there must have been some close and deep bond between us. For the past two years, in my desolate loneliness, she had been the one closest to me and having her around me had been a great comfort.

Born to poor parents with several siblings, she had started earning her keep from an early age. She worked at the Academy during the day and went to night school. When she had finished her high school course, she sat for the entrance examinations for Y University. Nobody including herself, had expected she would pass and even if she had there was no way in which she could pay the fees. But, she had said, she would sit for them just to see what they were like. When miraculously it turned out that she had been successful, Dr Kang was the one who was most delighted. He offered to pay her first registration fees. But for her, going to university would mean leaving her job, without which she could not carry on with her study.

Then I came up with an idea, which had the full approval of the director and the whole staff. She would keep her job at the Academy, working a couple of hours in the evenings in term time, and full time during the vacations. It worked. She was an intelligent, trustworthy and pleasant girl. She not only fulfilled her own tasks but helped out other members of staff wherever she could. Her job was mainly working as my assistant.

She proved to be a keen scholar. It was a great pleasure for me to observe her progress. In the full bloom of youth she was beautiful to look at. As we often talked about her studies I was more and more convinced that she would go far. As much as I undemonstratively trusted and loved her, she seemed to regard me with great affection. Soon I found her helping me not only as the official assistant but also with my private affairs. Even though she did not know exactly why, she knew I was financially in a difficult situation. Without once asking 'why', she became involved in my complicated pecuniary matters. Sometimes I sent her to Hae-ryŏn with a scribbled message asking for a loan, or on the *kae* days, she delivered my contribution as I did not wish to see my friends. Sometimes she reminded me saying, '*Onni*, don't forget the interest for Hae-ryŏn's twenty thousand Hwan is due tomorrow.' If she saw me flustered or unable to find the money, she would offer to help.

'I have a friend with a hair-dressing salon, and another who works in a publisher's office. Shall I go and see if they could help out for a few days?' She would come running back, out of breath, sweat pouring down her face, with the money.

When Suyŏn left after briefing me on the court proceedings and I was alone, I became submerged into a world of introspection. I chewed and chewed on the strange phrase, 'a convict of one year's imprisonment' until it seemed to become a part of me. He was now labelled as an 'infamous criminal', but it was only a superficial definition by the law. It hardly touched the core of the matter. There still remained the burning question of whether he had really been a spy or merely a fraud, and the answer lay beyond me. At the beginning of his arrest I had drawn some comfort from the fact that he was accused of fraud and not a spy, which would have had far-reaching impact. Not only would his punishment have been terrible but it would have had tragic consequences for so many other people.

But now I felt differently. If he was really a spy, he had at least some justification for his wicked deeds – he did it for what he believed to be a greater justice, patriotism. There would remain room for some credit for his human values. It was unbearable to think that he was simply a lier and fraud, that I had been a fool, thoroughly cheated by, and made perfect sacrifice for a proper roué. I had seen that he was extremely skilful at lying, but I had put up with it because I had thought of it as the inevitable means to protect a certain truth. But the short-lived affair with Hisun was too clumsy an adventure for such a master liar like him. Unless, as he made out to me, he was under threat with a gun pointed at his back, how could he dare to attempt such a foolish crime that would come out in the open within less than a month? And unless he had handed the money over to someone else, was it likely that he could have spent eight hundred thousand Hwan in one month, however luxurious their life might have been? At the end of it, why did he decide to come back to me? Did he really believe that I would still forgive him and take him back after finding out what had happened? He knew I was financially desperate and could no longer be a viable means of supporting him. He could well have left me for good. Was it not because of his love that he had returned to me?

Had he deliberately misled the police by making himself out to be a great villain? When he was arrested he had at first been suspected of being a spy. Knowing that the punishment for even the most depraved crime would be less severe, he could have pretended to be confessing his many sins – sex-offences, fraud, stealing and anything that came to his head. But was it at all likely that the police would take him at his word without checking his past records?

My thoughts were like a flowing river. It ran on deep into the night, and there were three key themes in its rhythm that repeatedly bobbed up to the surface and then submerged into the undercurrent one after another. 'Is he a spy?', 'Is he a fraud?' And 'My love, a convict!'

Towards the dawn, before I finally fell into a light sleep I had reached the conclusion that I could not simply label him as an evil man. There was some basis on which I could trust that he had in the past made some conscientious effort. His proficiency in foreign languages, if I could still believe what he had told me, was one such proof. In our early days he had told me that he was fluent in five foreign languages – English, German, French, Russian and Japanese. It had been at the time that I had started learning French. When I dabbled with some basic vocabulary he laughed and said that as soon as he was settled he would give me some lessons. Of course it had never occurred to me to test him for I had revered him. But he could hardly have been lying for something like this. That would have been too short-sighted. Anyway, a man who had made some serious effort to learn something could not be entirely bad. Besides the proficiency of languages, I remembered those poems written out in his beautiful handwriting that he now and again handed to me. A man who could write such poems could not be totally wicked.

If I were still alive when he came out of prison, what would become of us? He would then be removed from the class of the classless for he would have a definite identity, not false but real, a former convict, like Jean Valjean.

Turning the pages of a literary magazine that Chinmo had brought on his last visit, my eyes caught a line that gave me a momentary shock. It was an article about the life and work of the late poet Tongju Yun, who wrote Korean poems under Japanese rule, was persecuted for his writing and died young in a Japanese prison. There was a passage from 'The Star-counting Night', a poem that had become the prelude to our love so to speak. I asked Sŏnhi to get me by whatever means Yun's book of collected poems, and confirmed that it was his. Kwŏn had copied it out, and because it was spring when he gave it to me, he had changed the word, 'autumn' in the original to 'spring.' I shuddered at his craftiness. There was now little ground for thinking that the second poem, the third or any others had been his own. I felt bitter.

It took me a couple of days to come to terms with this fresh blow, but after I had regained my calm, I succeeded in persuading myself that I had no right to reject him now. Even if the poems were someone else's, a man who could appreciate such beautiful writing must have some goodness in him. After all, he had never said that they were his own. It was I who had assumed that he had written them specifically for me.

I should marry him when he came out. All I could hope for was that he would come out a reformed man. As a lawfully married man he would have no reason ever to lie. We would live a poor but honest life. I could postpone my death until then. If he still showed signs of falsity and kept on lying, I would teach him a lesson by my death. I resolved to be faithful to him.

With my mind made up thus, I spent several days without any tearful spells. I loved my room in the hospital. The four walls were white and my bed was by the window facing east and looked out over a garden with well-tended flower-beds and shrubs, and a woodland beyond it with the colours of early spring.

It was the day before my discharge. I was nervous at the thought of going back to the world. I needed to sort out my thoughts and prepare myself for it. I picked up my diary and leaning against the headboard of the bed began to scribble:

Now that the afternoon ward-round is over, it is so quiet here. All around me is like one huge space filled with silence except for the sounds of birds, like that of chisels of artists, as they work all day long with their material called 'a day' before them.

'Peck and jabber', 'peck and jabber', the sounds echo through the air. Shall I see and appreciate the outcome of their work, the meaning of the day, tonight, through the window in the western sky? The raptures and sorrows of human life – are they after all no more than the art work of the birds reflected in the sunset...?

There was a knock on the door and Fr. Osbourne walked in. I had not quite expected to see him again while I was in the hospital but I felt that he was a most welcome visitor. His smile, like gentle ripples that roll out towards the banks of a spring lake, spread out in the room. Suddenly the sounds of the birds seemed to have come to a halt. Were they pausing for inspiration before the next stage of their work?

I told him about Kwŏn's sentence and that even though I had not been able to see him for some time now I was not so anxious, as I was sure of his whereabouts. He said that he was deeply moved by my patience and devotion and that he particularly admired my courage for taking care of Kwŏn after Hisun had abandoned him. Encouraged by his praise, the only person in the whole world who appreciated my affliction, I went a step further and told him of my plans. I would take him on his release and marry him at once so that he would have the security of his own home.

My expectation of further praise did not materialize. He sat quietly for a moment in what I had come to think of as his characteristic pose when he was in a thoughtful mood – lightly closed eyes with long lashes delicately trembling. When he opened them after such a pause, they seemed to emanate a peculiarly clear light.

'Marriage should be based on mutual love and respect,' he said and after another pause added, 'Entering matrimony from one-sided love, sympathy, or charity is a dangerous thing to do.'

Soon after he left the sunset came. As if the meaning of that one day was summed up and sealed in those last words, I pondered them slowly as I looked out at the lingering sunset.

Chapter 12

A June Diary

1 June. The first day of the month that marks half-way through the year that I started in great distress. As if awakening from a long drawn-out nightmare I keep pinching myself to ensure that I don't fall asleep again. A succession of peaceful days continues. Now that I have worked out this month's budget my mind is at peace as my eyes leisurely follow the floating clouds and admire the luxurious green of the grass and trees. How delicious is the air in these pleasant evenings as the lingering sun dyes the western sky crimon. I wish I could forget the painful past that had deprived me of all my opportunities, youthful mirth and passion leaving behind only shameful memories. I feel like a bird released from a suffocating confinement, flying about free and singing.

5 June. Happy third anniversary to you, O, The Korean Academy! The inside and outside of you are vibrant with excitement today and my colleagues are all in jovial mood. I am leading, under the instructions of the director, the preparations for a tea party for the patrons and members of the Academy to commemorate your birthday! My heart is full of emotion. What miraculous progress and achievement you have made in the past three years! I am naturally proud to be a member of the staff that serves you, but there are more personal reasons for my rejoycing today.

Since I took my first step in social life three years ago with ambition and dreams for the future as bright as the green of

June, Dear Academy, you and I have grown up together like twins. I can say with clear conscience that I have served you with devotion. That is why I am so excited about your success as if it were my own, but there is something else. Serving you has been my job that I have held onto through my personal adversity, a job that kept me going and preserved my sanity in the height of my crisis. The pains I suffered when, due to unavoidable circumstances, I could not carry out my duty to you properly, and the sorrow I felt when I could not wholeheartedly join my colleagues in their mirth – how doggedly have I endured them all! While you have grown this much, what horrendous human experience have I gained!

You, dear Academy, stalwart as the Mother Earth to me, rejoice for me today for I am awakened from a dreadful nightmare. On your third birthday I wish you even more successful times ahead as I pledge afresh my devotion.

6 June. As we were talking at the staff meeting last week about a picnic, a treat for the staff as part of the anniversary celebrations, I proposed Samgak Mountain as the destination. I thought I would take advantage of the opportunity to see two years' growth of the magnolias. It had been agreed unanimously.

We set off in a Landrover borrowed from the X Foundation. We were too heavily loaded to climb up to the summit, so we decided to eat first half-way up, and then the more confident climbers could continue up later. In a glade in the wood by a small waterfall we spread out our feast and ate and played games.

'Rejoice in the splendid view, splendid water and splendid people' Dr Kang broke into an impromptu poem. Thanks to a heavy shower yesterday, the air was even fresher and the green more lustrous. We all sang to Mr Hong's accordion accompaniment. I sang until I thought my throat would burst and my heart was content.

Then I set off for the summit. I thought I would be going alone but Dr Kang joined me and then every one followed suit.

We walked up to the temple. The trees were not there where they should be. I felt like collapsing. My knees were weak. The abbot, who had been transferred there last year said that he had never seen any such trees.

'Young saplings like that – if they were not covered, they could have perished in the winter, do you think?' I asked.

'Yes, of course. The cold up here can be very severe,' was his disinterested reply. Like a drowning man clutching at a straw, I went on. 'Still, if the roots deep down were not entirely dead, do you think they could send out some new shoots – I mean even in a few years' time?' In his reply of an uncertain 'Maybe,' I felt the last gleam of hope being puffed out. I felt afresh the sense of betrayal.

I who had led the way up, was now bringing up the rear, falling far behind. The memories all came flooding back and made my heart ache for the precious chunk of my life, my pure passion and youth that had been trampled on and made mockery of and lost forever.

Come to think of it, there was no telling whether the saplings had really been magnolias, or ash trees or persimmon. A man who had copied out someone else's poem and handed them over pretending they were his own – what grounds did I have to trust him?

He had said he was fluent in five foreign languages, yet I had never seen him buy a book or even a magazine during the two years I had known him. If he had some interest in intellectual matters he could have read for hours on end in the Academy library instead of killing his time on the streets and in the tearooms. In fact, it occurred to me now, I have never had a truly memorable, intellectual conversation with him over the time I had known him. Occasionally his silly jokes or gossip made me laugh not because it was really witty but because hoodwinked with love as I was, I was ready to be impressed by whatever he said.

In his early days in the Kyŏng-woo Hotel, I found him once or twice so deeply absorbed in the books that I had borrowed for him from the library that he did not notice my approach until I went right up to him and tapped him on the shoulder. Had that been a play-acting too?

What about the telephone in his room which according to Hwaja, existed solely for sordid conversations with sleazy women? – Installed with the last penny of the precious money that I had saved for my sister's birthday! The awesome story of the interrogation he had been subjected to by the police was very likely a lie. And what did the night that he was supposed to have spent at Nagwŏn-dong mean? The moment he was assured that he had completely possessed me, his relationship with another woman had already started.

The hair? A strand of slightly curly hair less than three centimetres that was supposed to be from the armpit of his mother. Who knows where that came from? For all that I know it could well be the pubic hair of a whore! I have treasured it as if it were a holy relic, kept at page 395 of my Bible. If I were to be imprisoned as an accomplice of a spy one day, I thought, I would ask Sŏnhi to bring that Bible for me. There, sitting in the prison cell, unnoticed to anyone, I would freely stroke and worship it like the heroine of a fairy tale. What a joke!

'Ha ha ha...' 'Wha, ha ha ha ha...!' I broke into wild laughter like a mad woman. My friends thinking it was part of the picnic fun turned and laughed back to me.

I was beginning to see something that I had never dreamed of a month ago. The stuff that he had blown into the balloon of my love, making it float high and lofty had been entirely false, every bit of it.

By now I was wracking my brain to find some last straw, which was not a lie. A contemporary of my elder brother, Hyŏngsŏk, at Kyŏng-gi High school? A black wart the size of a sesame seed beneath his ear? Well, a tiny spot like that could be on any one's face. I walked up to Mr Yu who is a graduate of Kyŏng-gi, and asked him in a light, joking tone of voice, 'Mr Yu, is it true that at Kyŏng-gi there was a Japanese class shortly before the liberation?'

'What?' He spoke with mock severity. 'You're going to be in trouble, Miss Yun; if you slander the honourable tradition of somebody's school in that way, you could be sued for libel.'

'I mean it seriously. It concerns the choice of somebody's future husband.' I still pretended not to be serious. 'Are you sure about that? Didn't they take on some Japanese boys for an experiment or in the cause of supporting the slogan, "Japan and Korea are one nation"?'

'I swear on my life. You must have misunderstood the story of Seoul High school.'

Something snapped in my heart. That settled it. There was no need to think about it any more. I must give him up and try to forget the past. After all, two years that had felt like two thousand was indeed nothing in the time scale of a life span of sixty. I am learning rapidly.

7 June. Applying a sharp scalpel to the love in which I had been blind and uncritical had probably begun while I was in the hospital, not yesterday or day before. What Fr. Osbourne had said about marriage, 'based on mutual love and respect' had left a deep impression on me...It kept coming back. Even if I unreservedly trusted in his love, could I respect him? I had not made up my mind about this when I left the hospital.

Soon after my discharge I went to the prison to see him. It was my first visit since he was sentenced. Even taking into account that the meeting took place in the presence of the warden, it was a blatantly false show. I felt uncomfortable. There was no sign, on his side, of concern about my health. Not a word about me going into hospital. It was merely a succession of mentioning meaningless names as if the whole purpose was to impress the officers with the fact that he was a dear friend of so many important people.

'Professor Kim did so and so; Dr Kang said so and so; and when Mister Chang came back from the USA...' after which he concluded the interview by saying 'For the time being, let me have just ten thousand Hwan a month and that should be enough.' I said I would and left him. I felt bitter. What did he mean by 'just ten thousand Hwan' when I am trying to make even ten Hwan last longer? Does he mean to spend that much money just sitting in a prison cell? He knows better than anyone how I am harrowed by debts that have all been incurred because of him. Could he demand such a thing if he really cared for me? He could have said, 'I don't need much money here, so don't worry about me. Instead of sending me money pay off the debts as best as you can and look after yourself.'

Unable to get hold of the money, I kept putting off visiting him until one day a man in prison warder's uniform turned up at the Academy. He introduced himself as Mr Chŏlsu Kim's friend, Kim being Kwŏn's name, under which he is serving the sentence. Being a Yun himself, he said, he and I might have had some common ancestors in ancient times. Having heard so much about me from Kim, he said, he felt as if he knew me, and he handed me a letter from him. With his servile smiles and sneaky manners, he did not look at all sincere. I took an instant dislike to him, and the thoughts of Kwŏn's fraudulent tendency, crafty enough to bribe a prison warder, distressed me. I opened the letter, which consisted of three lines demanding fifteen thousand Hwan to be sent through this man. I told him to come back on the next day and then handed him the money. Two days later, I had another letter from Kwŏn through post. 'I have received two thousand Hwan via Yun. I seem to be relapsing into jaundice. Please send me fifteen thousand as soon as possible...' I was disgusted. They are all liars and cheats, I thought. Not only did I not send the money but I stopped visiting him altogether. If he was ill he would be seen to by the prison doctor. Other prisoners live without private provisions. Why couldn't he.

About that time, I learned from Yŏnok that Kijŏng had taken to bed, very ill, and from Sŏnhi that her mother, selling chickens in the market had pitiably asked her, on behalf of her daughter, Mr Kwŏn's whereabouts. That roused more anger in me. It was then that I positively began to doubt and measure him in terms of human values, weigh and analyse him.

For several days, I have been making a draft, on and off, of a letter to him and now I have posted it. It did not have to be long.

The time has come for me to renounce my association with you. Like the magnolias on Samgak Mountain, which have perished for good (though I shall never know for sure whether they were really magnolias), I will erase all memories of the past two years. If the past has been God's plan, I leave my future in his hands.

I have no wish to hear from you or see you again. I have reached this conclusion not through pressure from my family but of my own accord. Therefore it is final.

6th June, Sukey Yun.

9 June. I have been to two weddings this week, Sunja's and Haewŏn's, and felt terribly out of place. I shall never attend another. Sadly I realize I am outside such normal human conventions. I am destined to some abnormal fate. I must go away. Get out of this place and start a new life. Beyond the far end of the blue, blue sky, there is a wider world. I must go there.

One of my strong points is a passion for learning. I have the brains to back up that passion. For the past two years, through lack of interest in anything but one thing, him, I fear that my brain has gone rusty. But I can rub the rust off.

I have a longing to be buried in heaps of books and papers, all by myself, oblivious of the world around me. 'Hurry up, hurry up to that end,' my heart clamours. Before I go away, however, I have a task to fulfil. I must see Sŏnhi settled down with Chinmo. They are going to get married in the autumn. When I am alone and all around me is quiet, I think of her, calling, 'Sŏnhi, Sŏnhi.' My eyes brim with tears. How shall I part from her? For the next few months, I will give her everything – my thoughts and love, and help her to plan her wedding.

10 June. A letter from Kwŏn. Even though I can understand that he is conscious of the censorship of his incoming and outgoing letters, need he be so false? As if he had not received my letter, he is asking me to send him five thousand Hwan, a big drop from fifteen thousand. At first I thought I would write back saying that I am unable to extract that much out of my tightly worked-out budget as from now on I am set to live within the limits of my income, but in the end I decided to ignore his letter.

The rain has cleared and fresh air wafts through the open window. Trying hard to fight back depression. Don't look back, just look ahead.

14 June. A letter from Fr. Osbourne, which set my poor heart trembling with excitement. Apparently the Bishop is looking for a woman candidate to assist in his new project. He is going to start social work in a poor area in Kangwon Province. He would like to send her to England for training for a year or two. Fr. Osbourne says he could recommend me if I wished. 'Would I like to think about it?' he says. There is no question of thinking about it, is there? I am dying to get out of here on any excuse and social work would suit my temperament. I would like to say 'Yes, please,' at once but to show that my decision is made after serious consideration, I will put off writing for a day or two.

Today, I cannot see the view outside without deep emotion – clumps of cloud floating by in the sky, the avenue of planes below the window, and set back behind the town, the poor people's houses clustered closely along the slope of a bare hill. They pluck at my heartstrings with peculiar sharpness. Some day in future, sitting beneath a foreign sky, with what tenderness shall I miss them all. Even though I know I have to go away, the thought of leaving it all, the Academy, my beloved family and friends and the hills and rivers makes me weep.

But is it because of this love that I am now reluctant to say 'yes' to Fr. Osbourne's offer? Of course, not. Still bound in a tight net of debt, I am not yet free to go.

At the time of Kwŏn's arrest my debts were eight hundred thousand Hwan. I have reduced the great bulk since then but I still have to pay out a considerable sum each month for the *kae* and interests for other loans. I have worked out that at this rate, I shall be free of all debt by August next year. Before that I cannot think of going away. I must explain this to Fr. Os.

15 June. Why was I so excited? I mock myself of yesterday. I have written to Fr. Os. In a dream Kwŏn appeared with rugged face. I cannot shake off the image. I have never seen him like that. When he was angry, his face turned rather expressionless, blank. Is he going to haunt me every night in this way? Flowers in the vase are limp for I have not changed the water for several days.

21 June. A brief letter from Fr. Os. I made a wise decision, he says. The thought of having missed a good opportunity saddens me.

I gave Sŏnhi a nice birthday, her last one as Miss Yun. I cooked the dinner all day by myself and invited Chinmo. He was quite impressed with my cooking. I could not help feeling sad at the memories of that disastrous birthday two years ago. One thing leads to another. I could not help thinking about Kwŏn sitting in the prison cell still waiting for me to turn up, day after day, hope against hope. He will never believe that I have changed, will he? One day he will know I meant it.

24 June. Kwŏn appeared again in dream with an evil expression on his face. I was fiercely fighting back his attempt to get at me. Awakened by my scream, Sŏnhi woke me up. Drenched in sweat, my body turned into gooseflesh. The cool touch of rayon bed sheet on my skin made me shudder and the warmth of my body was unpleasant too. I felt ill. I am going to have a nervous breakdown, I thought. Unable to go back to sleep I lay awake all night.

If he were a truly gallant man as I had trusted and as he had made out to be at the beginning, he would not blame or resent me now for turning away from him or whatever course I chose. But, probably he was not. A man with the least decency could not have been so thoroughly wicked however he was forced to be. More likely he belongs to a species that flourishes in turbid currents and dances about boisterously in a dark world.

I have many unanswered questions about him, but whatever his true identity, there is little doubt that he is an evil man. Until now he has tried to show me that he is a good man but when he finally realizes that what I wrote to him was true, I tremble as I imagine his evil face after he has cast off the mask of a gentleman.

What will become of me? The seeds I have sown have not reached their harvest yet. I am not free from my commitments of the past two years. From the moment he gives me up what dreadful scheme will he plot to trap me? How well I know his skilful psychological tricks and manoeuvres...If he does not want to let me go free, but intends to trick me back, I feel sure that I shall be trapped sooner or later.

I have started going to the early mass again every day.

30 June. Ah, Myŏngsŏk's tragedy deepens. I hate him and then love him and feel sorry for him. I have sat up for two nights on a chair before my desk without getting into bed on the floor. When I was overwhelmed by exhaustion I rested my head on the desk, dozed off, and then awoke. It was to show Myŏngsŏk how I could stick to my own words. I had said 'I will not bring myself so low as to lie down on the same floor with a coward like you.' After sleepless nights, my work at the Academy suffered. My nerves are thin and I had to grit my teeth not to break into hysterics.

Myŏngsŏk came a few days ago. Somehow he had found out our address. Sometime ago father called in and told us a sad story about him. After eating a bowl of meat soup from a market stall, he had been very ill. His hands and feet had swollen and his face broke out in rashes.

'I can't bear to think of his suffering.' Father was distraught. Sŏnhi cried as she beat her chest. I kept a calm surface but inwardly I was sore with remorse. If only I had been able to spend on him half the money I had wasted on Kwŏn he could have been saved. He would have been a college student and a BA next year. Ah, how is it that I have squandered my life in this way, when my own family could have benefited so much from even a little bit of help.

So when four days ago, Myŏngsŏk unexpectedly walked into the courtyard calling 'Sister', Sŏnhi and I ran down the verandah to embrace him. His hands and clothes were so dirty he looked like a beggar. We sent him off to the public bath-house, while Sŏnhi went round to Chinmo's to borrow some spare clothes. No sooner had he eaten his fill than he stretched himself out unceremoniously on the floor and fell fast asleep. In our six-foot-square room there was hardly space for Sŏnhi and myself to lie down. After spending an uncomfortable night, we explained the situation to him. He seemed to appreciate it and agreed to go back to the country. We provided him with the bus fare and a little bit extra, and a spare set of clothes.

'Goodbye. Look after yourself, 'I said.

'As soon as we can, we will come down to see you,' added Sŏnhi.

In the evening we found him still there. This went on for four days, and on the last evening we found him sleeping drunk. He had done away with the decent clothes and was wearing his old rags. I was provoked. 'You are subhuman, base and cowardly,' I said. 'I will not bring myself so low as to lie down on the same floor with such a coward.' Then I sat up on the chair.

'So, you can't go until you exhaust your sisters' hospitality, is that it?' As I poured out such sharp words, I tried to read some sign of emotional upset in him but my venom might as well have been aimed at a brick wall. His nonchalant silence seemed to say, 'You'll never be able to physically lift my large body out of this room, so it's all right with me.'

Early this morning Sŏnhi went to Lady Lee's residence and fetched father as he is the only person Myŏngsŏk is still afraid of. As he stepped into the room father struck him in the face. 'Get out of here, you, shameless creature!'

Myŏngsŏk put his hands in front of his face and said, 'Please, don't hit me, I am still not well,' as he walked out of the room. His shoulders crouched forward and speaking in a strong country accent, it was a pathetic retreat for a man who was once the darling prince of his family. My heart ached all day. He must have spent all the money we gave him four days ago. So how did he get to the country? Is he sleeping underneath a bridge somewhere? I feel it is all my fault.

I want to live. I want to make a new start. If only I can be freed from debt I can catch up with my studies. It is not too late. I know I can do it. I remember Fr. Os. once saying that he could lend me interest-free money. Should I defy my pride and ask him whether it is still feasible?

Chapter 13

The Rally

Sŏnhi's marriage brought about a big change in my life. If my former life-style could be compared to that of a foal in the open field, now I lived as part of an orderly domesticity. Prior to the wedding there had been heated discussion in the family as to where I should go. Father insisted that the only proper thing was for me to come back to him however inconvenient it might be. Sŏnhi said I should come and live with her in her new home with Chinmo to which father objected saying it would be a disgrace for him to allow such a thing. As for me, all I wanted was to be left alone in a rented room. I longed to be free from all cares and human obligations, to be free to cry and laugh to my heart's content, to sit through the night reading and writing or go to bed at six in the evening if I so felt like it. Neither father nor my sister would let me alone. We were at an impasse until Chinmo came up with a practical solution. The house they were to have was rather big just for the two of them. They would be lonely on their own at times, so why didn't I come there as a lodger.

In this way I was installed in one of the spare rooms of Sŏnhi's new home. From the time when the suggestion was first made, I gave much thought as to my position in that family if I were to accept it. It was only when I was absolutely clear in my mind as to what to follow that I finally agreed to move in with them.

Until now, in my life with Sŏnhi, by some unspoken rule, I had been the boss of that simple domesticity, and partly because with her domesticated and caring nature, Sŏnhi took it upon herself to wait on me always.

In the new hierarchy, obviously my brother-in-law was at the top. Second was Sŏnhi as his wife and I was the third. As the third, I had to maintain a certain decorum and respect for them as my seniors. In return, however, I received love and care from them both. Unlike a hanger-on living off a newly-married couple, which I was indeed, I was treated with great love like that of parents for an only child, or like the love that the youngest sister gets from her elder brother and sister, or indeed both put together.

In general the three of us got on very well. Chinmo and I often argued heatedly about politics and other intellectual matters while Sŏnhi prepared tasty midnight snacks.

I had to give up my habit of roaming the streets to be home in time for the family supper. If I could not make it I phoned Chinmo at work, for private telephones were rare in those days, to let him know. Even so, there were times when I was inevitably late. At such times, I no longer gobbled up the cold rice with any bits of left-over side dishes. Sŏnhi herself brought a neat meal table with a warm bowl of rice, hot soup and other tasty dishes into my room. My room was kept warm and tidy, and my clothes were laundered as soon as I had put them in the laundry basket.

In the name of a lodger's fee, I was paying only a nominal sum, but I made sure that without fail I handed it over to Sŏnhi on the last day of each month. Even though she was my sister, she was now a married woman and I thought that a certain formality ought to be observed.

I borrowed a large sum of interest-free money from Fr. Osbourne to pay off my high interest debt. It made a big difference to my future prospects. By paying back the money a little at a time I would be free of debt by next spring.

Since becoming Sŏnhi's lodger, my health greatly improved. Though at times I felt restricted and missed the freedom of the past, regular meals and a good night's sleep were doing me a world of good. After passing on my old quilt to Kŭmok, the maid, I now slept on a silk mattress with a quilt padded with a thick layer of cotton-wool. On the cold winter nights, getting into a soft bed laid out on the hot *ondol* floor was a heavenly comfort.

Kŭmok was the maid at Sŏnhi's new home, on the fourth place in our domestic hierarchy. A girl of merely fourteen, she had already served in several homes. She was mature for her age and gave the impression of a withered old woman, but beneath her grim look, she had preserved the untainted innocence of a child. She reckoned she was lucky to have found a home like ours – only three adults with no kids. I had not liked Sŏnhi's decision that I should have Kŭmok sleeping in my room to look after me as I still slept badly. Though I seemed to rapidly recover physically, my shattered nerves were slow to heal. I often had nightmares, cried loudly, and woke up drenched in cold sweat.

On the first night with her, I could not help feeling uncomfortable as I scrutinized her. Her grim face was slightly pockmarked and had a perpetual frown, and her hands were chaffed and gnarled like twigs. But within a few days, we became close to each other, the frown on her face being replaced by a cheeky grin. Her goodness poured forth. Unlike a paid employee, she simply loved Sŏnhi and Chinmo and me. She was particularly devoted to me.

One day, coming home, I found a new bookcase in my room. Apparently it was a belated wedding gift from a friend of Chinmo but as he had no need for it at present, Sŏnhi had decided to put it in my room. Unable to afford to buy myself a bookcase, I had kept my books piled up against the wall in the corners of the room.

'Auntie,' Kŭmok came running out with a proud smile, 'I have put all your books on the shelf.' As I entered the room, I repressed a wry smile. I could not have expected the books be in any order but neither in such disorder. They were jumbled together with some upside down. She was illiterate to the extreme. She could not distinguish English books from Korean.

That evening I was absorbed in *A Farewell to Arms* when I felt her eyes on me. I put it down and looked at her. She must have stared at me for a long time.

'Is that an English book?' she said. I nodded.

'How I wish I could read. If only I could read letters from my father, I would envy nothing in the whole world.' She sighed and started to roll out the bedding. As I lay in bed, I thought, I might be able to teach her to read. When I suggested this the next day, she squeezed my hands tightly as she cried, 'Auntie!'

'Just to think that I shall be able to read my father's letters and books too, one day!' She could not contain her excitement and jumped up and down like a little child.

We set to work. Firstly, I explained to her the principle of how the consonants and vowels are combined to make one letter, and started with the first lots of consonants. But, alas, it was not as easy as I had imagined to teach a person who had missed the right time to learn certain things. Her unpractised brain did not seem to be able to take in or register the simplest thing. Until a week was out, she could not memorize the first five consonants. She tried hard day and night but as soon as she sounded, 'g, n, d, r, m', the first five sounds of the Korean Alphabet, she ended up in a fit of giggles as if tickled to death by her own voice.

After ten days, she gave it up. Instead she launched a new appeal, reciting it every night like a religious creed. 'Auntie, please promise me one thing that when you get married, you'll take me with you.

'Please promise me that you will not drop me.

'That's all I want in my life. I will want nothing. I don't need to learn to read or write.

'I will do anything for you, auntie.'

Even though I could not entirely shake off attacks of depression and melancholy, I became more cheerful and light-hearted after I had sent off the letter to Kwŏn in June. I often walked along the bank of the River Han deep in thought. '"Human life lies in the hands of Heaven", they say. It had been my great mistake from the beginning, and an unbearable burden to think that Kwŏn's life lay in my hands. "A man appointed to drown will drown in a saucer of water", the proverb says. If he had been fated to die, he would have already died in all sorts of ways. If he is to live, on the other hand, he will live through all kinds of dangers in future without my aid. He is far beyond me. I have done all I can for him, and from now on I will leave him in the hands of Heaven.'

As I crossed the bridge over the river, I stopped at one point and leaned on the parapet. Below me the dark stream flowed writhing like a huge reptile. I took the ruby ring off my finger. It had been there as if symbolizing the chains of fate. I would defy fate, I thought. Without a moment's hesitation I dropped it into the river.

As I typed the minutes of yesterday's Board meeting, from the notes made by Dr Kang, I learned that, at the meeting, Mr Sangjin Hyŏn's paper entitled 'The Prospects of Korean Diplomacy' had been chosen as the Academy Award winner of the year. Mr Hyŏn had been a member of the Academy for over a year now. He now and again turned up at the Reading Room. Tangled in a strange fate and always on the alert against people around me lest my words or behaviour gave some clue to my secret life, I had put on an attitude of coolness or indifference towards him. If I saw him in the library, I gave him a formal greeting as I did to the other members and clients, never giving him the chance to approach me and engage me in an intimate talk. He did not seem to mind, nor did he try to approach me other than as an officer of the library. He had not been to the Reading Room for a long time, but today he turned up at the office. It was obvious that he had heard the news and came to see the director. I can't explain just why I showed such an exaggerated reaction on seeing him.

'Congratulations! I am really pleased for you.' I must admit I was pleased indeed to see him particularly now as a liberated woman since I had cast the ring away the day before. He smiled gently as he asked whether he could see Dr Kang. He came out of the director's room a few minutes before closing time and as I walked out of the office, I saw him waiting outside.

'Are you in a talking mood today?' He said at once. He quickly searched my face and must have read consent. 'Let's go. I'll buy you some dinner.'

We sat in the Hanil-kwan Restaurant. He had a couple of drinks with the meal. I was painfully aware that while I had been in the dark valley, I had lost all my social confidence. My habit of shunning people now put me on the alert against him. He belonged to a different valley from mine, the bright side of the sun. I decided to keep my mouth shut and just to listen.

He had been quietly drinking for a while when he said, 'Why are you in such an anguish? What is it that makes you so sad – can you not tell me?'

'What penetrating eyes,' I thought, 'like a detective's, trying to get inside the defendant's mind. I am not letting him into mine.'

'What anguish? What makes you think that I am sad?' I said in a flippant, joking tone but he looked serious. He was intense without his usual touch of humour or relaxed banter.

'Do you think I don't know? Does a woman who's not in anguish walk soaking wet through rain from one end of the town to the other? A woman not in anguish – why would she choose the darkest corner in a tea-room and sit for three-quarters of an hour with closed eyes? Can you tell me why a woman who's not sad comes out of a cinema, after seeing a comedy, weeping?'

It was true since Kwŏn had been put in prison, I had often walked the streets aimlessly for hours on end, sometimes breaking down in tears in cinemas or tea-rooms.

'If you saw me you might have said "Hello", instead of following me all the way from one end of the town to the other like a detective.' This thought crossed my mind but I just waited his next words.

'I saw you walking with a gentleman in a traditional Korean suit. I thought you were going to marry him and expected the invitation, which never came. Can you blame me for following you without stopping you? Do you think I don't know that you try to keep me at distance? How could I approach you when you are being deliberately cold to me like that?'

He emptied his glass, smiled and changed his tone into a gentler one as he said, 'Today, you were different. More like you when you were a student. What's the matter? Why are you being like this? So elusive, like the "Peepy Bird".

'Do you know that song? I don't know what the bird looks like but I do know what it's like.'

He started singing the song in a low mumble. I knew every word of it because as a little girl I sang it solo at a school concert, and all children of my generation knew it.

As if to be seen, you sound so near,
Peepy, peepy, peepy bird, how sadly you sing.
When you leave here, pray where do you go.

To the place my mother has gone,
where the sun rises.

As if to be caught, you sound so close,
Peepy, peepy, peepy bird, what a mournful song.
When you leave here, pray where do you go.
To where my mother is,
Where the moon rises.

I had to repress my impulse to sing it with him. No words
were needed as I knew perfectly what he meant. He was still
humming it to himself even when we were out of the restaurant and walking towards the bus stop.

He suddenly stopped and looked at me. 'Look, Sukey. In
such a time and age as this why does a woman like you have
agonies?' It provoked an argument.

'In such a time and age as this, who does not have agonies?
– that would be more to the point, I should think.'

'Nonsense. I thought you were a clever woman but
you must be a dim-wit. A good-looking and intelligent
woman with a good education like you should not suffer.
What is there that you can't have or who is going to stop
you doing whatever you want? In all our history, has there
ever been a time when women had been so blessed with
opportunities?

'You might say this or that but you cannot deny that the
country's liberation brought the liberation of womenfolk and
it's now a women's paradise. Everything is within your grasp
if only you have the will. The competition is not as harsh as in
man's world. You have all the advantages, haven't you, Sukey?
– Good looks, intelligence and education...'

'I don't have any of those.'

'Huh, you are a proper idiot. Why don't you get married?'

Suddenly the memory of that night, three years ago, shortly before he went to the States, came back to my mind. I almost fancied we had gone back to that point in time.

'Well, why don't you,' I said. 'If you were married yourself and advised me to do likewise, I would at least be ready to listen'

'Ha ha ha.'

'Ha ha ha.' We both broke into helpless laughter. It was the purest and heartiest laughter I had had in a long time. A tight knot in my heart seemed to loosen as warmth spread through my body like alcohol.

'Listen to me,' he said. 'Do you know what is a "Life at three p.m."?'

'I suppose that comes from the dictionary of your home-made vocabulary? How can an idiot like me know such things?'

'Say, lunch time is one and supper time six. Carried away with a medley of things, one missed his lunch. Three o'clock − it is a bit of an awkward time, isn't it. Too late for going back to lunch and too early for supper. So there we are. That is "Life at three p.m."' He gave a chuckle. 'Now, what about some coffee?'

If we went on like this, talking freely, I felt, I would end up opening my heart and letting the secret out. I said I had to go. He did not seem to mind and saw me off on the bus. Through the back window I saw him walking away in measured strides.

I was well cared for at home and had a good job, so I could be content as far as appearances went. But in reality I was a broken woman in spiritual chaos, drifting aimlessly on a muddy current of memories in the aftermath of a flood. The one who helped me to sustain some mental stability in those days was Fr. Osbourne. I had to see him once a month to pay back by instalment the five hundred thousand Hwan I had borrowed.

He was a mysterious man – all foreigners are, I suppose, until you get to know them better. Sometimes our transaction took a few minutes. I handed over the money and he said, 'Thank you,' and we said 'Goodbye' and I turned and came away. At other times it extended to a long chat and developed into a fascinating discussion after which I felt enlightened and wiser. I had never had such profound conversations with any one before. Yes, there had been Mr Hyŏn but it had been in the days before my fall. The arguments Miae and I used to have with him seemed naive and I often looked back at them with nostalgia.

Fr. Osbourne said he was experiencing a change taking place in the faith and philosophy that he had held firmly all his life. Such ideas as 'Dogmatic Christians can do more harm to society than humanistic atheists,' or 'Jesus is a person who lived in particular historical time and it was not he himself who claimed that he was the son of God,' are now commonplace but in those days were like earth-shattering blasphemies to an uncritical believer like myself. But each shock was followed by the opening up of my inner vision into a new world.

He said that the Man, Jesus, was the person he admired most and another man who fascinated him most at present, besides Jesus was Nietzsche.

'How come,' I protested, 'That a priest devoted to Christ and his teachings can admire another man who is an emblem of anti-religion, nihilism? Your love must be like that of a butterfly.'

He smiled at my indignation and said, 'Well, you maybe right. I suppose it is my innate nature to roam about from one place to another instead of settling down and doing one thing. That's why a man born in England finds himself at this end of the earth.' After a pause he said, 'Sometimes, you find common ground in two extreme opposite doctrines that you'd think could never exist. I find infinite possibilities in such assumptions?'

On subjects such as religion or philosophy, he was too clever for me. I could not be his match. He knew this, and steered the discussion gently as he avoided using technical terms for my benefit. The subject where we found comfortable common ground was literature. He was most lively when we talked about an English novel. I could talk a lot about Korean literature. As far as Western literature was concerned I was a novice and I blindly followed his lead. It was thus that under his influence I began to read novels of his recommendation. He was passionate about Joseph Conrad, Thomas Mann and James Joyce. In this way I was getting to know him better and as I got to know him better a completely different person emerged from behind the mask of shy, modest, saintly foreigner.

Amongst the people he lived with, he was known as a saint. I soon found out that it was not because he was particularly pious in his faith or in recognition of his wisdom, but it originated from his charitable deeds and his indifference to material things and worldly conventions. He lived among poor people, most of his congregation being poor farmers. On the other hand he also had friends among the well-to-do. He treated them with equal cordiality as if to him such a thing as social class did not exist. Some of his church members living five miles away from Anp'yŏng came there on Saturday night to attend the Sunday morning mass. They slept the night on the matted floor of the study-cum-visitors' room of the clergy house.

Amongst his regular visitors were a couple of professors of English literature from universities in Seoul and some distinguished theologians. After talking late with him on their weekend visits, they also slept in this modest room amongst the farmers from the village. He kept his life-style to the basics and gave away what was left of his income to people in need.

In the leper colony that he had started in a village in Kangwŏn Province, a community of some thirty people had now established a modest form of self-supportive life by means of farming and raising poultry. Fr. Osbourne visited them fortnightly and gave them the Communion. What Chaehong had told me often came to my mind as to how Fr. Osbourne looked at home among the lepers whom the outside world regarded as monsters condemned by God. He happily spent the morning with them and for lunch he took a couple of boiled eggs with a cup of sweetened water offered by mangled, fingerless hands.

When he was in Seoul, I had a couple of occasions to walk with him through the streets after work. A dozen beggars approached and greeted him from under eaves or alley ways.

'Hello, Father, when did you come?'

'Are you well, Father? It's good to see you again.'

He replied to every one with gentle smile, thrust his hand into his inner breast pocket, took out a hundred Hwan note and politely handed it to him with two hands as if he was offering it to his superior.

I was to meet Fr. Osbourne in the evening at the Cathedral to pay him the December instalment. My sister asked me whether I could bring him over to her house for supper. She wanted to give him a treat as a token of the gratitude she felt. She often said that she would never forget his wise words to me when some time ago he had said that it was about time that I took more care of my own health.

It was at rather short notice, I thought, but if he had no other engagement that evening he might not mind coming over. I gave a hand with preparing a nice little feast. She was chopping, mincing and slicing all day. Then as I was setting off, it occurred to me that as it was Friday, he might wish to abstain from eating meat like some Christians do.

'How awful!' Sŏnhi was in despair. 'What shall we do with all these food?'

Chinmo popped his head round the door and said, 'Don't worry. If the Father can't come I can provide a replacement on the spot.'

'Who is that?' Sŏnhi and I looked at him earnestly.

'Mr Sangjin Hyŏn. He's as good as Fr. Osbourne in paying court to Sukey, isn't he, even though Hyŏn is a bit more ardent than the other.' Then he broke into laughter.

'You are crazy, *hyŏngbu*!' I protested as I flushed. 'Anyway I'll go and see what he says.' I ran out of the house.

From Shinchon bus terminal, if you followed the main road in the direction of the H University, you soon crossed a small stone bridge. A few metres further along the road, you could take the first turn left onto a small path weaving through some vegetable plots. After some three hundred metres or so this path joined onto another road, which in fact ran parallel to the main road you had just left. Follow it about two hundred metres and you came to a flight of five or six stone steps and the road ended there. Walk up the steps and you found yourself on a newish road running parallel to the steps. Turn right here and follow the road and you would come out back on the main road. Where the stone steps met this road was a new housing estate with a dozen smart houses in western style. Sŏnhi and Chinmo had recently moved into one of them and I came with them. Sŏnhi's new house had three fences, one on each side and another at the back, but not in the front. Step out the porch and you were right on the road. Kŭmok and I shared the room attached to the porch with our window opening onto the road.

On our first night there, a burglar came. Just after twelve I was about to fall asleep when I heard the sound of the glass panel of the outer window being cut. It was a double window. If you removed the frosted glass of the outer one, there was an inner sliding window of rice paper, easy to break, and behind it, on the window sill sat a clock, a transistor radio and a camera.

I raised the alarm and all the family woke up. The burglar ran away. Towards dawn, this silly person came back, though we could not be sure it was the same one. This time it was Kŭmok who was woken up by the glass-cutting sound. Scared, she called out as loud as she could, 'Burglar! Burglar! Auntie! Uncle!'

In the morning we found that the corners of her mouth were congealed with blood. In her fright she had tried to open her mouth too wide. We were all helpless with laughter. Either the burglar was stupid, assuming it was the same one, or the security in that area was poor, as he came back for several days in succession and did not get anything. We were too smart for him but it was a nuisance. In the name of the head of the house, I put on the window outside a little note:

Mr Burglar,

I am in sympathy with you for working hard every night in vain. Shall I give you a tip? However hard you try you won't get anything from this house in a hundred days. My wife suffers from insomnia and the very first scratch on the window makes her jump out of bed. She is becoming hysterical over your nightly visit and it's becoming hard on me. Why don't we meet somewhere face to face and I will treat you to a decent meal.

Head of the house.

Whether this note had any effect or it was thanks to Chinmo's request to the police for a night petrol in the area, the burglar stopped coming.

I had first noticed the nameplate, 'Woojin Hyŏn' above the gate of the house, a few metres down the road from the stone steps, when we were looking round the village, house hunting with an old man from the estate agent. It reminded me of Sangjin Hyŏn and ever since I could not pass the house without looking up at the plate. It was more than a month since we had moved into the new house when, one day, I came face to face with Mr Sangjin Hyŏn at the bus terminal. Instinctively I realized the name plate must have been his elder brother's.

'Fancy, "Two enemies meeting on a log-bridge" as they say.' He did not understand what I meant at first. I could no longer hide where I lived. When he stood in front of our house, he broke into laughter. Apparently he had seen my note stuck on the window and was so curious to know the writer of it that he had been meaning to call in.

He had lived there with his brother and his family for nearly two years, after selling their house in Tonamdong where Miae and I used to visit him.

I asked him in. Sŏnhi had heard a lot about him and Chinmo hit it off with him straight away. It was indeed strange that I had come to live in his neighbourhood out of all places.

Sometimes we were on the same bus coming home. On the evening rush hour buses, people were like goods piled on top of one another. When I did not have anything to hold onto, standing beside him I flopped about like a leaf in the wind. He would whisper to me, 'Hold onto me.' I shook my head as I jokingly whispered back, 'I am not a weakling who can't stand on my own feet.' He smiled and did not insist.

Fr. Osbourne was delighted with the invitation.

'I was worried that you might be fasting today.'

'I should be forgiven on a special occasion like this,' he said. All went pleasantly with the supper. Sŏnhi and Chinmo got on well with him. When I went out to see him off at the bus terminal the signboards of the Azalea tea-room caught my eyes. It had recently been refurbished and had reputation for good music. I offered to buy him coffee there. As we entered, the room was vibrating with the blast of the last bars of Beethoven's fifth symphony. I had meant to have a quick cup of coffee and go home but it was a couple of hours before we left.

'I wish I had clear views on things and knew how to find my own intellectual nourishment like you must do,' I said, and went on, 'My life has been so wasteful. All I have been obsessed with was my own comfort and selfish desires and I've done nothing for my family or society or the country, and I am now nearing thirty, and still just drifting. Some nights I lie awake thinking how pathetically I have squandered my life.

'In the same way as my past has been wasted my future will come and go too, won't it?'

'I think,' Fr. Osbourne said, 'a priest with too strong views can be more harmful to society than a woman with empty hands in search of a meaningful life. I started at a theological college when I was thirty. There, for a time, I thought I had at last grasped a truth worthy of all my life's dedication. But now, nearing forty, my convictions are beginning to shake and I doubt whether what I have believed is the truth, the real truth. I can't think that a man like me is in any better position than you are.'

'I suppose, that is how the meaning of life grows and expands,' I said. 'It makes me think of a never-ending sea voyage. Each time the ship anchors at a new harbour it gets ready to sail on and explore further. To give up at one port for good is to die. Likewise, when you stop thinking, you are as good as dead. Do you agree?' I went on talking as if to myself.

'At present I live at my sister's home comfortably enough as if I had no worries in the world. But at the bottom of my heart I know it is not where I want to stay. I must set sail again, but where to?

'As they say "one who has no experience of weeping all through the night has no right to talk about human sorrow."

Probably you have no such experience, so you would not appreciate such anguish, would you?'

'That's why I respect people with sorrows,' he said. 'And admire your courage through your hard experiences. Have you any idea of what you would like to do?' Then he added, 'By the way, have you given up the idea of taking your own life?'

'Yes, thanks to you. I've got over that stage now. I want to live, to make a new start but it all feels like useless dreams. I don't know how and where to start.'

'Didn't you study politics at college?'

'Yes, politics and diplomacy to be correct. But it means little to me now. Looking back, even my motivation for choosing that subject seems childish.

'My father had been at the height of his political career when I left high school and was ready to go to college. He was a marvellous orator and often made speeches in front of large audiences. I loved to be there, sitting among them. The structure and contents of his speeches were excellent and his clear, ringing voice arresting. He never had a manuscript before him, not even as much as a note. When he paused, the silence in the auditorium was so absolute that you could hear a pin drop. His speeches invariably ended amidst a terrific applause and cheers...'

Here I felt my voice quiver as memories of my father who had been the hero of my childhood, rose vividly before my eyes. Now he was a fallen star proving that the prosperity of human life was nothing more than a passing mirage. I continued in a deflated tone of voice.

'He was really fantastic. I thought that was politics – to be in the limelight, applauded and worshipped by the crowd. I wanted to become like him. In short, I chose politics for childish heroism.

'By the time I got through the hard competition of the entrance examinations, I had lost interest in the subject. I managed to keep up with the course at the minimum grades and spent an awful lot of time stealing into lectures on literature and philosophy in others' classrooms.'

The music had changed several times and I kept reminding myself that I ought to be going but I continued to talk.

'I must get away from here as soon as I can. I think that's the only way I can revive.'

'Abroad?'

'Yes.'

'To America?'

'That is the easiest.'

'What would you do there?'

'Library science is the easiest option. It is hardly a scholarly subject but my experience here will be advantage and librarianship is regarded as a decent job for women in America apparently. Besides, am I in a position to be fussy about the type of employment now? I will take anything that comes first and easiest. When I am settled down and independent, then I can change my ideas and interest, can't I, like you do?' He immediately understood what I meant by 'change my ideas...like you do,' and smiled.

After a long silence, he rather abruptly said, 'Why don't you write novel?'

This word had magic power that seemed to enter and hit some vital spot somewhere inside me. Yes, becoming a writer is one possibility. He talked on about various things but I was not paying much attention as a vague thought brewed up and was shaping itself that I was going to write some day. Strange, I thought. This man, a foreigner, had for the second time shown me a landmark with his words in the charting of the course of my life, as I recalled how his words about a marriage, on my last day at the hospital last June had set me off to critically analyse my relationship with Kwŏn.

YP Club Night was a monthly reunion of graduates, old and young, from the department of Political Science of Y University. This year the December meeting was combined with a celebration of the publication of Mr Hyŏn's paper, which had won the Academy award earlier in the year. Being out of practice at going to parties I was nervous at first, but I was soon swept into the friendly atmosphere and was enjoying myself thoroughly. Dr Kang was there, not only as the director of the Academy but also as a lecturer in the Department of Politics. Some members of the Board were present too. As I whispered to myself, 'I'm glad I came. It was the best thing that I've ever done to break off that dreadful chain,' my eyes brimmed with tears. I felt like embracing everyone and telling them my story.

The formal part of the evening closed with the singing of the college anthem. After that most of the elders left and the party carried on in an informal way. Soon there were only Mr Hyŏn and his close friends and a few younger ones. It was then that someone started playing a medley of popular classic music on the piano: Wings of the Songs, Ave Maria, Caro Mioben, Largo.

A few of us gathered round the piano and hummed the tunes. As the pianist broke into the prelude of La Traviata, there was a sudden hush, and all around was silent with expectation. I can't remember how it came about but I found myself singing with Mr Hyŏn the duet of Alfredo and Violetta in the first act. It was utterly unprepared and both the singers and the pianist were amateurs, so it was not very good but in some strange way we managed to keep up the spirit of the music, until conscious of the solemn atmosphere of the hall I broke into laughter and broke the solemnity. But the excitement I felt as we sang could not easily be dismissed.

Outside, the first snow of the year had fallen and lay on the ground and was still falling. Mr Hyŏn and I started walking towards home. We had not agreed on this but walked all the way. At first, in total silence, but past Sŏdaemun, he started singing the snow song. To begin with I just hummed but eventually joined in and we sang it together repeatedly.

Snow was falling over the hills and rivers
The whole world lay white, pure white
I walked with my lover aimlessly, endlessly
Till the night turned to dawn.
Now the snow is falling like it was then....

At the entrance to our village Mr Hyŏn suddenly came to a halt. The snow had stopped and all around us was a white expanse on which a bluish sheen of moonlight poured down. He took a deep breath, lifted his face to the moon and broke into a solo in a vibrating tenor, the last verse of a farewell song as if singing a finale of a magnificent opera.

Some nights when the hills and rivers are deep in snow,
I shall light a candle, and beneath its light shall weep alone
Ah, ah, you must go your way, and so must I mine.

In front of our house, he said, 'Good night,' turned round, and ran quickly down the stone steps like a man running away.

It was late but I did not feel tired. Without bothering to change I flopped down into the chair at the desk and started writing down my feelings in my diary. Then I took out the old ones and read them all, going over the story from the very beginning to the last – there had been things I could not even write down freely lest they might be found and read by some detectives.

Even though the story seemed to have ended, on my side at least, there was no telling how the seeds sown in the past two years might sprout and grow. It was my fate to bear it alone to the end. I could not share it with any one.

I did not have to hold back my tears. I let them flow freely so that it might wash down and soothe the pain of the scar.

It was past two o'clock. Kŭmok slept, breathing deeply. There was a light tap on the window, twice. I knew it was Mr Hyŏn. As if I had been waiting for him, I stepped out of the porch and stood before him. Reflecting the chilly light of setting moon cast on the snow, his face was extremely pale.

'Why are you not in bed?'

'I knew you would be coming.'

'You've been crying. Why are you persecuting yourself in this way? Pray, what is it?'

His voice was low but every word he uttered went straight to my heart, beating on it like a hammer. Suddenly, tiredness surged up with such enormous force that I felt like fainting.

'I won't say any more. I just want to hear from you one word, "Yes" or "No".'

I closed my eye as I leaned my head against the door frame. I did not know how long I had been like that.

'It is "No". Please go.'

He went away and never again appeared before my eyes. Soon after that his family moved away from the village.

Chapter 14

Vicissitude – A Chronicle of Christmas and the New Year

17 December. '*Onni*, a letter for you.'

From the way Suyŏn approached me I could sense that it was not a welcome letter. It was from Kwŏn. Thanks to a Christmas parole given to model prisoners, he was due to be released on 22nd of December. Whether or not he had received the letter I sent him last June announcing my intention to break with him, he had put down a detailed checklist of items that I should send in before his release. I did not bother to read them. I will not follow his instructions. I crushed the letter in my hand and closed my eyes to remind myself that I must never again get involved with him, I must try to wipe him out of my mind. His life now lay not in my hands but those of Heaven. Despite this firm resolve, I could not help shaking all over.

23 December. I have kept away from work. In no way, could I face the possibility of meeting him. But I cannot shake off the thought of him. Even at this very moment, he will be hanging around the Academy. He may have chosen a place from which he can spot me coming out of the front door. Oh, the horror! I feel more pity for him than hatred. Within the limits of my imagination, he must be the shabbiest and most miserable-looking beggar. Has he really got no place to go to in the whole world? What will become of him? Tong-hi Kwŏn, Changho Yu, and Chŏlsu Kim – which one of these is his real name? Do any of the women associated with him in the past two years know what is happening to him now? – Yuni's grandmother, Julie, Madame Kim, Hwaja...

Staff Christmas party. Suyŏn came to fetch me at the request of Dr Kang. If I was not too bad, would I mind making an appearance at the party even briefly? I braced myself and set out with her but my legs were so weak I could hardly walk. Obsessed by the thought of him roaming around my home ground, I saw him in every man with spectacles, every man of his stature, and every one pushing open the door of the Reading Room, and each time my heart thumped.

If we both go on living long enough we may come to face to face some day but I want to give him plenty of time to sort out his own life.

The party went all right, good fun at times and awkward and embarrassing at others. When it was nearly over Sŏnhi and Chinmo came to escort me home.

24 December. Afraid of a possible encounter with him, I stayed away from work yet again. But I had to go out because Chinmo was to be confirmed in the Anglican Cathedral at two o'clock. I had to be there. I was the one who had converted him to the church shortly before his marriage and even though he may not be a devout Christian, he seemed rather excited and nervous about it.

From the moment I stepped out the porch my heart beat fast. I ran all the way to the bus stop, and all the way to the church after getting off the bus at Sejongro. I felt as if he would run out some corner at any moment calling out, 'Sukey!'

When I saw Sŏnhi in the Cathedral shortly before two, I could sense she had something on mind. I urged her to come out with it. What she told me amounts to this: She had a phone call from Kwŏn during the morning.

'It is me, Tong-hi Kwŏn,' he said. He received a chilly reception. He said that he would not go into the past but as he was intending to leave Seoul, he would be grateful if we would let him have his clothes.

'Sukey is now engaged to a man who understands everything,' she said. 'We burned all your belongings in front of the grave of our mother as she swore to her soul that she would never see you again.' He put phone down as he said he wished to congratulate me.

Then on her way to church just now she had seen him twice through the window of a bus she was on. He was walking with a woman in a mink coat. In a way it was comforting to know that he was with someone rich rather than with beggars, I thought then.

Who was the woman? It is too absurd of me even to be jealous, but inexplicable tears rise to my eyes. I can forget about him at last? I must wish him well.

Christmas Eve – after Midnight Mass.

We came back, the three of us, from Midnight Mass, blissfully happy. Chinmo was quite moved by his first communion and I was too because it had been my first for a long time as I had recently lapsed from church-going. I felt sure that the Christmas blessings would carry us through a happy new year.

Foolish of me! Vicissitude. The ever-changing face of human life. It changes not only from day to night but more like minute by minute. The sunny smile of fortune a minute ago turns into black despair the next.

I was about to fall into a blissful sleep, when Sŏnhi came over to my room. She said she could not leave it until the morning and gave me the latest news. Apparently Chinmo had seen Kwŏn in the church at the mass. He was sitting a couple of rows in front of him at the men's side. I asked how could Chinmo know him, as they had never met. But it turns out that he had seen Kwŏn once in the Reading Room at the Academy and another time on the bus home. Kwŏn was sitting next to me in a crowded bus and even though I had not noticed Chinmo, he had had a good look at him as he wondered whether or not he should speak to me. Besides, Chinmo's description of his attire leaves no room for doubt. He was apparently wearing a brown jacket over a brown polo-neck jumper, without an overcoat. These were some of the items I had sent him after his arrest. Without an overcoat on this bitter night! When she saw my troubled looks, Sŏnhi said that as a clever deceiver, he had appeared like that to arouse my sympathy.

She went back to her room saying that I should not trouble myself about him, but how could I not? What troubles me most is the thought that he might be truly reformed. A man who came out of prison to find his lover gone cold, flown away beyond his reach. He has reformed just a little too late.

With nowhere to go he must be sleeping underneath a bridge, cold, hungry and sad. I am fighting back a tide of emotion. If I lose this battle, I may set out in the morning in search of him. Ought I not to take him back?

Another voice in me says I must be on my guard. Don't I know what a crafty man he is? Am I so naive as to believe that a year in prison could have reformed him? He may try to win my sympathy by means of pathetic appearances at first, but when he realizes that it does not work he will change his tactics and act differently.

Human vicissitude. How my mind wavers and changes.

29 December. How foolish I was to think that he has left me for good. He will not give up his scheming until he has squeezed out the last drop of my sympathy.

Miss Pak had phone calls from a man for two days running. He asked her whether she was a friend of mine and told her that he was a friend of my boyfriend Mr Kim. Apparently Kim, who is seriously ill, is desperately asking for me. He wants to tell me about something very important. Could Miss Pak not cooperate with him in bringing the estranged lovers together? Miss Pak does not know anything about what is going on around me. She does not know that the man I have been trying to avoid for the last few days is the one that I met in Onyang, nor does she know who this Kim is, the alleged boyfriend of mine. All she knows is that I am entangled in some tricky situation that she is too polite to ask me about. She handed me a slip of paper with a telephone number and the man's name and passed on the exact words of the message with no comment of her own. She is wonderful in that way.

Of course I won't ring back. I must not show any response as I know all too well that it will give him the clue for his next move.

Sŏnhi takes me to the door of the Academy. If I have some business outside druing the day I send Suyŏn instead, and in the evening I am escorted home by Chinmo.

Tonight as we turned off the main road into our alley I saw a man standing at the corner. As soon as we approached he turned and disappeared into the darkness. I think I have been followed. Chinmo didn't seem to notice. I am uneasy. I can't shake off the fear of a sinister presence shadowing me, slowly but surely until it catches me. I feel as if I am trapped in some crime story and will end up as its victim. In a couple of days, Sŏnhi and Chinmo are going down to his home in the country for the New Year and I will be left alone with Kŭmok. I am really scared at the prospect. Kwŏn – at the very thought of him I shudder. Tonight I am afraid to go to sleep lest he should appear in my dream with evil looks. I imagine him saying, 'You are being thoroughly protected now but it won't be long before you fall into my trap. Just wait and see, shall we?' and he guffaws.

The vicissitude of human life! How can it be possible that a noble appearance that had overcome me with love too years ago has turned into a symbol of evil and fear?

New Year's Day. It has been a very special New Year's Eve. It was not the first time that Suyǒn had slept in my room. When this happened, Kǔmok slept in the spare room for visitors. Suyǒn and I have become very close since Sǒnhi's wedding day.

Looking back, it was the most beautiful wedding I had ever seen and a sad occasion to me. My poor parents could hardly give her a decent wedding present, but she did not complain and bore it with a graceful smile. She was such a beautiful bride and everybody admired her.

After the wedding I went to the railway station to see them off on their honeymoon. My effort not to show my tears was quite useless. After taking their seats on the train and putting Sǒnhi by the window, Chinmo came back to me.

'Look at you, crying like a big baby,' he said teasingly. 'Go home now and we'll see you on Saturday.' He went back on the train, and as it started moving Sǒnhi put out her hand through the open window to hold mine. I could see she also was trying hard to hold back her tears for it would ruin her eye make-up. Her hand was warm and soft. The moment she let go of it I felt like falling. When the train went out of my sight I didn't know which way to turn. I stood on the spot as if dazed, when some one came running down the flight of steps and wildly caught me by the shoulders. It was Suyǒn.

'*Onni*! I knew you would be like this. I meant to be here before the train left but couldn't quite make it even though I've run all the way.' She was breathless. 'Let's go.'

I had no desire to go anywhere or do anything. I let her manage my afternoon. She took me to a cheap cinema and then we sat in the Renaissance, a tea-room popular for its classic music. And in the evening she slept in my room and comforted me when I cried calling my sister in my sleep. Since then she has become like a member of the family, always welcome to stay and sleep or join in a family meal.

It was a wild night. Outside a gale must be raging. The wind was smashing against the telegraph post, and a piece of corrugated iron, probably blown off someone's roof was rolling about scratching on some hard surface.

A night sending off the old year and letting the new one in – I had never before had such complex emotions on New Year's Eve. What kept me awake were not only these emotions but the wild wind. I hate winds at the best of times. They make me restless. It is worse in the night. I imagine the air filled with rancorous ghosts howling, gnashing, cursing and tearing at each other. The spirits of people who had died resentful deaths, jealous of the happy people they left behind may even try and snatch the chance to play some mischief on them. Who knows if I may be picked on as the prey of such malice? How unsettling it all was.

'*Onni*, why aren't you sleeping?' Suyŏn had been lying so quiet I thought she was asleep.

'Sleep has deserted me. Why aren't you?'

Without replying to this she sat up bolt upright. 'Bother the sleep. Why don't we just talk?'

I got up and lit the blue night light on my desk. She looked up at me as she pushed back the long hair that had fallen over her face in bed. She had bright, intelligent eyes. She has grown more beautiful during the past year or so. She leads an exhausting life but she is like a flower bud in spring. There is that mysterious sap of youth that pushes the spring buds through the hard crust of the earth. Compared to her, I felt, I was like frost-bitten autumn grass.

'I have kept a secret from you,' she said.

'?'

'That woman called Hisun. When I saw her attacking you in that way, I didn't know what to do. I could not jump in and interfere when I had no clue to what it was about. So I went to see your sister. First I begged her not to tell you that I had been, and then I told her exactly what I had seen.'

'I see. So it was you!'

'I felt guilty, as if I was going behind your back but I could not just hang around doing nothing. I had no idea of who she was and what it was about. When I mentioned a woman with a mink muffler, your sister seemed to know her at once.'

Suyŏn did not sound as if she was asking for my forgiveness but more like demanding an explanation. I thought the time had come. I told her the whole story from the beginning to the end.

'What makes me sad and upset most now is not what happened in the past, or the fear of meeting him one of these days, but how could the me of one year ago become the me of the present? What am I but a changed, unfaithful woman?

'I make out as if I took Fr. Osbourne's comment about marriage, that it should be based on mutual love and respect, as advice to break off my relationship with Kwŏn, and by pointing out how he had wronged me in the past try to justify my abandoning him. Aren't these all excuses for my betrayal and cover for my guilty conscience?

'A year ago I was prepared to give myself to him whatever suffering that might have meant. Now I desperately try to get away from that suffering. I thought my life would be worthy because of a rare fidelity, straight and strong like bamboo.

'As the poet would say, "Hills and rivers are as ever, but humanity has changed!" Vicissitude, I suppose, is the right word.

'Nothing stands still. My mind changes by the minute, and I can't trust myself. Who knows? My heart may change overnight and in the morning I may set out in search of him and kneel down before him?'

We put out the light and went back to bed. Outside, the wind had not abated in the least. Resentful ghosts writhing in anguish, smashing against walls, as they dashed about criss-cross in all four directions, hoarsely crying.

'Poor man, he may be sleeping beneath some bridge, hungry and freezing without even a winter coat in this weather...' Weak tears flowed down my cheek and onto the pillow. Lest I woke up Suyŏn I quietly swallowed my sobs. But she was not asleep. In the dark she pushed her handkerchief into my palm. She must have been quietly weeping herself. She snuffled as she released a deep sigh. Had she been thinking of some comforting words for me as she silently wept or was it an impromptu. She gave me lengthy and truly impressive advice.

'Do you believe that blind fidelity or sacrifice can be a virtue? What does one sacrifice oneself for? Isn't it because the cause one is offering oneself for is something worthy, valuable?

'Could one sacrifice oneself for the sake of a worthless piece of wooden stick for instance? Take for example, the fidelity and chastity of widows, especially those widowed as no more than girls, which was so highly valued in our tradition, and consider why fewer people do it nowadays.

'In the old days the intellectual gap between an educated husband and his wife with no schooling must have been enormous, like the gap between earth and sky. A woman dared not go over the threshold of her husband's intellectual world. It was enshrouded in mystery. He must have looked wonderful to her, like God. Naturally, if he died she would remain faithful to his memory and his ghost all her life. What else? It was the only worthwhile life she could lead.

'In the modern world, things are different. Women get educated and some even have professional careers. So the mystery about the men's world is disappearing. Man is no longer such a wonderful being.

'The bamboo is a traditional image of unyielding fidelity, but bamboo is not an easy plant to grow. It is very fussy about its living conditions. It does not take to every soil and climate. If the climate is not to its liking it refuses to grow in the first place.

'God does not test us beyond what we can endure and you jolly well know that you cannot endure that burden again. If you volunteer to take it on again at this stage, you will only end up in swamp from which there will be no salvation for you. That cannot be God's will.'

I was impressed and moved by her logic and persuasiveness. When had she trained herself in this way? Without interrupting once, I attentively heard her through.

'I like the plain saying,' she went on. '"You feel different before and after going to the loo." It hits the nail on the head.

'Vicissitude, that is the biology of the universe. Life itself is ever-changing. Without change, what could the universe be? By the laws of nature water flows. Can you stop it? It's just you who is sad and crying about it.

'*Onni*, please be brave, and try to forget about it?'

The eastern window turned white. The wind outside seemed to have calmed down. The ghosts having had their bout overnight must have lost their venom at the approach of the dawn. Suyŏn and I had passed New Year's Eve without a wink of sleep.

A New Year! The sun, though changed not a bit from yesterday, had risen in the name of New Year. Exhausted, Suyŏn fell into a deep sleep. I went to early mass wading through a thick fog that made me think of the chaos before Creation.

Chapter 15

Living on Borrowed Time

When I had taken the poison with the intention of taking my life, it could have ended there. It was only by a sheer quirk of fate that I was still around. I was living on borrowed time. I often reflected on this. Is it possible that a life on borrowed time turns out to be more substantial and wholesome than the real one?

The latest news of Myŏngsŏk was that he had quarrelled with his host, our closest relation in Susim, and had been turned out of the house and moved into the servants' quarters, where he had to cook his own meals. I had been intending to send him some money, however little, regularly, as soon as my financial situation got better.

I went to see him one Saturday in February. Most of the day it was drizzling with rain that hurried along the spring. The bus from Chŏnan to Pyŏngch'ŏn via Susim was jam-packed with a market-day crowd. It was not until it stopped at a place called Salti, where a lot of them got off that I managed to find a seat to sit in the back. Even though I was sure we were not far from Susim, I wasn't quite sure whether the bus would stop there. I looked around and asked a man sitting opposite.

'Could you tell me whether the bus stops at the entrance to Susim?'

'Yes, lady,' he said as he closely examined my face. He was wearing shapeless, shabby clothes and his face was tanned to copper-brown. Deep lines on his forehead reminded me of the furrows of a winter field.

'Who are you going to see there?'

'Mr Hijun Yun. Do you know him?'

He nodded as he said, 'Yes, m'am.' Then he closed his mouth and sat expressionless.

'He is my great–uncle,' I added but all I got out of him was a meek 'Yes, m'am.'

Within a minute of getting off the bus, while I gave a quick brush to my hair and put on a scarf, I realized to my amazement, the man had disappeared. I knew the way to the village well enough. I would have to walk along a narrow winding path between paddies, cross a wooden bridge over a small river, turn right on the river bank, follow the dyke road for half a mile and turn at the foot of a low hill on my left. I would see it from there.

Before I reached the bridge, I had another strange encounter. In the falling dusk, out of nowhere a figure with giant stature appeared on the dyke some way ahead of me. As if sending out signals aimed at me it waved its arms up and down as it strode along. The way its four limbs flailed made me think of a mad man. He had a piece of whitish cloth flapping on his head. I felt like turning and running but the small parcels I was carrying weighed me down. The giant was speeding his steps so hard that I could hear his panting breath and I judged that running away would not get me anywhere.

Then he called out loudly, 'Is that you, sister, Sukey?'

'Myŏngsŏk? You, idiot!' I collapsed on the spot like a deflated balloon and as the tension went out with a pop, I burst into helpless laughter.

'What a nice surprise, sister.' He ran up and grabbed my hands and took the parcels off me.

'How did you know I was coming?'

'Someone told me.'

'I thought you were a mad man coming to get at me, silly boy. What a way to walk. And what is this flapping thing on your head?' I snatched off the cloth.

'It's only a hankie. Because it's raining.' I felt so close to him. Who else on earth would give me such a whole-hearted welcome? Because he had no umbrella he had come running to meet me with a cloth on his head. Blood was certainly thicker than water. I handed all my parcels over to him and walked along the narrow road behind him.

As soon as we entered the village, I saw half a dozen urchins following us with furtive looks.

'In the village, they call me "Mr Loony".' He broke into a chuckle. 'They can't just call me "mad man", you see. Because our generation name is that of the older people, most of young ones call me uncle.'

I gave a wry smile and said, 'The famous "Mr Loony" has a visitor for once. What a day! Is that why these kids are following us?'

He grinned and turning stamped his foot. 'What do you want, stupid boys? Go home at once!' Without a murmur the children dispersed into the dusk. 'They are not really bad.' he said.

Despite his protest I took him with me to pay a formal greeting to our great uncle. Before him I bowed low, and asked after him and his family.

'I regret that it came to this. You may think badly of me, but I and my family have tried as best as we could. I have sent a letter to your father asking him to take Myŏngsŏk away from here as soon as possible. He bullies and scares my grandchildren to death. They are only kids of six and eight – what do they know about anything?'

From his title he was one generation above our father, so that father called him uncle though he was only five years older.

His only son had died in an accident a few years ago leaving a widow and two young children. My great-uncle was renowned for making a big fuss about his grandsons. He had no formal schooling but had the air of dignity and authority of the gentry. Myŏngsŏk who had been sitting with a mocking grin abruptly broke in. 'Why don't you just shut your trap, uncle. You sound so stupid.'

'Look at him,' uncle said. 'Is that how a gentleman's son should speak to his elders? That's nothing. How can I tell you what he's like?'

'You make me sick with the way you want to be treated like a gentleman. Why don't you behave like one?'

'Shut up, Myŏngsŏk!' Unaware of myself, I shrieked and then shrank. As a gentleman's daughter, how dare I raise my voice before an elder? I apologized.

'Please forgive me for raising my voice, uncle.'

'If we go on in this way, that rascal and I will end up by becoming enemies, or our two families will. It is best if your father hurries up and takes him away.'

'I am deeply ashamed, uncle. If you would excuse me I will go down with him and try to put some sense into his head.'

Womenfolk, uncle's wife and their daughter-in-law came and told me that my supper and bed were ready in the inner quarters. I diplomatically declined the offer and bade them all goodbye, saying that I had to catch the first bus in the morning and wouldn't be able to see them, and went down to Myŏngsŏk's place.

In the servants' quarters, there were two rooms side by side and at the end of one of them a kitchen only in name, a confined space with a straw mat hanging down where a door should be that could barely keep rain and wind out. One of the rooms had a light. Myŏngsŏk went into his and struck a match to light the tiny oil lamp. The meanness of the room revealed in the light was far worse than I had imagined. In the middle of the room lay a quilt, its cotton padding broken and lumped up. In one corner lay some clothes like rags and the satchel he used to take to high school. That was all.

The wall paper was mildewed, and torn with patches of the mud-and-straw wall showing here and there. The over-heated *ondol* floor was like a furnace. With clothes in tatters that showed his bare knees and elbows, as he stood in the middle of the room with expressionless face, he was like a scarecrow.

As I repressed my emotions, which was ready to explode, I took out the stuff I had brought. I suggested sending in some of the cake Sŏnhi had made to our uncle but he said abruptly, 'There's no need to.' I took out some item of clothing and asked him to try them on. 'I will, tomorrow,' he said and pushed them aside. I put before him a couple of cooking pots and jars of chillie sauce and bean paste.

'You needn't bring things like that.' He was not at all pleased. 'I won't starve as long as I live here. People are mostly our relations and I can get one meal here and another there.'

I could no longer contain my anger.

'Why should a man like you with all your limbs sound scrounge off other people? Are you a beggar? Is that what you want to be all your life? How many times have I told you that it was about time you set about earning your living and leading a decent life of your own?

'I know you've been unlucky with your family, but if you have some sense, and will-power, you can make your own living. A fully grown-up young man – why can't you do that? At your age lots of men have families and support their parents.' Throughout this outburst, his face showed no expression, like a man waiting for the spell of a passing shower to be over. On my side, even while shouting, I was conscious that I had no right to chide him.

'I know, I am no one to tell you off, but at least I'm not a parasite like you. Even if you can't do much good for others, you have to try not to make a nuisance of yourself, don't you?' My voice had lost its force.

After standing like a totem pole in the middle of the room he sat down with his back against the wall while I continued with my nagging, though in a quieter tone.

'How can you live in a room like this? Why can't you repair that wall? It is no more than a morning's work. That wouldn't hurt you. A decent life with money that you earned yourself – don't you think that's a good idea?'

He never once responded. Instead he was leafing through the pages of an old English dictionary. At first I thought he was urgently looking up certain words. Then I saw him scribbling in it with a pencil.

'What are you doing?'

Only then he shut the book as he grinned and said, 'It's nothing. Just in case things get pinched...the place is full of petty thieves.'

I snatched it from him. Written at random on the margins of the pages were tiny letters like sesame seeds, as if in code, of the inventory of his poor possessions. Even if everything was put down there, how would he ever find out later what he had written?

'He's mentally infirm.' At this thought a flush of tears surged up to my eyes. Regardless of my weeping he went out and round the wall I could hear him urinating. When he came in he said, 'What about some sleep?' as he prepared himself for bed.

'You go to sleep. I am OK,' I said. I could hear snoring in the next room.

'Who is in the next room?'

'That's the Hulk.'

'What's a Hulk?'

'He's a labourer from outside, and he works so badly that they call him "Hulk". He's a migrant who was passing here a couple of weeks ago. He was looking for work and our greedy uncle hired him on the spot thinking he'd be strong because he's so big, but it turns out that he can't lift heavy things at all.'

'In this stupid place, people call each other by their nick-names, do they? "Mr Loony", "Hulk"?' Earlier I had been stung at the thought of my brother being called 'Mr Loony'. How dare they?, I had thought.

'Country bumpkins – they are all like that, not worth both-ering with.' He sounded as if he was looking down at them from a superior position.

'Aren't you a country bumpkin? You're not any better than the labourer, are you?' I wanted to strike at his vain sense of superiority.

'Pah! Of course I am not one of them. I'm not going to end up by being a peasant, and anyway farming doesn't suit my temperament.'

'I can't believe this. What makes you so arrogant? You hav-en't a penny or a foot of land to your name, yet you look down on your neighbours with contempt and suspicion. You are terrible to our great uncle. However bad he maybe he is your guardian, so to speak, on behalf of our father.'

'Ugh, don't mention that baboon. He makes me sick. A crafty, cunning old thing. Do you think he let me stay here for his love of me? If you don't know let me tell you. He has his dark plans worked out – when father gets into a good position, he is going to send those brats of his up to Seoul for our father to send them to good schools and look after their education. You should see him going around bragging about his great nephew who was a member of parliament... Hum, the country bumpkins.'

'Shut up. Can't you speak without bringing in "country bumpkins" every other word?' It was obvious that I was wasting my breath. I would never make him see things in my way. There was an unbridgeable abbys between us.

I put my coat round my shoulders, leaned against the wall and closed my eyes. As I opened them I saw Myŏngsŏk deep in sleep with the clotted quilt haphazardly wrapped around him. I closely examined his face, pale under the dim light from the tiny wick of the oil lamp. Traces of his once princely looks still remained after the strife of life – long eyelashes, straight, high-bridged nose and cupid's lips.

I blew out the lamp, leaned against the wall and tried to sleep, as I calmly surrendered to my sorrow. As soon as dawn broke, I got up and after brushing my hair and putting some cream on my face set off. I wanted to get away before the family of my great-uncle appeared to make a fuss over me.

In spite of my insistence that he should not bother to get up but go on sleeping, Myŏngsŏk came with me as far as to the main road where the bus stop was. While waiting for it, we had a bowl of soup with rice in it for our breakfast at the roadside inn.

'Please think about what I said last night, Myŏngsŏk, will you? Try to live like a decent human being.' Probably from an intention to cheer me up before I went away, he was attentive and agreeable now.

'Take this. Buy yourself some socks and other things and keep this separately to use only in emergencies. You must learn to do your own washing instead of depending on other people. I don't know when I will see you again – maybe not for a long time. Don't get it into your head that you can count on me just because I am generous for once now.'

'I understand,' he said.

A few minutes before the bus arrived we saw a man coming running along the path from the village, as if in a great hurry.

I recognized him as the man with a copper-coloured face on the bus the day before. Myŏngsŏk said 'hello' to him. It all became clear to me. He was the man Myŏngsŏk had referred as the 'Hulk', and was the very person who had disappeared in a flash when he got off the bus, and must have run home to tell Myŏngsŏk of my coming.

'Good morning,' I said.

'Good morning to you, lady,' he replied and stood beside Myŏngsŏk ill at ease, blinking his eyes, which reminded me of a toad.

'Where are you off to as early as this?' Myŏngsŏk asked.

'I am going to Ch'ŏngju to fetch my daughter, sir. I have a promise from the lady at that inn to take her on.' He pointed at the eating place we had just come out from. 'Before I came here, I left her at a restaurant in Ch'ŏngju. Working in an eating place is a hard life all the same whether it is here or there but I so much want to have her living near me.'

As I sat next to him on the bus the words that my father often said came to mind. 'Even brushing past the sleeve of someone in the marketplace is due to a bond from your previous life.' I could not just sit there and ignore him for an hour or more.

'How old is your daughter?'

'Fourteen.' I had thought he would have little to say but once he was put at ease he had so much to tell and did not stop talking. A common attribute of a lonely heart – I recognize the symptoms, I thought. There was a mountain of stories that was ready to spill out when it found a right outlet. I let him speak.

'I was born to be poor. At the age of fifty-five, there was not a day when I was not hungry. There is not a corner of the country where my feet have not trodden and no kind of rough work that I haven't put my hand to. I carried along with me a wife and a brood of kids, all about a year or so between them, everywhere I went, and lost them one by one, some dying of starvation and some of illness, and two years ago my wife died. That was also due to starvation, so to speak, as a family of three, we were huddled up without food for three days underneath a bridge.' He turned his eyes to the window as he blinked his eyes, and then went on. 'I was left with my daughter. I thought to myself what wouldn't I do, just to keep her, my only remaining child alive? So I took a job at a port in Pusan, which involved carrying heavy loads. I had an accident there in which some of my ribs were broken. I was laid up and lived on food earned by my daughter, only twelve then, by working as a kitchen helper at a tavern.

'I got better eventually but I can't carry heavy things, so what use am I as a labourer?'

'You must know a lot about human life through your own experiencee, I guess.' At this complimentary remark, a proud smile rose to his lips as his talk became livelier.

'Yes, indeed. Lots and lots. If I could write I should like to write books about it all. As the song goes,

The world is a desert,
I, a travellers on it, going through
Troubled miles after sorrowful miles
How sad life is.

'That hits the nail on the head.' He was showing off a bit, I thought. So at ease with me, he seemed ready to sing it aloud if I asked him to.

'Are you getting on all right at my great-uncle's?' At this he started.

'Please, lady, lower your form of address to me,' he said as he visibly corrected his posture and sat up straight in his seat. 'The merciful heaven guided my steps that way and Master Hijun Yun is indeed my saviour.'

I felt I had had enough of his story. I offered him a boiled sweet from my packet.

'I am so grateful to you, lady,' he said as he popped one into his mouth and his story came to an end.

Pretending I was sleepy, I closed my eyes. 'Please, lady, lower your form of address to me.' His voice still rang in my ears. Why did he keep saying that when he was an old man, old enough to be my father?

Suddenly, I saw what he had in common with a well-established professor of economics. Out of the many facets of human life, they both had a thorough understanding, through lifelong experience and observations, of one aspect of it, the money. The professor had gained insight into the function of money: how to manipulate it to make the country's industry prosper and the state rich, and he had become a professor, and was respected by everybody. You addressed a professor in the highest form and still nervous lest your language was not respectful enough. But this man, who had borne the pain with his flesh and bones all through his life and gained insight into what became of a man if he had no money, was so humble that he kept asking me to lower my form of address.

The forsythia and azalea, rampant in the gardens of the Tŏksu Palace, had been replaced by the soft green silk of May. After work, I met Fr. Osbourne in the Cathedral garden. He was leaving Korea on the following day. We strolled into the Palace grounds, which were next door to the Cathedral. Once we took our seats on a bench beneath a large gingko tree we sat silently as if attentive to the whispers of birds and rustling breeze going through its pure, green leaves. I had thought there would be a plenty to talk about. Starting with obvious questions such as his feelings as he was about to leave the country and people which he had served with such love and devotion for the past eight years. I would further question him about his religious conviction and his future plans when he was back in England, and properly express my gratitude to him. That's what I had thought.

At first, I was waiting for him to say something, but then I thought that after all it was for me to steer the conversation but I could not find the first words. When I realized the daylight had been taken over by the evening air, I felt that words were quite irrelevant. We had sat for nearly two hours in silence, sad in some way, yet blissful in another.

'How the birds sing.' He said in a quiet voice. I had noticed their noises had grown more forceful with the approach of the evening.

I wanted to say, 'They are making such a racket, yet how peaceful it is here,' but could not bring out the word. With that the last chance to say something was lost.

'I am supposed to have dinner with the bishop, so I had better go,' saying thus he stood up. I felt as if I was hit by a hammer on the back of my head. 'What an idiot!,' I thought. 'How can I let him go just like this? I should have brought some little present or something.'

There was nothing I could do except walk out of the gate of the palace with him.

'The bishop has arranged a farewell service early tomorrow morning and seems to have invited several people. Then I shall leave for the airport at ten.'

Next morning I went to the mass, but did not have a chance to speak to him. I thought that after reporting at the office first, I might be able to take some time off to go and see him off at the airport. But it was not to be. As soon as I was in the office, Dr Kang called me to his room.

'My students at the American Eighth Army are coming to look round the library during the morning,' he said. 'Would you like to put a few items of interest on display, and can we

give them some coffee? There will be about twenty altogether.'
I said, 'Yes, of course.' It was not the first time that his students
had been to the library and I knew exactly what to do. It was
a pity that in no way could I go to the airport. I went back at
once to the Cathedral to find Fr. Osbourne.

'I was going to the airport, but it turns out that I can't leave
the office as we are expecting some visitors this morning.'

'I understand,' he said. At his calm, unruffled response, I felt
tears rising.

'Goog-bye,' he said.

'Goodbye, Father, and a safe journey.' I turned away. It was
only when I got on the bus that I realized I had missed for good
the chance to properly thank him for all the help I got from him.

As the saying goes, 'It never rains, but it pours.'

Two disasters tumbled in one on top of the other in one day.

Dr Kang, who had been out teaching, came back earlier
than expected. His face was extremely grim and serious. I went
to his office to report on a few visitors and telephone calls I
had received during his absence. He mechanically nodded but
was not really paying attention to what I was saying. I went
to my desk. Obviously something was wrong but I could not
guess what it was. Five minutes passed before he pressed the
bell to call me in, but it felt like ages.

'Yes, sir?'

'Miss Yun!'

'?'

'Can you answer me this? If they don't want to study why
do they come to college paying such an enormous registration
fees?' It came as a great relief to realize that I had not been the
direct cause of his distress. I had never known him so upset. I
did not know what to say. So I just stood there and waited his
next words. He seemed to realize that he had vented his anger

on me who had nothing to do with it. He gave a wry smile as if in token of apology.

'I have written a note of resignation.' He handed me a sheet of paper, which read:

To the Chancellor of Y University.

Since my appointment, I have tried my utmost to maintain the high academic standards of this university. However, due to lack of my ability I find myself unable to fulfil my duties satisfactorily. I therefore submit my notice of resignation.

Sincerely Yours,
Kijin Kang

I swallowed a sigh as I handed it back. Probably I was one of the few people who appreciated Dr Kang's personality. He was a highly principled man who could not tolerate insincerity or the attitude of getting ahead by artful means which had become the social mores in the aftermath of the Civil War. He took great trouble to uphold the principles whether it be the trivial office rules or the management policy of the Academy. He painstakingly trained his staff to differentiate between private and official matters. If a member of his staff was off for ten days due to illness, he readily allowed him an eleventh day to ensure his full recovery, even if it meant great inconvenience to himself, but he reprimanded someone who was ten minutes late after lunch.

He strictly upheld the rule that books must not be taken out of the Reading Room even by the staff without special permission. If the books he borrowed for special reasons were due back he brought them in to be re-stamped. If they were overdue and he had not been warned or notified, he scolded me for not carrying out my duties properly.

His conviction that scholarship should not be compromised with politics had put him into sticky corners many times. Since his first day as director, he had been subject to enticement to be drawn into political organizations or government bodies. His efforts to steer the Academy clear of political influence by constantly rejecting these invitations had earned him unpopularity and slander.

In a way he made his life hard for himself. Some people around him criticized him for being narrow-minded, cold and unrealistic. I had known all this and often thought that his temperament, uncompromising, puritanical, and idealistic, had something in common with my own.

'"Sir, can we skip the lecture today?" "We have some urgent matters to discuss, if you don't mind", amid idiotic giggles. If they had something to discuss they could do it during the break or at lunch time. Do they think I have nothing better to do than to stand there being mocked?

'"That's fine by me. Do as you please", I said and walked out. Don't you think their attitude is fundamentally wrong?' Now that he had vented his anger, he was weakly smiling at me. Meanwhile he had sealed his notice in an envelope.

'Please post this for me at once.'

He had confided his worries to me, so I felt I ought to say something.

'I know that on the whole, students don't work as hard as they should. I did not take my studies seriously either in my time. But you cannot expect that all the people attending college will turn out to be scholars, can you? The important thing is that there amongst the noisy rebels must be a few to whom your lectures are important. You carry on for their sake if for no one else.'

'Please, sir. Could you not reconsider it and revoke your resignation just this once?'

'No, I will not.' It was final. I carried out his order and posted the letter.

In this uneasy atmosphere the morning passed quickly. His gloomy looks did not lift all morning and he remained in his office during the lunch hour.

Then in the afternoon the other thing happened.

As I came back from lunch I sensed some commotion in front of the caretaker's room by the main entrance. I heard Mr Shin, the caretaker shouting, 'What do you want?' and then Mr Yang, his assistant speak in a lower voice, 'He says Miss Yun is his elder sister.' I guessed that there had already been a little squabble before the head caretaker was called to the scene. My heart missed a beat. I briskly walked up to the entrance. The two men were at loggerheads with a man dressed like a beggar trying to stop him entering the building. It was Myŏngsŏk indeed. He looked like the beggar of all beggars. In my embarrassment I pulled him by the sleeve and pushed him into the ladies' toilet. It was the nearest door. I would think up what to do with him once he was out of sight. I was going to tell Dr Kang that I had to go as I had an urgent family matter to deal with and then take him out. I went to my desk to put away a few things when I heard a thunderous shout of Dr Kang in the corridor.

'What the hell are you doing in there?! Who are you?!' Myŏngsŏk must have poked out his head out of the ladies toilet just as Dr Kang was passing. Things had gone hopelessly wrong. Dr Kang accused the caretaker for letting a man like that slip into the building. What with my colleagues coming back from lunch and curious readers coming out the Reading Room to see what was going on, the corridor became a bottle-neck. Amidst this confusion Myŏngsŏk stood lost and frightened like a cockerel brought to the market with its wings clipped. My colleagues stood around as they looked at me awaiting an explanation. Dr Kang called the caretaker and his assistant to his room and closed the door.

I thought I would never get over my shame this time. I had no courage to enter the director's room. I took my handbag and as I went out spoke to Miss Pak.

'Ŏnni, I am sorry. Please tell Dr Kang that I had to go.'

I stood in the street with Myŏngsŏk and did not know where to turn. It was not far from where I lived but it was not my own home and I was afraid of causing trouble for Sŏnhi. In the afternoon sun of August, the peak of summer, the asphalt underfoot felt warm and soft. We could not stand there much longer but where should we go? Just then a bus drew up. I got on and Myŏngsŏk followed, dragging his shoe from which the worn-out sole had become loose at the heel and flopped like a dog's tongue each time he took a step.

It was after I got on the bus that I realized it was going to Nokbŏnli, a western suburb of Seoul. When we got there, my destination became clear. We were not far from the Anglican Church cemetery where our mother's grave was, before her remains were exhumed and reburied at our ancestoral graveyard in the following year. The thought that we were far from the Academy gave me a sense of relief and my mind, which had gone numb started functioning again. He must be hungry, I thought. We went into a small eating place and I ordered meat soup, rice and some side dishes. He ate it all, every bit, now and again casting nervous glances at me. We went out and started walking again.

'Where are we going?'

'Don't you recognize this road?'

We turned off the main road onto a path through meadows, rounded the foot of a low hill, went over a slope and crossed a narrow stream. This was a spot of sacred memories. During the early years after mother's death, father often brought Hyŏngsŏk,

Sŏnhi and me, and sometimes Myŏngsŏk as well, then a toddler, to visit her grave. After paying our respect, we used to come down here, wash our hands and have a picnic by the stream. In my memory, the stream had been wider and with more water.

When I reached mother's grave with Myŏngsŏk trailing behind, I collapsed at the foot of it and broke down into unrestrained cries calling, 'Mum, mum, mummy!' into the air like a calf calling its mother.

Before the grave of the mother who had given birth to both of us, I was crying and he just watched dry-eyed like a spectator. The thought of a dried-up person like a barren land made me even sadder. Soon I had to calm myself down and think up something for him. He must go back to the country, setting off at once, for there was nowhere for him to stay the night in Seoul. I turned to him.

'You have seen it all yourself, so I won't tell you what an embarrassing situation you have put me in. It is now clear that I can't bear to stay there any longer.

'I keep repeating this – Try to live as a man who has no parents, no sisters....what do you keep coming up to Seoul for?' Then I was choking again with pity for him. 'Anyway, how are you keeping these days? It's your turn to say something. It's a busy time in the country. You must be busy too?'

'I am alright,' he said. 'If you can spare the money for the fare, I will go back by the evening train.'

'Knowing perfectly well that you will have to go back feeling sad like this, why did you come in the first place? You really are thoughtless.'

'It is like this,' he said. 'In the evening, I go to bed thinking to myself, I am alone in the world, I have no family, no nothing and I must learn to live alone. In the morning, I go out to the field thinking I might do some work. Then I feel a bit lonely, so I walk up to the main road just to have a look at what's going

on there. Then a bus comes and I hop on. Where can I go but
to Seoul? Sometimes I go to the house where we used to live,
but it's all changed around there, you wouldn't recognize it.
Sometimes I go to places in the city and look up people who
used to be friendly with father. They turn me away at the gate
and don't offer as much as a snack. So I just wander round'

Fresh tears surged up. I emptied my purse and took off my
wrist watch, and told him to go and sell it for whatever he could
get and go back.

After sending him away, I lay down on the ground by the
grave for a long time with my eyes fixed at a spot in the sky.
Then I sprang up, took out a pen and paper out of my bag and
started writing:

Dear Chaehong,

*I don't know why the thought of you sprang to my mind just
at this moment. I am deeply troubled and need to pour out my
heart to somebody.*

*You will remember that I once told you about my younger
brother. He turned up at the Academy today. He looked like
the beggar of all beggars. It so happened that I was out when
he arrived. You can imagine what a commotion it caused at the
entrance. No one would believe that it could be my brother. I
had nowhere to take him so I brought him to our mother's grave.*

*How could this be the place where my mother's body lies
who in her life time had loved her children with such devotion?
Desolate wind, mindless clouds, and meaningless birds' song...
Her youngest child whom she had adored as she kissed him
and squeezed him with love came and stood here as a tramp,
but there was no response from her. My loud cries for her could
not reach her soul but after resounding over the top of the hill
dispersed into a void.*

He is a beggar not only in appearance, but his heart is barren. Cut off from his unusually blissful infancy, he has been without the blessings of the rain and sun throughout his boyhood and youth. It was his environment that pushed him into this. He was not only the most beautiful of all our siblings but the most intelligent and with the most sensitive nature.

Life has been cruel to him and now even his own family refuses to let him into their house, treating him like an illegitimate child.

God? He does not know such a thing. A lump of clay thrown into some shady corner, God's light has not even touched him.

When are you coming up? Please could you make some time to see me then? I may need your help and advice. I feel like a wrecked ship, both my mind and body are exhausted. That explains this bad writing.

Yours,
Sukey Yun.

For some reason unknown to me Chaehong had taken a year off college and was undergoing a practice period as a catechist in a country village, Chinwŏn in Ch'ungch'ŏng Province. They had recently built a new church there and since his arrival, the congregation had trebled and they were very enthusiastic, I had read it in the Church News. As an only son and without father he had his mother to take care of. Any form of material help from him was unthinkable but I needed his wisdom and advice. Even though he was only a year older than me, he seemed far superior intellectually and in practicality. When we were in Ch'ŏngju as refugees, while I found it hard going to keep up with schoolwork and the preparation for the university entrance exams, he was reading all sorts of books apparently into the small hours of the morning.

'He reads too much, that's the trouble with him,' his mother used to say.

When I came home exhausted, my sister embraced me and escorted me into my room and brought in my supper table. In the future, she said, we must do something more positive to help Myŏngsŏk.

'You look more dead than alive. Go to bed now,' she said as she went away. I had not told her, but I had already decided that the time had come for me to leave the Academy. I would never get over the shame I had felt today. I dreaded facing the director in the morning. Even though nothing had been said there had lingered an uncertain impression about my affair with Kwŏn, which needed some form of explanation. There had been Hisun's attack and on top of these, now another mysterious appearance of a man in rags. Unless I opened up my heart to my friends at work and explained these mysteries, which was obviously impossible, I thought, I could not remain their colleague. In the night, I got up and wrote out my resignation.

When he saw me in the morning, Mr Yang came up and apologized as if what had happened had been his fault.

'Oh, no, Mr Yang, I'm the one who ought to apologize. You must have had a hard time of it.'

As I entered the office, the playful Mr Yu said, 'Miss Yun, you're as good as dead. "Miss Yun, gone with the wind!"' as he drew his hand across his throat as a gesture of the sack I would get. To hide my shame, I gave him a bright smile.

'You know, the director was awful to us all day,' he said. I could well believe that.

Familiar footsteps in his room. He was just coming in. Before he had time to call me, I knocked on the door and went in.

'I am sorry about yesterday, sir.' Now that I had decided to go, I was not afraid to face him. A benign look on his face made me momentarily wonder whether I was being foolish.

'Was that your brother?' he said. Of course he had the right to demand an explanation but I was not going to give it him.

'Please, do not ask me any questions, Dr Kang. It is far too complicated for words. There is one thing, though, that I want you to be assured of. That is that I haven't done anything against my conscience and I have done everything to the best of my ability as far as it was possible...' I handed him my note of resignation. 'It will take me a few days to tidy up and hand over my work to my successor, presumably Suyŏn for the time being.'

Without giving him a chance to speak I told him just what I wanted to tell him while he sat nonplussed with his eyes as large as saucers. If it went on a minute longer I would burst into tears. So I said, 'Please forgive me,' as I went out of the room.

At the news of my resignation my colleagues were aghast. As if on behalf of them Mr Yu said, 'Miss Yun, you are not doing this because I teased you a bit earlier on, are you? Come on, tell us, what is the matter with you?' The director invited me to reconsider and Miss Pak supported him saying that the motive of my resignation was too feeble, but nothing could revoke it.

The most urgent thing for me was to find another job to be able to pay for my lodgings at least. I should never find one half as good as the one I just had given up. Going through the daily papers I saw a little advert: 'Female office worker with typing skills and competence in English conversation.'

With little difficulty I got the job in an American trade firm. The office was in the Bando Hotel and my pay was about a half of what I used to get at the Academy.

Five days after I wrote to Chaehong, I received a short reply. He would like to see Myŏngsŏk himself, so could I send him to Chinwŏn as soon as possible.

Sometime after that I had another letter telling me that Myŏngsŏk was now with him and that he was likely to stay there for some time. Two weeks after the second letter I went down to Chinwŏn to find out how the two of them were getting on.

The church stood on the top of a low hill surrounded by acacia trees, which reminded me of the ones in Ch'ŏngju and brought back memories of my youth. The church was built in traditional Korean style. The large beams inside and the eaves still smelt of fresh wood. Across the courtyard was a three-roomed thatched cottage and Chaehong lived in one room, looked after by a seventy-year-old lady who obviously was a great admirer of him. As his guest, Myŏngsŏk was wearing clean clothes washed and pressed by the lady and sharing his room.

'You two must have a lot to talk about, so I will first give you that chance,' said Chaehong as he left the room. No sooner had he closed the door than Myŏngsŏk said in a low voice. 'You must never believe anything that man says, and never even consider paying him any money for my board, not a penny. If you have that money give it to me.'

I felt weak. Because Chaehong had not told me that Myŏngsŏk was causing any trouble, I had foolishly thought he might have changed under Chaehong's good influence. I sought a chance to talk quietly with Chaehong but Myŏngsŏk followed me everywhere so as not to give me that chance.

'I told you never to believe anything he says.' Myŏngsŏk openly showed his hostility. I sought Chaehong's eyes to have some form of communication, even if only a wink, but he seemed to ignore my efforts. It was a battle of nerves. Then half an hour before the bus was due Chaehong solemnly spoke.

'Before you go, I had better report you on what has happened during the past weeks.'

He called Myŏngsŏk who was a few yards away. 'Hey, Myŏngsŏk, you should join us and hear what I have got to tell your sister. It is so that we avoid any kind of misunderstanding.'

The three of us sat in the shade of an acacia tree. Chaehong looked thinner and pale than I had known him. Only his large eyes were bright.

'One evening a couple of weeks ago, a man dressed like a beggar turned up in heavy rain. When he told me his name I knew at once who he was.

'His clothes and shoes were soaked through. They would have been of no use even if washed and dried, so I put them in the bin and gave him some spare clothes of mine, and shoes, though they were not new ones.'

He turned to Myŏngsŏk. 'Is that right, so far? Would you like to add anything?'

Myŏngsŏk ignored him as a sarcastic smile slid over his lips.

'We have an old lady of seventy here. She sweeps the yard every morning and evening, cooks the meals and does the washing. She is a devout member of the church. What is Myŏngsŏk to her that she should feed him and wash his clothes? She only does it because he is my guest.

'What does Myŏngsŏk do all day? Nothing, absolutely nothing. As he is staying here at the cost of the church I thought it might be a good thing for him to look now and again at the Bible or the prayer books, so I gave them to him – mind you, I never forced him. As far as I know he has never touched them. He has never once put a step inside the church.'

Here he turned to Myŏngsŏk again. 'I am not lying, am I?' Then he went on as if talking to an imaginary fourth person. 'Frankly I am one of those who care for Sukey. When I realized that she was distressed because of her brother, I simply offered to help. If he has no place to go or is unhappy where he is, I thought, I could let him stay here for a while in my room and share my meals. I think Myŏngsŏk suspects that I am being paid by Sukey for doing this. I want to make it clear that I have not received a penny from her so far.

'All he does everyday is to eat, sleep and smoke. I believe it is the same wherever you are. You have to do something towards your keep.'

Then he turned to Myŏngsŏk again. 'If you are not happy here or not sure about it you should go away.' Here his officious tone became more relaxed as he quickly glanced at me. His eyes were saying, 'Please understand. I am being tough on purpose.'

'Now, what would you like to do, Myŏngsŏk? Would you like to leave with your sister or stay on for a bit longer? You decide. I have said all I wanted to say.'

Myŏngsŏk sat with a blank face without showing the least inclination to go.

'If you want to stay, I think, it would have to be under some conditions. From now on you will have to be a bit more cooperative if you want to be fed.

'You will have to help the old lady to sweep up the yard. And now and again make an appearance in church, if only to save my face. It is not unreasonable, is it, considering that you are staying here as the guest of the catechist.'

I took out some clothes that I had brought and some tins of meat. He pushed the clothes aside and gathered up the tins. 'I will keep these.' I glanced to Chaehong as if to say, 'He's hopeless, isn't he?' To which he seemed to reply, 'Don't worry and leave him with me. I will write to you.'

The bus arrived. A couple of passengers got off and I got on. A few days later I had a long letter from Chaehong:

....I could see at once that Myŏngsŏk had long since closed his heart to the world. The door has been locked for so long that it looks as though it has gone all rusty, but once that door is opened up, nobody can foretell what precious treasures might be found behind it. Would you say I am being too ambitious

to hope to open that door with my own hand some day? I am terribly interested in him.

If you have no objections, I hope to keep him here for a few months and, through him, I would like to test my own patience, love and faith....

Occasional charity is like giving alms to beggars now and again. It can do no good. It can only foster expectation and dependency. If you want me to have a try with him, I want you to leave him entirely with me. Do not write or send him any gifts.

The other thing is that, as you know, I have no means of feeding any one for a long time. I would appreciate it if you could send me by post, anonymously, a small amount of money, just enough to cover his food, once a month.....

The atmosphere at my new work was so strikingly different from the place I had left that I did not know how to adapt myself to it. I did not make friends with anyone for a month. I did not feel myself like a person but a tiny part of a big machine. From morning till evening I sat in front of a typewriter and struck the keys. I had got on well with a Mr Dickson, the deputy manager, at the interview but once I started working there I never had any further personal contact with him. I worked with other Korean employees under the command of a Korean supervisor named Min, who came in and out the room I was working in at any time. For some reason he reminded me of the word 'pimp'.

Sharing the office with me, both as my senior clerks, Miss Yang and Miss Chŏn were not only refined in their make-up and choice of clothes but very good looking. From the first day I had no great appeal to them. It was obvious that they were disappointed in me. They must have thought what sort of a woman is this with no make-up and making no effort to be charming, like a county bumpkin. They might have said to each other, 'I don't know how she got the job in the first place.' But they were decent to me as they explained the office rules and gave me instructions as to how to do certain things.

When there was time to spare I read while they faced each other and constantly chatted, their chins resting on their propped-up hands. The contents of their chat was matters that seemed to belong to a different world.

'At the Bar Casino, so and so...at the Sky Lounge Charlie did this and that...Monsieur Buchez...' It went on like that.

Each time Min came into the room he exchanged with them what seemed to me extremely crude jokes as he fingered their shoulders, cheeks or waist as if it was the most natural thing in the world. His style grated on my nerves. At the thought that it was not the right place for me, I was depressed and missed the Academy dreadfully. It was clear in my mind that I could not carry on like this for long, I must go far far away and now that I had cleared up all my debts, I was free to go. But to where? Save money from the pittance I got from the job and go to America? You might as well aim to pluck the stars standing on a ladder. Besides, why did it have to be America?

About this time there appeared in one of the papers a series of report of an assignment on the Hǔksan Islands. It curiously stirred my imagination and interest. Until then I had never known such a place existed – an archipelago off the south-west coast, consisting of over forty islets, fourteen of them inhabited with a total population of twelve thousand. Cut off completely from the world outside they lived amidst the grandeur of nature. The flora and fauna were exquisite and mysterious. Harsh living conditions were part of their physiology.

Some years ago, an Irish priest had settled there and things had begun to change as he started a church and a school. Apart from the newspaper report, I collected more details about the place through my own inquiries. My mind was finally made up. 'I will go to Hŭksan Island. I will give everything I can to people who need it. That would be a worthy life.'

Like a shipwrecked seaman who, exhausted after long drift, suddenly sees the gleam of a distant lighthouse and goes blind with tears of joy, I was blind to all the troubles around me. I could not wait for the day I would leave this world and start a new life. I was mentally adapting to the life there – a place where a handful of rice is novelty and where people lived all through the year on potatoes dipped in salt with whatever they got from the sea.

'I shall learn to dive like the sea–divers and crack open clams and oysters, and learn to pluck the sea–plants from the sea bed. I can teach, be a nurse and cook.'

I wrote to the priest telling him of my intentions, but because there was not a regular postal service, and particularly when the seas were rough the post could be delayed for weeks, it was over a month before I received a reply. He was very pleased with my letter even though he expressed doubts over whether I could really survive such a hard life. In any event, he thought it would be best if we met before we made any final arrangement. As he had some business to attend in Seoul, he was hoping to come up at Christmas. He would contact me then and arrange a meeting.

One afternoon, I entered the narrow road between the old Parliament building and the Ministry of Communications building and turned right into the quiet alleyway that let up to the Anglican Cathedral and its convent. I was walking along the slightly uphill road lost in thought. Suddenly I was startled by something like an electric shock. Looking up I saw, about twenty feet ahead, approaching me, a figure that was all too familiar. It was as if he had dropped from the air or sprung up from under the earth. It was at the spot where the lane gently curved left. It was my first face-to-face encounter with Kwŏn since his release.

Earlier in March he had phoned me at the Academy. At his first 'Hello,' I had recognized his voice and he did not need to add, 'It's me.' 'I want you just to listen to me,' he said.

'No, I won't,' I had rejected him quietly as I put the phone down. That had been the last of him.

On this afternoon, the usually quiet road was absolutely empty. It was as if by some unknown hand all living things had been cleared out to provide the stage for this encounter.

If he had looked like a poor man dressed in shabby clothes or a monk's habit, I might have knelt before him. He was exactly as he had been three years before – a smart suit with a hat, highly-polished black shoes and carrying under his arm a thick brown envelope with bits of what could be seen as manuscript paper sticking out. He did not show any expression on his face, probably waiting for my first move as the basis on which he would begin to act.

'Just the same!' I thought that with this one sarcastic remark I would go past him and ignore him, but once my mouth opened, my whole body shook violently as my anger exploded like a volcano.

'He still hasn't cast off his mask and goes about as a lecturer, ugh!'

'Devil!' 'Liar!' 'Sex-maniac!' I uttered each word with sharp articulation between clear intervals. I was going to add, 'Spy,' but refrained. A spy deserved at least some credit in that he was risking his life for what he believed in. A rogue like him did not even rank with spies. I was driven mad by the impulse to be cruel. I was dying to find the strong words that would be daggers into his heart.

'What gutless woman is he hanging onto now? How many more whores is he going to devour? God, strike him dead!'

When I had spat out all this almost in one breath, I felt a chill on the back of my neck. I was seized by fear, utter terror, as I imagined him running up to squeeze my neck in his hands. If that happened nobody would ever know. It was eerily quiet all around.

'Murder – !' I let out a scream as I ran back down the road. I ran until I was in front of the police post at the corner as if I was going to report a murder. Only when I became conscious of the curious eyes of the officer on duty did I come to myself. What was I going to do there? I could not help a wry smile rising to my lips. Too scared to stay out on my own I caught a taxi home.

This was no land for me to settle down in peace. I had to get away from the predatory eyes of a serpent. 'I must go, and go at the earliest possible opportunity!'

'I think she fancies Sudol,' said Sŏnhi after making sure that Kŭmok entering the bathroom had locked the door from the inside. Since I left the Academy, Sudol came round to our house a couple of days a week to polish my shoes. Early in the morning he came through our alley crying 'Shoe Shine!' When he reached our house he called from outside my window, 'Auntie, polish your shoes.' It was usually before I was up, so Kŭmok gave him my shoes and sometimes she asked him to polish Chinmo's as well.

He had suddenly shot up during the last year and his pet-name of 'Tiny Tot' no longer suited him. When he was not carrying the shoe-shine box, and was wearing his school uniform, he was a tall, handsome boy.

'Really?' Encouraged by my interest, Sŏnhi had plenty to say.

'After he's been, she becomes very lively and chatty. I've noticed it quite clearly.'

'That's interesting.' I said. 'When he started coming here, I noticed her being cheeky to him and nagging at him pointing

out spots and saying, "It's not done properly here, and there. More recently she seemed to have stopped that."
'It's not just that she doesn't nag anymore but she sits by him as if spellbound.'
'It's natural at her age, isn't it?'
'A piece of cake from the day before – she keeps it wrapped up in a hanky and hidden behind the cupboard. She's never done such a thing before. Is it because she's hungry? No, it's obviously for him. And, last week, he called one afternoon. I gave him my shoes to polish. There were some noodles left over from lunch. She asked me if she could give it to him. I said, "yes", and she got a small table ready in the kitchen. After that she was so happy, she kept breaking into smiles.'
'Go and fetch the cake wrapped in a hankie. Let me have a bite of it, I am starving.' I burst into laughter. Sŏnhi shushed me as she put her finger across my mouth. 'Pretend you don't know. She has her pride just like you and me. If she sensed that we are laughing about it in this way, she'd be really hurt.' Nevertheless Sŏnhi went on with some more gossip.
'Shall I tell you what she does sometimes? She has seen me now and again massaging my face with pieces of cucumber or water-melon peels. When she has a nap, she goes to sleep with her face covered in melon peels, her pock-marked face. I shouldn't be laughing like this. I feel really sorry for her.'
'All in all, she's a good girl. We're lucky to have her,' I said. 'It would be nice if they can eventually marry each other.'
'I don't think it will work,' Sŏnhi said. 'There's too big an intellectual gap between them. I am wondering how to break down that thick wall of illiteracy she is imprisoned in.'
'Promise me, Sŏnhi, you will go on with it even when I am not here.' It was a slip of the tongue that I regretted instantly.

'What do you mean by when you are not here? Where are you going to be? To America?' She noticed my sad smile and at once tensed up.

'What are you up to? Can't you ever be frank with me?'

Unable to tell her about my plans for Hŭksan Island I said that I had some vague idea of doing something but it was not yet properly thought out and not worth telling about.

Kŭmok came in and Sŏnhi went back to her room. Straight out of the bath, her cheeks were rosy pink and her eyes sparkling. Either because I was so used to seeing her or because she was now in bloom I no longer found her as dismal-looking as she was at first. She might be ignorant bookwise but she was clever in domestic matters. She had learned from Sŏnhi to cook and prepare attractive and tasty meals and she kept the house spotless. She had steadily saved through joining several *kae*, so that if she carried on as she was, in a couple of years' time she would have a handsome lump sum to start a home of her own.

I was looking out of the window of my fourth floor office. The scene below, I thought, would have seemed unfamiliar to people whose mentality, like mine, still belonged to the previous century.

On the street were waves of motorcars, through which people swam like fish. Now that my mind had bidden farewell to my present life, I had lost interest in such sights, like old garments from which the colours had been faded. I had no place among them. They had no relevance to me. We had become strangers, I thought.

'What are you thinking about, Miss Yun? You look very serious.' Miss Yang addressed me as she came closer. Miss Chŏn was off sick and she must have been missing their usual chat. It was the first attempt at friendship I had received. I smiled brightly to show that I was pleased, and made room for her to sit.

'I am not really serious. I just get carried away when I look down on the streets from here. Look at all those cars and people – what are they all dashing about like that for?'

We sat side by side and chatted in a desultory manner. She asked me about my background and past experience and I light-heartedly replied. Then we went back to our desks as some more work came in. At another break towards the end of the day, she asked me why I, with a background like mine, had chosen a job like this. The earlier chat seemed to have brought us closer.

'Things turned out that way. It's my fate, I suppose.' Then I added, 'If your job is just a means of earning your bread, it doesn't matter much whatever it is, does it. Anyway, I don't think I will carry on like this for much longer.'

'Miss Yun, you are not what you look, are you? You are smart.' At this moment our minds clicked and I felt that all the barriers between us had fallen away. We carried on like two old friends.

'This time next year, probably I shall be cracking open oysters, sitting on a rock on Hŭksan Islands.'

'Hŭksan Island? You want to go there? You're fantastic. I'd never have thought you were such a romantic. Oh, I wish I was going there!'

'I didn't mean to be romantic. For me such thing as romance has "gone with the wind" a long time ago.' She was delighted at my outburst and broke into laughter.

When it was time to go, she went into the ladies to readjust her make-up while I just picked up my handbag. Until now, I had just said 'Goodnight' to them and walked out, but today I felt that would be mean. While I was hesitating she came out, obviously in a hurry to catch up with me.

'Let's go.' She said as she stood beside me. 'If you have no other engagement, would you like to meet me tonight? At "Autumn Leaves" at eight o'clock.'

'Autumn Leaves' was a tea-room in the most fashionable part of Myŏngdong area. I was there at the appointed time, pushed the door and entered. She was not yet in sight. I took up an empty seat and looked round. With no special features or taste in its deco, it was just a typical tea-room of the day, plain white walls with a counter by the door, comfortable chairs and a few pot plants. I didn't like the background music. A few tables away from me sat a young couple. The girl approaching them with a coffee tray had a striking resemblance to Miss Yang. Not trusting my eyes, I looked up at her again. Sensing my disbelief, she stopped in the act of serving and gave me a wink.

'I am sorry to have kept you waiting.' When she finished serving she came over and sat beside me. She addressed me less formally but with more affection.

'This is my evening job – from eight to eleven. I liked what you said earlier, "If your job is a means of earning your bread, it doesn't matter whatever it is."' She looked dazzlingly beautiful.

'About this time of the night, it is fairly quiet but after nine, it is packed. Then I won't be able to come and talk to you like this. You will get to know me better eventually, I hope.'

She was showing me her evening world. Each time new customers arrived or old ones left she got up to welcome them or say goodbye. She brought me a cup of coffee. 'This is a complimentary cup from me.' It was quiet and she was able to sit with me and tell me her life story.

'If I didn't do this, a family of six would sit and starve. In an eight-matted rented room, I have, beside my widowed mother, a brother at high school and three sisters, the youngest being in the fourth year at the primary school.

'My mother is from a family of the gentry, and never knew the harshness of life outside her family. She remains unchanged in both her mental attitude and practicality, even though she has been widowed seven years. She's just not equipped to face the modern world. She waits on me as the head of the family. I have such great respect for her, and I treasure my brother and sisters.

'Sometime ago, my brother left home. He had been unhappy for several days saying that because he was behind with school fees, he was likely to be banned from sitting for the end-of-term exams.

'Anyway, he was missing for several days and we thought he might be staying with some friends until we got a letter from the head-master demanding an explanation for his absence. Only then did we go through his belongings. In one of the drawers we found a letter. He said that he was leaving home to lighten my burden at least a bit and to save one mouth to be fed, and that he would try to earn money and come back as a self-sufficient man.'

As if in an effort to keep her emotion under control, she stopped talking as she softly closed her eyes. Then she went on.

'My mother, whose principle it is never to show herself crying even when her heart is bursting with anguish, was weeping every night as she tried to smother the sound. It was unbearable. I reported to the police and he was brought home.

'He had been in towns near the demilitarized zone, hanging round the army camps. It looks as though he was hoping to pick up some saleable stuff from the army dumps and take it to the market to sell.

'Mother brought him up like a delicate treasure and pampered him. Even though outwardly he is tall and strong, he's a baby inside. As he walked into the house followed by the police officer, I ran up and thrashed him. With no resistance he took it all. I beat him until I was exhausted. Driven by a swirl of emotions I was mad and blind.

'My mother not knowing what to do, just hovered around clasping her hands. Then while, exhausted, I was panting for breath, she pleaded with him. "Darling, please say, 'Forgive me, sister.' You little know how we have been worried about you."

With no fuss he said, 'Please, sister, forgive me. I am sorry.' After being beaten like that he was begging my forgiveness. Forgiveness for what for heaven's sake? What had he done wrong?

'I never show my tears to my mother or my brother and sisters because I can't bear showing any weakness as the head of the family, but that day tears were blinding me. I bit my lips till they bled, still I could not contain them. To fight them back, I raised my voice and shouted at him.

'"Who told you to worry about me? Do you think I can't see you through the university? If you ever get such a cheeky notion into your head again, I'll really kill you."

'That night, mother didn't get a wink of sleep as she sat by him massaging his arms and legs, and stroking his bruises, in the bright moonlight that poured into the room.

'Next morning, I walked into the house of a man called Kwangbok Kim and borrowed thirty thousand Hwan, paid up the school fees and pressed the rest into my mother's hand.

'Kwangbok Kim, you'll see him here one day – a middle-aged rich widower and the most insinuating and ugliest-looking businessman.

'What's the good of pride? In my kind of reality with five lives depending on me and keeping them alive is my sacred mission, pride is a vice that destroys the reality.'

She tightened her lips as she swallowed hard.

'You said your choice of the Hŭksan Islands was not from a romantic idea. What I envy you is not the romance but a situation in which you can feel free to go when you choose. How good it would be to feel free!'

My heart was tight. I thought of Myŏngsŏk. To lighten the atmosphere I changed the subject.

'What about Miss Chŏn? Is she hard up too?'

'No, she's not. In some ways she's like a teenager going through adolescence. She has both her parents and they lead an upper-middle-class life. But she makes out as if she's sad and serious. Funny, isn't' she? But she's a good sort. She's never crafty or ill-meaning to any one. If she'd wanted to she could have finished her course at college but she gave it up, didn't she, to take a rubbish job as a typist' She stopped short, grinned at me. 'Upsa, sorry! I didn't mean to insult you, another typist.' At this we both laughed.

After that I often sat late at 'Autumn Leaves' relaxing. I could only admire her graceful manners. Often there were male customers doggedly hanging round pestering her. She had an air of dignity and confidence as she dealt with them amicably, maintaining the balance between the politeness of a waitress and her personal integrity.

The worlds we had lived until then were as different as two separate cultures but once we had opened the doors of each other's worlds we became very close and even felt fascination towards these new worlds.

At the beginning of October, I had a letter from Chaehong asking me to visit him.

I arrived at Chinwŏn on a Saturday shortly before Evensong. I was to stay the night with the old lady in her room. After putting down my overnight bag in the room and washing my hands I entered the church, and knelt down. The congregation entered one by one gradually filling up the place. In the first row on the male side, I saw Myŏngsŏk. On Sunday he would sit in the same place at the early mass, eleven o'clock mass and again at the Evensong.

As Chaehong had suggested I had been sending some money for his food but had never written to him. On this visit, too, at Chaehong's request, I avoided any chance to talk to my brother seriously. All I said was 'Are you all right?' when I first saw him, and 'Have some more,' when we were eating together. But I could see clearly that some change had come over him, and he was still in the process of some transformation. In the first place, his attitude to Chaehong, the old lady and the other people around him was not sarcastic or hostile as before. It was simple and straightforward. It was a quiet visit and the change in Myŏngsŏk was not explained until the end of November when Chaehong came up to Seoul.

Our talk started at a tea-room around six o'clock and went on until eleven. He seemed to be pleased with the change in Myŏngsŏk and optimistic about his future.

'The beginning was the hardest. Once over the first hurdle, things went fairly smoothly. Of course, I have to wait and see a further development, but at present I am optimistic.

'I had been cruel to him though not intentionally. You wouldn't have liked me if you had seen me being like that, and, of course, you would have taken him away.'

'I see. That's why you didn't invite me earlier or allow me to write to him?' He ignored my comment as he continued.

'My diagnosis of his symptoms was that his mind was not normal. A normal mind is one that feels sad about a sad situation, I believed. So my first step was to make him feel sorry for himself by constantly reminding him of the situation he was in: he was rejected by his own parents and family; he was a man with nowhere to go; he was so perverse that he could not get on with other people; and what awaited at the end of such a life. Of course, I didn't point out these things in crude words but through a sort of smoke screen aiming at the core of his psychology.'

I felt tight in my throat at the thought of my poor brother who, like an orphan, had no choice but to depend on others while loneliness penetrated into his bones. Chaehong went on.

'We often quarrelled violently.'

'I'm surprised that he stayed on.'

'It's simple, I just won, because he had the weakness of having nowhere to go if he walked out, however hateful it might be. He once told me that he'd rather die than go back to your great-uncle's. I kept on attacking him aiming at the last drop of his resistance.' Regardless of my sadness he went on with the story of his victory like an elated hero.

'That last drop persisted for a long time. Then suddenly he gave in and was in low spirits.'

'My poor brother!'

'He was now sad. He seemed to droop. He sat vacantly staring ahead him as his thoughts ticked away. He was no longer arrogant or loud spoken and at night he was restless and heaved deep sighs.

'I knew the time had come. I wanted to be like a mother who appears in front of her child who is lost in the wilderness. I wanted to be a saviour to firmly grip his lonely and scared heart and fill it with love and hope. As you know I am not a very attentive, caring kind of person. More than once, I thought I should ask for your help, but I said to myself, "No, it can't be. There must be only one saviour for if there are two, there will be trouble." So I decided to take it onto myself.

'At the same time as giving him sympathy, comfort and encouragement, I started talking about God's love. I had entered into his desolate heart and held it firmly, so I was like the helmsman steering the course. It was easy then. He was within my control.

'My idea of mission is to catch people by their intellect, not by giving them material benefit. I hate the practice of luring poor people into church in the expectation of some windfall. I want to drop a seed in the soil of a thinking mind so that it sprouts and grows and naturally turns towards the light of God.

But in the case of Myŏngsŏk, I must admit that I had to bend my principles. In a manner of speaking, I tempted a hungry person by holding a bowl of rice before his nose.

'But you'd agree, wouldn't you, that to settle down a mad man you may have to use a whip. If an anaesthetic is necessary to stop him from falling off the bed you have to use it.'

As if he was repenting on the cruel methods he had used, Chaehong fell silent for a moment.

'Now Myŏngsŏk and I are friends. We are close to each other. Looking back, my first impression of his dismissive attitude toward the world and perverse views of things was a form of self-defence, an inferiority complex formed over many years. He had lost confidence in himself to face the world in a normal sort of way.

'I made him read the lessons during the service. At first he flatly refused but once he had proved that he could do it, he loved it. He reads well and has a good clear voice. I plan to make him a server and take him with me when I go visiting so that through the contact with good people, he may gain more self-confidence.' As if tireless he carried on. 'A long time ago he casually said something hinting that he would like to be a priest. At that time, I was not sure about him myself and thought it was too early to make any decision, so I let it pass, but now I am beginning to believe that he meant it and it is a possibility. What do you think?'

He had been talking all evening without giving me a chance to put a word in edgeways.

(He wants to be a priest! My poor brother has found something he wants to do.) Tears rose to my eyes. Where his own family had failed to give him any hope in life, someone not even related to him had performed a miracle.

'I have nothing to say. Just tell me what to do, whether it be advice or orders or reproach, and I will take it. Just a "Thank

you" is far from being adequate to express my true feelings.'
Embarrassed to have shown tears in my eyes, I attempted to
change the atmosphere.

'Let's go.' I said. 'I will buy you some supper.'

Over the meal, our conversation was still centred on
Myŏngsŏk.

'There is no doubt that he is basically a gifted man. His
memory, perception and imagination ....he's brilliant. He has a
store of hidden knowledge, which amazes me sometimes. When
we talk about serious things, his sincerity is quite touching.'

(Fancy, there is someone in the world, who appreciates my
brother's talent!)

Chaehong went on. 'There is no problem in keeping him
there with me until next March. I will give him some instructions on Christian doctrine and I expect our friendship will be
strengthened with time. The question is what will become of
him after that. You see, I have to go back in March to finish
my last term at college.'

'I see.' I said weakly as I felt despair rising in me. 'Good
things have to come to an end sooner or later, I suppose, just
as bad things do. To tell you the truth, I am going to bring my
present life to an end before that'

'What does that mean?' His eyes widened.

'I haven't told my sister yet, but I am planning to go off to a
small island for good.' I explained my plan to go to Hŭksan. 'I
need some purpose in life for which I can burn and grind my body
and soul to smithereens, or my disease will remain incurable.'

'What disease?'

'You won't believe it, will you? My mind has long since
been diseased. Feelings of futility, a hollow heart, insomnia,
lethargy, hating my fellowman. The list of symptoms is endless,
worse than Myŏngsŏk, I suppose. Only I don't show it like he
does.

'If one can define an abnormal state of mind, madness, I am ten times madder, a hundred times worse than he is. There is no hope for me. The difference between us is that I know what can cure me.' I smiled wryly, but Chaehong who had suddenly become serious did not smile back.

'It looks as if madness is a monopoly of my family,' I said jokingly but he still did not smile.

I said, 'I just want a new start, that's all. A new start is only possible by leaving behind the people and the circumstances that I have been attatched to.'

(All these people that I have loved so much and the jobs and duties for which I have been so faithful – I have to part with them.) At this thought my throat tightened as tears rose.

'Well, I am not going straight away, and there are things yet to be sorted out, so please don't worry about me. Tell me more about Myŏngsŏk.' I tried to disperse the solemn atmosphere I had brought on.

'My original idea was that when I graduated and ordained, I would take him with me to the parish I will be assigned to. There I would continue to instruct him and let him help me with the parish work. After some time, if he still shows an inclination to become a priest, I would recommend him to the Anglican theological seminary. If he proved to be promising, he would have the privileges of studying and lodging free of fees. That was what I had in mind, but...'

'But what?'

'Apparently the bishop has arranged for me to go and study in Australia for two years after my graduation.

'I see.' I should have been very pleased for him but I could not readily offer my congratulations.

'Myŏngsŏk is the first human project I have taken up as an aspirant to the priesthood myself. It would be such a shame if I had to drop him at this stage. I can't...'

He closed his eyes as he rested his chin in his raised hands, and remained silent for a few minutes whether in scheming something or in prayers.

When he opened his eyes, he said, 'I have got some vague ideas, but I won't bother to tell you about them now. As we have some time until March, I will try what I can and you do whatever you can.'

A letter arrived from the priest on Hŭksan Islands whom I had been expecting to meet in December. Due to unforeseen circumstances his visit to Seoul had been indefinitely postponed. It was a big blow feeling as if the rope to which my shattered body and soul had been clinging onto suddenly snapped. I was confused and frightened as if I had dropped and smashed my lamp from the top of a cliff in snow-storm. I flopped down and floundered. It was just then that another beam of light as if by magic from nowhere appeared before me. It was in an unusual form to be sure but undoubtedly a light.

A few day before Christmas I received a letter of proposal from Fr. Osbourne. Since his return to England, I had exchanged a couple of letters with him, but being a man of few words, they had been simple. He had told me that he had settled down in a small country parish and that he often thought about me. But we were now far apart and beyond reach. I had not expected our relationship to develop any further.

I was flustered at first. I thought it would never be possible. But when a couple of hours had passed and I had regained my composure, it seemed to be a perfectly natural thing to happen. There had been a trace of unconfessed love. I had not known what his feelings were but on my side there had been a strong feelings beyond mere respect. The only person in the whole world who understood you – when that person was a man, how could you dismiss the possibility of love? Now the possibility had turned into a confessed love, I was faced with enormous practical difficulties. To announce it to the world and to be accepted by it – the prospect of complications and pressures from the people dear to me was quite daunting. Staunch defenders of traditional conventions, not one member of my family or any of my friends would approve of it. I was afraid to be labelled as a rebel and a disgrace. In a respected society in a country that upheld the single, unmixed blood of their people throughout history as a national pride, a marriage with a foreigner was unthinkable.

I was fretful all through the whole month of January, as I turned it over in my mind. It was Miss Yang who first sensed my restlessness, and the one who helped me to make a decision. By now we were the closest of friends and knew every detail of each other's past.

'Go, Miss Yun,' she said. 'It's your happiness that matters. What have other people got to do with it? If you are not sure about his character or in doubt of his love, that's a different matter.'

Then she said, 'How I envy your freedom. You have no family depending on you and no parent following your every step pushing a spoon into your hand saying, "Please eat a little bit more." If only I could get away from this damned land of poverty!

'What kind of life is this!? Do you love it so much that you want to get stuck here? You must have some leisure in your life. Only then can you cultivate your talents and interests and live a decent life.'

She was two years younger than me but much more mature in many ways. There was, in her approach to life, as she firmly set her feet on the reality, a formidable air of authority. She had faith in her own judgement, and I learned from her that a person with such confidence was not inclined to compromise or anxious to please those around her. It was rather that her environment came to comply with her ways. Thanks to her encouragement, I wrote to Fr. Osbourne accepting his proposal but warning him about the practical difficulties ahead.

Once I had made up my mind, I gave up the idea of the Hŭksan Islands and like a ship about to sail, was filled with hope and buoyancy. Spring was approaching. In the past, every year when spring came round I had suffered depression like a seasonal disease, but this year I had no trace of it. My life was too full.

Spring was deepening and time flew like a dream. Through his frequent letters, twice, even three times a week I could feel the extent of his love and got to know him better each time. I was convinced that at last I had found the port where my soul should anchor and rest for good.

'You seem to get a lot of letters these days?' Sŏnhi said one evening when we were sitting round supper table. In fact I had been looking for the right moment to talk about it with her and her husband. When I told them that I had had a proposal from Fr. Osbourne, they broke into laughter as if at a good joke. The subject was lightly dismissed.

The following evening my sister came to my room with a serious face.

'So, you mean you will really go?'

'Yes.' At my definite answer, she let out a deep sigh as her eyes brimmed with tears. I had never seen such a sad face since her marriage.

'"A pagoda built with great care and devotion tumbles down" as the saying goes. There is no end to it.' As if to restrain herself, she sat with tightly-pressed lips.

'It has fallen long since, don't you remember? Just think your sister is dead.' I said half jokingly, at which she flew into hysterics.

'In your whole life have you ever done any good for your parents or your family? In everything you do, you think only of yourself....'

I sat quietly as she flung at me hurtful words, until she was exhausted and left the room in tears. Kŭmok, not knowing what it was all about cautiously unrolled my bedding and I crawled into it. Naturally I could not sleep. It was only the first hurdle of many. If at the first trouble I felt so crushed, how was I going to endure the rest that would follow? I was loosing confidence. If Sŏnhi kept on objecting, I would have to give in, I thought.

After midnight, on my way to the toilet, I passed the room where Sŏnhi and Chinmo slept. They were quarrelling and I could guess it was over me. I stopped and eavesdropped.

'I am saying this as a man who knows her very well indeed.'

'Whoever you are, you can say that because it's not your own sister. If you don't know how I brought her up you will never understand what I feel.' She was sniffling.

'Just think about it calmly, and rationally. Who is the most important person in this? Whose happiness are we concerned about? Yours? Your father's?

'A lonely, farmer's son myself with no brothers or sisters do you think I don't wish to have my clever sister-in-law, married happily and living near us? But I would put her happiness before mine.

'To be honest, I don't think there are many men around here capable of making a woman like that happy. I think she's made the right decision.'

I held my breath and retreated as I felt a lump in my throat. Chinmo had always been good to me but I had never felt more grateful. In the morning, from Sŏnhi's manners, I guessed that in the end she had been won over. Now that I had her approval, I believed, things would develop much more smoothly.

To save father from a big shock we decided to tell him that I was going to England to study. And then, if I decided to marry James there, he would take the news with less pain.

At lunch time, on the way to the usual noodle restaurant across the road, I saw, on a roadside stall, a pile of well-ripened plums, the first of the season. Without a moment's hesitation, I bought fifty of them, wrote on a piece of paper, 'To my darling sister, with love, Sukey,' and went home. I had remembered her saying, a few days before, that she had a craving for plums. She was with child and it had a strong emotional effect on me. The thought tugged at my heartstrings and I would happily take any amount of trouble to give her whatever she fancied.

A baby of Sŏnhi's flesh and blood who would call me auntie was on the way. It was coming to fill up the hollow in Sŏnhi's heart that would be made by my departure.

Sŏnhi was delighted at the sight of the plums. Behind her, as she picked up the piece of paper and looked at it, stood Kŭmok with a happy face, and from behind her Sudol called, 'Auntie,' also beaming. Apparently he had dropped in, so they were about to have lunch together.

I looked at my watch. There was not enough time for me to sit down and join them.

'You are not going back without lunch?'

'I haven't got the time.'

'Silly girl. Am I dying for them? You could have waited until home time.' We looked into each other's smiling eyes. We needed no words.

'Auntie, I hear you are going to England?' put in Sudol.

'That's right.'

'I am happy for you. When you go, I bet, your sister will cry, won't she?'

'She will. Even if I am not here, you won't stop coming round, Sudol, will you?' I said and with a playful wink added, 'Not only would my sister miss you but Kŭmok would miss you even more.'

'Of course I won't,' said he and blushed while Kŭmok turned scarlet as with a child-like whimper she protested, 'Oh, auntie,' and squeezed my arm.

'Well, I have to go now.' I briskly walked out of the alleyway filled with warmth not only towards Sŏnhi but also for Kŭmok and Sudol.

A sort of meditation or a habit of serious thinking first developed in me probably when I was about five, coinciding with the star-gazing that started shortly after my mother's death.

In my small head, there was little room for me to figure out the significance of her death but I wondered why my mother, whom I was waiting so hard to see again, did not come back even for a brief moment, and eventually I came to my own conclusion that once dead, one could never come back.

I used to sit by the window and look up into the sky, my elbows propped on the sill and my chin resting in my upturned hands.

The sun had dyed the western sky crimson on its way out. Even before it was fully out of sight, a star was switched on with a click.

'Where had it come from?' 'One star, one me.'

With such murmurs my star-gazing would start. As I observed them, various thoughts criss-crossed my mind.

'Two stars, two me. I hope father will soon be home bringing lots of mandarin oranges....'

'Three stars, three me. How long before the school holidays? I bet my brother and sister will take me skating on the river....'

'Nine stars, nine me. If you eat uncooked rice, your mother dies – granny said so. Is it because I ate the rice out of the chest in the store room that my mother died? No, it can't be, because I started going there after she died, not before....'

While I had been thus absorbed in chasing after new stars, my surroundings had gone dark and the number of stars reached far beyond my counting ability. Suddenly they were like silver powder sprinkled by a magic hand, ready to pour down over me. I was overpowered by a giddiness.

While the number of the stars increased, the number of my wishes and thoughts that had once been more than I could count seemed to have dwindled one by one until there remained only one with a strong intensity – the desire to have my mother back.

'Is she really not coming back? Is it possible that she isn't...?'

The more I became convinced that she never would, the more intense grew my longing to see her face just once more. I looked up at the sky again. It felt much more friendly now than it had earlier on. If I stared into it long enough, I felt that mother's face might appear up there among the stars.

That magic feeling that I had felt then as a five year old had not only remained, but steadily grown into a belief as I grew older and imagination started to enter into my thoughts. In my last year at primary school, I learned a little poem from a text book which I loved so much that I still remember every word of it with all the fascination it had to me then.

Lured by the cool breeze – I stepped out into the courtyard
Just in time to see the crescent moon
and stars emerge out of the cloud.

The moon has set and
only the stars twinkle together.
I wonder whose star that one is.
And which of them is mine?

Standing silently, alone
I count them one by one.

I had recited it endlessly as I pondered what the poet could have meant by 'I wonder whose star that one is, and which of them is mine?' until I found an answer that pleased me.

'There are as many stars in the sky as there are people on earth. When you die, your soul goes up to heaven and takes up one star as your dwelling place, and at the same time, the soul that had been in that star comes down to be born on earth to fill up the empty space left by the dead.'

I half believed this childish invention, and even now when I look up at the starry sky, I fall into reverie and get carried away into the fairy tale world of my childhood invention.

I would choose a star as my mother's and stare at it endlessly as I continued an imaginary conversation with her.

Of late I had given up my elder brother, Hyŏngsŏk for dead and started searching the sky for his star. A man with whom all communication had been cut off for more than ten years, how could I expect him to be still alive?

Then one day a letter came. It was unbelievable. Some mischievous person could be playing a trick on us. Even so, the writing 'Your son, Hyŏngsŏk' at the end of it was all too familiar to our eyes.

'Your brother, Hyŏngsŏk is alive!' As he entered Sŏnhi's house father was breathless. Written in a mixture of Korean and English, the content of the letter was simple.

. . .due to a combination of complicated circumstances, I have been an unfilial son. Please forgive me, father. I cannot explain all this in a letter, but when I see you, fairly soon I hope, I will tell you all about it. For now, only trust me, father, that I have lived a manly and honest life, and I am healthy.

Driven by unavoidable circumstances, the submission of my dissertation has been delayed, and it was not accepted until last June. Fifteen years after leaving my homeland I have at last fulfilled my dream of becoming a qualified doctor.

I return all the pride and honour to you, father, and my beloved family. Please write to me at this address, and I will send a longer letter.

Your son,
Hyŏngsŏk.

Sŏnhi and I embraced each other and danced and wept at the same time. It was Sunday and my brother-in-law was at home. Sŏnhi and I prepared a special supper to celebrate the happy occasion, and on behalf of the family I wrote a long emotional letter to him in English.

Father stayed long after supper.

'How are your procedures going?' he asked me.

'All is going well, father,' I said

'I had better get going.' He let out a deep sigh as he stood up to go. I walked with him to the bus stop. He was silent all the way until he was about to get on the bus when he said,

'To be honest with you, I'd rather you didn't go to England. Even if it means returning with a doctorate or even with a star plucked out of the sky...A woman nearing thirty, you should get married. I am already seventy. How many more years will I live? Sŏnhi is now a married woman, so I don't worry about her so much as you and Myŏngsŏk. If Hyŏngsŏk comes back soon, and if I can live with him, you and Myŏngsŏk all together under the same roof for a few months, I will die a happy man.'

Earlier, during the season of planting out the rice seedlings when plentiful rainfall was of vital importance, the country had been hit by a severe drought, which was said to be the worst in thirty years, but now when the plants were beginning to settle, the floods, said to be the worst for ten years, came to uproot them.

For me, life was even and peaceful. The procedures for going to England were progressing smoothly and our family fortune, which had seemed to be doomed were looking up.

Even though father was as poor as ever, with the expectation of a reunion with his long-lost son, he looked bright and cheerful.

I was looking out, from the high office window, the scene below – water everywhere. For a brief moment the sun peeked out, only to be overcome by thick, black clouds and heavy streaks of rain pelted down. In no time a river was forming around the drain.

'How exciting! Look at that. Like the Pastoral Symphony' I shouted delightedly. Then I felt a sudden chill down my neck. I turned around to meet the disapproving eyes of Miss Yang from the other side of the room.

'?'

'Miss Yun!'

'?'

'However clever you may be, you're childish. What do you mean by "exciting"? You may not have any worries about your daily meals, but thousands of people will face hunger because of that bloody rain.'

But for the presence of Miss Chŏn, I would have liked to grab her hands and beg for forgiveness. Every day the papers reported the adversities of the afflicted people, the damage to the crops and the poor prospects for the harvest. The prices of food were going up and people were worried and grew mean. In the market, it was said that you could not buy grain even if you were prepared to pay two or three times the normal price. The stories of hungry and starving multitudes were not a tale of other people. My own brother and father could be among them.

After spending a miserable afternoon, I held Miss Yang's hand on the way home.

'Please forgive me, Miss Yang'

'For what?'

'What I said at lunchtime. It was so thoughtless of me.'

'*Aigoo*, Miss Yun, still brooding over it? You, silly woman. I told you, you're still a baby.'

I felt forgiven and happier. We went into a noodle hut and chatted over a bowl of soup.

'Any more news of your brother?'

'Umn. I am busy these days writing letters on behalf of each member of the family. I told him all about the decline of our family fortunes and how we have suffered. He says my letters gave him more shock and pain than all the adventures and hardships he had been through himself put together. He just can't wait to be reunited with his family.

'Last month he sent father two hundred dollars. He's only just started working in a hospital as a junior doctor so what more can you expect?'

'That's wonderful. You're OK now. You don't need to worry about anything. Does he say when he is coming back?'

'Not immediately, I don't think. But he's hoping to invite father over there as soon as he can afford it. In one of his letters he says that he will take over the care of his father from his good sisters, and will make up for his negligence of his filial duty of past years.'

'I'm so happy for you.'

August was over and with it the fiendish season of monsoon. Clear and high, the sky heralded autumn. The papers reported that considering the flood damage, the prospects for the harvest were not too bad. It was about this time that a new wave of alarm seized the country as a cholera epidemic raged up. It was said that once infected, the death rate was one hundred percent. Inoculation tents were pitched in streets.

On the twentieth of September, there wasn't a cloud in the sky. I was daydreaming as I thought how could there be tragedy for people living under such a splendid canopy, when my father, his face the colour of the earth, stumbled in holding a telegram that read 'Myŏngsŏk died of infection.'

Chaehong, having changed his original plan of coming back to Seoul in March stayed on until June, so Myŏngsŏk had continued his stay until then. By this time the friendship between them was deep, and Chaehong had worked out a plan for Myŏngsŏk's future.

Among the elder generation of Anglican priests, there was one called Father Song. He had been a close friend of Chaehong's father and Chaehong called him uncle. Father Song had, in his parish in Sang-ju, a small establishment, a training centre for lay readers. After being trained there and recommended by their instructor, Father Song, one could go to the theological seminary.

Chaehong had succeeded in persuading Father Song to take Myŏngsŏk on from the September term. Myŏngsŏk had become quite a different person. He had a strong faith. At last he had emerged and stood before God as a man with self-control and his own will.

However, he had nowhere to go until September other than Susim about which he had said he would rather die than go back, but he had parted with Chaehong and gone there with the promise of a new start in autumn. He must have had will power to endure the intervening three months. He died not knowing the news of Hyŏngsŏk as we had kept it from him lest it unsettled his plans and revived his sense of dependency on the family.

When Sŏnhi and I accompanied father to the village of Susim, Myŏngsŏk's body had been removed by the district medical team, in the presence of our great uncle as his guardian.

In the room where he had lived, smelling strongly of disinfectant, I saw strewn around, bits of straw and peels of garlic and an aluminium bowl. The clotted quilt and rag-like clothes would have been burned.

For the arrival of his ashes we stood at the entrance to the village. Some of the villagers also stood around us with grave faces, mostly our kinsfolk, with a few outsiders. I heard their casual chatter, not paying much attention, until suddenly some of their words struck me like lightening.

'They say garlic and chilli sauce are just the thing for this disease.'

The speaker, as his eyes met mine, flinched and added 'He might have been all right if he had had them.'

I did not need to hear or see any more to guess the painful truth.

With the spread of the epidemic, absurd home remedies were passed around, and the desire to live, strengthened by the death-knell, made people ready to try anything. The innocent looking aluminium bowl and garlic peels lying about in his room – what did they mean?

I also recalled a casual remark earlier that day by the daughter-in-law of my great uncle.

'The day before he died, he came round to the kitchen in the evening. His eyes were sunken deep and his face was as white as a sheet of paper. He asked for some garlic and chilli sauce. I thought he was going to make himself some hot soup. I offered him a boiling bowl of soup but he declined it. So I gave him a bowl of chilli sauce and told him to help himself to the garlic.'

I had heard a similar case a week before. A patient, after eating a large quantity of these things had died of damaged intestines. Crunching and swallowing one by one these pungent cloves dipped in chilli, in the sole hope of beating the virus – What will-power, what strong desire for life. What could be more plaintive and heroic than such an act in human life?

I did not tell this to Sŏnhi nor father. It was to remain a secret that I would bear alone, and when I had found his star in the sky, I would exchange some thoughts about it with him.

Myŏngsŏk, finally embraced by father as a handful of ashes in a container, was buried in a sunny spot, not far from the graves of our grandmother and mother, where many generations of our ancestors had been interred.

'I should have gone before him, worthless father that I am. I tried and tried to be a decent father to him but...' Father unrestrainedly cried before the grave.

'Myŏngsŏk, Myŏngsŏk, my poor, poor brother....' Sŏnhi wept as she mumbled and wrung her hands.

I sat dry-eyed, thinking that before I left the country I would come back alone bringing a handful of cosmos seeds to sprinkle all around his grave. Every autumn it would be covered in white flowers and nobody would know how they came to be there.

This small piece of earth shall be adorned by white flowers and lit by moonlight and starlight – the sacred ground where my beloved brother's ashes are buried.

'Father, you should get going,' I urged him 'it's getting late.'

'Let me be,' he said, 'time does not matter.'

I sat on. As I looked up into the sky that had already darkened and filled with stars I was carried away on the wings of imagination into the depth of thoughts concerning the populace on earth and the sky. Among the multitude of stars that seemed as if to pour down, a peculiarly tiny one caught my eyes. I recognized it as Myŏngsŏk's. One moment it sent me a wink, looking pale as if he was still smarting from the sores he had received in twenty seven sorrowful years on earth. But another moment, he sent me a bright smile, like that of a hero, as he whispered,

'Sister, don't shed tears for me any more, or sigh, for as you see I have come close to mother now.'

Indeed, very close to Myŏngsŏk's, there was a larger star, which I thought of as that of my mother, but it did not send any word or message.

Which one was the baby's that was to be born to Sŏnhi soon?

The positions of the stars were not fixed. As they moved about according to their rules, I might see Myŏngsŏk's star in another part of the sky tomorrow.

The Anglican Cathedral in Seoul, an elegant nineteenth-century Romanesque construction, was my spiritual home. Its interior had been the cradle of my infancy. My grandmother had been a catechist in the early days of the Anglican mission in Korea and my father the cathedral warden for many years. I was baptized there as an infant, went with mother to mass and attended the Sunday School. I still hear the fine, vibrant voice of mother like a reed pipe as she sang the hymns.

This was where I first experienced a sense of holy awe as I gazed fixedly at the holy pictures in the golden mosaic behind the altar on which golden candle flames flickered.

In the centre of the nave there was a large Crucifix, hanging suspended in mid-air from the high ceiling, with a human figure on it, his head, crowned with thorns, drooping forward. Beneath it a lady in a neat nun's habit, sitting straight in a tall-backed chair, had taught us, the Sunday School children, and I had often been carried away, spellbound, as I gazed up at the Cross.

This same crucifix had survived all the fierce retreats and counter-attacks of the Civil War, and still hung exactly as it had been those many years ago. It had had an extremely moving power over me. During the two years when I had thought I was carrying the cross of love, I had spent many hours in meditation beneath it as I opened up my lonely heart to the figure on it.

The cathedral had been a place of comfort to me. On Sundays I had sat in the most inconspicuous corner, submerged in my own solitary thoughts.

On this particular Sunday, my mind had seized like a gramophone needle that had stuck in a groove of a scratched record, and went over the same passage again and again. '...forgive us our trespasses as we forgive those who trespass against us, and lead us not into temptation but deliver us from evil...' While one part of my mind stayed in this groove another part was creating a scene with an imaginary God whom I had grabbed hold of.

'You jolly well know, don't you, that you have been perfectly horrid to me? You have been so cruel. Why did you have to be so cruel to me? You, who know everything about me, even my secret thoughts, I don't need to say anything, need I? You alone know how exhausted I am and what a dear price I have paid in the name of Love. Promise me, please, that you will take special care of me from now on and save me from falling into any evil again...'

Completely out of tune with the mass taking place around me I had been wandering in regions of fantasy. The service had reached the Communion. To the singing of a Communion hymn, the congregation was lining up to receive it. I felt shameless as I stood to join them.

After receiving the communion I returned to my seat, knelt and continued with my protest. I lifted my eyes and turned them to the Cross. Hung from the ceiling of a high dome and above the light from the windows, it was always in half darkness. There, I seemed to see a gentle smile like that of a loving father rising on the face of the figure on the Cross.

I well remembered a smile like that. When I was a little girl, I had often obstinately argued with my father, protesting and persisting in making him see things in my way. He had loved me for doing this. When he finally admitted defeat, touched by my eagerness and proud of my logic, he would say as a smile just like that spread over his face, 'All right, all rright, child, you made your point.'

It did not matter if it was all my imagination. I was happy that I had won over the Father and secured his blessing for my new life. I came out of the church in a blissful mood.

Outside, the clear blue autumn sky was dazzling. In the churchyard, the huge gingko tree, a hundred years old, with its leaves turned golden-yellow stood in a glorious harmony with the sky. I walked beneath it, where the leaves were falling one by one, towards the main gate. Outside, unexpectedly, I saw Hwaja, the maid from the Kyŏng-woo Hotel, waiting for me. My instant reaction was a sinking heart, but after a moment I could sense that she was not there with any evil intent.

In the early days, when Kwŏn had taken lodgings there, I had learned to read her face – the mischievous expression as she lightly tapped him on the shoulder and said, 'For the sake of literature'; her cool, lofty and detached look, with a pout, when she suspected his relationship with another woman; the shameless face, as she had put on a metal mask, when she demanded money for an abortion; and the expression when she felt respect for me yet mixed with pity – on all these occasions, her face had vividly betrayed what was in her mind. At the same time I knew that she was never crafty or scheming.

This morning what I read there was a plain amicability on seeing, after a long time, an acquaintance. She said that she had come to see me about Kwŏn and could we have a cup of coffee together. I could not refuse. Inevitably, the memory of the occasion when I had sat opposite her at the tea-room across the road from the Academy depressed me but I led her to a tea-room nearby the Cathedral.

'Mr Kwŏn's on the brink of death. He so much wishes to see you just once more…Sometimes he call out 'Sukey, Sukey' in his sleep.'

It was like being struck with a hammer on the back of my head. But I was on guard not to betray it. I sat quietly with my lips lightly pressed. It could be a trick to kidnap me. I looked at her face again and could read no other intention beyond what she was saying.

'I am not in a position to tell you what to do, but I thought you might be willing to grant a dying man's wish, so I told him I would look for you, but in the wide city of Seoul where would I find you? Apparently you asked the people at your former work not to give your address to anyone. Then he told me I might find you here. So here I am, but if you don't want to see him, I will understand.'

In my desperate effort not to show my emotion I did not even ask what was the matter with him.

She went on, 'I bumped into him one day in the street.' Here she stopped short. Sensitive to her expression I knew what she was thinking. She thought I suspected her of secretly carrying on with him even after she had taken the money from me.

'Believe me, it was the first time I saw him since I left Kyŏng-woo.' Then she went on. This occasion, she said, he had looked shabby and extremely unwell. Apparently he had been to the dentist and wanted to lie down. So she took him to her place, and there was no need to say their cohabitation started. She said she was earning her living by helping at a restaurant.

She did not belong to high society but she was by nature a compassionate woman. Even though in an underhand way she had loved him once, and now he was in a difficult situation, I knew that she was not the sort of person who would turn him out but look after him even if not as a lover.

In an alley off the poor quarter behind Yongsan railway station, he was lying in a six-foot-square *ondol* floored room as if dead. The room smelt rancid and the floor had not been heated despite the chilly weather.

As if reading my thoughts Hwaja said, 'His inside is on fire, he says, and he wouldn't let me light the stove. That's why it's so cold,' and closed the door from outside. At first I was nervous because of my suspicion that I might have been kidnapped, but soon it became obvious that I had not.

He was a pathetic sight. Lying on his side, he seemed unable to move his body nor could he lie flat on his back. He managed to shift his face with difficulty to look up at mine.

'Sukey, please forgive me for the wrongs I have done to you. I wanted to say this one word to you in person, so I wandered all over Seoul.' Then his eyes dropped onto the floor as he went on. 'Please say that you forgive me for my ugly past and for hurting you so much, so that I can close my eyes in peace.'

That was all. After saying this he said not another word. A long silence, except for the bubbling sounds of phlegm in his chest and his weak breathing.

'I forgive you,' I said, but could not add 'Mr Kwŏn', a name that I had been so fond of calling two years ago.

'Thank you, Sukey,' he said and another silence fell. I could not find another word to add, so I left him, thinking that I would never see him again.

But when I got home, and went over what I had seen in a calmer frame of mind, I felt choked with pity for him and regretted that I had been so mean and heartless to a dying man as to utter a few cold words, 'I forgive you,' and leave him. His pathetic appearance with sunken eyes and coarse whiskers lying under a shabby quilt kept coming back before my eyes. His face once so fine and attractive – where had it gone? How was it that that charming appearance that had once captivated the hearts of so many women could turn into an exhausted body lying on a cold floor?

After turning over all through the night without a wink of sleep, I went back to the house at the first light. Of all the questions still unanswered, there was one in particular that I wanted to clear up.

'There is one thing of which I want the truth. Can you tell me honestly whether or not what you told me at first was true?'

His eyes closed, he remained silent for a long time. As if dead, even his breathing seemed to have stopped. Then he opened his eyes as he spoke in a very quiet voice.

'Sukey, please do not question me about the past, it is too cruel...It is not so simple as to be answered with a simple "yes" or "no". What is true is that I came from the other side and my name is Changho Yu.'

After an interval he spoke again in a wavering voice.

'When the country is reunited, I beg you to go and seek my mother.' I saw a streak of tears running out of his closed eyes. My heart was smarting but I knew that if I got tangled with my emotion at this point, I would fall again to be its slave and would never be free again. I increased my guard as I tried to regain my composure. Unaware of myself, I had taken out a handkerchief to wipe away his tears but if his hand gripped my wrist, I should never be able to shake it off. I crushed it and held it tight in my fist.

'My mother's name is Changsun Sohn. Don't tell her the truth about my miserable, dirty life, but tell her that I was adopted into a good family like yours as son-in-law, and had a happy life.

'I am a criminal but what drove me into this was the tragedy of my divided country. To keep alive a worthless life like mine, I had no alternative.' He was visibly exhausted by talking too much or by aroused emotion. He sounded very weak as he went on, 'Just remember that I had a mother who adored me. How I missed her every morning and night – who could ever know that? I was not even able to cry for her to my heart's content...' He could not carry on but broke down and sobbed calling, 'Mother, mother....'

For a moment a thought crossed my mind that he might be just acting to captivate my heart, but immediately another thought rose that he would never get up again, and I brushed aside all my suspicions.

After a while I rose to my feet.

'Calm yourself and goodbye. I am going abroad very soon without any definite plan to come back, so I can't promise you anything.' 'Besides, I don't wish to commit myself to lying again to your mother.' – I was going to add this but lest I sounded to be reproaching him, I omitted it.

'Even so, you will come back one day even for a short visit to see our reunited motherland. In the north there will be boating parties in spring on the Taedong River...' His voice faded into a mumble whether because he was recovering his breath or falling asleep.

As if someone had gripped hold of the lower trunk of a deep-rooted tree and wildly jerked it from side to side, a violent pain from deep down shook my whole body. It was a pain of the earth being torn asunder, a pain of the sky being smashed and falling down. I took a deep breath. As I repeated this to keep my pain under control, the wings of my thoughts spread out and flew hither and thither.

How terribly had I loved. I should never be able to pull out its roots. If I gave up my attempt to escape, and settled down there, I thought, it would be less painful. But never to become again a slave of love, I was choosing a harder and more painful way. That was my fate.

During the two years while I was going through a fever of love, there had been a recurring theme in my mind, 'the tragedy of a divided nation'. The sight of Kwŏn lying like a bird with broken wings was, I thought, regardless of his rights and wrongs, a symbol of the national tragedy. At this point, it hardly mattered whether he had really been an active spy or one fallen out, or simply a liar. His tears of penitence were enough to wash away whatever sins he had committed.

Myself, perfectly normal from outside but broken and devastated inside could also be seen as a part of that tragedy. We were both victims of the unnatural division of our motherland, and in that sense, were both sinless sinners going through an extremely severe course of punishment.

We were not the only ones. How many millions of people had suffered and died unfair deaths, and how many more were still suffering the consequences of that division? For what justifiable causes had the country been divided, its people aiming guns at their own flesh and blood, wandering from north to south and from south to north in that dreadful way?

I felt I ought to fold up the wings of my thoughts and leave the place soon. Kwŏn and I were both wrecked. The only difference between us was that while he lay in utter despair, I had a faint glimmer of hope and a will to make a new start.

He lay still. Whether he heard or not, I said, 'Goodbye,' and left the room.

Hwaja stood outside the door. I pushed some notes into her hand and told her that I was soon to leave the country. Looking somewhat sad and forlorn she followed me out of the gate.

'He came in with a bullet wound in his left shoulder a couple of weeks ago,' she said. Only then did I understand why he lay in that awkward position. She had probably expected more curiosity from me but all she got was a stony face. Regardless, she went on as she walked beside me along the alleyway, probably lonely and wanting someone to whom she could open her mind. She said, she had gathered that he was shot while trying to steal some goods from the US Eighth Army base not far from their home. But the word 'bullet wound' reminded me of what Kwŏn had once told me about being followed by former colleagues holding a gun at his back.

'He never talks about what goes on inside him, so I never know what he's up to or where he goes. Not that I particularly want to know. What's the use of knowing if it will only give me headaches?

'He refuses to go and see the doctor, forbids me to bring one round, so what can I do? It's only a flesh wound, he says, and will heal gradually. He takes penicillin daily and I change the dressing. Sometimes he seems to be getting better and other times worse. From what I can see, he's made up his mind to die. He so much wanted to see you for once, and I thought I should help him to have his last wish granted.

'When he was going about pretending he was the only son of a millionaire and a lecturer, and flirting with all sorts of women, I nearly died of jealousy. I had to put my finger in it whatever I did. That's how it started. Naturally I had him most because we lived under the same roof. When I think about how he lied in those days, I feel like killing him sometimes, but a sick man now, eating food pushed before him, often with unkind words, without any protest, I feel sorry for him, so I am nice to him occasionally.

'He's a nuisance, to be honest, and a liability to my job. I wish he'd go away, but he has nowhere to go, has he? Unless of course, if you want to take him on?' Here she looked up at my face with a mischievous smile.

'He loved you best, but I had him most, so I will see to him to the last. You, Miss Yun, go and start a new life.'

She was a far superior woman to me. I was a Pharisee and she was a Samaritan, and Mary Magdalene. I held her hands firmly in mine as I said, 'Thank you and goodbye.'

Is painful and sorrowful experience a step forward to sublimation of human soul? If, after experiencing some great suffering, one remains the same as before, it is an opportunity wasted. I believe that human suffering is rewarded in whatever form.

Like when the peak of a sultry summer is over and is followed by cool, refreshing autumn breeze, over my constitution coming out of a fever, came a welcome change. At first it was like a mere chink of blue sky peering through thick layers of cloud. It grew to the size of an eye and then bigger and bigger till it overcame the cloud and eventually cleared it away. My reason overcame the turmoil and swirl of my emotions and spread out blue and lucid. I was hopeful. I was confident that once I left the present scene, a new life would be possible.

Chapter 16

Departure

Once I got my passport and visa, and the date of my departure was fixed, I felt a sense of alienation. I no longer belonged anywhere. Every corner and familiar sights roused affection and nostalgia – an especially beautiful state, known only to the one who is to part from it, never to return. In the glow of this last love, even ugly sights or evil ones looked so beautiful that I could embrace them all. This parting emotion was now and again interrupted by spells of disbelief and doubt. Where was I going? Even though I said I would come back if I did not like England, was it likely once I was there? Who was this Fr. Osbourne? What did I really know about him? From a photograph, his large deep eyes seemed sharp and severe one moment and boundlessly benign at the next. Whatever was the case he was the only person in the whole world awaiting my arrival at the opposite end of the Earth. At this thought I felt comfort and a fatalistic longing.

My reason for choosing the thirty-first of December as the day of my departure had been two-fold. I wanted to belong to my mother country till the last possible hour of that year and to start my second life on the dot of the new one. The other reason was so that I could see the birth of Sŏnhi's baby.

On the twentieth of December, ten days before I was due to go, she gave birth to a baby daughter.

It was past eleven in the night when I heard my brother-in-law calling my name in a grave voice.

'Sukey, please, come here at once!' I ran into their room. Her contractions had started.

'Sŏnhi!' I went over and seized her hands. The three of us looked at one another and broke into nervous but happy smiles. Our minds were as one in the wish for a safe delivery.

Her suitcase had been packed and ready and it had been arranged for her to be admitted to hospital at any time. We did not know what to do next, so kept glancing at each other smiling. Chinmo looked the most flustered of the three.

'What should I do? Shall I go and call a taxi? Sukey, will you bring your sister to the gate and wait till I come back?'

Sŏnhi patted him on his lap and in a gentle voice as if calming a small boy, said there was still time and he need not go yet. Still restless, he walked up and down from one end of the room to the other until suddenly he went out. Sŏnhi and I wondered what he was up to. He came back bringing the Book of Common Prayers. Having joined the church shortly before their marriage, he had hardly shown much enthusiasm. Now on seeing him enter the room with a prayer book and a solemn face, Sŏnhi and I burst into laughter and laughed until our sides ached. Nevertheless we soon knelt down with him. I did not know what to do but opened the book at random and started with 'Lord, have mercy upon us,' and carried on reading bits of prayers, picking them out from here and there. It was comforting.

At last she was taken to hospital and after eight hours, gave birth to a little girl. When Sŏnhi was brought into the maternity ward after the delivery, her face was as white as paper but she looked happy. Chinmo, who was unable to go home because of the curfew, and not allowed into the delivery ward had spent the night walking up and down the corridor, came up to her bed. His unshaven face was grubby but beamed with happiness.

A nurse came in with the baby. 'Look at her, isn't she neat?'

Before her parents, I stepped up to her to take it. A small bundle of life was put into my arms. The moment I held it, unaware of myself I pressed it tight to my bossom.

'Let her mummy hold her first,' said the nurse as she was about to take the bundle away from me.

'I will hold her a little while longer,' I said as I looked at my sister and Chinmo. They at once knew what I meant.

'Let her,' said Sŏnhi to the nurse. 'It is a very special niece for her. She has even put off going abroad to see this baby.' A wry smile came to her face. The nurse went away with a pleasant smile. I put the baby into her mother's arms. The moment she settled in her mother's bosom, she opened up her eyes to the full and gave a large yawn.

I drifted, as if mindless, as the current of the wave of Christmas tide and the end of the year swept past around me, and did some last shopping with Miae with whom I had become close again. I paid a last visit to my mother's grave and dug a handful of frozen earth as a memorial to take with me. I stood before Myŏngsŏk's grave and sprinkled seeds of white cosmos generously over and around it. No doubt some would be eaten by the birds, and being such a ferocious winter, some would perish, but, I believed, at least some would survive and flower next autumn.

As I finally cleared my desk and drawers, I let tears flow freely as I thought I should never, never have to cry like this again.

The traces of thirty years of my life here was summed up in one and a half suitcases.

At 2 p.m. on the thirty-first of December, a small crowd of friends gathered in the foyer of the Bando Hotel, from where I was to catch the airport bus. They were the people dear to me with whom I had grown up and lived as they enriched my life. Among them I terribly missed my brother, Myŏngsŏk. My eyes roaming round as if in search of him met those of Chaehong.

Obviously he had read my mind. He quickly turned his eyes away.

After Myŏngsŏk had gone back to Susim with his heart full of hope and anticipation for September when he would start his new life, I had gone to see him once not knowing that it was to be our last meeting. Nor could he imagine that it was to be the last conversation he would have with me. He was only sorry for himself because he would miss me while I was away. He had walked with me along the dyke to the bus stop on the main road where he was to see me off. What he had said then in a voice unusually assured and dignified, rang in my ears.

'Sister, I hope you will come back and marry Chaehong. He has been my salvation. He is to me like a father, an elder-brother and a best friend put together. I will follow his advice and counsel all my life and I will be fine.'

At the Bando, the send-off party had to be split up as some of them had to go back. Because of a meeting he could not miss, Dr Kang said he had to go as he held out his hand.

'Goodbye, Dr Kang. Thank you for everything. I feel I owe you so much.' I held his hand.

'Don't worry about that. You have plenty of time to come back and pay it all off.' Typical of him, I thought – a mixture of dignity, affection and a sense of humour. As he turned away, Miss Yang approached. We held each other's hands tightly.

'Since we became friends I have been so happy. Until I met you I had not known what real friendship could mean in one's life. I have been so happy. But an unlucky woman like me, how can I expect such happiness last for long?

'I can't even afford to buy a decent present to a dearest friend whom I don't know when I'll ever see again. This is only a cheap stuff but unusual and Korean.' She handed me a small package – three rectangular pieces of polished brass, the size of a match box. They were brooches carved into Chinese ideo-grams, *Soo* – longevity, *Bok* – Happiness and *Hee* – Felicity.

'Thank you, Miss Yang. They are lovely. I will wear them with pride and in remembrance of you.' I held her shoulders and lightly kissed her on the cheek.

'Call me, Chŏnghi, and I will think of you as my elder-sister, always.'

The bus for the airport arrived. The remaining people got on. Sŏnhi, slow to recover after her delivery, had come so far as to Bando against her doctor's advice but should not risk her health by going further. In place of my brother-in-law, who was to go with me to the airport, Suyŏn agreed to take her home.

Wrapped from head to toe, in a fur muffler and dark purple overcoat, except for her eyes and nose, she was weeping uncon-trollably as she stood outside the bus. The moment it started, she tried hard to smile but her effort ended up in wild crying. Since last night we had avoided talking as if we were cross with each another. If we opened our mouths, we felt we would break down. So now we were parting without even properly saying 'Goodbye.' Through the back window of the bus now speeding up I saw Suyŏn escort her into a taxi, enter it behind her and slam the door. I fought back my tears. I did not want to show a tearful face to my friends. I smiled all the way.

At the airport, father and mother with Chinhi were waiting for me.

Mother said, 'We were hoping to be able to get you some-thing but...' and father said, 'I am a worthless father.'

I could not help feeling sad and neglected. I was setting off to go thousands of miles away and my parents had not given me as much as a pair of shoes. If it had been Chinhi, would they have done the same however hard-up they might be?

'Don't worry, father.' I said cheerfully.

'Come back a successful woman.' His eyes brimmed with tears. I turned and hugged Chinhi. To my mind, she was still a baby, who I and Sŏnhi used to make a fuss of, teaching her to sing and do cute tricks. Now I hardly knew her. She was slim and tall in high-school uniform. I should not have blamed my poor parents but myself. What good had I ever done for Chinhi? If she had been my full sister would I have allowed her to become a stranger to me?

'Chinhi, work hard at school, and be good to father and mother, and make up for me as well, won't you?'

'Goodbye, sister.' Tears rose to her eyes.

I walked up to Mr Sangjin Hyŏn, and told him the truth for the first time.

'I am going to marry an Englishman.'

'Really? Congratulations!' He held out his hand as he smiled a large, kindly smile. I felt so proud that my friendship with a man had lasted in so pure, honourable and scrupulous a fashion. I held his hand and heartily shook it. 'Goodbye, and be happy.'

The thirty-first of December 1963, 6.30 p.m., the huge aircraft that bore me was slowly leaving the ground of the country that had given me birth and reared me for thirty years. At the moment it separated from the ground I fancied a loud voice calling my name from the control tower.

'Yun – Sukey –,' and it resounded, 'Yu – n – su – key,' in female voice one moment and male the next and then in mixed voices. Suddenly it changed into the chorus of a song we used to sing in primary school. It rang in my ears so loud that it seemed my ear–drum would burst.

> Clear and calm flows the stream
> Skirting round the little hill
> There in childhood, I fished with a tiny net.
> Sweet memories of the gone-by days

mingle with tears of sorrow
As I bid farewell to my homeland.
Adieu, my home, adieu, adieu
Adieu, my home, adieu, adieu.

I closed my eyes as I tightened my lips and fists and swallowed hard.

Adieu, My Mother Country, Father and Sister, Adieu.

The end.